THE SUICIDE ROOM

ABOUT THE AUTHOR

XAVIER VIDAL

Born in Barcelona, where he attended medical school and became a medical doctor, Xavier was awarded a Fulbright scholarship, and lived and studied in the United States for several years, obtaining two Masters degrees from Harvard University.

For 20 years he worked as General Manager for several biotech companies and international advertising agencies.

Through the years he has written screenplays for films, theater plays, musical theater shows (book, music, and lyrics, as he is also a musician and composer), newspaper articles, and novels. He has written articles about New Zealand as a foreign correspondent for the digital edition of *La Vanguardia*, one of the main newspapers in Spain.

His novel UXMALA was selected as Finalist in the VII HISPANIA Historical Novel Literary Prize (2019).

Xavier lives in Auckland (New Zealand) with his family.

OTHER NOVELS by XAVIER VIDAL

The BICYCLE CHRONICLES
(Subinspector Morillo Series)

THE SUICIDE ROOM
CHOPIN'S SECRET

Stand-alone Novels

UXMALA
VOICES FROM ETERNITY
LACROIX

For more information on Xavier Vidal and his books, please visit:

www.xaviervidalworld.com

THE SUICIDE ROOM

Xavier Vidal

Published by Xavier Vidal

New Zealand, 2021

This is a work of fiction.
Similarities to real people, places,
or events are entirely coincidental.

THE SUICIDE ROOM

First edition. October 10, 2021.

ISBN: 9780473593353

Written by Xavier Vidal

Published by Xavier Vidal, 2021
New Zealand

Book and cover design by Xavier Vidal

TO MY FATHER, VICENÇ

With love and gratitude

Always an inspiration and an example of integrity,
kindness, and endless scientific curiosity,
to guide me throughout my life.

There is much of him in sub-inspector Morillo,
the main character in the novel.

I just hope there is also much of him in me.

CHAPTER 1

Barcelona. 1912

The thick carpet muffled the sound of footsteps as if it were a living being who only wanted to engulf the unwary who ventured to step on it.

The gentleman's booties had seen better days but still kept a certain shine that evoked more prosperous times. His leather soles slid gently over the carpet, almost skidding on it, and although his pace was slow, he walked with determination, even with firm resignation.

In other parts of the hotel, electricity was lavishly wasted, but that long hallway was in permanent semidarkness, despite the small gas lamps, a row of iron skeleton arms coming out of the wall and holding small fireballs.

Lighting was becoming poorer, and when he reached the end of the hallway, he could barely make out the traces of the large paintings hanging on the walls, making it hard for him to guess what or whom they pictured.

The gentleman looked up and stopped in front of one of them, in which two women of easy virtue sat on each other's lap in a loving attitude, smoking from long nozzles.

Leaning on his cane, he looked at it for a few seconds and even seemed to recognize it, as his lips curled in a hint of a smile.

He was a middle-aged gentleman of distinguished bearing. A long black flannel coat covered a suit sporting several skillfully sewed patches that would have not survived close inspection. A short top hat bobbed in his head but never fell, as his hands repositioned it in a nervous and automatic twitch several times per minute.

The physiognomy of his face represented the prototype of early twentieth-century urban man, thin sharp nose, bushy mustache, and well-kept goatee always pointing downward, giving his face a somewhat feline appearance.

The bellboy, a thirteen-year-old kid who walked a few steps ahead of him stopped to wait for him and gave a respectful cough to get his attention.

When the gentleman looked away from the painting, the boy waved his hand, showing him the way.

"If you care to follow me, sir. This way, please."

The gentleman placed the cane under his arm and followed the bellboy to a thick black wooden door. The bellboy rapped on a large gilded brass circle adorned with Art Nouveau arabesques placed in the center of the door, in what surely was a prearranged code.

The gold ornaments came to life and rotated a few centimeters, letting out a thread of light through the slit, from which a pair of eyes studied the gentleman carefully. The peephole closed and the sound of bolts unlatching gave way to a head peering through the half-open door.

The clean-shaven man's face further accentuated the contrast with his abundant hair combed back and held in place by a more than generous amount of gel.

"I'll escort the gentleman from here, boy," he told the bellboy.

"What is your name, kid?" the gentleman asked, with his hand in his pocket, as if he was about to tip him, but the man stopped him, holding his hand by the wrist.

"There is no need, sir," he said, to the boy's disappointment. "Agustín, go back to the front desk," he ordered, and the bellboy instantly obeyed.

He waited until the boy disappeared to open the door completely, stepping aside to let the gentleman pass.

The corridor behind the door was even darker, and he

could not even see the color of the floor tiles, which he only sensed by the sound his heels made upon walking on them.

They came to a large riveted iron gate, which only opened from the inside and the man unlatched a few bolts and had to push with his shoulder to get it moving.

The gentleman descended a long stretch in a gentle slope, without losing sight of the back of the man walking in front of him. It surprised him he was not wearing the hotel staff uniform, but did not care.

With all its twists and turns, the hallway had ceased to be a corridor to become a passageway. The slope became steeper and he could feel an intense musty smell. He barely passed any other door during the long haul, or if he did, he could not see them because of the low prevailing light.

After what felt like an eternal five or ten-minute walk, the corridor narrowed and ascended again, ending in a large rectangular space, at whose end he noticed some rough steps carved into the natural rock, climbing up a narrow curved passageway.

"Wait for me here, if you please," the man said, stepping forward and up the stairs. Seconds later, he reappeared and gestured with his hand, inviting him to come up.

The gentleman looked around, surprised by the rapid transition from hotel hallway into a cavernous environment, and climbed the stairs, arriving at a varnished wooden door, marked with a golden brass symbol.

It was a beautiful Art Nouveau arabesque, a convoluted figure that could both suggest the body and filmy dress of a nymph as well as a few clouds or the undulations of a crest wave in a stormy sea.

The man turned the doorknob and slowly opened the door, nodding the gentleman to invite him to get in.

"I hope you will find the room to your liking," he said, stepping aside. The gentleman paused under the doorway and holding the hat in his hands took two steps inside.

There could not be a greater contrast between the dark,

damp passage and the interior of the room. His feet immediately noticed the thick fluffy carpets covering the floor and reveled in them.

The lighting offered by two small gas lamps was soft but not to the point of being insufficient, giving the room a warm orange air.

There were no windows, and it surprised him the walls were not lined with dark fabric so common at the time, but rather with bright glazed black tiles that reflected sparkles of gaslight.

A modest bookcase held several thick volumes, most likely encyclopedias, accompanied by some smaller books, perfectly arranged by height.

"If you want to hang your coat and hat, you can do it here," the man said, pointing to a hanger next to a large secretary desk with several drawers.

"You will find everything you need here," he said, opening and quickly closing a large drawer under the desk.

"Over that little side table, there is an excellent assortment of brandy and cognac at your disposal and we trust you will find everything to your liking.

Take your time, and on behalf of our establishment, let me thank you for honoring us with your trust. It has been a pleasure to have you as a customer," he said and turned around and left the room, closing the door behind him.

The gentleman placed his hat and coat on an overstuffed couch by the door, and approached the bookcase, reviewing the spines of the smaller books. Some were literature classics, while others were novels of recent publication, and upon noticing it he could not suppress an approving smile.

He sat in front of the desk and started to open the main drawer but stopped and slammed it shut, not daring to look inside.

Taking a deep breath he turned his head to look around, resting his head in his hands until a new sigh of resignation brought him back to the present.

He reached out to the secretary desk and checked the

contents of each drawer until he found a paper sheet with the seal of the establishment. He placed it on the desk with a trembling hand, while extracting a fountain pen from his other pocket.

It wasn't long before he had relived his deepest feelings and arranged them on the paper in the form of the wobbly lines of a brief letter he read several times before he signed it and sealed it with his tears, dissolving the ink strokes on the paper.

He put the fountain pen back into his pocket and folded the letter into small folds. A deep sigh accompanied him on a short walk around the room, which ended back at the table.

His determination grew with each passing minute, and he slowly but completely opened the drawer, this time putting his hand inside.

The barrel of the little Belgian-made Browning 1900 pistol was the first thing he saw and the last thing he would remember.

It was not a new weapon, it was scratched and its worn grip betrayed the many mouths it had silenced.

His hand stroked the dark metal and accompanied the pistol as he carried it to his mouth.

He introduced the barrel until it almost disappeared down his throat, closed his eyes and pulled the trigger.

CHAPTER 2

Barcelona. Today.

Thed receptionist looked away from her computer screen and offered him a glass to drink while he waited.

"I won't say no. I didn't have breakfast and I can't think of a better way to start my day," Gerard said, thanking her with his best smile.

"Very well then, if you go out to the elevator landing, you will find a water fountain on the right, next to the toilets. Here you have the glass," the young girl said, handing him an empty plastic cup.

"*When she offered me a glass, I did not expect the offer to be so literal,*" Gerard thought, without voicing his thoughts, although the girl seemed to read the disappointment in his eyes and tried to justify herself.

"Glasses always get stolen, so our manager is asking me to ration them," she said apologetically.

Gerard took the cup and walked toward the landing when he heard a familiar voice behind him.

"Good morning, Gerard. Thank you for coming so quickly." It was Matías Vendrell, Chief Editor of the contemporary art magazine "*Breaking Molds*", approaching him with an outstretched hand.

"I see you already poured yourself a drink, perfect. Come to my office, please" he said, taking the empty cup from his hands and giving it back to the receptionist, who gave him a look of resignation.

The editor's office was a model of Spartan austerity. Gerard knew there used to be a table somewhere, for he had seen it on previous visits, but if that was the case, it must be hidden under mountains of magazines and documents.

He remembered his first day working at the magazine, a welcome relief after being dismissed from the newspaper he worked at, for reasons never sufficiently clarified, and after years as a freelance journalist, accepting any job, however small or quirky it might be, provided they paid well.

Despite it all, he had never been satisfied with his collaboration with the magazine, where he wrote art reviews about exhibition openings in art galleries.

It was not the investigative journalism to which he aspired, but the work was comfortable, and allowed him to travel throughout the country covering events, kept him busy a few days a month, and paid the rent.

In addition, openings normally offered attendees an abundance of snacks, which helped him keep his subsistence budget pleasantly lightened.

Matías pulled up a chair and sat opposite him.

"I called you because I have good and bad news and wanted to talk to you personally".

"Start with the bad ones," Gerard said.

"Can I offer you something to drink?" he said, getting up to pour a can of soda he took from a minibar fridge hidden under a mountain of magazines.

"Oh no, sorry, I forgot the receptionist already offered you a drink," he said, putting the drink back and closing the refrigerator door before Gerard's glazed and thirsty look.

"Sales have not been what we expected. Competition from digital magazines is very strong. Print may have its days numbered, I don't know, but in any case, since the multinational acquired our company, the Americans demand immediate results, and one of their first measures is to change the publication frequency from monthly to quarterly."

Gerard could not quite guess where he was going with that but kept listening attentively.

"That's the bad news? Bad for the magazine, or also bad for me? How can it affect me?"

"No, that's the good news. Good, because it means they will not pull the plug on the magazine and we'll keep going, albeit with a more relaxed frequency."

"So what's the bad news?" Gerard asked, fearing the worst.

Matías cleared his throat before continuing.

"Fewer issues per year, and fewer pages per issue, which means we have to be very selective with what we publish. In summary, we must cancel your section," he said, gazing into his eyes.

"Your type of section, cultural agendas, and art exhibition reviews no longer make sense in a quarterly publication. We cannot compete against the immediacy of digital magazines. Besides, I'm sure you were tired of traveling around the country from opening to opening."

Gerard had a blank stare. His eyes were open, but in his mind his gaze was pursuing a flock of flying hors d'oeuvre and mini sandwiches that flew away from him, disappearing into the horizon.

"We have to prioritize other issues, change our editorial approach. We need to focus on theme reports and research. You have always supported that option, so it should be good news for you," Matías said, rising from his chair, to show the meeting was over.

"But, will I keep working for you guys? Do you have any particular assignment?"

"Well, I'm sure some will come, although not at this moment."

Gerard let out a deep sigh that was not lost to the editor.

"We're still open to your presenting us your ideas and suggestions about possible articles. Bring us information about what you have on your plate and we will assess whether it fits our editorial line," Matías said, stepping boldly toward the door.

Gerard got the hint and stood up.

"Do you have any good idea you can share with us now?" Matías asked, reaching out to shake his hand in farewell.

"Yes..., well, there are a couple of subjects I've been working on for months, like how archeological findings in the city's underground are silenced, to protect the commercial interests of large real estate companies or how dirty politics and speculation have almost destroyed the city's immense Art Nouveau legacy, squandering its cultural and touristic potential," Gerard said.

"As long as you do not get into politics or go against the powers that be," Matías interrupted him. "Remember the nasty consequences it has always had for you."

There was no need to be reminded. His dismissal from the newspaper was still very recent, and Gerard suspected the real reason had to do with his investigations about political corruption at the state government level. His articles had annoyed some powerful leaders in the capital city, and they pulled some strings that eventually entangled around his neck, choking him.

Gerard shook his hand but could not help throwing him a contemptuous look upon feeling the compassionate slaps Matías gave on his shoulder as he accompanied him out of the office.

"Now I have to leave you, I have a conference call to attend. Let's stay in touch" he said, closing his office door.

Gerard stood there, trying to absorb the news and the more than likely dire consequences for his home economy. Finally, he took a deep breath and headed for the door.

The receptionist saw him and raised her hand, offering him a plastic cup with a fake half-smile.

Gerard declined her offer with a slight nod.

"No thank you, I won't be needing it. I'll drink from the bottle," he said, leaving the office.

CHAPTER 3

"Can Pocapena" Farmhouse, Argentona. Today.

The huge attic occupied much of the main building and was poorly lit. Gerard wondered why all the attics of the world always had to be gloomy, dark and have a musty smell.

Sunlight leaked through gaps between the tiles and the giant wooden beams that supported the roof.

The dust in permanent suspension made those anonymous rays of light visible and helped you find your way through the jumble of furniture and old bundles piled up everywhere and covered with dusty tarpaulins.

Or at least that's how he remembered it from his childhood when he'd come up to play with his cousins and hid among the bundles that stored there since time immemorial, veritable storage of dusty family memories.

Where were all those bundles now? He could barely see some furniture left alive; a wardrobe with its doors open like enormous arms but with empty entrails, a rocking chair without a backrest, through which one could probably travel to another dimension, the mortal remains of a pair of bicycles belonging to an indeterminate period given there were not enough parts left to estimate their age, and a host of objects in an advanced state of disintegration and hard to catalog.

"I cannot understand you could sell everything," Gerard exclaimed, dropping his coffee cup, unable to hide his anger. The cup hit the plate spilling some of its contents, and Gerard got up and approached his aunt, standing by the sink in the giant kitchen of the family farmhouse, in the small town of Argentona.

Gerard took a deep breath and tried to control himself.

He had been relatively happy in that farmhouse, a solid traditional Catalan construction that had seen the centuries go by, growing and mutating to adapt to the different architectural styles and prevailing aesthetic tastes in each era.
They built much of the main building in Art Nouveau style, with a white facade topped by battlements and small corner towers.

Since he was a child, Gerard had always seen it as his private castle, the one where he fought next to the many cousins with whom he shared the house, confronting imaginary monsters that stalked him from the outside, while dreaming that one day he would conquer the world with his fountain pen as his only weapon.

The two families shared the huge estate for years, but when his father died prematurely, Gerard still a child, the pressure and ghosts of the past tormented his mother so much she decided to abandon the farmhouse and move to nearby Barcelona, leaving his sister Carmen and her many offspring, in charge of the family mansion, despite having serious doubts about it.

When Gerard turned twenty-five years old, ran acute leukemia ended his mother's life, without even giving her a chance to fight. From that moment on, Gerard's relationship with his aunt Carmen deteriorated rapidly, as the woman made it clear her priority would be to manage the house as if it were her private kingdom, setting the ground for her own children to inherit it.

Gerard knew his mother's testament clearly specified the farm could not be sold and that it would remain in the family as long as her sister Carmen was alive, and that she could continue to live in it with her kids until the end of her days, when it would then be transferred to all the cousins in equal parts, including Gerard.

In recent years Gerard had avoided visiting the farmhouse except for the occasional family celebration, as his only happy childhood memories in that house related to his mother's presence in it.

Gerard was aware he was losing respect for his old aunt Carmen, who possessed the commendable virtue of making him lose patience with surprising ease.

He had never felt affection for his aunt Carmen, but out of respect for her mother, he had always tolerated her impertinences and her blatant favoritism toward her children.

"You've disposed of almost everything stored in the attic. They were family heirlooms. At least we could have done an inventory, to know to whom each thing belonged," Gerard said.

"Am I not of the family? Are you implying I have done something wrong? May I remind you that since your mother died I administer the house, as she left in writing, which empowers me to decide what to do with old toys and useless junk, after years or centuries gathering dust in the attic," aunt Carmen said, raising her voice.

"If I remember correctly, there were paintings, and also boxes with crockery and cutlery, and God knows what else," Gerard said, unable to refrain from slamming his hand on the table.

Aunt Carmen seemed undaunted and maintained her haughty tone.

"There was nothing of value, only trinket and old gadgets. If there was something valuable, don't you think we would have known many years ago?" Carmen said, keeping her gaze fixed Gerard's furious face.

"What I cannot believe is that you would sell the trunks without even checking with me," Gerard insisted.

"They were only old books; they weren't worth anything. And if that's what you're implying, I didn't do it for money, they gave me next to nothing. It was just spring cleaning," she apologized.

"But my parents' books were there, books I could now use in my work, and who knows how many more things I did not even have a chance to value. Besides, I've played with those trunks since I was little, nobody else had ever been interested in them."

"Gerard, I don't want to discuss this anymore. I'm sorry, but it was just old junk," she said, settling the argument.

"What do you know about books?" Gerard thought, "if the closest thing to literature you've ever read are the journals in your psychiatrist's waiting room."

Aunt Carmen walked to the living room, indicating the conversation was over, an unequivocal sign to suggest that Gerard leave the house.

As he walked toward the door, Gerard did not take his eyes from her, from her disturbing half-smile, which he was sure was hiding something. The woman also followed him with her gaze, her hands playing with the huge iron key that activated the lock on the main door of the farmhouse.

Gerard could not forget that rusty key, as impractical as it was spectacular, that must have weighed almost a kilogram, and that always surprised their visitors, both for its antiquity and its gigantic size.

"If you love them so much, you can visit the bookseller I sold them to, he has a stall in the Sant Antoni Market. I'll give you the address, but don't bore me again with your nonsense," she said, before disappearing upstairs.

Gerard clenched his fists, trying to control his rage. He could still see his mother smiling at him and wandering happily around the house, and that image made him repress his desire to respond to the old woman with words he could later regret... not having said.

Out of respect for his mother's memory, he decided to settle the issue right there and set out to track the books in the Sant Antoni Market as soon as he had some free time.

CHAPTER 4

Sant Pau-Santa Creu Public Library. Today.

E very five minutes, he lost his gaze in the heights and had to force himself to concentrate. The majesty of the enormous room was distracting. The huge pointed arches holding the framework of wooden beams and the warmth of the stone always transported him to past periods.

He could not help but think of the medieval knights and damsels in distress that had strolled through those halls from the time when Christopher Columbus roamed the city in search of financial support for his voyages.

Gerard had had a chance to reflect on his immediate future. He needed projects that would generate income, without giving up his dreams or his commitment to the truth, the main reason he had devoted his life to journalism.

He decided to take advantage of the impasse Lady Luck had put him in, to pick up the thread of his past research on those issues that had always obsessed him, hoping that if he researched them, and accumulated enough evidence, success would come and it would be the media chasing him and not vice-versa. He thought of writing a long series of articles and perhaps compile them into a collection.

He closed the book he was holding and put it down next to the column of other volumes he had borrowed. They were all about Art Nouveau in Catalonia, the European

14

cultural, artistic and architectural movement that in the late nineteenth century flourished in Catalonia.

The region was regaining its historical identity, and its bourgeoisie had the economic means to finance the construction of iconic buildings and residences, built by architects who would pass on to posterity, such as Gaudí, Puig i Cadafalch and Domènech i Montaner.

The legacy of those artists amazed him; hundreds of government buildings, factories or private homes built in a style where whimsical rounded forms and a riotous cult to form and nature in all its versions prevailed, with abundant floral, animal or mythological motifs of great beauty and sensitivity.

UNESCO had declared many of them World Heritage Sites and had become one of Barcelona's biggest tourist attractions.

It outraged Gerard to find out that after the Spanish Civil War, during the forty years of Francisco Franco's dictatorship, the dictator's obsession with the systematic elimination of all the Catalan nation identity symbols implied the destruction of many of those architectural gems.

It also infuriated him to ascertain how real estate speculation and political corruption continued with the shameful obliteration of many buildings, lost forever in a stinking cloudy past, depriving future generations of a priceless legacy.

Gerard pushed aside the mountain of books in front of him and turned to the pages of his notebook. He had found nothing of relevance, only the usual mentions about demolished buildings, and a few names of local councilors involved in the processes.

He dropped all the books on the metal cart, except one he borrowed and he walked out on the street to stretch his legs and find a place to eat. The library was on Hospital Street, a few blocks from the famous Las Ramblas avenue, near city landmarks such as the Gothic Quarter, the Cathedral and the Gran Teatre del Liceu.

In those narrow streets, old taverns abounded, as full of character and personality as littered with waste on the floor, especially near the bar. He entered one and took a risk by ordering the daily special.

We all must die of something, he said to himself, and today it was as good a day as any.

He sat at a very worn white marble table, as close to the door as possible, to get more of the scarce natural light able to reach down those narrow streets. While he waited for his food he leafed through the photographs in the book he had borrowed from the library, an illustrated guide to old Art Nouveau Barcelona.

He enjoyed letting his gaze travel down those black and white streets, oozing sadness, always full of passersby, entranced and with a serious stance in front of the lens of those old unusual cameras they had so rarely seen.

He stopped at a page dedicated to the long-gone Fine Arts Palace (Palau de Belles Arts), a magnificent and imposing building, demolished in 1942 on orders from the dictator himself, who considered it "*a symbol of Catalan nationalism*".

Gerard would have shed tears at so many examples of barbarism and ignorance by those old fascists. Letting his eyes wander along those photographs allowed him to somehow relive a lost forever past, and he tried to imagine what the Barcelonians of the time pictured there felt.

He admired the elegant lines of the Palace of Fine Arts, which seemed to have been six or seven stories high, with its main hall able to accommodate several thousand people, under huge chandeliers. The large stained glass windows in the frontal wall filtered the sunlight as if it were an urban cathedral and gave the atmosphere a ghostly dreamy aura.

Under the windows, a giant pipe organ further strengthened his perception of the place as a center of pagan worship. Dozens of metal pipes of different thicknesses rose into the stained glass windows, the pipes seemingly emitting light instead of sound, feeding the environment with golden reflections.

It was a captivating photograph, but there was nobody in it, which surprised him because it was very unusual for the time, when any photograph became a social event attracting crowds of onlookers.

The sound of his mobile phone interrupted his thoughts.

"Hi Max," he said automatically after seeing his friend's name on the screen.

"What are you up to? I already heard about the magazine. They're a bunch of ignorants, they have sold their souls to the capital but they won't get very far. Soon they will regret what they did to you," he told his friend, trying to comfort him.

"Sounds a bit threatening, doesn't it? Anyway, it doesn't really matter. Life gives me an opportunity to move on and do the things I believe in, whether or not they buy my articles," Gerard said.

"I'm glad to see you take it that way. I hope you're honest with yourself and buy it," his friend added.

After a few minutes of small talk, Gerard filled him in on his recent visit to the family mansion.

"From what you're telling me, that woman wouldn't be out of place as a housekeeper in a grim gothic mansion," Max said, "although, on second thought, aunt Carmen is not exactly a very scary name."

"Let's change the subject. Do you want to meet this Sunday to go explore the Sant Antoni market? I don't want to let too much time go by before I get back my family trunks."

Max maintained the suspense during a few seconds of silence.

"All right, but first we'll take an apéritif, and then we can visit all the stalls selling books and antiques, whatever you want. If you can't find it there, it doesn't exist," Max sentenced.

"Ok, but let's meet at ten because I know you. Weekends you never get up before noon."

"You mean I should change my habits and wake up early, putting an end to my all-nighter reputation?"

"No, what I want is to be there early and have more time for the apéritif. It's your turn to pay."

CHAPTER 5

Sant Antoni Market. Barcelona. Today.

I t was way past 10:00 am and the streets of the Sant Antoni quarter were busy with pedestrians out to buy the newspaper, bread, to have breakfast, or just out for a walk.

Max not showing up was nothing new; the amazing thing was he deigned to call to give an explanation.

"Did you not sleep well last night?" Gerard asked.

"How did you know? Are you a psychic or something?" Max said dully. "I don't know what I had for dinner last night, but my stomach is very upset. I haven't slept at all. I couldn't stop getting up and sitting down. In fact, I've been sitting down most of the night, and not exactly in a chair, if you know what I mean."

"I can imagine the scene, please spare me the details."

"With all the pain in my heart, I'm afraid I must pass on having an apéritif with you this morning, I'm sorry."

"The lengths some people will go to avoid paying for drinks when it's their turn," Gerard joked.

"Chill out, man. Just put it on my tab and next time we'll make it double. Really, I feel very sick, but I'm sure you'll manage in the market without me. Uaghhhhh! I have to go, it's an emergency, bye!"

With a smile on his lips, Gerard tried to erase from his mind the grotesque image of his friend and his urgent indisposition. He felt sorry for him, but he wanted to make the most out of the morning.

He went into a bar to have breakfast, and he was soon back on the street, letting himself be dragged by the flow of people moving toward the market.

Sant Antoni's Sunday market was a popular fair set up every Sunday under the canopies surrounding the enclosure of the food market. It dated from 1936, initially born as a point of purchase, sale, and exchange of literature, having done much to awaken the love of reading in many generations of children in Barcelona. During the dictatorship, it was the place where all books banned by dictator Franco.

Currently, it was a swarm of people, mainly parents, and children who came to exchange trading cards of all kinds, and also collectors in search of old books, movies or curiosities.

Gerard had been there just a few times, and he enjoyed visiting the stalls, stopping at those specializing in antique books or art books, trying not to be carried away by the human flood.

It didn't take him long to locate the bookseller his aunt Carmen told him about. A rickety table made with a wooden plank over two trestles, behind which he saw shelves full of antique volumes whose spines were almost illegible and boxes filled with old books.

Gerard rummaged through the piles of books on the table and found an old treaty on Art Nouveau architecture that interested him.

"How much do you want for this?" he asked the bookseller.

The old man, his hair almost albino white, was dressed in an old dark navy blue work coat which looked as old as his books, the wrinkles on his face comparing to the yellowed pages of old parchment.

"How much do you offer?"

"*So you expect me to bargain,*" Gerard thought. Despite being uncomfortable in those types of transactions, he considered himself one of the few fortunate people born with the expert negotiator gene in his DNA.

His strategy was to hide his desire to get back his parents' trunks. That way he hoped to get a better price when it was time to bargain.

"I don't know how much to offer, but not much. These are old books and not exactly incunabula. The thing is that I'm interested in this subject," Gerard said, his confession breaking one of the main rules of a good negotiator.

The old man approached him, took the book in his hand and opened it by the first page.

"So you are interested in Art Nouveau? This is an early century book, from the year 1900 approximately."

"Yes, I know. I'm very interested in this period. I'm a writer and I'm gathering information for an article, but I cannot spend much, although the subject has fascinated me for years. Please tell me how much you want and I'll pay you. I won't argue with you," Gerard said, in another demonstration of his brilliant negotiating techniques.

The old man did not answer, but looked at him in silence, as he turned the book in his hands. "I have the feeling you didn't come here only to buy this book."

"What do you mean? Is that obvious?" Gerard surrendered. "It's true. I'm here to ask you about some trunks full of books you purchased a few days ago from a farmhouse in Argentona."

The smile disappeared from the old man's face.

"That was some character, that woman," he sighed.

"I don't know whether to take your sigh as a sign of admiration or desperation, but that woman is my aunt," Gerard said, to which the old man replied rolling his eyes.

"The trunks belonged to my parents, and they only contained my grandparents' old books, of no economic value, but lots of sentimental value for me," Gerard said, trying to be persuasive.

"Wait a moment," the old man said, and with surprising agility, he ducked under the wooden board, and walked to several bundles stored under the table and covered with a dark green canvas.

He lifted the canvas to show several cardboard boxes crushed by the weight of the books and a medium size wooden trunk. He approached the trunk and patted it.

"I want to help you. If that woman is your aunt, I feel sorry for you. This is the only trunk left from the lot. I already sold the other two."

Gerard could not hide his disappointment.

"But this is the biggest of all three, and I filled it up with more books that will interest you. They're all from around 1900. There's a little of everything, Art Nouveau, architecture, design, and even several literature classics that had just been published. The bestsellers of the time, we might say."

"But I'm only interested in those that were originally in the trunk. Can I just choose some and leave the rest?" Gerard asked.

"I don't remember which ones I added. Besides, I prefer to sell them all in one lot, I cannot be selling single pieces, I wouldn't make any profit. Keep in mind I buy entire libraries that often come from inheritances, in which books are sold by the pound, and heirs only want to make a profit from selling the lot. It's a shame, but the story is always the same."

"I'm not sure. I would be buying blindly, and adding insult to injury, I would buy back something that rightfully belongs to my family, which is the height of stupidity," Gerard said, unaware that his comment might annoy the bookseller and crown his negotiating master class.

"Don't worry," the old man said, showing an enigmatic but friendly smile. "As I said, I want to help you. I like you, and even though they're not incunabula, I know you will appreciate these books. That's why I'll sell you the trunk and all its contents for only fifty euros."

Gerard still hesitated. It infuriated him to have to pay for something a few days earlier was his, but if he was in that predicament it was thanks to his aunt Carmen's extreme greed, when she had no remorse getting rid of family heirlooms for money.

"Please consider that only the wooden chest alone is worth more than that. It's from the last century, with and its corners are reinforced with golden rivets, all original. You won't regret it, it's like buying a surprise box," the old man said, knowing he was about to close the deal.

Gerard reached for his wallet and pulled out a fifty euro note. He had no job, no income, not even good short-term prospects, but he couldn't afford to let that trunk go or he risked losing it like the other two.

He did not give it more thought and handed the note to the old man, who smiled gently and crouched to push the trunk out from under the table.

"It's locked. Do you have the key?" Gerard said, noting that the chest had a large external lock. "What if it's full of rocks instead of books."

The old man smiled nervously again.

"That is part of the fun and the surprise. I believe I lost the key. That's why I sell it so cheaply but believe me, it's full of books."

Gerard shook his hand, cold and wrinkled. He bent down and to his relief he saw the chest had leather side handles. He tried to take several steps and carry it on his shoulders, but couldn't even lift it above his waist. He did not get very far, so he put it down on the ground and looked out into the street to stop a taxi.

If he added up the cost of the chest, plus the cost of the taxi, plus breakfast, he did not want to know how much each book would end up costing him, if what he would find inside turned out to be books after all, although the thought he was getting his parents' books back made it all worthwhile.

When he closed the cab door, he turned to the bookstall. The old man was still there, watching him from a distance, with his dirty dark blue coat, leaning on the table filled with books and with the same half-smile that had not disappeared from his mouth.

CHAPTER 6

Barcelona. 1912.

The dark stairs were so narrow there was only room for one person. Young subinspector Morillo had climbed three floors and wheezed as if they had been forty.

The bicycle ride from his police station in the Eixample district, in the upper part of Barcelona, to Tallers Street, had been exhausting, even though the journey was mostly downhill. Heavy traffic and cobblestoned streets turned any trip, however short it might be, into a massage session at the hands of a steamroller.

The notice had come in that very morning, and he hoped to be among the first to reach the scene. He did not want to see potential evidence altered by the intrusion of onlookers.

A man was waiting for him in the dark hallway of the fourth floor and motioned him to hurry.

"I am the manager of this establishment. Thank God you're here," he said, pulling Morillo's coat sleeve, to which he resisted, wanting to show who was the authority.

Morillo knew the apartment was a well-known brothel, whose existence was tolerated given the high political and social status of many clients but the contrast between the lugubrious outside and the exuberance of the interior surprised him.

He was in a large entrance hall, where a small and elegant dark wooden desk next to a huge porcelain vase decorated with oriental motifs welcomed all guests.

He walked along a carpeted hallway, its walls dressed in a dark maroon cloth that had a velvety touch, which he knew because he could not resist running his hands over them.

Several disheveled female heads sporting layers of thick make-up showed up through the many half-open doors and disappeared as he walked by, the doors closing in his wake.

The manager waved and stopped in front of a closed door.

"Here we are. We have touched nothing since one of the women in charge of cleaning found them."

Subinspector Morillo winced slightly upon hearing the man had used the plural.

"Did you say, she found *them*? Is there more than one corpse? The person who gave notice to the police station only spoke of one person, a male."

The manager seemed flustered. "I wouldn't know. It was not me who reported it, but whoever did it, was trying to draw as little attention as possible. Our establishment is a nursing home, visited by well-known and respectable people who seek discretion and anonymity. That has always been our main hallmark and we try to preserve it at all costs."

"A nursing home, you say? Some kind of spa where you prioritize the relief of the ailments of the soul over those of the body?" Morillo asked, unable to repress a slight smile.

"Ehhh, we could say so. Although we do not forget the body either. Not in vain it is considered the temple of the soul," the manager sentenced.

"The temple of the soul... It turns out you're a philosopher," he said, and pulling out a handkerchief from his pocket he grabbed the doorknob to open the door.

"For the love of God. Do you fear you will get stained? We clean our rooms several times a day, everything is spick and span," the manager said, taking offense.

"I do it to avoid altering the dactylogram, in case we decide to take it. Has anyone touched this door since they discovered the bodies?"

"Only the cleaning lady and myself, at your service. Nobody else. If you do not mind my asking, what is a dactisam?"

"Dactylogram. A police technique patented twenty years ago in Argentina, which allows us to study a person's fingerprints for identification."

"And wouldn't it be better to study the face to identify someone? At the end of the day, it is easier to recognize someone by his face than by his hands, isn't it?" the manager said.

The subinspector considered for a moment whether that conversation was worthwhile continuing.

"Yes, you're probably right. Wait here, please, and don't let anyone in before I get out," he said, entering the room and closing the door behind him.

The room was in semidarkness and he could only make out a small sofa and a coat stand, from which a coat and a dark hat hung. The room was tiny, but he soon realized it was only an anteroom and that the master bedroom hid behind huge red velvet curtains.

He pushed them aside with one hand, slowly poking his head, not knowing if he would find the bloody scene of a savage butchery or a more conservative scenario.

The room was lit by a small electric lamp covered by a purple screen, tinting the atmosphere with an eerie and somewhat sickly hue.

To his left, there was a couch, on which several pieces of both male and female clothing piled up, next to a dresser against the wall, in front of a giant bed with an imposing dark wooden headboard. Under the crumpled sheets and blankets, he noticed some bulges.

He approached the bed carefully, looking down to avoid stepping on any possible incriminating evidence. As he looked up and to his left, his heart thudded to be facing a man of medium height standing in front of him.

He quickly drew the gun hidden under his coat, regretting not having entered the room holding it already.

The man did not move, and although something in him felt familiar, it was hard to see clearly in the prevailing gloom. "Do not move! Who are you?" he asked, pointing his weapon at him.

He took a step forward, but upon seeing the reflection of the same bed behind him, he realized it was a full-length mirror placed in front of the bed.

Lowering the gun, he thanked God for having entered the room alone, saving him from the embarrassment. He walked to the only window in the room and pulled back a few centimeters the heavy curtain that almost hermetically isolated it from the light.

He turned, his eyes following the white light beam that impacted directly on the crumpled sheets as if a divine hand tried to show him where he should direct his attention to.

As he waited for his vision to adapt to the glare he amused himself watching huge dust motes dancing in the light beam.

Under a thick dark green silk bed cover, several legs protruded, two hairy legs clearly belonging to a man, and a thin leg embedded in white stockings that could only belong to a young woman.

He examined the surface of the bedcover and went around the bed, picking up some small evidence that he saved in a small metal box he pulled from his pocket. Then he came to the foot of the bed and slowly lifted the bed cover, exposing a pair of naked and bloodied bodies.

A man about sixty or seventy years old lay stretched on his back. On top of him, a young woman about twenty-five or thirty years old, her legs spread, straddled him and had her face smashed by what looked like a frontal shot fired at close range.

From what he could see, the man showed no apparent injury to his face, but his body was bloody, although its position made it difficult to assess whether he had suffered other wounds of relevance.

Next to the two bodies, there was a small gun, but he

decided not to touch it until he could pick it up and store it under good conditions. He sniffed it and found it had been recently fired, but did not know how many times. The girl must have died instantly, but the man's cause of death was not apparent.

An autopsy would give him more information, but now he had to keep digging. The sheets must have been white once, but now they were red with pink nuances, having absorbed a large amount of spilled blood.

He walked to the bed's headboard to examine the man more closely and noticed the rosettes carved in the dark wood, splintered and smashed. One had a hole that foreshadowed the lighter color of natural unvarnished wood inside.

From his pocket, he took a small folding blade knife and poked the softwood in the hole, until he felt something metallic. It was probably a bullet, but considering the angle, it could not be the bullet that had shattered the girl's face, which was in the opposite direction.

As he examined the head of the man lying in bed, he immediately saw part of the huge open hole in the occipital skull region, exposing part of his brain mass.

He could only think of two options to explain the terrible impact, either they had beaten him with a blunt weapon or it was the exit wound of a bullet.

The answer was clear.

CHAPTER 7

Police Station. Eixample district. Barcelona. 1912

The morning was cold and Morillo entered the police station premises rubbing his hands, despite being sheathed in the ridiculous fingerless gloves he got as a Christmas present from his sister.

"Hey, "Bicycle man", the captain wanted to see you as soon as you got here," another subinspector shouted from the stairway to the station.

He found the nickname "Bicycle man" not funny at all, but had to admit it defined him perfectly, for not a day went by when he did not ride his bicycle, both to travel home or to many of the crime scenes he had to visit.

Climbing the stairs two at a time he reached his unit's floor, and after hanging his coat, he opened the desk drawer where he kept the evidence he had gathered in the alleged nursing home.

He had waited several hours for the removal of the bodies instructed by the judge and it would still take a few days for the medical examiner to send him the autopsy report. He wanted to spend the morning processing the evidence and preparing a lengthy report for his superiors.

Somehow he had the feeling this would neither be a normal case nor one more of the hundreds of murders occurring every month in brothels and seedy joints across the city.

He placed several metal boxes on the table and a leather briefcase containing various objects he had collected at the crime scene.

The close examination of the male's clothing had produced no results, and he carried no identification documents with him.

Identifying the woman was easier. When he interrogated the occupants of the adjoining rooms, he learned the young girl came from some Northern European country.

The manager insisted she was a young therapist, highly skilled in the arts of relaxation, but Morillo saw it more as a linguistic issue since perhaps in those latitudes prostitutes were known by a different name.

It was clear the girl had died before the man did because it would have been impossible for her to kill anyone, considering how her face ended up after receiving a close-range shot in it.

It was also more than likely they were having sex, although he did not know whether it had been before or after the alleged therapeutic relaxation session, which reinforced his idea that this was the typical case of an extramarital affair with a tragic ending.

To him, the key was to find out the male's cause of death. If it was suicide, why kill the woman first? To leave no witnesses? And why would he do it during sex? Why not commit suicide in private, as it is customary?

"Morillo, to my office immediately!" someone shouted from one end of the premises, bringing him suddenly back to reality. It was the voice of captain Botell, his immediate superior. He had forgotten to report to his office.

In a hurry, he put all the evidence boxes back in the drawer, tucked his shirt into his pants, and ran his hand through his bushy mustache, an unconscious gesture he made whenever he was nervous.

"With your permission," he said, giving a few knocks on the captain's office door.

"Sit down, please," he said, in a surprisingly friendly tone. After a minute of small talk about the weather, the captain went straight to the matter at hand.

"I suppose you're already working on your report about yesterday's case, am I right?"

"Yes sir, you are," Morillo lied. "I started, but I'm still analyzing the evidence I collected at the crime scene. If you would allow me, I would like to request a little more time. I believe there are unusual elements in this case that deserve an in-depth analysis."

"Is that so? And have you formulated any theories already?"

Not yet, sir, but several indications do not fit entirely in what might be a logical explanation. You see, sir, the male's death can only be because of three causes, suicide, accident or murder."

"You will never make superintendent if all you can do is reaching such brilliant conclusions. Even my grandmother, may she rest in peace, could have gone further," the captain interrupted him.

"I personally lean toward suicide, but right now I cannot rule out any of them."

"Nonsense, Morillo. Don't waste your time. This is a textbook case. A poor devil falls into the hands of an unscrupulous prostitute who kills him in the heat of fornication and then she commits suicide, regretting her crime. We've seen it a thousand times," the captain said, trying to settle the issue.

"True, but it could also be exactly the opposite. A man of social relevance puts an end to his life for whatever reason, and he does it in the arms of his lover, taking her to the grave with him," Morillo said.

"You have no evidence whatsoever that it was so. Do we know the identity of the man?" the captain asked.

"No sir, he had no documents on him. We will try to identify him by reviewing all missing persons' reports and asking the neighbors."

"As I said, don't waste your time. If he was someone important, we would have known already. And if he was not, I won't spend the very few resources of this department to investigate a simple murder in a brothel, the ravings of a lunatic who decides to end his life and that of his lover," the captain said, rising to end the meeting.

"In any case, I'm still waiting for the autopsy report, which I'm sure will bring light to the case," Morillo said as he stood.

"Autopsy? I doubt it will reveal anything new. We should not waste our time on that. You'd better devote your efforts to investigate the anarchists. That is a real threat to the population, and the mayor is pushing the commissioner very hard to get some tangible results soon. I think I will assign you to the team of deputy superintendent Zamora, who could use some extra hands. What do you think?" the captain asked, patting him on the shoulder as he walked him to the door.

"Whatever your orders are, sir, but I would still like to devote time to this case. It won't take long, I can combine the two tasks."

"No. I have already told you about my firm decision. You have until tomorrow morning to submit your report and then forget about the case. Besides, working on deputy superintendent Zamora's team will give you much more internal visibility and it will help you a lot when the time comes for promotion. I will see it in a much different light. You know what I mean," and giving him a nudge in the arm he pushed him out of his office and closed the door.

Morillo stood there, looking around. That was neither fair nor normal. He was ever more convinced that something smelled rotten in that affair. And he only had one day to prove it.

CHAPTER 8

There was a lot of work ahead and very little time to carry it out. He could not do it alone, so he resorted to the old "divide and conquer" to get it all done within the deadline the captain had given him.

He knew he would be returning favors for years, but he convinced another subinspector and a corporal to help him with the basic investigation. He sent them both to discreetly interview all workers and neighbors of the so-called relaxation center. Meanwhile, he would dive in the archives of missing persons in search of someone who could fit the profile of the strangers that lay in the morgue.

A cautious man, he decided to write beforehand a preliminary version of his report, in case the captain shortened the deadline he had given him and not wait for the next day, which had already happened a few times.

Happiness did not last long when he found out the only typewriter in the whole police station, a heavy cast iron Remington was being monopolized by a substitute typist, which entailed having to drop his handwritten report in the pile of pending jobs and wait one or two days for her to start typing.

On second thought, it was not such a bad idea, since delaying delivery because the report was in the slow process of being typed would buy him some time.

He hurried to draft a conventional report by hand, in which he embodied the same doubts and theories he had already shared with the captain during his recent conversation. He dropped it at the bottom of the tray of pending jobs to be typed, not rushing the typist in the least, and went out to check the missing person files.

The morning went by reviewing all entries for the last year and a half in the voluminous registry book. It was a tedious process, since he had to write the classifying number for each case, and go to a filing cabinet to locate the corresponding folder to retrieve all data from it, such as the text of the complaint, the statements of the family members, the physical description and other details about the disappearance.

Since it was very unusual to have photographs of the missing persons, he knew most of his investigation would rely upon verbal descriptions, often dodgy.

Starting with the male he gathered information on over sixty cases where age and general characteristics of the missing persons could fit with the subject in question. He spent most of the afternoon trying to reduce that group down to a more manageable number, but he found it very difficult to identify common traits.

Applying logic, he soon could separate them into two groups based on their profession. The largest group included people from different trades, such as shopkeepers, merchants, schoolteachers or carpenters, while he identified a much smaller group comprising industrialists of some renown or social status.

He had to decide and take risks, so he concentrated on that second group, being the smallest and most interesting for him.

More commonalities appeared within that small group. Most were impoverished industrialists, or who had gone through financial difficulties in the months prior to their disappearance, which could favor the suicide thesis in many of the cases.

He also realized most of them had no partners or offspring, and complaints had been filed by second-line relatives, like brothers or cousins, or court-appointed.

Not having direct relatives meant not having direct

heirs. He thought it would be interesting to find out if any of them had written a will, although that job would take many days, and time was a luxury he did not have the benefit of.

It was late and soon he would have to quit the investigation for that day, but he waited until his two collaborators returned and updated him on the outcome of their inquiries.

The main conclusion after questioning workers and neighbors was that there was more traffic in that nursing home than in a train station at rush hour.

Despite the discretion with which they handled the visits, everyone knew it was a brothel, assiduously frequented by high class, wealthy individuals and politicians covering the whole political spectrum.

It had been impossible to establish the identity of the male. The absence of any distinguishing physical trait made recollection by neighbors and employees very difficult.

He decided to call it a day, thanked his colleagues for their collaboration, and went down to pick up his bicycle from the storage room in the lobby, where they allowed him to park it.

As he was walking away from the big city, pedaling uphill between fields of crops delimited by small stone walls, he could not get the list of missing persons out of his head, trying to find some link between them that could connect them to the deceased.

He reached his home, a modest space in an annex to a stately farmhouse in the Horta district, whose owners rented it to him for the peace of mind it gave them having a police subinspector as a tenant.

He took the bicycle on his shoulders as he opened the door and entered the house, leaving it near the entrance.

That night he could not sleep. He hoped the autopsy report would help him with the investigation. He decided to visit the coroner first thing in the morning, to get some preliminary information before receiving his final autopsy report.

The next morning he got up very early. The first rays of sunlight found him pedaling along dirt roads toward the city. He went straight to the Laboratory of Forensic Medicine of Barcelona, created in 1887, which handled all autopsies requested by the authorities.

An orderly informed him the coroner was busy, and he had to wait over an hour for him to show up. Although Morillo suspected the coroner had come straight from home, he avoided the subject in his presence.

Dr. Ernesto Vilaseca was a relatively young medical examiner, whom Morillo had worked with in several cases. Although they could not be considered friends, there was mutual professional respect between them and a certain degree of sympathy.

The coroner cleared a chair full of reports and papers so Morillo could sit. That office was even messier than his own, Morillo thought, pleased to feel increasingly comfortable in such a chaotic environment.

He noticed a large framed photograph, on a bookshelf behind the desk. It was a portrait of the famous escape artist Harry Houdini, in his underwear and loaded with chains and shackles. Morillo could not help smiling at it, as he was also a big fan of magic.

Although it surprised him to find the picture of an artist in a coroner's office, he had to admit he was not in a funeral parlor, and love of show business was nobody's exclusive domain.

"What brings you here, subinspector?" he mumbled, as he pulled a pack of cigarette paper and started rolling one, which Morillo declined with a wave of his hand.

"I have taken the liberty to visit you and call upon your expertize. We have worked together in several cases, but I believe this is the first time I'm in your forensic laboratory," Morillo said, breaking the ice.

"Is that so? Well, I don't blame you. I can think of much nicer places to hold a meeting. The company here is boring. I'd say this place is… dead," he said, openly laughing at his own joke, and Morillo joined him, even considering the joke in bad taste and inappropriate.

"My reason for being here is to inquire about the autopsy of two bodies you received yesterday afternoon. Have you reached any preliminary conclusion?" Morillo said, going straight to the point.

"As you will understand, subinspector, I haven't yet had time to get to it in depth, I hope to do so today. Although I have many cases waiting for me downstairs, I'm fortunate because none of my clients will grow impatient if I keep them waiting too long, don't you think?" and started laughing outrageously again.

Morillo smiled out of courtesy, convinced he was not improvising those tasteless jokes, but he must have used them ad nauseam.

"I understand, the last thing I want is to interfere with your work but, would you be able to venture any speculative theory? I'm sure nothing can escape a man of your great experience," he said, trying to play the always-infallible adulation card.

"You're flattering me, but yes I would, I won't deny it. Let me think. Yes. Based on my preliminary external examination of the bodies, and in the absence of necropsy data, I can categorically claim several things," he said solemnly.

Morillo approached the desk, listening with growing interest.

"The female has a facial wound, a fatal one, most likely caused by a gunshot, fired at close range. I would say it was a shotgun, in all probability."

Morillo look surprised. "Couldn't it be a handgun?"

"Highly unlikely, to be honest, judging by the type and size of the facial injury," the coroner said, and Morillo preferred not to interrupt him again.

"I don't expect big surprises when performing her autopsy, the cause of her death is clear. As for the male, I'll need the autopsy to confirm or disprove my theories. The cause of death appears to be an intracranial injury, caused by a projectile impact inside out."

"In other words, are you suggesting he could have committed suicide?" Morillo asked.

"Precisely. Either that or he was a fakir who enjoyed eating large-caliber bullets for breakfast," he said, laughing ostentatiously.

Given Morillo's sensibility, he was getting fed up with those unpleasant jokes, but he played along. He had worked with that coroner before but had never seen his comedian side, although his sense of humor was black and outdated.

"But there is something else," the coroner said, again drawing Morillo's attention. "I think I'm not mistaken when I say I observe two exit orifices in the occipital skull region, although the wound is so large I must study it more closely."

Morillo was pensive for a few seconds. "Do you mean he received two shots through his mouth?"

"That is my expert opinion. Perhaps the alleged suicide victim wanted to make sure he was doing things right and pulled the trigger a second time," he said, laughed out loud again. "He must have been a very meticulous man."

That was too much for Morillo, such disrespect for the deceased coming from a professional bothered him, but the relentless doctor kept going at it.

"And the police report says they found the female on top of the male in coital position? Despite the position they found them in, I do not see traces of penetration or them having maintained relations of a sexual nature, although I will have to examine the issue deeper. Perhaps the female lost interest when she saw her male was losing… his head a little," and this time his laughter was the last straw that broke the camel's back for Morillo, his knuckles white from clenching his fists, to avoid antagonizing the coroner until he had received his report.

He rose from his chair and headed for the door.

"If you'll excuse me, doctor, I have duties to attend. I am very grateful to you for sharing with me your preliminary conclusions. I will wait to receive the final report, which I will read with utmost interest," he said from the door while putting on his coat.

"Whatever you need, subinspector. I'm glad to have been of service," he said from behind his desk.

"You cannot imagine how much," Morillo replied, walking out the door.

CHAPTER 9

Gerard's apartment. Barcelona. Present

Gerard came home dragging the trunk as if he was carrying a corpse, and as soon as he was in the living room, he dropped it and plopped down on the sofa, exhausted from the effort.

He lived in an austere attic in the upper part of Dos de Mayo Street, its modesty amply compensated by its biggest and probably only advantage, its extraordinary views. From its tiny balcony, and climbing on a stool, Gerard could see a piece of the Mediterranean Sea in the distance, squashed between two horrifying apartment buildings.

It was a bachelor's apartment, and nothing betrayed an unlikely feminine presence. He had had some steady partners, but none with enough patience to endure his many absences, both physical and psychological.

His absolute devotion to his journalistic investigations drove him to almost abandon all social life, something incompatible with maintaining a healthy relationship with a woman.

He had never overcome his parents' deaths, gone too early, and his vicious relationship with his aunt Carmen and his cousins had only made things worse.

His unjustified dismissal from the newspaper made his character bitter, and that bitterness acted as the best repellent against any woman who tried to approach him wanting to maintain a stable relationship.

But he hoped the new setback he just suffered after losing his work in the magazine could be the wake-up call he needed to give his life a positive turn. He had to reinvent himself, find a taste for life again. It was never too late to try.

He went to the kitchen and opened a can of sweet peanuts, one of his few declared vices, and swallowed a big chunk before going back to examining the trunk.

The trunk looked smaller than what he remembered, which he attributed to the change in scale and perspective that comes with leaving childhood behind.

It was a dark wooden trunk, dirty and battered from the passing of time, but still had a sturdy appearance. Edges reinforced with metal pieces that had once been golden, two leather straps surrounding it crosswise, and in the front, two rusty locks.

How could that old man sell him a locked trunk with no key? He began to wonder how could he have been so gullible.

It was not enough having paid money for a trunk he owned by right, but he now had to deal again with his aunt Carmen to figure out where could the damn keys be.

The keyhole was not huge, so he tried all the keys he had at hand but to no avail.

If what the old man had told him was true, and the trunk itself was more valuable than what he paid for the entire set, he did not want to damage the lock by picking it, but after leveraging with a fork, he disengaged the moving lock tabs and they snapped open.

He lifted the lid and a strong smell of dust and mold made him sneeze. He smiled upon seeing the seller had not fooled him. The chest was full of books.

He forgot any remorse he might have had about his purchase and surrendered completely to discovering what was inside the chest. He felt like little boy Jim Hawkins in Treasure Island, rummaging through pirate John Silver's chest, although he could not remember if a chest like that

41

ever appeared in the book. The feeling was exhilarating and for a moment it took him back to his childhood.

Gerard started placing the books on the dining table as he examined them. There were several thick architecture treatises, which he separated from the rest for later review, and also some very old novels displaying beautiful Art Nouveau illustrations, which greatly pleased him.

How was it possible that having climbed so many times to play at the farmhouse attic during his childhood, he was never interested in exploring the contents of those trunks?

He wondered whether the books were part of some of his great-grandparents' private collection, or belonged to a member of the high bourgeoisie since most novels were in their original language version.

He found a copy of "Le Fantôme de l'Opéra" by Gaston Leroux from 1910, one of "The Secret Garden" by Frances Hodgson Burnett, from 1911, the 1908 classic "Uncle Tom's Cabin" by Harriet Beecher Stowe, a copy of "White Fang" by Jack London, from 1906, Sir Arthur Conan Doyle's "The Hound of the Baskervilles's", from 1902, an Italian copy of Emilio Salgari's "Le Tigri de Mompracem" and Joseph Conrad's "Lord Jim", both from 1900, and the well-known "The Wonderful Wizard of Oz" by Lyman Frank Baum, also from 1900.

It surprised him to find among them a 1906 copy in French of Guillaume Apollinaire's "Les Onze Mille Verges", a scandalous novel which had secretly circulated among Europe's high bourgeoisie circles during that period, considered by many as pornographic. Could that forbidden book really have belonged to one of his ancestors?

Most had publication dates around the turn of the century and seemed to be first editions, in the original version and in very good condition, which made him think they would be valuable for a good collector.

It pained him to admit it, but it seemed his ancestors bought books by the meter, to fill their shelves and boast about their cultural level in front of their friends.

When he closed the trunk he was amazed at the number of literary classics published during those prolific years. He wished he could have lived in such a turbulent but fascinating period.

He was hungry and momentarily abandoned the books to go into the kitchen to fix himself a delicious dinner with fried eggs, bread, more fried eggs and some fruit, which he enjoyed sitting in front of the TV, watching the nine o'clock news.

After the break, he went back to the trunk and busied himself leafing through some novels, many of which had pages stuck together, although he thought in most cases it was not due to moisture, but to their virginity, having never been read.

He unwittingly spent more time with Apollinaire's forbidden book, a novel so hot and shattering that it was the equivalent to ten kilos of hot pepper swallowed with warm vinegar. He was shocked at the atrocities recounted in its pages, but his curiosity got the better of his stomach and he spent almost one hour reading it.

It was a brutal and gut-wrenching book, not suitable for sensitive people or those with restless stomachs. He reached the last page, closed it and was about to put it on the pile of books he had been taking out of the trunk when something caught his attention.

The last page was folded, not letting the back cover close. He took it in his hands and flattened the page with his fingertips.

He could feel something hidden under the lining.

CHAPTER 10

Taking the thinnest kitchen knife he could find he carefully lifted off the paper, which was not glued but only held under a tab from the thick back cover.

He found a small sheet of yellowed paper folded in two folds which appeared to have been hidden there in a hurry, without even gluing the lining back.

The only reason it had not become loose before was nobody had opened the book since someone hid the paper there.

He thought it was probably a note from the bookbinder, but he unfolded it slowly, almost reverently. The paper had a letterhead engraved on one corner, but it was faded and he could not recognize what it was.

His surprise grew when he realized it was a handwritten letter, written in tiny print, in downward sloping crooked lines.

It was clear whoever wrote it, did it in a hurry; in some parts the black fountain pen ink had smeared, drawing whimsical gray clouds on the paper.

Had his fingertips caressed it while the ink was still wet or did a teardrop rain on the paper surface?

His excitement grew along with his impatience. He got up to go look for his reading glasses and stood next to a floor lamp beside the sofa.

The letter displayed the elegant calligraphy of the

period, and the handwriting was legible, betraying how well-bred his owner was.

"*To whom it may concern,*

I write this letter in Barcelona, on January 6th, 1912, the day of the Epiphany of Our Lord. It is with great sadness that I am forced to write what I am certain will be my brief last words. I should have never let events reach this point, but my many vices have always outweighed my few virtues, and now I have no option but to pay the highest price for them.

It is against my will that I take this decision in order to expiate my misdemeanors, suffer punishment for my greed and to protect my family from a discredit that in no way do they deserve. Blackmail is always vile, but I face it courageously, aware as I am that my penance will ease the burden my descendants will have to bear, both personally, because they will not endure the scorn of seeing their ruined and humiliated father begging in the streets, and financially, for although they will be deprived of their inheritance, they will never know the troubles wealth carries alongside. I hope they live the modest and virtuous life that I did not know how to live and never forget the sacrifice I am about to carry out just for their wellbeing.

To my dear wife, one last tender kiss and the forgiveness I beg from her. To my daughter, hoping that the future holds for her something better than what I could not provide, I ask her forgiveness too.

May this letter be written proof that I am forced to do it, having been criminally stripped from all my properties under threat to my family, hoping that progress and the greater maturity of our society will allow the future reparation of the terrible injustices perpetrated here and the punishment of those responsible, putting an end to this ignominious reign of terror.

It is time, I must not keep the lady of the house waiting, she should not be infuriated.

P. "

The letter was signed with blurry initials, which appeared to read V.P. or perhaps only P.

Gerard held the letter in his hands while he meditated on those words, the farewell message of a repented father and husband. It had the wrenching tone of someone who, regretting his mistakes, is saying goodbye to his loved ones, hoping to get their forgiveness, an inherent feeling to human nature that seemed to never change despite the passing of the centuries.

Could it be from one of his ancestors? Was he reading the last words of some old relative? The mere possibility was, at the very least, exciting.

Gerard could feel between those lines there was more that deserved to be investigated. The mysterious letter spoke of blackmail, of a man forced to take action against his will, of criminal acts, of punishment requests for the guilty ones.

But above all, it was a full-fledged farewell letter; it appeared to be a suicide note.

CHAPTER 11

Casa Xamot. Barcelona. 1912

The clattering of the popular Blue Tram alerted the few residents in the area of its presence, as it slowly climbed Tibidabo Avenue, a budding arteriole in Barcelona's upper part, winding at the foot of the Tibidabo Mountain, where a modest amusement park had opened.

Recently urbanized by Dr. Andreu, a pharmacist who made his fortune helping Barcelonians fight cough with something as innocent as pills, of which he sold tons, the avenue was becoming populated with some of the most spectacular Art Nouveau mansions built by the wealthy Barcelona bourgeoisie and designed by the best architects.

Concealed from the outside behind an undulating wall, the Xamot Mansion's white walls adorned with floral motifs stood majestically at the top of the Avenue.

It was a huge house in Art Nouveau style and alpine inspiration, with a pointed roof and the incline so typical of Swiss buildings.

The local press had criticized the suitability of such building in a Mediterranean city like Barcelona, where snow only made an appearance twice each century.

The vagaries of the upper classes had no limits, and the Xamot family had spared no resources to secure the services of one of the most popular modernist architects of the period, Puig i Cadafalch and provide their estate with the greatest luxuries and comforts.

Immense manicured gardens surrounded the house, and at the main access to the property a building acted as the gatehouse, but it might have easily sheltered several families given its enormous dimensions.

The guard was a middle-aged man who lived alone, whose duties went beyond surveillance and included gardening, general property maintenance, and acting as chauffeur for Mrs. Xamot's automobile, an imposing brand new 1912 Cadillac directly imported from the United States, whose distinctive feature was being the first car equipped with an electric starter instead of the dangerous manual start lever.

It was midnight, time for the guard to leave his house to make one last round through the gardens and along the perimeter of the main house, as was his custom. His two dogs accompanied him, two mastiff hunters with an accumulated age of over one hundred canine years, who had seen better times.

It took him about twenty minutes to complete his round, which always ended with him checking all access points to the mansion were locked, before retiring to the gatehouse to sleep.

He entered the mansion and came out shortly after carrying a food bowl for the dogs with leftovers from his dinner. It was his way of keeping them well-fed while not generating much garbage, which he would then have to incinerate in the garden, adding to his already long list of duties.

When he reached the spot where he usually deposited the dog food, the dogs were nowhere in sight. He called them softly, and taking two fingers to his mouth he blew the muffled whistle he used to get their attention, but they did not come.

Those old mongrels were older than he wanted to admit since they already lived with the family when they built the mansion.

He bent down to pick up a stone and banged the metal bowl with it, but no one answered. He put the bowl down on the ground and walked around the perimeter of the house, with the same result.

He decided to check the gardens where sometimes the dogs would play chasing little mice and rabbits.

A trail crossed the wide central avenue, dominated by a large pond where the familiar murmur of a water jet provided background music to the nocturnal symphony of crickets and cicadas.

Gravel crunched beneath his feet and the guard kept whistling to call the dogs. He thought he heard movement between the bushes under the small pine grove to his right. He headed there and soon he made out a shape on the ground, facing the gnarled trunk of a large pine tree.

Upon arriving he found the lifeless body of one of the dogs. He turned it around, but could not see any wounds and attributed its death to old age. Nonetheless, his senses were on alert and he looked around, whistling again softly.

He explored the surroundings and suddenly heard branches brushing, which could only come from the hedges near the main house, so he headed there, giving a little detour through the central promenade.

The muffled howls from the other animal sounded as if the dog was crying, and he ran toward the point from which they originated.

Forced to find his way solely by ear, he walked into the woods, feeling the branches scratch his face and arms. When he reached the spot from which the howls came he assumed he was in a small clearing between the bushes since the faint moon glow seemed barely able to break through the thicket and reach him.

He could no longer hear anything. He reached for the only weapon he carried, a wooden cane, and brandished it aloft, pricking up his ears in case he heard the animal cries again, as he cursed himself for not having taken a lantern.

Soon he heard a faint sound coming from the ground, beside him, a soft and repetitive sound, like a light dripping.

He looked up and his heart sank when he saw a dark mass hanging over his head, swaying in the night breeze. He thought he knew what it was, but he feared to be right. He reached out and felt the mass with the tip of his cane. It was soft, and when he touched it, the bulge moved, letting out a faint moan.

The guard was beside himself. Someone had hung the poor animal, and it seemed to be agonizing. He jumped to try to reach it, but the body crashed down accompanied by the dry sound of a rope rubbing against the tree branch, followed by a strong lash.

The animal's body fell on top of him, and they both rolled on the ground, the guard slapping blindly, trying to shake off the flesh mass.

A burst of lucidity made him think if the animal was hanging there, the person who committed such a barbaric act could still be there too.

He jumped up, his heart racing and almost coming out through his mouth and he waved his cane blindly from side to side. How soon had he forgotten his military training, he thought, and started running toward the house.

Gravel from the central promenade blew up in the air as he ran by without even bothering to hide, going straight to the mansion's front door, whose porticoed entrance stairway he climbed in a single jump.

He found the main door locked, which reassured him a little. He thought of going to the gatehouse at the estate main entrance to collect his service weapon, but his instinct told him it was not there where danger lurked and his duty was to protect Mrs. Xamot above all else.

He went around the house at a brisk pace, checking all the windows and doors until he completed the circle and arrived back at the front door. His next step would be to go to the gatehouse to get his gun and a lantern and search the whole state.

The piercing screech of a moving hinge made him turn around quickly and his blood froze upon seeing the front door was slowly opening, as if pushed by an invisible hand.

The assailant was inside the house. He hesitated an instant, assessing his options. Enter the house and confront him, armed only with a cane, or go get his gun, wasting precious time; that was the dilemma.

The answer came to him suddenly, when he heard crunching gravel behind him and had just enough time to turn around and stand in the way of a thick long blade, which penetrated cleanly and deeply through his entrails, rummaging inside with precise movements and staying there while severing what little still held him to life.

During the lapse between when life escaped from his own eyes until they went off, the guard looked straight into the eyes of his assailant and collapsed into his arms, as he placed his lifeless body on the ground.

The trail of blooddrops the saber left on the gravel headed toward the house.

CHAPTER 12

Subinspector Morillo did not use his bicycle this time. He thought that one advantage of not wearing a uniform was he could move around the city without being identified as a policeman, although often his bearing, his staff, and his trademark bowler hat betrayed him.

He traveled along with corporal Roura, a young officer of about twenty-five years of age who was enjoying one of the few opportunities he had to escape from his routine, accompanying a true secret police subinspector in one of his missions.

The horse-drawn tram climbed with difficulty up the steep Balmes street, pulled by a single suffering horse, when under normal circumstances it should have had a companion.

The horse snorted while dragging a wagon full of passengers, and at the end of its itinerary, it stopped outside "La Rotonda", a building under construction.

Feeling sorry for the exhausted horse, whom his tandem partner had abandoned, they followed on foot up Tibidabo Avenue until they reached the iron gate giving access to the estate known as Casa Xamot.

Several municipal police officers controlled the street access because despite being an exclusive area with low population density and undergoing an urbanization process, the incident had attracted numerous onlookers who crowded in front of the gate looking for some morning entertainment.

When he saw them arrive, the officer guarding the gate greeted them and let them in. In front of the gatehouse, they met subinspector Aromí, who summarized the facts for them, starting with the murder of the guard, whose disemboweled body covered with a white sheet was still in front of the main house.

"We also found his two dogs dead. One of them down there, probably poisoned with a piece of meat, and the other, stabbed and hanged from a tree in that thicket there," he said, pointing toward the grove flanking the side of the house.

"With the guard out of the way, we believe the murderer entered and left the house through the front door because no access has been forced. He headed for Mrs. Xamot's chambers upstairs and savagely attacked her in her bed."

"Who gave notice to the police?" Morillo asked.

"The only maid who slept in the house that night, as the other employees had the night off. After discovering the murderer the girl fled to look for the guard, but when she found him dead in front of the house, she went out to the street prey to hysteria. A municipal police patrol found her several blocks away. If you want to interrogate her, we keep her in custody in the main room, or maybe you would rather examine the cadaver of the guard first," the agent said.

Morillo decided to prioritize the living over the dead, and climbed the steps of the huge outdoor marble staircase, flanked by rows of twisted columns supporting a roof that covered the access to the mansion in case of rain.

The interior was a perfect showcase of the prototype of an Art Nouveau house; wavy moldings and ceilings, overstuffed furniture and a profusion of ornaments, floral and nature motifs coexisting with minimalist forms and geometric elements of great elegance.

Not a single glass on windows or doors was simple and transparent, all were colorful stained glass windows showing highly elaborate craftsmanship.

Morillo stopped for a few seconds, fascinated by the dreamlike atmosphere of the room, where the exterior light filtered through the stained glass fell on the furniture and ornaments as a fine rainbow colored rain, giving the whole a surreal aspect.

A huge carpet with floral arabesques covered most of the floor in the room. Morillo wondered what kind of ostentation desire could bring those wealthy owners to cover with Persian rugs floors such as those, in which beautiful tile mosaics could rival in beauty with those of the Roman villas of two thousand years ago.

At the back of the room, a uniformed officer stood guard by a young woman who waited sitting in a chair, dressed in blue with a white apron. She seemed to hurt on her side and to have dressed in haste, and her agitated state betrayed the strong emotions she had experienced.

"Are you all right, miss?" Morillo asked, showing reassuring interest.

She replied with a slight shrug.

"Can I get you something, food, some water?"

She shook her head from side to side as her only answer, which made Morillo think the interrogation would not last very long.

She turned and Morillo was pleasantly surprised to be facing a pair of beautiful clear eyes, thin lips and a look of serene intelligence. Her skin had some cuts and bruises, but they were not enough to distort her honest beauty.

"Good morning, madam, I'm subinspector Morillo of the secret police. Apologies beforehand, as I fear my colleagues may have already asked you several times, but please, give me a summarized narration about what happened, I beg you."

The young girl smoothed her apron over her legs and nervously summarized her version of the events.

Like she did every night, she had just gone up to Mrs. Xamot's chambers to make sure she would need nothing else. She ran with her through the list of chores for the next morning and helped her to bed. She went downstairs to the kitchen to complete the list of supplies she would order from the grocery store.

As she went down to her room in the basement, she noticed the front door was ajar, even though she was sure it was closed when she went down the stairs to the kitchen.

She figured the guard had entered the house to complete his round or to collect some item, which happened frequently, given his multiple responsibilities in the house.

Retracing her steps, from the landing of the stairs she noticed the door to Mrs. Xamot's chambers was ajar. The guard would have never entered the lady's room if she was already in bed. Something strange was happening, but overconfidence made her lower her guard and she entered the room.

In the dim light from a small bed lamp, she saw Mrs. Xamot writhing on her bed, struggling with a dark shadow straddling her and beating her with brutality. Even from a distance, she could see the bloodstains on the sheets.

The young maid could not suppress a scream, but terror left her paralyzed.

Upon hearing her, the assailant stopped and turned to face her. She could only see his piercing eyes, for he was wearing a firmly seated dark cap, covering the rest with what looked like a handkerchief or a black scarf. He wore a large black coat.

"Agnes, help, help me!" the lady shouted, barely able to vocalize, her mouth shattered.

Such desperate shout made her react, and acting instinctively she ran to the small fireplace a few steps from where she stood, grabbed the iron poker and pounced on the assailant with the courage and unconsciousness only youth may confer.

She was lucky because her first blow struck something consistent, and she hoped it was the skull of that savage. Mrs. Xamot was screaming, but now unintelligibly, spitting blood spurts every time she tried.

The man turned to the maid, still mounted on the

woman, punching her face savagely. He reached inside his coat and pulled an object that to her looked like a huge dark knife.

The man seemed to ignore Agnes, perhaps underestimating the threat she posed, or because of her feminine gender. Enraged, she raised the poker again and landed a second blow on the assailant, this time clearly impacting on his head, causing him to fall on his side on the bed.

Jumping from the bed, the man chased the girl to the door and when he reached her, he dealt a blow to her stomach and pushed her against a couch. Without pause, he lifted a chair and smashed it against the girl's ribs, and she felt an immediate flash of pain accompanied by a beautiful sight of multicolored lights, almost losing consciousness.

The murderer bent to finish her off, but Mrs. Xamot screamed again, trying to sit up and tearing down a large jug of water and several glasses on a tray. The man left Agnes for unconscious and turned his attention to the revived house owner, running to the bed and jumping again on top of her.

From that moment on, Agnes could not remember all the details, only that she rose as she could, and decided that the most sensible thing was to get out to seek help, since trying to help her lady would have meant certain death for the two of them.

Pushed by terror and fueled by pure survival instinct, she ran to the bedroom door, pulled the key from the inside lock and got out, slamming the door. She took two turns of the key from the outside and left the key blocking the lock and ran down the stairs, almost tripping but finally climbing them down the traditional way.

She expected to hear footsteps running after her, but only heard furious blows against the bedroom door which would not hold the assassin for long.

She left the house down the great marble staircase, screaming and calling the guard. When she ran into his bloodied body lying in front of the house, it stirred up her hysterics and helped her run with renewed energy to the estate's main entrance. She walked past the gatehouse and soon hit the streets, running down the avenue until she found two municipal policemen.

"You have been extremely brave," Morillo said, "and extremely foolish too, if you don't mind my saying," he added.

"What did you expect me to do? Your comment offends me. Had I stayed there, we would both be dead by now."

The courage of that young woman impressed him, and he liked her firm mood and her strong and determined character more than he cared to admit.

"Can you remember any other detail that might be of help?" Morillo asked, with little hope.

"Yes. When I hit him the second time, I pulled his cap and I could see his hair was abundant and reddish. He was a redhead," she said, excited at having remembered.

"It's a good detail. Anything else? Would you mind telling me the age?" Morillo asked.

"You never ask a lady her age," she replied, blushing.

"I mean the age of the assailant, not yours since it is obvious you cannot be over twenty," Morillo lied, although he should not be too far out.

"I could not see him well, but I would say about thirty-five or forty years."

"Do you think you could recognize him if you saw him again?"

"It was very dark, but I will never forget his gaze when he attacked me. If I can look into his eyes, I would recognize him anywhere."

"Excellent. I'm afraid I must trouble you a few more times, requesting your presence at the police station to further study the matter. If you would care to give me your address, I'll see to it that corporal Roura escorts you to your home and I remain personally at your disposal for whatever you need, any time, day or night.

Corporal Roura looked at him in puzzlement. Such display of interest and solicitude toward a mere maid could only mean one thing, but he would not make his life difficult by questioning a subinspector, because deep down he shared his admiration for the young lady.

CHAPTER 13

Police Station. Barcelona

The preliminary report mentioned Mrs. Isabel Xamot, the widow of a wealthy industrialist who had died two years before, as the owner of the mansion.

The woman was admitted to the Hospital de Sant Pau with serious injuries, and doctors feared for her life. When the maid ran for help, the assailant picked the lock and fled, leaving the woman badly injured.

Mrs. Xamot had no children or known relatives. Morillo wondered who would inherit the mansion and the many real estate and industrial properties she administered since the death of her husband.

Two days had gone by since the incident, without major breakthroughs in the investigation. Apart from the damage to the house, they had found no evidence on the ground and the only data they had was the testimony of the maid.

After an extensive consultation of police records, Morillo found no other similar attacks that could suggest the action of a maniac or serial killer.

He decided to investigate the life of the deceased husband, industrialist Ramón Xamot, an engineer who had made a fortune in the steel industry during the industrial revolution.

They considered his death by falling from a great height

into a bucket full of molten iron a consequence of doom, but there were also voices defending the suicide hypothesis.

He frequented the city power circles, and could be regularly seen at the Can Tunis racetrack and the Casino de la Rabassada and liked to gamble, often losing large amounts of money in both places.

"Do not obsess over this case," his friend subinspector Aromí told him, pulling a chair in front of him and lighting a cigarette. "A botched robbery at a high-class mansion, something we see quite often."

Morillo leaned back in his chair.

"I don't know, something doesn't fit. According to the witness, the assailant attacked Mrs. Xamot brutally but seemed unwilling to kill her, or he could have done it earlier and much faster," Morillo said.

"He must be a crazy psychopath, or a sex offender eager to have some fun with the little widow, you know what I mean, but the maid's sudden appearance interrupted him," Aromí sentenced.

It did not convince Morillo. His instinct told him there was more to it.

"What do you know about the late husband? What is your theory about how he died?" he asked Aromí.

"It was never clear. The official version spoke of a fatal accident during a routine visit to the steelworks. The medical report didn't cast much light since all they could find of him were his glasses, which came out flying as he dove straight into the pool of molten iron."

Morillo denied it, unable to conceal his doubts.

"I remember the controversy about who would inherit his fortune, because a few days earlier he had changed his will, leaving a substantial part of it to the city council, mainly real estate properties. His young wife only received breadcrumbs, so she hired the best lawyers to claim her part and after a lengthy lawsuit she got her right to a greater piece of the pie recognized. Among other properties, she kept the mansion they were building on Tibidabo Avenue, which the deceased never got to enjoy," Aromí explained.

"How could he enjoy it if he was dead?" Morillo joked, to which Aromí did not know how to respond.

"I meant the deceased never enjoyed it when he was alive. The fact is, he paid for it, but never got to enjoy it," Aromí said, ditching the subject.

"It is odd that having no descendants, he left nothing to the Church like many wealthy people often do, don't you think?" Morillo said.

"Yes, it would have been normal, but apparently our friend was not a very religious man. The matters of the spirit are often at odds with steelworks," Aromí joked, standing up.

He put his bowler hat and his coat on and banged his staff on the floor. His attire had become the unofficial uniform of the secret police, no longer guaranteeing their anonymity and letting people recognize them everywhere.

"Well, I have to go. They have assigned me to street work for two weeks, and I do nothing but tailing suspects and my kidneys are reminding me they can't take any more moisture and cold temperatures. Those damned anarchists, they seem to know we're following them and they're making me go round in circles like a merry-go-round. I had never walked so many kilometers in my life. Sometimes I wish they would make up their minds once and for all and planted the damn bomb so I could begin a proper investigation instead of following them all day as if I were their go-between," Aromí complained.

"Don't talk nonsense, preventing a massacre is always preferable to investigate it when it has already happened."

"I'd push the bomb up their asses, and would make it explode when they went to the bathroom, that's the best way to prevent massacres. Bye," Aromí said, heading for the stairs, where he bumped into a young boy of about sixteen, dressed with the standard delivery boy uniform, high black boots, jacket buttoned to the neck and a leather briefcase hanging from his shoulder.

"Hello *Bicycle man*, do you have anything for me?" Aromí asked, stopping next to the boy, who had a special bond with Morillo because they had a shared nickname.

"No sir, today I just bring a letter to subinspector Morillo."

"Well, in that case, I'm out of here," he said, disappearing down the stairs.

The messenger handed Morillo a thick envelope and he made a gesture to tip him but found no money in his pockets.

"Put it on my tab," he told the boy, whose facial expression suggested the same scene had taken place more than once.

When he was alone he opened the envelope. It was the autopsy report, signed by Dr. Vilaseca.

"Will he use any of his infamous jokes? I hope he shows more seriousness writing reports than in person," Morillo thought, ready to read the report.

That report could be the proof he needed to confirm the death of the unknown subject was not accidental but a suicide. The report would provide him with arguments to go to captain Botell and ask him to be reassigned to the case.

As he turned the pages, avoiding the technicalities of the wordy technical forensics language, his face was changing color and his expression went from shock to anger without barely realizing it. It was not possible, that report could not be right.

He flipped straight to the page where Dr. Vilaseca listed his conclusions. The cause of death in the male was a shot in the head at close range, a mortal shot, but did not mention the second shot with which they finished the job. He did not even consider the possibility of reasonable doubt or other alternatives such as suicide.

Dr. Vilaseca peppered his report with his characteristic statements, like saying the murder was committed "without violence", which, besides being contradictory, it reinforced the theory the man was killed while comfortably stretched in bed, enjoying the pleasures of the flesh.

He then went in some detail about the semen traces

found on the woman's body, and the various skin erosions in her genitalia, which according to the doctor showed there had been sex with substantial infatuation.

Morillo could not suspend his astonishment. Why would the doctor hide the victim had received a second shot in his head? And why would he declare now there had been sex when he had previously assured him he had found no evidence of it?

He had to speak to Dr. Vilaseca and clarify his strange change of position and question him about his contradictory conclusions. The fastest way would be to call him over the phone, no easy task given the limited availability of phone lines.

The police station had a single switchboard from which to place calls, as long as there was a request in advance and always handled by an operator. He would send "Bicycle man" to the Laboratory of Forensic Medicine to let the doctor know and invite him to a conference call at an agreed time and date.

He went down to the ground floor to request the call and as he came back, he saw from afar someone leaving Lieutenant Botell's office. He was astonished to see it was the coroner, Dr. Vilaseca.

He ran to him, calling his name aloud.

"Dr. Vilaseca, please wait!" he shouted, while the doctor climbed down the stairs.

Morillo caught him when he was between the two floors and grabbed his arm, which seemed to greatly disturb the coroner.

"Will you please let me go?" he snapped.

"It is imperative I talk to you, it'll only take a minute."

"I'm sorry, I have no time, they're expecting me in the lab," he said, and breaking free of the hand holding him, he walked downstairs.

Morillo did not give up and held him again.

"Please, just a minute. It's about your autopsy report. It has nothing to do with what we discussed the other day, your conclusions are completely the opposite. How is that possible?" Morillo asked, his stare begging for an honest answer.

Dr. Vilaseca seemed to ponder his words and replied tersely.

"My current conclusions are final. My preliminary conclusions were just that, educated guesses, and you should not take them into consideration," he added, looking around as if to make sure no one was watching them.

"But... I cannot believe the evidence be so disparate. You told me there were two clear shots, and that..."

"Do not continue. I have already told you all I can share with you," the coroner interrupted him, walking down the stairs, although he stopped again after a few steps.

"Truth is never found in the official archives; sometimes it is shackled under several locks, and searching for it becomes a Chinese torture. I'm sorry, I've told you everything I could," he added, and flashing an enigmatic smile he left Morillo standing halfway down the stairs and walked out on to the street.

That was really a very odd man, Morillo thought.

CHAPTER 14

Laboratory of Forensic Medicine. Barcelona. 1912.

The bicycle rattled over the rocks in the road, as Morillo tried to dodge loose pieces of rubble until he was near the Laboratory of Forensic Medicine building and stopped. Hiding the bicycle behind a stone wall bordering a nearby field, he continued on foot for the last hundred meters.

Making a detour to find a rear access, he soon found it. With his set of police lock picks in his hands, it didn't take him long to pick the lock on a small service door.

He entered the building and walked down a narrow dark corridor until he reached a set of stairs and climbed them, guided by the glow coming from the upper floor.

As he approached the front of the building, he soon recognized the path he followed days earlier to the coroner's office. He feared to bump into a night watchman, but everything seemed calm.

In front of Dr. Vilaseca's office, he reached into his pocket for his set of lock picks, expecting to put it to good use again, but the door opened with a soft click when he pushed it.

Not waiting for his eyes to adjust to the darkness, he risked turning on the lamp on the desk, covering the screen with his jacket to keep the glow from being seen from the street.

As he turned, his heart sank; sitting in the chair behind the desk, a figure was watching him.

Instinctively, he drew his gun and pointed at the shape, thinking it should have been the opposite since he was the intruder.

The figure did not move, but through the gloom he made out it was the coroner, watching him motionless, with glassy eyes. Morillo came closer, still pointing his gun at him, surprised by his immobility.

"Doctor Vilaseca, you must wonder why I show up here this way... but I also wonder why are you here working in the dark at such late hour," Morillo said, trying to make conversation.

He walked around the desk table, surprised to see the doctor's gaze did not follow him and kept looking straight ahead. He walked toward him and touched his arm with the barrel of his gun.

The swivel chair moved and the coroner's body slumped to the other side, falling to the ground, dragging a mountain of folders along.

Morillo ran to him. Despite the low light, the large bloodstains on his chest were visible. He unbuttoned his shirt and saw two large incised wounds; they had stabbed him with a large knife.

He spent one second to assess the options before him. His obligation was to report the discovery of the corpse, but he would have to justify his presence there at such a late hour.

Not reporting it, he risked someone would discover him, which would turn him a suspect. It would be hard for him to explain captain Botell why he was still investigating the case despite having been assigned to other tasks.

He decided the wisest course would be to fulfill his obligation and to report the crime, but first he would do some checking; after all, that was what he had come there for.

The body was already a little stiff, which meant death probably had occurred a few hours earlier. He went through

66

the mountains of papers and documents stacked on the desk.

He didn't know what he was looking for, but he had the remote hope the coroner might have collected his real autopsy findings in a logbook or a notebook.

He found nothing related to the case, but he had to admit the coroner clearly had the edge in terms of office disorder.

After picking the lock in several file cabinets, in one of them he found folders containing autopsy reports, but classified by numbers, with no identification names.

In his jacket he had the report the messenger had given him and wrote the number.

He went through the file cabinets until he found that number and flipped through the report. No doubt it was the original autopsy report, albeit only a slightly extended version of the same one the coroner had sent him, a summary of the main sections.

Defeated, he sat in the chair facing the desk, the same where he sat during his last visit. Sitting there in front of a corpse and do nothing to report the crime made him feel bad. His police soul and his professional ethics required him to report and investigate the murder, instead of blindly going on with his unauthorized investigation.

Not having found any relevant clues, he decided to close the issue. He walked to the corpse and picked up the piles of sheets and objects dragged by the fall, placing them back on the desk and the shelf; papers, folders, pencil holders, Houdini's framed shot, an ashtray.

Looking at the photograph of the famous escapist brought a smile to his face. Nothing was impossible for Houdini. He admired his serene expression, facing a new challenge almost naked, his hands and feet bound with thick chains and padlocks, and always coming out of it victorious. Morillo envied his extreme skill, he wished he could have some of that physical and spiritual strength to get to the bottom of any enigma, as the great illusionist would do.

He could not take his eyes off the photograph, although it had nothing to do with his case. He went back to the corpse and inspected it.

Besides the chest wounds, he had been severely beaten in the face, one blow having broken his nose, shifted to one side, and he had bled profusely from an eyebrow and several cuts on the cheeks.

The man appeared to have suffered tortures and being savagely beaten before receiving the fatal stab wounds.

A thought suddenly assaulted him, so he closed his eyes trying to capture its essence before it disappeared.

The coroner's last words to him were still ringing in his head. *"Truth is never found in the official archives, sometimes it is shackled under several locks, and searching for it becomes a Chinese torture."*

Strange words; but the coroner was a strange man, so it should not surprise him. Official archives, Chinese torture, padlocks, was he trying to tell him something with all that nonsense?

The official records were in front of him, in the file cabinet, and all he found in them was but the official version. *"Truth is never found in the official archives"*, in that he had to agree with the coroner, but where was the truth then?

The allusion to Chinese torture could not refer to the fact they tortured the coroner before he died, it was impossible he could have predicted his own fate. His reference to the truth being shackled under locks could refer to the fact that whoever knows the truth keeps it a secret, but that was a no-brainer.

His eyes returned to Houdini's photograph, in which he could see several padlocks. Probably the coroner, like him, an admirer of the great escape artist, had used them as inspiration for his metaphor.

When thinking about Houdini, one of his most spectacular numbers and a recent worldwide success came to his mind, his escape from inside the Chinese Water Torture Cell. Too many coincidences.

Was it possible that with his last words the coroner could refer to Houdini? He really must have been a big fan. Or maybe there was something else?

He took the framed photograph in his hands, a black and white still covered by glass and printed in such thick paper it looked like cardboard.

Lifting the small metal tabs holding it was hard, but inside he found two folded sheets of paper hidden between the photograph and the wooden back.

They were handwritten notes. It looked like an autopsy report draft, the coroner's original notes, to be handed later to a staff secretary to be typed.

The handwriting was quite legible for a doctor, and Morillo approached the lamp to read it better. They were brief notes, first impressions, only a list of short sentences, with no prose.

He quickly skimmed through the first parts and went straight to the conclusions on the second page.

The autopsy befitted a man and a woman. The man had two gunshot wounds. One of them by a gun fired from inside the oral cavity and shattering his skull, but the second, fired from a longer distance, was done post-mortem, that is, when the subject had already been dead for hours.

He could recover none of the bullets, as the impacts had cranial exit wounds, but the coroner suggested two different weapons were used.

The woman showed no signs suggestive of sexual intercourse in the hours before her death. Finally, he ruled the woman died from a close-range gunshot to her face, probably by a sawed-off shotgun.

At the end of the last page, he had written a registry number. Morillo leaned toward the autopsy registry book still open on the desk and compared the number with the one corresponding to his case. The numbers matched.

The coroner had given him a clue after all. The veiled reference to Houdini allowed him to find his notes and his real autopsy conclusions.

Why had he not spoken clearly? Why fabricating a false report stating the total opposite of truth? Who forced him to write it? Who was he hiding his true conclusions from?

Morillo was torn again between reporting what happened, enduring the captain's wrath, or escaping without leaving a trace of his presence there, and to secretly continue with his investigations about the more than evident suicide.

The fact the coroner hid his true report, and was probably killed to silence him, showed he was facing someone very powerful and dangerous, and you could never be too careful. He could not and should not trust anyone.

He made his decision. Picking up his jacket from above the lamp he put the coroner's notes in the inside pocket of his jacket, placed the photograph back in the library shelf and walked quietly out the door, undoing the path he had followed earlier until he was out on the street.

Once there, he could only pray his bicycle would still be in the field where he had hidden it, otherwise, he would have a long and cold nocturnal walk ahead.

CHAPTER 15

Barcelona. Present

Gerard devoted a few days to an intensive job search. It took him over two hours to update his resumé, instead of the fifteen minutes he had imagined. The damn document had the unpleasant virtue of sounding worse every time he re-read it.

It was hard for him to simplify his academic and work-life down to a few dates and lines. As a writer, it was much easier for him to write about others than about himself.

To him, writing a CV meant the height of exhibitionism, the equivalent of exposing himself naked in a store window, with thousands of onlookers squashing their noses against the windows and taking pictures with their cameras mobile phones, smiling or laughing loudly, pointing at him.

He reconnected with old contacts, sent dozens of emails offering his services for all types of projects and placed many calls to friends and acquaintances. The response was nothing short of disappointing.

The few who bothered to answer, did it in terms of false politeness, with no true intention of offering him anything. Nobody would worry about him, his personal situation was not a priority for anyone.

But the worst were those he had believed to be his friends who, upon receiving his call seemed to be strangely uncomfortable, as if talking to someone without a job would be contagious, making empty help promises they had no intention of keeping.

After that call, they would automatically place him in a permanent quarantine, from where they would only release him if he were to find a new job or succeed, at which time they would get out of their lairs to ingratiate themselves with him, with an intensity in direct proportion to the importance of the job or the project.

Sickened by the realization he was sadly alone and dependent on nothing more than his own resources and initiative, he resigned himself to keep going and emerging stronger from that new test fate had thrown his way.

The day had been long and disappointing. He sat on the couch with a glass of iced tea and relaxed watching an inconsequential comedy on television. So much futility stunned him, and before losing his dignity even further he switched it off and turned to the old trunk, still in the same place he had left it the day he brought it home.

His mind dragged him back to a sea of doubt, from whose depths he kept thinking perhaps the suicide letter was the last and desperate note of one of his great-great-grandparents. Just to think there could be a family connection, made his head boil with uncertainty.

He moved closer to the trunk. It was beautiful, it had character. It was difficult to pinpoint what period it could be from, because of its timeless design, and although it denoted classicism, it would not have been out of place in a pirate galleon or it could have belonged to Don Quixote himself.

After running his hand over the lid, caressing and feeling its texture, he took a kitchen rag and busied himself cleaning the trunk surface, dirty and obscured by the passage of time.

He soon realized the layer of dirt covering it could be traced back at least to the Middle Ages. He dipped a corner of the cloth into his glass of lemon tea, and after moistening the material he rubbed hard on the lid, smiling with satisfaction when he noticed the patina of dirt faded, its color clearing considerably, recovering some of its past splendor.

After rubbing for thirty minutes, the trunk had rejuvenated a few centuries. Satisfied, he noticed a roughness in the central area of the lid. On closer examination, he thought there was some kind of engraving, although it could also be scratches or damage because of use.

He used a small magnifying glass he kept since his teens, the one he used with his collection of fossils and insects and confirmed his suspicions, there were engraved symbols on the trunk lid.

The old trick, rubbing a crayon on a sheet of paper placed against the surface of the trunk seemed infallible, and it pleased him to see it not only worked in detective movies but also in real life.

It was hard to tell what it was, but he could make out some arabesques and a large incomplete circle, on top of which a series of letters were part of a crown-shaped inscription.

He moved the paper away in front of his eyes, unable to focus. The new technologies would have to come to his aid. He took a photograph of the symbol with his cell phone and emailed it to himself.

From his laptop computer, he retrieved the photograph and opened it in an Internet search engine, which in seconds tracked cyberspace to locate similar images.

The process was even faster than he expected. A few seconds later the computer screen showed a grid displaying hundreds of small images, supposedly related to the photograph he had taken.

It was obvious many of them were there for some strange cyber reason that escaped him. Some were commercial logos that clearly did not match up, others showed remote mountainous landscapes and some even bordered on the pornographic. His initial enthusiasm cooled off after sailing through such a display of options, each crazier than the next.

He had already viewed several pages and was about to log off when his eyes fell on an image that flashed through his visual field. He went back a few pages and clicked on the image to enlarge it.

It was an old sepia color image, showing two small white square towers topped by battlements, as in a medieval castle, although it looked more modern.

Between the two towers, a large iron gate and above it, a gigantic iron circle supported by Art Nouveau arabesques, on which large iron letters clearly read: "LA RABASSADA CASINO AMUSEMENTS" . The design was virtually identical.

He devoted the next day almost entirely to research about the place.

He found out it was a Casino opened in 1911 on top of the mountains of Collserola, the natural park surrounding Barcelona from behind and pushes it gently into the sea, like a giant hand afraid to hurt it, in whose palm the life of the city throbbed.

It was a major project, a quirk of the Catalan bourgeoisie of the time, eager to have a Casino that would rival the big and prestigious European casinos.

Built in the middle of the woods, in an idyllic natural environment, it not only offered the possibility to play roulette and all the most popular games of chance, but it also had a modern amusement park within its grounds, offering several of the most modern and spectacular amusements and rides in Europe.

Among them, a dizzying roller coaster, or the Water Chute, a free-fall ride in which carts would run down a steep slope to a halt when they reached an artificial lake, to the delight of the customers who ended up completely soaked.

The Casino attracted the largest national and international fortunes of the time, industrialists, politicians, financiers, and celebrities of the moment, who did not hesitate to rush to this privileged location to happily squander their fortunes in any currency.

The repeated bans against gambling issued by the Central Government in Madrid and the continued legal and bureaucratic barriers imposed on the Catalan entrepreneurs who owned the casino prevented it from establishing itself as the international gambling benchmark it was destined to become.

The definitive ban on gambling issued by the dictatorship of General Primo de Rivera in 1924 struck it the final blow. Condemned to operate only as a hotel and amusement park, it languished for years, and during the Spanish Civil War, the government destined the building to military use. After the war, its decline accelerated, with the frequent looting and pillaging of everything of value left in the premises.

After years of neglect, in the forties took place its final demolition, all materials from its majestic remains being used for decorating the neighboring houses, while the rest was sold for scrap.

As he delved into the study of the Casino and the socially turbulent but culturally wonderful Art Nouveau period, Gerard saw his interest and fascination for that building and that period of history grow.

The following weeks he expanded his research visiting libraries, diving in bookstores, delving into ancient books, examining blueprints in municipal registries and reading newspapers and publications of that period.

He collected the little information he could find about the Casino and its environment, its activities, its structure, and he was even fortunate to get a partial list of employees from the hotel that had been attached to the Casino.

It surprised him to read about the increase in crime in the area, as the Casino business grew. Attracted by the sweet aroma of fresh currency, many brothels flourished around the premises.

Being nestled among forests and mountains and away from the city did not encourage safety, and daily news appeared in newspapers about thefts and assaults perpetrated around the Casino and in the roads leading to it.

Of particular interest to him were the news about corpses found near the Casino, most of them individuals assaulted, robbed and killed, whose bodies showed up later, abandoned on the mountain.

Most never came to be identified and became part of the never published lists of that mysterious Barcelona, where opulence was magnified and the lurid was silenced.

Such events were not enough to turn Barcelona into a lawless city on the style of the cities born in the American West. The assaults always took place far from the city, in the mountains, and citizens saw it as something distant and associated with gambling and prostitution, therefore it never came to cause social alarm beyond jocular comments, jokes and brief newspaper accounts.

Gerard knew he had finally found the central theme that would give meaning to his research about Art Nouveau Barcelona and real estate speculation.

An aura of mystery and seduction had grown around the legendary and long-gone Grand Casino de la Rabassada, hiding it from the eyes of historians and the few who remembered its existence. It was the dark veil of death, which Gerard could feel ever closer, fluttering around him.

Those lost walls and rooms had been mute witnesses to events that were part of the black legend of the city, what the official history always strives to bury under shovelfuls of oblivion and denial.

He felt it was the duty of researchers and scholars like him, to rescue that part of history and expose it to the light of truth and established facts.

Gerard thought justice was only meaningful when the truth was revealed, and he felt the enigmatic Casino was still alive, its soul still beating in some remote corner of space-time, calling him to reveal its secrets.

He was always willing to listen, he would never turn his back on someone who needed help, nor on a good story, especially one in which he sensed the elements he played with were nothing less than life and death, perhaps that of one of his direct ancestors.

Now he realized what his next step had to be, to visit the Casino ruins and investigate directly on the field.

It was time to stir up the old ghosts.

CHAPTER 16

Hospital de Sant Pau. Barcelona. 1912

The next hours passed by slowly for Morillo. After his escape from the Laboratory of Forensic Medicine, whenever lieutenant Botell called him to his office he feared the worst.

As days went by his anxiety diminished, and he concentrated in the Xamot House assault's investigation and tried to keep what happened in the forensic laboratory out of his mind.

After his decision not to report the coroner's death, any time he expected news about the discovery of his body, but they never came. When he dared to ask about him, the official story was the coroner had gone out on a trip, a lie which deepened his concern and made him even more cautious.

It was clear someone inside the department was covering up certain crimes, and until he could figure out who did it and why, he could trust no one and had to draw as little attention as possible.

"Subinspector, I bring news from the hospital," corporal Roura said, showing up at the door. "Mrs. Xamot is awake, although her condition still is extremely serious."

Morillo put his fears aside and stood up.

"Has she uttered a word in front of her doctors?"

"I don't know, I have no confirmation about it."

"Who's with her?"

"Two municipal police officers relieved me and I came and let you know," the corporal said.

"Do you know them?"

"Only one. I don't know his name, but I've seen him before."

Morillo saw the opportunity he needed. Perhaps he could still question her, even if only for a few minutes. There was no time to waste.

"Let's move on. Come with me, corporal."

"Sir, it's raining, and the bicycle..." the corporal said.

"Forget about the bicycle. Wait here, while I go to the administration department," Morillo said.

He pulled some strings and got authorization to use a police car to travel to the hospital, leaving the bicycle or the bus, their usual means of transportation, for some other time.

The imposing St. Paul's Hospital grounds never failed to impress him, not in vain it was the world's largest Art Nouveau complex.

The original hospital dated from 1400 A.C., but the current Art Nouveau buildings had been built at the onset of the XXth century as a true miniature town; a group of individual pavilions among gardens, distributed along a main central avenue, flanked by an imposing main building at the entrance to the enclosure.

It was one of those buildings whose overwhelming beauty diverted his attention and sometimes even made him forget the reason for his presence there.

This time it was not the case. He was determined to find out what happened. A ruthless murderer was on the loose, and it was vitally important to question a witness of such caliber, the victim herself.

He also thought about meeting again with the maid, and although she could add little to what she had already told them, he wanted to see her again, and that should be reason enough. But now he had another priority.

Once they passed under the arches of the main building,

they accessed the tree-lined boulevard, rushing across the gravel road until they reached San Rafael's Pavilion.

Morillo strode up the steps, closely followed by the corporal who despite his youth was puffing as if he had been running all the way from the police station.

In the lobby, he spoke with a nurse hidden behind a counter who told him where he would find Mrs. Xamot.

White wooden doors gave access to a huge ward, with a vaulted roof and lined with bright green tiles. All along the room, through large windows reaching up to the ceiling, the light descended from the heights but never quite reached the beds down on the floor, which remained in a likely intentional semi-darkness, to avoid disturbing the patients.

The first visual impact shocked him; two long rows of beds pushed against the wall, twelve on each side, all exactly alike.

Morillo and the corporal strolled down the center aisle as they watched in silence the twenty-four heads sticking out between the white sheets of those endless bed rows, stretching as far as the eye could see.

Someone was sitting beside each bed, a family member, a white coiffed nurse or a nun, but no patient could complain of being neglected or poorly accompanied.

When they reached the back end of the room, a small door led to a smaller room, from which two flights of stairs started. A municipal police officer was on duty at the foot of the narrow staircase climbing upstairs.

After showing him his identification, the officer told Morillo the upper room was an isolated chamber, its only access being through that flight of stairs.

Morillo asked Roura to wait for him there and the corporal started chatting with the municipal police officer.

At the top of the stairs he came to a closed-door painted in the same green color as the tiles, green supposedly being a soothing color, but it made Morillo uncomfortable, accustomed as he was to the simplicity of the yellowed white walls of the police station.

He entered the room without knocking. The room was

spacious and circular, occupying the top floor of a small tower. Three large windows looked out onto the gardens, but from such a height, he only saw the treetops.

The bed was at the back of the room, but he did not see the patient, surrounded by four doctors and two nurses leaning over her. The oldest doctor, a heavyset man with a big slicked mustache turned to him and motioning for him to stop, walked up to where he was.

"I'm sorry but I must ask you to leave the room," he said, in a tone that overruled any objection.

"I'm subinspector Morillo. How is Mrs. Xamot? I wouldn't want to impose on you. I just want to ask her a few brief questions."

"She is in no condition to speak to anyone. Sir, I beg you, please leave the room right away," the doctor insisted.

"And whom do I owe the pleasure?" Morillo asked, hardening his tone.

"I'm Dr. Oleguer Papiol, Head of Digestive Surgery in this hospital. I do not want to have to ask you again. The patient is in critical condition and needs absolute rest."

"If that's the case, why are there so many people around her? Are they all indispensable?" Morillo asked.

The doctor seemed very upset by the arrogance in his question. "They are medical students. In your sublime ignorance, you may not know it, but this is a university hospital, and we can proudly claim we train future doctors, who do the rounds with the senior doctors responsible for their training. I'm sorry, but I cannot waste another minute talking to you. Get out of here, please. We will let you know should any new development occur," the doctor said, pushing him toward the door, gently but firmly.

Morillo considered the possibility of confronting that presumptuous chieftain but preferred to keep a cool head and avoid antagonizing him. He would find another way to achieve his objective.

Two hours later, they still had no access to the patient and Morillo was losing his patience. He could not afford to spend a whole day waiting for them to let them see her.

They went out to the gardens and walked around the pavilion up to the back of the tower. The windows to Ms. Xamot's bedroom were on the first floor.

"I don't see any other possible access from the outside," corporal Roura said.

"No, the staircase inside is the only way."

"That guy, Dr. Papiol, doesn't look like he'll make things easy for us to see the victim," the corporal said.

"Yes, so much irascibility is surprising. But many doctors are like that, they believe they are gods in the Olympus."

"The Olympus Theater down by the harbor?" an innocent Roura asked.

"Uh... no, I mean another Olympus, in Greece."

"Never been in that town, but I wouldn't mind taking my bicycle and going there for a visit one of these weekends," the corporal said.

"I'm afraid Greece is a bit too away far to go there by bicycle."

"Do not underestimate me, boss. Once I ran over twenty straight kilometers on my bicycle, and I only stopped once to pee," the corporal continued, his loquacity increasing after having found a topic of mutual interest.

Morillo wondered what the minimum level of studies required to enter the force was these days, but settled the debate immediately.

"Corporal, listen to me. You know the municipal police officer at the door, don't you?" Morillo asked, and the corporal nodded.

"Good. How about if we talk him into taking a break tonight and we relieve him and his partner from his night shift?" Morillo asked with a smile.

"And who would replace them?" the corporal asked.

Despite being slow-minded, Morillo's silence and his lingering smile gave Roura the answer.

"Tell me, corporal, you haven't gone up to the room yet, have you?" Morillo asked.

"No, you know I haven't."

"The doctors there have never seen you, have they?"

"No, I guess not."

"Tell me, do you have any plans for tonight?"

CHAPTER 17

It wasn't too hard for corporal Roura to convince the municipal police officer that night surveillance would be more effective in the hands of a member of the secret police and a corporal, plus he promised a generous tip for his cooperation, although he didn't have the slightest idea what to give him.

At eleven p.m. the nurse accompanying Mrs. Xamot came down the stairs. Although it surprised her not to find the usual guard, she told Roura she would be gone just a few minutes.

The corporal ran to a window overlooking the garden, waved his arm and returned to his post. Less than a minute later, Morillo entered through a side door.

"If the nurse returns, keep her here and send me a signal," he said, walking up the stairs and opening the door in silence.

The room was gloomy and the only light came from a lamp at the head of the bed.

Mrs. Xamot seemed to be asleep, but the large hematomas, her broken nose, her eyelids like two bruised spheres the size of two tangerines and the swelling that distorted her face, they all attested to the viciousness of the assailant and the severity of the injuries.

If her visible parts were in that pitiful condition, Morillo could not even imagine how her internal organs would be.

"Mrs. Xamot, can you hear me?" he whispered as he

dabbed her shoulder. The woman did not answer, she seemed deeply asleep, or perhaps unconscious.

Morillo insisted and seemed to notice movement in the corner of her lips. He approached them to get a better listen, and heard the woman trying to speak, but it could well be just moans of pain.

"Could you look at your assailant?" he asked, keeping his ear close to the woman's lips. He thought he heard an answer, but did not understand whether it was a simple yes or just a whimper.

"Did you know him?" he asked, staying close to her lips.

"Eeeee" she said, in a whisper that Morillo found painful to hear. Did she say yes? That's what he thought he heard. If so, it could be an acquaintance of her late husband or a family member. He had to keep talking to her at all costs.

In the silence of the dark room, the sudden sound of distant voices startled him. Corporal Roura was probably engaged in a discussion with the returning nurse. The muffled sound of footsteps coming up the stairs forced him to make a quick decision.

He barely had time, he had to hide and try to flee during an unguarded moment or when the nurse left the room again.

He looked around and saw a wooden door to what was probably a wardrobe closet and hid inside.

It turned out to be a small toilet which he discovered after taking a few steps in complete darkness, hands in front of him, feeling everything around him. Upon hitting against what felt like a porcelain toilet bowl, he hid his hands immediately.

He walked back to the door and put his ear against the wood. He could hear footsteps and the sound of sheets and concluded the nurse was fixing the patient's bed. The wait could be long, so he sat on the floor and kept his ear to the door.

On top of the sound of sheets, he heard the metallic

sound of springs clanging. It must have been the bedframe springs, he thought, but how could they squeak like that? It sounded more like a couple frolicking than a patient in a coma.

He peeped through the keyhole, but it was tiny and did not overlook the bed but a sidewall. His limited field of vision only reached as far as the glow of the lamp drawing its elongated wake on the dark wall, no matter how hard he tried to look beyond.

Suddenly he saw the light blinking and a series of shadows coming into the beam of light, like huge shadow puppets. It could be the shadow of the nurse's silhouette, but the nature of the movement felt strange, and when associated with the spring noises, his police instinct blew all alerts.

Something was happening out there, so he stood up, grabbed the door handle and opened it slowly, praying for the hinges not to squeak.

As his field of vision widened, he saw the shadows projected on the wall and when he had a direct view of the bed, he saw a dark shadow on the bedhead, wrestling with the patient.

It did not take more than a split second for his brain to process it was not the nurse, but somebody else who was trying to put an end to Mrs. Xamot's life.

He fully opened the door with a kick and lunged at the guy trying to catch him by surprise from the back. He had no time to draw his gun, but he could lift his staff as he ran toward the bed.

It all happened in less than a heartbeat. The man was choking Mrs. Xamot, crushing her head under a thick pillow. He barely had time to turn, surprised by the sudden appearance of Morillo darting over him, brandishing a huge staff which he downed hard on his shoulder, making him roll on the ground.

Morillo could not stop his momentum and he struck against the bed and fell on the legs of the poor woman, who was no longer in a position to complain.

With one hand he threw the pillow to the floor, while with his other hand he checked the woman's carotid for her pulse.

In those three seconds, the assailant got up and jumped on Morillo, both wallowing on the bed, crushing even further the unfortunate woman's body.

The assailant was much stronger than him, and unless he subdued him soon, he would not hold on much longer. He hoped corporal Roura would come up to help him, but didn't know if he could count on him, so he tried to pull away from the assailant to get his hands on his gun.

Morillo rolled back and felt he had reached the end of the bed and fell into the void, banging his head against the floor.

In the brief moment it took him to open his eyes, he saw the shining blade of a large knife, in the hands of the man dressed in black who jumped on him again.

He turned away instinctively and reached into his jacket, looking for his gun, which soon was aiming at the target provided by that buffalo charging into him. The gun muzzle flash shone in the dark, a burst of confidence that made him think he could have killed him.

He looked forward but did not see him, not in front of him, nor on the bed. The excruciating pain he felt in his arm told him the threat came from his side, an onslaught that sent him rolling again.

Through the cut that pierced the fabric of his coat he felt the warm, moist touch of blood oozing from the wound.

Unable to sit still, he raised the gun and fired twice blindly, pointing in the direction where he thought the assailant came from, and he believed he had hit the target because for a moment there was silence.

His staff was on the floor at the foot of the bed and he bent down to pick it up with his left hand. A new brief flash from the huge machete blade betrayed his position and as soon as Morillo sensed it, he did not even think and his staff described a wide arc striking with full force against the attacker's arm.

He saw how the knife came out flying and how the staff, after hitting the murderer in the arm, hit against his right cheek, sending the black cap covering his head flying up in the air.

The force of the blow forced Morillo to let go of his gun, which fell to the floor beside him.

Wanting to finish what he started, he reached down to pick it up, but he paused, and during the split second that savage face remained in front of him, their eyes met and Morillo felt pure distilled hatred concentrated on those dark pupils staring at him, shining as if they were on fire.

As soon as he felt the gun in his hands he turned to the assailant, raising his arm to aim, but the shadow was already a few steps from the door, running toward the stairs.

He wanted to aim before shooting, but after those few seconds of hesitation, when he fired, the bullet hit the door frame.

There was no debate, the priority was always the victim. He ran to the bed, but there was nothing he could do for that poor woman. If there had been any breath of life left in her a few minutes earlier, it had completely vanished, smothered by the crushing and the abuse endured during the fight.

He ran to the stairs and climbed down the two sections on two long strides. Only the gaslight from the street lamps outside, seeping through the windows, illuminated the small lobby.

At the foot of the stairs, he tripped over a bulge on the floor, corporal Roura's body. He turned it around, relieved to see that, although unconscious, he was still breathing and had a pulse.

He looked around but saw no one. The assassin only had two possible escape routes. One, the door to the large common room where all patients were sleeping, but judging by the silence he heard, he dismissed it as an escape route.

The other route, the one he probably used, was the same

Morillo took to get in when Roura alerted him, the small staircase leading down to the labyrinth of underground passageways interconnecting all buildings together.

It was a dark network of endless underground corridors, where few dared to venture into, especially at night. Morillo considered whether it was worth pursuing the killer through that underworld, when in the one above he had an eyewitness probably dead and a badly wounded fellow cop who needed immediate medical attention.

He suppressed his desire to go down to the maze and acted responsibly. Despite the disaster his action had proved to be, at least he had got two vital pieces of information for the case.

With his staff he had put a mark on the killer's face with something more than just a huge scar, which could facilitate his future identification.

On the other hand, although he had fled with astonishing speed, in the dim light from the table lamp he had had time to glimpse the color of his hair, a flaming red.

CHAPTER 18

M rs. Xamot's death did not make the cover of any newspaper, it did not even deserve to make the headlines on the inside pages. In a society dominated by men, a young widow's death did not even seem to generate interest with the family of the victim, since Isabel Xamot had no children or known relatives who could claim her inheritance.

Subinspector Morillo had to strive to build a credible story to explain his and corporal Roura's presence in the hospital at night.

He explained that their presence there was a part of their investigation, with the good fortune he surprised the assailant in the middle of his criminal act and force him to flee, although paying a high price for it, the death of the witness and a police corporal admitted into the hospital with very serious injuries.

Mrs. Xamot had failed to overcome the new injuries caused by the second attack. Morillo obviated the details about the punches and blows she suffered while being trampled like a carpet.

Corporal Roura had two stab wounds in the abdomen and had lost a lot of blood, but since he was already in the hospital, he underwent emergency surgery and although his prognosis was serious, doctors did not fear for his life.

A few days later, routine police work prevailed, and the hospital events seemed a distant memory. Morillo was reassigned to new ordinary cases, which occupied most of his time.

Deep inside he could not get out of his head the issues that really obsessed him, the death of the unknown subject and the prostitute, the obscure silencing of the coroner's death, the crude manipulation of the autopsy report, Mrs. Xamot's attempted murder in her mansion and her ultimate death in the hospital at the hands of the same killer who attacked her at home and who also killed her guard.

Morillo performed his routine work effectively but without getting involved more than strictly necessary, and he spent all his spare time in his secret ongoing investigation of those cases.

One of the persons he met with was Agnes, Mrs. Xamot's beautiful maid, the first person to have seen the face of the redhead murderer.

She had lost her job after the passing of Mrs. Xamot, and Morillo felt he had bonded with her, not only because he had also seen the red-haired murderer, but because being with her gave him a rewarding sense of tranquility, an inner peace he had not felt in years.

Perhaps that is why his visits to the young lady became increasingly frequent, and to avoid drawing too much attention, they began to meet in discrete public places such as parks, or secluded coffee shops away from the downtown area.

Morillo could not forget the murderer knew Agnes could recognize him, and if he had returned to complete his work and finish Mrs. Xamot, he was convinced he would try the same with Agnes, or with himself, since he had also seen his face.

Both had become targets for the assassin and their lives were in danger, although Morillo did not speak openly about it, because he could hardly trust anyone within the police department.

"What a mess you got yourself into at Hospital de Sant Pau the other day," subinspector Aromí said, slapping him on the shoulder as he passed by him.

"I didn't mean to, you know how things went."

"Yes, I know. I'm sorry you lost your main witness. Although poor Roura took the worst part, but I heard he will make it," Aromí said.

"Yes, this afternoon I'll go to visit him. He is young and strong, nothing that rest and good food won't cure."

"Could you take a good look at the assailant?"

"Yes. That bastard will pay for what he's doing," Morillo said, closing a folder and dropping it on the table.

"If I can be of any help, you know, I'm here if you need me."

"Thanks, I know," Morillo said, with a pensive countenance. "Tell me, do you think there may be some relationship between the two killings in the whorehouse and Mrs. Xamot's? Do you see anything in common? Someone who could benefit from their deaths?"

"To be honest, I don't know. The death of the couple seems to be a simple case of a murder in a brothel. Maybe it was a fight between lovers, out of spite, jealousy, or a simple theft, who knows? Mrs. Xamot's death though, strikes me more like a botched robbery attempt, by the arrival of the guard first and then the maid. Don't look any further for hidden motives. Truth normally lies in the simplest explanations," Aromí said, leaning on the table.

It was clear to Morillo he would not convince his colleague with his theories about those facts, nor was he sure he wanted to.

"I've been studying for days the files for missing persons, violent deaths, apparent suicides, murders of unknown subjects, but they were no beggars, but people of a certain social status. And now, Mrs. Xamot leaves a big inheritance no one can claim. Who benefits the most with all this? The Government? Perhaps some of those strangers assassinated were also industrialists without family or heirs, with no one to claim their properties. Isabel Xamot would also fall into that category," Morillo said.

"What you're trying to say?"

"I have never believed in coincidences. I believe this is the work of a potential serial murderer."

"Have you talked to the captain about your theory?"

"Yes, several times, but he doesn't even want to hear about it."

Captain Botell's last words when he asked him for resources to continue that line of research, were still ringing in his ears.

"I believe I told you very clearly to forget about this absurd issue," the captain said. "In a large city like this there will always be murders of unknown people, but to think there is a plot hatched against powerful industrialists and decent people in our community, borders with absolute idiocy. You disappoint me, Morillo. I figured you were smarter than that."

Those words stung like salt and vinegar on a wound, but he still tried to reason with his boss.

"Sir, maybe you could use your connections with the Mayor and ask him to allow me to investigate within the Circle of Economy and interview several of its members. I'm convinced I could get some good leads and at the very least, warn them of the danger."

"And create unnecessary alarm among the most important and influential group of people in the city? You are crazier than I thought. Soon I'll see you controlling the traffic of cattle in the Pyrences Mountains or investigating thefts of pig food in the pig farms north of the city. Yes, I believe by assigning you to those cases we will all benefit from your enormous potential as an investigator," the captain had said, ditching the issue and accompanying him to his office door.

Morillo pulled his characteristic round frame glasses and cleaned them with a pocket-handkerchief, which instead of cleaning seemed to smudge them even more so.

"How can I have access to such influential people, without having to resort to the captain's contacts?" Morillo wondered aloud.

Aromí smiled as he headed for the exit door.

"You can't. They're on a higher level, unattainable for mere mortals like us. They belong to other circles, they are

93

regulars at the Hippodrome races, spend half their lives losing money at the Casino, and in the evenings, they attend private parties held in their mansions uptown. What I'm telling you, a different world," Aromi said, making a farewell gesture with his hand as he went out the door.

Morillo remained pensive, dancing around what his colleague had just said. The Hippodrome was a very popular public place, but there would be too many people watching, and it was unlikely one could go unnoticed.

On the other hand, being invited to one of those private evening parties would be more difficult than to see the captain winning a sympathy award.

However, the Casino de la Rabassada was a good option, one he had not considered until then.

Inaugurated recently, it was located in the mountains of Collserola, several kilometers away from Barcelona, in a very discreet enclave in the woods.

Given gambling was the activity carried out there, the Casino held an aura of discretion and confidentiality that would make his inquiries a lot easier. Besides, industrialists, politicians, members of the nobility and many foreigners of good standing frequented it.

He reproached himself for not having thought about that option before, but it was a good alternative, so he made his decision.

It was already dark when he reached the hospital. After showing his identification, the nurse guarding the entrance to the Digestive Surgery Pavilion pointed him in the direction where Roura was.

He entered a huge ward with ten beds on both sides, which looked more like a boarding school dorm than as a hospital ward.

It was already late, and the nurse had allowed him to stay just a few minutes, so the visit would be very brief.

The corporal was awake and when he saw him coming down the center aisle, he raised a hand in greeting.

"How do you feel, Roura? You look good," Morillo said sincerely, pulling up a chair and sitting by the bedside.

"I didn't think I was coming out of this alive, I swear," Roura said, shaking his head.

"Does it hurt much?" Morillo asked, pointing to the injured man's abdomen, as the man smiled with the proud smile of one who feels worthy of admiration for his acts and eager to squeeze the most out of his brief moment of glory.

"It hurts a lot, but I try to bear it with fortitude. The doctors told me that luckily the stab wounds did not reach any vital organs, you know, the heart, the brain," he said grandiosely.

Morillo considered for a second how hard it could be for a stab in the abdomen to jeopardize such a distant organ as the brain, but he chose not to bring it up with the corporal and maintained a respectful silence.

"Do you remember anything about what happened?"

"All of it. Unfortunately, I remember everything," he said with a grimace.

"After giving you the signal as soon as the nurse left, you arrived and went up to the room. I stood at the foot of the stairs, making sure no one came. I walked to the door to the large Pavilion ward, through which the nurse had to return and the truth is, I did not pay attention to anything else. That's when I heard a noise behind me. As I turned around, I met this guy in front of me. He just looked at me and stabbed me in the belly, that damned son of a..." Roura said, wincing in pain.

Morillo helped him sit up in bed.

"Relax, please don't be tense."

"Yes, thanks. The wound hurts a lot when I move. Well, the thing is the guy must have come up the stairs coming from the underground passages. I jumped on him and we wrestled, but I felt weak, lost a lot of blood and I couldn't do much. He stabbed me again, but then I fell to the ground and cannot remember anything else, I probably lost consciousness."

"Fortunately, the murderer left you for dead and did not finish you, or you wouldn't be here to tell the tale," Morillo said.

"Yes, I even have to thank the son of a bitch for being so stupid. But going back to your question, I looked deep into his eyes, and I'll never forget that stare. The skin around the eyes was very white, and he was quite stocky, otherwise I could have beat him easily," Roura said.

"Of course, that I have no doubt of. I'll put you under surveillance day and night. The murderer may decide to return and pay you a visit," Morillo said.

"If he does, here I am. They don't let me have my gun, but I keep my service nightstick under the pillow," he said very seriously, while Morillo smiled.

"I think the nightstick will be more useful to you to defend yourself from the nurse, whom I see coming down the aisle to kick me out of here. Get all the rest you can and get well soon, I need you back in my team," he said, patting him on the shoulder.

"If it were up to me, I would go with you right now, but I think I may be here for one month, maybe less," Roura said heavy-hearted.

"Time goes by fast," Morillo said, signaling the nurse to let her know he would leave immediately. "I'm following a lead that I think can provide us with a lot of information."

"Really?"

"Yes, but for that, I have to catch up on my gambling chops, because I only know how to play dominoes."

"What?"

"Rest and recover. I'll see you again in a few days," Morillo said, starting to walk down the aisle, following in the footsteps of the nurse who was walking in front of him.

The following day a new phase in the investigation began.

His next stop, the luxurious and mysterious Casino de la Rabassada.

CHAPTER 19

Grand Casino Rabassada ruins. Barcelona. Today.

The morning was cold, as befitted the season, but Gerard did not remember as particularly capricious a fall as the one they were having, where freezing temperatures alternated with mild days emulating the heat and humidity of the tropics.

He drove his small rickety vehicle up the road to Mount Tibidabo, suffering and sweating every time he had to step on the accelerator to get the car to climb the slopes with a minimum of dignity.

At times like these, he was convinced his mortal soul and that of his rickety car were one and only, both entering a state of spiritual communion that united them beyond time and space.

Gerard came to feel in his flesh the suffering of the engine trying to do its very best by multiplying its revolutions above what was mechanically advisable. His mind and heart focused on the curves and slopes before him and encouraged the vehicle as if it were an extension of him and not an artificial machine.

He could not help it, climbing a mountain road with that piece of junk was a constant suffering that left Gerard in a state of mental and physical exhaustion comparable to having gone up the slope dragging the car with his teeth.

When he finally reached Vallvidrera, a small town

whose houses balanced precariously on top of the mountain, he slowly rolled through the streets and across the only existing traffic light in the area, feeling as if he was crossing victoriously the finish line in the last stage of the Paris-Dakar rally.

After driving for a few minutes through a pleasant grove, he saw through the trees the crumbling remains of what had been two large buildings, on a promontory overlooking a bend of almost three hundred sixty degrees.

Slowing down, he drove by them looking through the car window. How impressive it was to see the decline of those noble early century buildings. What once had been stately mansions were now two-and-a-half walls, about to collapse, or engulfed by the vegetation that grew wild all around them, whichever came first.

He could not suppress a shiver being in front of what remained of the imposing iron gate to the abandoned property, supported by two pillars on which two frightening powerful glyphs rested, a mixture of a lion and a winged dragon, still faithfully guarding the entrance to the house, alien to the prevailing desolation.

They were scary and he was glad to leave them behind, trusting their image would remain only in the rearview mirror of his vehicle and not in his retina.

A little over a kilometer from there he reached the first Casino ruins. He almost missed them because all that was visible from the road was a few meters of a wall, partially hidden by vegetation, part of what used to be the main facade of the hotel attached to the Casino.

The road ditch was very narrow there, so he kept driving until he could park the car in a bend of the road and walked back.

The remains of the wall were minimal, an empty door and some window frames, decorated with arabesques of Moorish style, chipped and badly damaged, generously decorated by local graffiti artists, which had splashed them with bright colors.

Looking out those windows or crossing that door was

like entering a magical, mysterious jungle world, in the most literal sense of the word, because the vegetation had grown with such exuberance that Gerard thought he was entering the Amazon jungle and not the Collserola mountain range.

Behind the wall, there was nothing, just forest. It was like a modest movie set in which only a fake wall stood, and no one had bothered to build the rest of the building.

He crossed the doorway of what had once been the main entrance to the hotel and tried to imagine what he would have experienced had he been there a century earlier, who would have come out to greet him, to help him with his luggage, the luxurious atmosphere that existed.

That world had vanished decades ago, devoured both by the greed and avarice of some and by Mother Nature's voracity which now reclaimed what was hers in her own right.

The vegetation was thick, and it was hard for him to find a way through it. Among the brambles he divined a narrow path going down the mountainside. He followed it, trying not to slip on the wet ground, surprised to realize how just within minutes of being there he had stopped listening to the sound of vehicles passing by along the nearby road.

All around him, the noisy silence so characteristic of the jungle; crunches, rubbing branches, leaves swaying in the wind, the song of tireless crickets, the croaking of what Gerard hoped were just birds, and so many other sounds of unknown origin appearing magically in those thickets.

The steep slope softened, and the road became wider, soon turning into a stone and gravel path that seemed to have been traveled with some frequency.

He stood there for a moment trying to find his way, and when he looked up, he glimpsed through the branches of trees a vertical straight structure that could only be of human origin.

Excitedly, he quickened his pace to get closer and stopped to examine it. They were the remains of a large building, half-hidden among the trees. The walls, painted in shades of ocher, still kept much of their original color.

The path kept going down and around that structure, crossing under the ruins of an arch supporting what looked like a terrace and parts of a balustrade which at the same time acted as a roof for that building.

He left the path to examine the terrace and the arch, just the skeleton of what had once been a bridge leading to one of the large casino terraces. All that was left standing from that bridge were the two large beams shaping the arch, as the flooring they had sustained between them had collapsed years earlier.

Beyond the arches, he saw the terrace surface, where the pavement seemed in good condition, still retaining many of its tiles.

To get there and across the skeleton bridge, he had to walk balancing on a narrow beam just a few centimeters wide at a height of over four meters. Gerard assessed the risk and decided to try.

He felt like an explorer walking over a river full of piranhas, crossing a suspension bridge made of lianas and rotten wood beams, except in this case there was no wood, nor lianas, nor piranhas, but a drop deep enough to break all his bones should he fall.

He trusted his sense of balance, so he took a first step, followed by a second and a third, but as soon as he lost sight of the mainland behind him, he stopped.

It was one of those situations where he had to decide whether it was better to move forward step by step like a drunken tightrope walker or do it closing his eyes, gaining momentum and running.

Against all caution, he chose the second option but kept his eyes open. The distance was short, so the momentum he took was enough for him to jump and reach the apparent safety of the terrace tiles. He felt the floor at his feet and it looked solid, so he ambled on the terrace toward the railing.

The view from there was magnificent.

He was above the treetops and from there he could see the green mantle of the Collserola mountain range extending in all its splendor.

How many couples in love, at the turn of the century, would have looked out that same balcony to the serenity of the forest, while the ladies strolled, sheltered from the sun under their umbrellas, and men tilted their top hats as they played pretentiously with their batons.

The warmth of the sun on his face was a nice feeling, and Gerard closed his eyes to enjoy it, before going back to the humid forest and keep walking down the path.

A dull roar made him suddenly open his eyes. No doubt it was of animal origin, and it seemed to come from somewhere behind him.

Gerard turned but saw nothing. He blamed his nervousness or the sounds of a forest so full of life, or maybe it was one of the many wild boars that abounded in those places, causing so much damage to crops and gardens in the residential developments in the area.

When he heard the roar again, this time it was much closer and then he saw it for the first time, a pair of eyes gleaming through the bushes, visible at plain sight from where he was. Just what he needed, meeting a wild boar in the middle of that godforsaken forest.

He took a few steps approaching the two beams that had supported the bridge over sixty years ago. A huge black beast poked through the thick bushes, watching him with open and drooling jaws.

Gerard stopped and stared at the animal. It was not a boar, it was a dog, and although he was not a dog expert, its appearance told him it must be at least a Doberman or some other breed of a similar criminal record.

Trying to remember the tips he had seen on television programs about how to treat those animals, he could not remember any. The only thing that came to mind was that music tamed the savage beasts, but he was sure if he began to sing, far from improving, the situation would worsen considerably.

He opted for caution, sitting still and waiting for his opponent to make a move, which didn't take long. The huge animal came out of the forest and walked to the bridge structure. There were only two parallel beams crossing the gap between the mountainside and the terrace.

It reassured Gerard to think no animal would dare to cross that open space walking on a beam a few centimeters wide.

When the fearsome beast leaned on his front legs over one beam, Gerard felt a chill, but when the animal began to walk on it, the chill became a trickle of sweat running down his spine.

He had to act before the animal would end up crossing the beam and reached its breakfast. Gerard climbed on the other beam, only one and a half meter from the first one and started walking, his arms outstretched for balance until he stopped halfway and turned to look to the dog next to him.

They were both balancing on two beams running in parallel over an abyss almost five meters high. When Gerard took a step forward, the dog retreated and kept giving him that wild menacing look. How was it possible for that creepy beast to hold the balance so well? he thought.

Whether he moved forward or backward, the animal would keep chasing him. The only solution was to knock the dog over, although he had nothing at hand he could use to poke it.

In his pocket, he only carried a change purse and his car keys. He threw the purse and hit the dog on its back, starting a shower of coins to the void, but all he did was to infuriate the dog even further.

He watched in horror as the animal flexed its hind legs, preparing to jump to the beam on which Gerard was standing. The dog stopped barking, and that bothered Gerard. It was the preamble to the jump; the dog was getting ready, and this forced him to do the same if he didn't want to end up between its jaws.

The dog jumped hard and fell on the beam, balancing on its tummy while it desperately shook its hind legs trying not to fall. Gerard didn't have time to think; when he saw the dog landing on his beam, he jumped and switched to the other beam, but lost his balance and fell forward, hanging by his hands in the void.

He was holding on tight, but the dog had stood on the beam and was getting ready to jump back again toward him.

Gerard had no choice, and with tremendous efforts, he rose freehand and sat on the beam. He took one of his shoes off and when the dog started his jump, he threw it hard at the animal. The shoe hit its snout, and as the dog fell to the void, with a sharp howl manifesting its opinion about Gerard.

After hitting the ground, weak moans attested to the dog's agony. Gerard stood up, and walking on the beam with a bare foot he arrived to the mainland.

He detoured through the woods and ran to the path under the bridge, to where the dog had fallen, but it was nowhere to be seen. He was sure that was the right spot. Five meters above him, he saw the two beams crossing from side to side, and there was his shoe, but no trace of the animal.

After following the path, he reached a clearing in front of the facade of the little tower, full of trash and abandoned utensils, which probably belonged to some vagabond.

At the base of the tower, Gerard saw a wooden door ajar, and he peered inside. He waited for his eyes to adjust to the darkness and soon began to make out shapes.

The gravel under his feet crunched as he looked at the walls completely covered in ghoulish graffiti, faces of monstrous and misshapen beings, with giant eyes and malignant expressions watching him from all angles. The only non-painted wall was the ceiling, and only because it was over five meters high.

There was an old mattress in a corner, so wrinkled it was difficult to recognize its shape, and next to it a beach

103

chair with its fabric torn. It smelled of dirt, of humanity, of moisture and burning wood, as if someone had lit a wood fire that had already extinguished.

The place was a homeless shelter, he thought, which it bothered him, it made him feel like an intruder, as if he were invading someone's home uninvited.

Something moved a few meters in front of him, above the mattress. He thought maybe someone was sleeping, but it did not seem so, given he saw no bulge on the mattress. He was about to leave that room when he thought he heard a whimper and went back to check.

As he approached the mattress, his own body blocked the little light coming through the open door and cast a huge shadow that hindered his vision. The mattress was empty, covered only by some old threadbare blankets.

He carefully reached out and raised the blanket from a corner. His heart sank when he found the Doberman's bloodied body, trying to open its jaws in a pathetic and futile effort to attack him, even when the animal was closer to the paradise of dead dogs than to the one for the living. How could the dog have gotten up there?

Gerard could not continue inspecting the place. A very strong blow to the back of his head knocked him down. He dropped the blanket, which fell on the dying animal, covering it again, and darkness was complete.

CHAPTER 20

W hen he opened his eyes, he did not know whether he was alive or he was already keeping the dog company in the Valhalla of Dobermans. He did not hear any barking or groaning, thus he still counted on being on planet Earth.

He felt a concrete floor under his back but could see nothing, and his main concern was to find out whether it was due to the prevailing darkness or if something had happened to his eyesight. His head was about to explode and his body was so bruised that it hurt even to think about it.

He stood up with great difficulty. He only saw shadows but noticed a high spot through which light entered, a small trap door high in the ceiling.

When his eyes adjusted to the dim light, he noticed the curved enclosure walls, and the vaulted ceiling. He was at the bottom of what probably was an enormous cistern about ten meters high, whose length he estimated to be over thirty meters.

"Hello, anybody here?" he shouted lamely. The resonance of his voice against the walls confirmed it was a large empty space. It could be an old rainwater collection tank or a huge cistern to supply drinking water to the Casino.

A metallic screech accompanied a beam of natural light shot from above, illuminating a spot on the floor as if someone had turned on a theater spotlight focused on the artist on the stage. Gerard looked up and saw the ceiling hatch had opened, and he made out the silhouette of a person leaning out.

"Who's there? Help!" Gerard shouted, not knowing whom he was addressing, and gesturing with his arm toward the ceiling. "I'm wounded, help me, please."

"Shut up and listen," a gravelly voice said, sounding cavernous because of the effect of resonance within the enclosed space.

"If you are still alive, it's because I wanted it so, but I can change my mind easily. You have already caused enough harm. Go away and forget about this place."

"I'm sorry about your dog. It was chasing me and it scared me. It was an accident," Gerard tried to apologize, assuming he was talking to the dog owner.

"True. Accidents happen and they will keep happening, no one can avoid them. It's something you should never forget," the voice stated in a threatening tone.

"How did I get here? What happened to me?" Gerard shouted.

"What should concern you is not what happened but what has not happened yet," the voice replied.

"Get me out of here, please."

"No one is holding you. The exit is at the end of the room. Leave and don't look back. Next time you won't be able to, because there won't be a next time."

The echo of his voice was still ringing when the silhouette disappeared and the hatch closed with a sharp squeal of rusty metal.

Darkness invaded everything again, but his eyes were now more used to it. He looked around. He headed toward the faint glow coming through some openings at the top of the wall, as the floor creaked under his feet although he did not dare to reach down and find out what he was walking on.

He reached a brick wall, boarding up what should have been one of the tank walls. At the base of the brick wall, there was a tiny wooden door, so small it was more a trapdoor for cats or a Lilliputian scale door.

Gerard pushed it with his foot and it seemed to give a little, so he gave it a hard kick and opened it up a few centimeters. He bent down and pushed with all his bruised body until the opening was enough for him to crawl out.

It relieved him to be outdoors, under a thick grove. Judging by the mountain slope he deduced he was well below the spot where he encountered the dog. To go back to his car, he would have to walk uphill.

He had the unpleasant feeling he was being watched from that gloomy forest, a very unsettling feeling. He wanted to go back to the tower to look for clues, but he knew what awaited him there and he did not want to go through the same experience again.

The option of going to the police did not cross his mind. Despite having been attacked by a wild animal first and then by a wild human, he did not want to involve the police, for he would not even know where to begin to explain what happened, or why he was there.

He needed more time to dig deeper into the past of that mysterious building, and for that, he should return to inspect the site, but not alone. Next time he would bring reinforcements.

He decided to go back to his car, but taking a good detour to explore that area, the bottom of the valley, therefore he walked in a straight line, perpendicular to the slope, without descending any further. After having studied the old Casino blueprints at the Registry, he assumed he should be near the area where the amusements were.

It had once been a large esplanade, from which people accessed the main rides, but there was no longer any trace of them, dynamited and invaded by the vegetation.

He thought he recognized a flat area, and when he found a large concrete base hidden under the undergrowth, it confirmed his suspicions; it was the bottom of the gigantic pool where the Water Chute barges landed on the water.

As he went down the slope, he soon found the entrance to one of the old roller coaster tunnels. It was in a surprisingly good condition, and he ventured to enter and walk inside. The light from the other exit appeared a few meters below. It was a very short tunnel.

From the old black and white photographs he had studied, he knew that about forty meters away there had to be a much longer tunnel. Unlike the brick buildings and the wooden stalls, blown up to pieces during the forties, the tunnels had not disappeared.

Something looming in the undergrowth caught his attention. It was a small quadrangular construction made of concrete, covered by a rusty iron fence blocking the access. Through the bars he could see a ladder made of iron rings stuck to the wall, going down several meters and disappearing into the darkness of what looked like a bottomless pit.

He yanked the gate hard but found it impossible to lift it. It was blocked with two locks.

CHAPTER 21

Visibility was diminishing because the sun was going down. It was not possible; he had arrived at nine in the morning and couldn't have been there for over two hours. For the first time he looked at his watch, it was half-past seven in the afternoon.

He couldn't have been so long into the forest, and he assumed he had been unconscious for several hours before he awoke in the tank. He decided to walk up toward the road because the last thing he wanted was for the night to catch him there.

Searching through the underbrush looking for a path, a few meters from where he was he saw two large dark eyes watching him, two big openings partially covered by vegetation.

One was bricked up, but there were two small holes halfway up he could look through. He had no flashlight and could not see a thing but he shouted several times and from the resonance, he deduced it was one of the tunnels. Why was this tunnel bricked up, and the others were not?

He walked up to the other entrance, which was easily accessible, and entered the tunnel, but had to stop because it was too dark. It had brick walls, and he could barely stand inside without touching the vaulted ceiling with his head. From what little he could see, the ground was free of debris and surprisingly clean.

If life were a movie, he could pick a wood stick from the ground, tie a rag around its tip, and use a lighter to get a powerful torch whose light would last at least an hour without extinguishing. However, this was not a movie, and in real life, things were not so simple.

Gerard had always wanted to be in one of those B series adventure films, exploring a cave amidst monstrous howls, but the reality was what it was.

He had no lighter, didn't have a torch, and could hear no spooky howls. Although that last part fit in his story, as he was hearing grunts, and they seemed real.

A chill ran through his body. That was not his imagination. There was something else in that tunnel, and it didn't seem human.

He ran out of there without waiting to find out what it was. He reached the edge of the forest, and without wasting time seeking for a path he ran uphill, pushing through the bushes, scratching his hands and face with branches hitting him and brambles digging its thorns on his skin, tearing his clothes.

He soon saw in the distance the big dark shadow of the casino ruins, the tower in whose terrace he had spent such wonderful moments that same morning. He reached the clearing in the forest next to the tower entrance, and there he had to stop in his tracks once again.

Before him, he had another giant black dog, probably a Doberman. He could not believe it, twice in the same day, it was a horrible "déjà vu". It could not be the same animal, he had seen it fall to the void, almost torn apart after hitting the ground, but it looked identical.

The animal was drifting toward him. It didn't bark, but it didn't have to, to scare the hell out of Gerard. Its open jaws, its razor-sharp teeth, and those eyes, those two red dots that pierced him, not letting him look away.

The dog was moving in short steps as if it could savor every second of suffering it was inflicting on him as if it could taste the bitter taste of terror flowing freely through Gerard's veins.

It was just two meters away from Gerard and soon it would launch the attack, but Gerard couldn't move, exhausted from running up the forest and paralyzed by fear.

"Rob!" a man's voice shouted. "Here!"

The animal stopped in its tracks, still keeping its eyes fixed on Gerard.

"Here!" the voice shouted again, making the animal step back slowly, without looking away from its target.

Gerard took a deep breath, relieved to see the dog receding, and almost suffocated for having held his breath for so long.

He saw someone coming out of the trees, a small skinny guy, wearing several layers of clothes of different colors and sizes, and a beard that should reach down to his navel at least. The animal continued to retreat until it was next to the man, who stroked and patted it on the side.

"Thank you," Gerard stammered. The man stared at him in silence.

"Do you live here?" Gerard asked, trying to start a friendly conversation, but got no response.

"Do you speak my language?" he asked, suspecting he was an illegal immigrant.

"Enough to know you crazy reckless," the man replied, with a strong foreign accent Gerard associated with some Eastern European country.

"I'm sorry. I was just walking, but I am out of here," he apologized.

"You lucky today Rob obey me. Not always obeys," the man snapped.

Gerard gulped, suddenly aware of the risk he could be running.

"I'm sorry about your other dog," Gerard said, trying to ingratiate with him.

"What other dog?"

"The other dog, the one who suffered the accident."

"Only have this dog, no other dog. You crazy," the man said.

Gerard tried to identify something in the voice or the appearance of the man to confirm whether it was the same who had spoken to him through the trapdoor in the tank,

111

but they were very different. This one had a softer voice, was less burly, and had a heavy foreign accent, while the other had spoken with no accent.

"Don't you have two identical dogs? Or a colleague who lives in this area?"

"Me live alone, no more dogs, only one, only Rob," the man insisted, getting nervous, and making Gerard nervous too.

"Do you live there in the tower?"

"Over two years. You police?" the man asked, suspiciously.

"No, no. I'm a researcher, I'm a writer, and I'm interested in the history of this place, that's all. I don't want to bother you or anyone else who may live here".

"Nobody else here, just me," he replied angrily.

"But this morning a dog attacked me, and then I woke up locked in a tank somewhere down there, near the tunnels, and a man threatened me. Do you know anyone else who lives here in these forests? Perhaps even in the tunnels?"

"The tunnels? You go, you go from here right away and not come back," the man shouted, furiously, pointing his finger at the path, toward the road.

With his other hand, he was restraining the dog, whose taut muscles were visible through its sweaty skin.

Gerard was eager to stay and continue investigating, he suspected the man knew much more than he was telling, which was nothing, but the sun had almost set, darkness had spread through the woods and it was about to drop its cloak. Under no circumstances Gerard wanted to spend the night there.

"Okay, calm down, I'm already leaving. And hold that dog, please, even if you only have one," he said, starting to walk, and passing by them without looking away from the dog, which was also following him with its eyes. He walked up the path, turning a few times to look over his shoulder at the little man and his dog, who were standing, watching him from afar.

The path narrowed, but he knew the road was close. He turned one last time to look at them but they were gone, there was no one at the end of the path, already invaded by the darkness rising from the bottom of the valley.

Gerard had the feeling the adventure movie had become a horror movie, the kind that never ends well, so he ran up the hill through the bushes until he reached the remains of the hotel wall, got out the door opening and hit the road, with little traffic at such late hour.

He kept running down the ditch, fearing the worst, but to his relief, his car was still there. Before getting in he looked through the windows to make sure no surprises were waiting for him inside. He had seen too many movies not to know what usually happens in such cases, and that environment was more terrifying than Transylvania.

A few minutes later he was devouring kilometers and unfolding the road bends that separated him from the warm and welcoming lights of Barcelona city.

He knew he would soon return to the Casino; he had to, he had the feeling that's where the key to the mystery undoubtedly laid, but he could not do it alone.

But he had to come back with the 7th Cavalry, or else, at least with a faithful squire like Sancho Panza, to accompany him in his quixotic madness.

CHAPTER 22

The following days were difficult. He could not take out of his head what happened in the Casino ruins. He would wake up at night sweating, believing that the diabolical dog was inside the room, in front of his bed.

He thought of going to the police, but he was not sure what his complaint should be.

He had been assaulted while investigating on a piece of land that had to be someone's private property, attacked by a wild dog of which there was no record, nor had he any evidence to incriminate the homeless man who lived in the tower ruins.

He didn't have a case, so he shelved the issue and concentrate on gathering information about the Casino.

"Tell me how can I help you," Enriqueta Castells said, an elegant and fragile woman near her retirement age, that indeterminate and subjective age with which society stigmatizes those it wants to make believe are occupying a space that should rightfully belong to young people.

He had arranged a meeting with Enriqueta in a coffee shop in Barcelona's Gothic Quarter, in one of the traditional "granjas", where one could taste an incredible "suizo", a big bowl of hot thick chocolate, on which Gerard loved to dip "melindros", sweet pastries that had delighted people for generations.

Enriqueta was a distant descendant of a family that had

lived in a mansion in the Collserola forest, near the Casino.

Interested in studying that part of Barcelona's lost or hidden history, she had done a lot of research and had written a popular book about the Casino and that troubled and exciting period.

"The house belonged to the great-grandparents of my late husband, or rather to his family. They say it was originally a farmhouse dating from the tenth or eleventh century," she said with ill-concealed pride.

"Is it still standing?" Gerard asked.

Enriqueta laughed somewhat artificially.

"Real estate speculation demolished it during the times of Mayor Porcinoles, many years ago. You should investigate that. No one has ever quantified the cost all the damage that was done during that period has had and will have, for Barcelona," she complained, not knowing she had pushed the activation button on a particularly sensitive issue for Gerard, who could not refrain himself and began a dissertation.

"Tell me about it, I've been delving into the issue for years. Those were dark years for the city. In the name of progress and urban development, they destroyed countless Art Nouveau jewels to satisfy the dark financial interests of municipalities, construction companies, unscrupulous politicians and their court of crooks and speculators. God only knows for how many generations we must pay the price for those years of frivolity, corruption, and institutional myopia," Gerard said.

"More like blindness," she pointed out.

"True, blindness. Sometimes I wonder whether we have made any progress since then, seeing the never-ending corruption cases and the low level of our current political class."

"It is the sad legacy of years of Spanish tradition. This country elevates rogues to the category of heroes, we thrive on the easy, the comfortable, what doesn't cost any effort, and we even rejoice over it. In the end, is nothing more than the realization that we lack moral principles," she sentenced, in what sounded like a speech she had repeated on many occasions

For the next hour, they discussed animatedly urban and city history issues, but Gerard started diverting the conversation toward the Casino.

Enriqueta told him many stories related to the Casino, anecdotes overheard in her family during her childhood, stories passed from parents to children and whose veracity nobody doubted, although with little documentary evidence to support them.

Enriqueta had interviewed many people during the documentation phase preparing her book, and she offered Gerard the possibility of sharing her notebooks with him, where she had collected all those conversations.

"I have put together a list of names and contacts of people I interviewed, descendants of former employees of the hotel and Casino since it's practically impossible to find someone alive who had worked directly in the Casino. If any of them were still alive today, they would be over a hundred years old, unless it was someone who was a child at the time and who had known the Casino in its final years, after the Spanish civil war, when the building was destined to military uses, among others," the woman explained.

The conversation led to more trivial subjects, the day-to-day of the Casino, the European aristocrats who frequented it, the celebrities of the period who let themselves be seen in its premises, the great fortunes lost there, those who lost their life or had it taken away, and about the black legend surrounding the Casino already during that period.

"Do you think the story about those who took their lives there is true?" Gerard asked.

She looked at him with suspicion, but soon seemed to relax and opened up to him.

"Of course, I have no doubts. In fact, my father told us that my grandfather had known Casino employees who had seen the famous suicide room."

Gerard could not contain his excitement.

"Is that possible? Did it really exist?"

Enriqueta smiled, pleased to see she had captured his full attention and was ready to squeeze thoroughly her minutes of glory.

"Yes, it did. It existed, but nobody knows where it was located. I have not found it out, nor have I met anyone who could locate it accurately or with credibility".

"Was it inside the Casino?"

"No, that's for sure. It would have been too risky, if not noisy. It could not be so close to where the gambling took place. Keep in mind that discretion was absolutely fundamental."

"Then? What's your theory?"

"The truth is, I don't have any, although I would love to have one. My personal opinion is that it probably was in one of the auxiliary buildings into the Casino grounds, but away from the main building and the hotel. Perhaps near the amusement park area, I don't know. In any case, nothing remains, the systematic destruction of the whole enclosure eliminated any trace of it. All we have left is the imagination, and that aura of mystery and romance that surrounds the legend of the suicide room," Enriqueta sentenced, ditching the issue.

"How many people do you think lost their lives there?"

"It's impossible to know. Many people believe the room is just a legend, that it never existed. According to the comments I heard in my family, I would say perhaps dozens of victims," she said, lowering her voice as if she feared someone was listening to them.

"Why do you call them victims? If they committed suicide, we shouldn't consider them victims, don't you think?"

Enriqueta remained silent. Suddenly, she seemed uncomfortable talking about that subject and looked askance at the tables around.

"We are in a public place, we should not be talking about these issues," she said, opening her purse to take out a wallet to pay.

"Please, allow me. I invite you, by all means," Gerard said, placing his hand over hers to stop her from opening her purse.

"Do you think there were victims? That not all casualties were suicides? Is that what you suggest?" Gerard said, still holding her hand.

Enriqueta shifted uncomfortably in her place, but seemed willing to talk, although it was clear those would be her last words before leaving.

"I shouldn't be telling you this, because it's just my personal opinion and I could be wrong. People said there were great interests at stake there, and that so much more than just money from the roulette was in play there."

"What you have learned?" Gerard pressed her.

"Only that, that gambling may have been just a front, a subterfuge to hide a different business," and after saying it, she closed her purse and picked up her jacket, a clear sign she wanted to leave.

"What other type of business? Who was behind all that?"

"I shouldn't be saying more, there are still descendants..., he's still alive," she said dryly.

"Who? Whom are you referring to?" Gerard insisted, gently holding her again by the wrist.

Enriqueta got up, took her hands away from his, and without even saying goodbye she left and didn't look back.

"How come you wrote nothing about it in your book?" Gerard shouted when she was near the street door. Enriqueta stopped and turned to him.

"I don't want to die so young," she said, grinning nervously, and she left the cafeteria.

CHAPTER 23

To die so young. The concept of youth some people had could not be more relative, Gerard thought, after hearing such highly subjective commentary from the mature Enriqueta.

He needed to think, so as soon as he was alone, he turned to the infallible therapy consisting in asking for another "suizo" and drowning his sorrows in the hot creaminess of the chocolate, in which he mercilessly sank the pastries, only to devour them ruthlessly until there wasn't any left on the plate.

Next, he ran through the list of current contacts Enriqueta had given him, a list with only ten names on it.

In some entries, there was a telephone number written, in others only one address, and next to each name an arrow pointed to the name of the Casino employee whom they were related to.

Some of those employees had been waiters in the hotel, there was also a croupier in the game room, a shoeshine boy, an Italian-French chef, a musician in the dance band, a hotel governess, an administrative, a gardener, and three staff employees who worked in maintenance and operation of several of the rides.

He had a lot of work ahead, and little time, so he got down to business.

He devoted the next days to try to locate each of the components of the list, or rather their descendants, which was no easy task.

From some, he only had an old address, and it would

take several attempts to get to them. Others lived outside Barcelona and hopefully, he could talk to them on the phone, so he began with that group.

The first on the list was a music student at the Conservatory. She had inherited the talent of her great-grandfather Fabian, a professional musician who had played the double bass in the Casino orchestra for a few years.

The orchestra entertained guests during meals in the hotel restaurant and also performed during musical sessions held in the Casino Theater, mainly dance music. The girl could not help him much, because her great-grandfather had died when she was very young and she never met him.

Through the stories told by her grandfather, an amateur musician himself, she learned of the lavish parties held in the Casino and of the marathon dance sessions that stretched until the wee hours of the morning, to the despair of musicians, who often did not receive overtime pay, left at the mercy of the generosity of the organizers, who used to reward them with tips.

She offered to email him some pictures she kept from the Casino orchestra.

The only interesting data she could contribute was that often the Casino hosted private parties with restricted access with her great-grandfather's orchestra providing entertainment, of which he never wanted to share any details with the family.

Of the other descendants from the hotel waiters, two refused to cooperate, providing suspiciously similar excuses, arguing they had no interest in removing their ancestors' history, putting an end to the conversation.

He spoke to the grandson of Sergio Bianchi, who had been a member of the original kitchen team of the Casino hotel, who met with him at a well-known Italian restaurant in Barcelona.

He was a kind old man, delighted that somebody could be interested again in his grandfather, a very young Italian chef who had studied haute cuisine in the best schools in

Paris and was part of a select group of French and local chefs hired by the Casino to create the fantastic menus that diners could choose to eat a la carte.

After his stint at the Casino, during the Spanish Civil War, his grandfather returned to Paris but had to flee again when World War II cannons roared throughout Europe, and he returned to Barcelona, where he settled permanently as a cook.

He married and had two sons and finally got to fulfill his dream of starting his own restaurant in the city center, still in existence and functioning at full capacity, run by one of Sergio's Catalan descendants, also a cook.

The old man invited him to the restaurant, and he proudly showed him the black and white photographs hanging from the walls, two of which showed his grandfather posing in front of the stove at the enormous and well-equipped Casino kitchen along with his colleagues.

All wore immaculate white aprons, keeping in perfect balance over their heads their huge chef hats, of a spectacular white, broken only by the black and bushy mustaches most of them wore above their lips, so popular at the time.

When Gerard asked him whether his grandfather interacted with clients and guests of the Casino or the hotel, the old man told him he knew his grandfather spent most of his time in the kitchen, and when he got out, it was only to go home or to stay and sleep on bunks fitted in the pantry.

As a curiosity, he told him sometimes his grandfather's team had to cook mysterious food rations with an unknown destiny. They were probably for private parties or meetings, but his grandfather had no chance to attend any of them, except on two occasions when they requested his presence.

When asked about it, his grandfather gave no details about those services nor told them who the recipients were, always jokingly saying that "*A cook is like a priest or a doctor, he cannot reveal the events he witnesses or the secrets entrusted to him. The doctor looks after the body and the priest looks after the soul, but the cook feeds the two of them, is the essential piece, the vital link without which life would not exist."*

Fermín, one of the casino employees who had operated a ride, had an only son who had died years ago leaving no offspring, which closed that line of investigation.

Aurelio's descendants, whose grand-grandfather had worked as a croupier at the casino, felt uncomfortable talking about their ancestor. At the onset of the Spanish Civil War, Aurelio left Catalunya and fought in the dictator's side, which opened an insurmountable gap between him and several of his relatives.

He died shortly after the war and Gerard could uncover nothing remarkable from that side, just a few tidbits about a popular equestrian roulette played in the Casino, in which people bet large sums of money on metal horses revolving in an endless circular race.

They told him the roulette worked day and night, but especially at night, and especially in games that took place outside normal Casino operation hours.

Aurelio did not last long as a croupier at the roulette table because he lost his job under never fully clarified circumstances. He was not a very talkative person and since he never married, his direct family came through his brother's side. Another dead end for Gerard.

The next name on the list was Juana Caballero, who had worked as a governess and was responsible for cleaning and room service at the Casino hotel. He did not have her grand granddaughter's phone, but he had an address.

He was standing at the door of a small, modest house in the Horta district. It was a pleasant surprise to discover there were still houses like that left in the big city, small islands lost in time, rooted in a past that would never return, refusing to be swept away by the waters of progress, waters he thought sometimes seemed more like sewers.

He opened the gate leading to the street and accessed a small inner garden dominated by the twisted and perhaps millenary trunk of an ancient olive tree, surrounded by well-kept flowers. He walked to the front door and rang the bell.

After waiting a while, the door opened, and he stood before the fresh and pleasant face of a woman of about thirty-five, smiling at him.

"Good afternoon, I'm looking for the relatives of a Juana Caballero," Gerard said, bowing his head.

"I am," she replied without losing her smile.

"I beg your pardon?"

"I'm the only close relative left in Catalonia, or at least the youngest, but I'm afraid you are late because my great-grandmother died many years ago."

"I'm sorry, I didn't know. In fact, I knew hardly anything about her, that's why I was interested in talking to you."

"I'm sorry too, but I won't talk to you," the young woman said, motioning to close the door.

"But why?" Gerard asked uncomprehendingly.

"You see, my great-grandmother raised me well; since I was a kid, she taught me I should never talk to strangers," she said, and her lips curled into a thin smile as she stood motionless under the doorframe, waiting for him to react.

"Ah, of course, excuse me, how could I have forgotten to introduce myself? Excuse me, please," he apologized, making her blush, although she kept her smile.

"My name is Gerard Bach, and I am... I am many things, but mainly I'm a writer. I'm researching the old Casino de la Rabassada, visiting the relatives of people who were related to the Casino".

"Yes, I see," she interrupted him. "You're not the first person who comes to me with that story."

Gerard sensed some animosity in her comment and tried to neutralize it.

"I know you talked to Enriqueta Castells; in fact, it was she who gave me your contact."

"Do not remind me about it. Several meetings, God knows how many hours of conversation and sharing memories, and when she published her book, there was not even a mention about my great-grandmother, not a damn one," she said, with growing anger.

"I'm sorry, I don't know why she didn't do it, but please, I have no relationship with her. In the first place, I'm not writing any book, although I don't rule it out. I write articles and stories in specialized journals, or at least that's what I did until recently, but I'm here for a different reason because this is a subject that interests me on a personal note."

She seemed to consider his explanation for a few moments and finally relaxed her countenance and hinted a smile.

"I'm afraid I have to leave," Gerard said, suddenly serious as he turned around.

"So soon? What's the matter?" she asked, surprised at the serious expression on Gerard's face.

"I didn't have the pleasure of meeting your great-grandmother, but if I had, I'm sure she would have advised me against talking to strangers," he said, gazing at her.

She closed her eyes for a second and burst out laughing.

"I have no doubt she would have said that. My name is Eva," she said, smiling again and reaching out to shake his hand.

Sitting in front of two steaming cups of coffee, in a small room at the back of the house, next to a pleasant terrace and a back garden somewhat larger than the front one, they spent a long time engaged in small talk.

Gerard noticed the house decoration looked as if the century-old great-grandmother still lived there, and not a young woman. Unlike the front garden, the back garden seemed quite neglected, with weeds that had not been cut since dinosaurs still roamed the garden.

Eva told him she had kept the house as her great-grandmother left it, and only stayed there during the periods she had to work in Barcelona, given the rest of the family lived in Andalusia.

"The truth is that talking about my great-grandmother

bothers me a little. She lived a simple and hard life, working from dawn to dusk to support her family, my grandmother and sisters. It bothers me to see so much interest in her now that she is dead, when nobody paid any attention to her when she was alive," Eva said, with a very serious expression.

Gerard noticed the change in mood and had a feeling that if he kept asking, what had got off to a good start could twist and turn into another dead end, and he had high hopes for that lead.

"It's getting late. I thank you for your time and hope you will forgive any inconvenience I may have caused you," Gerard said, finishing his coffee as he rose.

Eva also rose and smiled at him.

"First, call me Eva, please. And second, there is nothing to forgive, it's no bother at all."

"Okay, Eva. But I really must go, although I'd very much like to meet again, perhaps to have another coffee with no rush. Would you like that?" Gerard asked, leaving his business card on the table.

Eva seemed to consider her answer, but her smile gave her away.

"Yes, I would like it. Call me in a couple of days and let's talk," she said, writing her phone number on a piece of paper torn from an old newspaper.

"Thank you, I will," Gerard replied, letting her accompany him to the door and shaking hands with her again.

He crossed the front garden, and when he reached the street gate, he turned his head.

The girl had vanished, although he thought he saw someone hidden behind the curtains in one of the front windows.

Without turning back again, he closed the gate and disappeared walking down the street.

CHAPTER 24

Gran Casino de la Rabassada. Barcelona. 1912.

I t was early morning, and the day had dawned cold and foggy. Morillo had traveled a considerable distance, riding his bicycle to the top of the Avenida de la República Argentina, still in the city of Barcelona.

That was the origin for the tram line that climbed the Collserola Mountain to the Casino de la Rabassada, hidden in a small valley between mountains.

He could not go further on his bicycle, because what came next were over seven kilometers of a steep dirt road, which would have demanded too much of his legs and he was already puffing and out of breath.

He had preferred to keep his investigation about the Casino a secret, even with his superiors, so he didn't even think about requesting a police car nor did he leave any details at the police station about his whereabouts during the next two days.

Despite the early hour, the cross street where the tram departed from was a hustle and bustle of people and onlookers who came to watch the car preparation ceremony and the arrival of the passengers.

Some arrived in horse-drawn carriages, although most did it on foot. The apparition of a motor vehicle always generated huge excitement, and the driver, tooting the horn more for show off than to warn of his presence, made his way through the crowd, which separated meekly into two halves, like the waters of the Red Sea before Moses.

The area had seen a proliferation of small food businesses selling drinks, cigarettes, and snacks, and they all had an abundant clientele. The most popular establishment even offered an exciting and innovative entertainment to those awaiting the tram departure, chessboards on the street, which used to generate more passion among the many bystanders than among players.

Morillo entered one of the modest coffee shops and parked his bicycle in the back room, talking for a few minutes with one waiter, a good friend whose father had also been a cop. If he left the bicycle on the street, in less than a minute it would have passed into the hands of a new owner, so he preferred to play it safe and leave it under the custody of a friend.

He hastened to take his place among the tram passengers and even got to sit in one of the wooden benches next to the window, thanks to his distinctive police appearance, his bowler hat, his staff, and his bushy mustache.

The tram started with a loud rattle, and it was so hard for it to negotiate the first slopes of the journey that Morillo and his fellow passengers sympathized with the whimpers and groans of the wooden and metal car parts and suffered the car's hardships as if they were their own.

When the car faced the straight stretches, the vehicle picked up some speed, albeit relative, since even the peasants they met walking at a slow pace along the way overtook them easily.

Once the road abandoned the city and headed toward the mountain, as kilometers started falling, the slope became steeper and in direct proportion to the passenger's satisfaction to have been able to find a sit and not be walking or pedaling uphill.

Their arrival at what was popularly known as the "revolt de la paella" (frying pan bend), a famous upward sloping bend of over 180°, generated witty murmurs and admiration comments among passengers. The tram stopped at mid-bend and seemed to take a breath to undertake the rest of the journey.

The electric cable feeding the tram sizzled loudly over their heads, dropping a cascade of sparks that forced more than one careless passenger to take his arms off the window and hide inside.

After a relaxing drive through the Mediterranean forests of the Collserola mountain range, enjoying superb views of the city of Barcelona, that appeared to doze sticking her feet in the surrounding sea, they reached the summit and the tram headed for a few stretches of road that for the first time showed a downhill slope.

The tram car seemed to have caught momentum and slid downhill with a soft rattle. There was silence, as the sensation of speed the passengers experienced was considerable, although the overall speed of the vehicle could not be measured in double digits yet.

After some gentle undulations of the road, a long straight regaled visitors with a spectacular view of the Casino, which stood to their right, a set of buildings at the foot of the road, penetrating down into the mountain and the woods.

The tram stopped right in front of the main entrance to the Casino and passengers competed to get off, standing enraptured as they contemplated the imposing gateway, a huge grate topped by a circular wrought iron structure whose perimeter read "The Rabassada, Casino, Amusements."

The complex was decorated with large international flags since much of the Casino's illustrious clientele was composed of wealthy foreign nobles and industrialists.

Two large towers, housing the box office, flanked the entrance gate. From there Morillo had a view of the whole complex, whose distribution he had memorized the day before.

He saw the buildings housing the Casino and gambling halls, the large and luxurious restaurant, an exclusive hotel on the upper floors and a theater and music hall that could easily accommodate five hundred people.

All Casino and hotel buildings overlooked the Collserola mountain range, a splendid viewpoint amid nature, over the sea of green forests that were lost in the distance, in soft undulations dying in a green horizon behind which the city of Barcelona hid, gently trapped between those mountains and the blue Mediterranean waters.

Once inside the enclosure, Morillo walked up to the huge panoramic terrace, where two spectacular semi-circular staircases originated, flanked by all kinds of exotic plants, descending gently toward a huge esplanade stretching at their feet.

Morillo leaned over the balustrade of the terrace, and stood there a few minutes in silence, absorbing the majesty of the surroundings and admiring such an incredible work of engineering in the mountain's heart.

Hidden from view from the road, the Casino also housed one of the most modern and spectacular amusement parks in Europe.

Morillo had read about those never before seen rides like the "Scenic Railway", a roller coaster over one kilometer long with steep slopes and tunnels, whose route passed through the forest and over the trees, or the "Water Chute" a small barge that fell down a ramp seventy meters high to dive into a giant artificial lake, to the wet delight of the daring visitors, or more classic amusements such as the "Maison Hantée" (Haunted House), the distorting mirrors of the Palace of Laughter, or "Lawn-Tennis", among many others.

Morillo was fascinated, and somewhat uncomfortable in an environment of luxury and ostentation that was very alien to him.

He headed for the main Casino building to start his investigations at the nerve center, the most strategic universal enclave of any modern society, especially in Spain, the bar.

CHAPTER 25

He entered the annex building and walked down a long corridor with large windows on both sides, crossing his path with many gentlemen of distinguished bearing, dressed in tuxedos, wearing top hats or the classic straw hat.

Morillo nodded to greet them as if he knew them, attempting to blend in as soon as possible into that group.

It surprised him there could be so much bustle that early in the morning, since he had assumed gambling and vice were night creatures, but the place seemed to be full of life at all hours.

He peered into the restaurant, more out of curiosity than intending to eat. The army of uniformed waiters in a straight line impressed him, all on watch and awaiting customers, holding napkins on their half-raised forearm.

With a seating capacity for eight hundred diners, the tables were dressed with pristine white tablecloths and already set to welcome them. He saw printed menus on each table, but he didn't dare to come in and read them, and when a waiter approached, he pretended to be looking for someone and left the room.

The Casino cafeteria was his next stop. Even if he didn't know where it was, the smell of tobacco would have guided him there with no difficulty. The place was small and peppered with lots of tiny round white marble tables. He walked to the bar, where he ordered a long black coffee.

With the cup in his hand, he approached a group of gentlemen sitting around a table, engaged in a social gathering, while smoking cigars and drinking liquor already at that early morning hour.

A good way to start the day, Morillo thought, although from the haggard appearance some of them had, maybe it was not that the day had started for them but that the night was not over yet.

He sat quietly beside them, and when people no longer paid any attention to him, he knew he had successfully blended into the group.

The conversation alternated between sports and matters of local and international politics. Morillo stepped into the debate several times, trying to keep a rather neutral and conciliatory position, to avoid drawing attention in excess.

After more than an hour, he tried to steer the conversation to his terrain.

"Have you heard about the discovery of a dead man and woman at a building on Tallers Street?" he asked, not making a big issue of it, hoping to detect any unusual reaction.

"I read about it in the press," one of them said, a fat individual wearing thick glasses. Morillo did not observe in them any gesture denoting nervousness and none of them took the matter any further.

"Yes? Did you know the deceased?" Morillo asked.

"Don't make me laugh. How do you expect me to know him? It's well known that the place was not exactly a cultural Athenaeum," the man said, seemingly offended but smiling mischievously, prompting the accomplice laughter of the majority. Morillo played along.

"Yes, of course. But strangely, no one claimed or identified the body of the man when it was clear he was a man of good standing," Morillo said, looking at them all to provoke their reply.

"It could happen to any of us," a slim and flustered subject said, his hair grizzled and disheveled, holding a cigarette while he played with the golden chain of an expensive pocket watch seemingly trying to escape from the vest.

"Not if we're not regulars in such circles," Morillo said, trying to bring some sense.

"We're all exposed," the same individual spoke again, looking nervously at his companions.

"What do you mean?" Morillo asked.

The fat man stood up and motioned to the waiter to bring the bill.

"Gentlemen, I'm going for a walk along the Railway esplanade and then I will try to tempt again the luck yesterday proved to be so elusive," he said, diverting the conversation and ditching the issue. He pulled a large leather wallet from his jacket and paid for the drinks for the whole group, which soon dispersed.

Morillo had the feeling they were hiding something, or at least that there was something they did not want to talk about. He would need more time to gain their trust, so he decided to spend the night at the hotel and stay for two days.

He went to the hotel reception to book a room, and a young employee informed him about the rates.

"Is that the cheapest room you have?" Morillo asked, somewhat scared after knowing the room rate.

"If you prefer, the building of the Foreign Circle, further down the road, can offer you slightly cheaper rooms. Otherwise, there are private homes in the area offering rooms for rent, but they are farther away," the boy told him.

"No, that's all right. I will only stay one night, so I'll take it," he said, signing on the card, wondering how he would pay that bill and if there was any possibility, however remote, that the police department could pick a part of the cost.

"Are you here for business, pleasure or a little of both?" the employee asked him, as he signaled a bellboy. "Agustín, come here and accompany the gentleman to his room."

"Actually, I'm recovering from a surgical operation and my doctor prescribed rest and taking the medicinal waters of the Collserola fountains," Morillo lied.

"You've come to the ideal place to find rest and tranquility... provided you can stay away from the Casino and the amusements," the employee joked.

Morillo smiled and followed the young bellboy who accompanied him upstairs to room number fourteen.

"Here we are. If you need anything, ring the bell you will find next to the bed," the boy said, standing still by the door, waiting for a tip in which he did not trust much.

"Thanks," Morillo said, entering the room and closing the door behind him.

"I knew it," the boy muttered, walking down the stairs.

Morillo toured the room, although he could only do so with his eyes, given its tiny dimensions. He had been so insistent in getting a cheap room, that they had probably given him one for hotel employees.

He sat on the bed and thought about what happened and what still lay ahead.

He had to make good use of his time, for if there was something he was short of, it was time and money.

CHAPTER 26

The sun was setting over the mountains, and soon it would be dark. Morillo had made little progress in his investigation.

After walking through the amusement park area engaging in conversation with as many people as he could, he had returned to the cafeteria to continue making fleeting friendships among the clientele.

None of them shed any new light on the case. There were rumors about people having disappeared, but no one took chances at venturing any theory, much less give any names. He had to access the Casino gambling halls. Perhaps he could meet someone there who had information.

The gambling halls were in the wings of the main building, spacious rooms with Art Nouveau decoration, with large windows offering blinding natural light during the day, and starkly illuminated at night with humble electric light bulbs under flower-shaped glass covers.

The Casino was an access-restricted private club, but when Morillo showed his room key, the employee at the door gently let him in.

In the center of the huge room, he saw several gambling tables lined with green mats, one of them sporting a roulette surrounded by several concentric circles of small metal horses and their riders, spinning in an endless race, the Klondike, one of the Casino's most popular games.

There were several rooms dedicated to roulette, the

main game in all casinos of the time, played on huge long tables, already very crowded that afternoon, not only with players and casino employees but also onlookers like him.

He walked through the different rooms without stopping at any of the tables, and motioned to a bellboy, asking for a cigarette and a lighter. The boy, dressed in the universal bell boy uniform, red tunic, blue trousers, and cap, came back with a pack of cigarettes and a matchbox, and he lit one fast.

Morillo recognized the boy, and after taking a few puffs on the cigarette, this time he reached into his pocket and gave him the only loose coin he could find, without even looking at his face, in what he thought was a good imitation of the haughty attitude of the high bourgeoisie.

The boy looked at the coin and then back at him, but refrained from making any comment about Morillo's generosity, and returned to his place beside the main roulette table.

Hours went by quickly. Despite having played none of those games, he could soon follow the basic mechanics and was caught by the morbid fascination the combination of intrigue, gambling, risk and courage exercised over all those present, not only the players but also the public.

Several times he had to remind himself he was there on an official mission, such was the attraction power those games had over whoever watched them.

A few cigarettes and root beer glasses later, and since his meager budget would not allow him to bet a single penny on those gambling tables, he moved away from temptation and went back to the bar to take a bite.

His strategy had been to target those who had lost at the roulette, who often rose from the table with an expression between offended and embarrassed. Initially, they were not eager to talk, but soon they were glad to have someone who would listen to their sorrows and sympathized with their misfortune.

After speaking with several of them, the common denominator and their greatest consolation were knowing there had always been someone more unfortunate than them, someone who had lost an even larger sum.

They told him dramatic stories about individuals who, having lost vast fortunes in a single night, had to surrender not only their money but also their properties.

They had no problem mentioning specific names, like March, Morell, Galiardo and other illustrious names of the Catalan bourgeoisie, along with some foreigners belonging to noble families or related to international banking and members of European diplomatic bodies.

Most of them were well-known figures who, after their experiences in the Casino had kept a certain social life and public presence.

However, Morillo found out there was another group of strangers of whom nobody knew their nationality nor their lifestyle, who had also left a bitter mark on the Casino, leaving a dark trail of huge losses behind.

During dinner at the bar, he had a chat again with some of his earlier counterparts, and whenever the opportunity presented, he mentioned the redheaded man, trying to figure out if by any chance someone remembered any relevant casino client who could fit that description, but he had no luck.

He was very tired, and a considerable headache threatened to settle permanently into his head, so he decided to call it a night, hoping the next morning would bring him better luck.

Back in his room, he sat on the edge of the bed. A simple hunch had brought him to the Casino, hiding it from his superiors, but all that could end up costing him dearly, not only the hotel bill, likely to be expensive, but regarding his professional future in the police department.

He decided the next day at noon he would return to Barcelona. It wouldn't be difficult for him to justify an absence of a day and a half, but prolonging it further could backfire.

However, he realized he missed Agnes a lot; he felt an enormous desire to see her and even to share with her some of his suspicions, but the fact she was still a witness and party to the case stopped him, so he continued leaving her out of it.

He undressed to get into bed. As was usual with him, he did not use pajamas, so he remained in his traditional integral underwear set of maximum decency, covering him from neck to ankles.

All the discomfort around physiological emergencies it entailed, was largely compensated by the warmth it provided on cold winter nights.

Turning off the light, he got into bed and pulled the blanket almost to his eyebrows and as sleep was gaining ground, he enjoyed feeling he was slowly losing consciousness of his surroundings.

He used to take advantage of that state to fall sleep having positive and pleasant thoughts, to let the brain own them during the night, so they could have more chances of coming true the next day.

Morillo began to fall asleep with the image of Agnes' beautiful smiling face as he stretched his arm to hold her hand.

The noise distracted him momentarily, but he could forgive Agnes everything, even that she made a noise, although his dreams never had a soundtrack before, so the noise had to come from the other side, the real world.

Opening one eye he looked around. The room was dark, but he tried to sharpen the ear and all he heard was the sound of distant footsteps fading away. It could be any hotel guest walking down the hall, and he did not pay more attention to it.

He tried to fall asleep again but soon had the uncomfortable feeling sleep had definitely flown away, so he reached up and turned the light switch until the bulb in the middle of the room blinded him.

With the watch in his hands, he put his glasses on and saw it was nearly two in the morning, which meant he had just nodded off for an hour. He got up to get a glass of water from a jug on a small table on the other side of the bed, next to a urinal and a washbasin.

When he came back around the bed he saw a piece of paper on the floor, next to the door. He didn't remember it there when he went to bed. He bent down to pick it up; it was a handwritten note on a crumpled paper. Someone had passed it under the door, not too long ago.

He unfolded the sheet and read it. It seemed written in haste and with a trembling hand.

"Don't ask more questions, or you will find the answer".

CHAPTER 27

Morillo did not understand the message but wondered whether he should consider it friendly advice or a threat.

He opened the door and looked out to both sides but saw no one. On one side there was no exit, and down the other side, he saw the stairs. He ventured out and walked to the end of the corridor.

Everything was silent, and he was about to walk back to his room when the soft sound of a closing door made him turn.

"Damn," he muttered, seeing the door to his room had just closed, leaving him alone in the corridor, wearing only full-body underpants, more befitting the Wild West pioneers.

He had no lock picks on him, so he had no choice but to go down to reception to ask them to open the door for him. He walked to the staircase and leaned carefully. He saw no one and started down the steps very slowly until he glimpsed the deserted front desk.

His only option was to approach the counter, so he gathered courage and took a few steps forward. Once there, he thanked the Lord for everyone was in bed at such a late hour, where he should also be.

He hesitated before ringing the bell to call the clerk on duty, and when he was about to, he heard a noise behind his back and turned.

Across the hall, someone watched him from a small

door ajar. Startled, Morillo walked up to it, absurdly covering his private parts with his hands, when he was more than dressed wearing those underpants.

He opened the door slowly and came eye to eye with the little bellboy who had accompanied him to his room earlier that day.

"What are you doing here so late, boy?"

"I live here, sir."

"What are you doing up at this hour?"

"I heard a noise, and I came out to take a look."

"And do you always sleep dressed in your hotel uniform?"

"I dressed quickly, I can do it very fast."

Morillo did not want to keep tempting his fate, since being found in his underwear, in the room of a bellboy, early in the morning, it would be impossible to justify, even for him.

"I locked myself out of my room. Do you have a master key? Can you help me?"

"Of course, sir, I'll go up right away and open the door for you," the boy said, heading toward the front desk.

Morillo turned around and ran up the stairs, praying not to cross his path with anyone. He was lucky, and after a few minutes of waiting in the corridor, hidden behind a huge decorative vase, the sound of a bunch of keys announced the arrival of the bellboy, who opened the door.

"Thank you boy, I owe you a tip," Morillo said, pointing to the side of his underwear, to show the boy he had no pockets where to keep any coins.

The boy was disappointed and started to leave, but Morillo stopped him.

"Just a moment. Have you seen anyone go down the stairs in the last few minutes?"

"No sir, but I was in my room with the door closed, I can't see anything from there."

"Do you know if there is any other message for me?"

"No sir, no more messages," the boy replied nervously.

Morillo immediately grabbed him by the lapel of his

tunic.

"No more messages? Have I ever mentioned I had already received one?" Morillo said, raising his voice to impress the boy.

"Errr... I know nothing, sir," the child said, very agitated.

"Tell me the truth, and tomorrow I will reward you generously, believe me."

Seeing the boy seemed unimpressed, he shelved the subtleties.

"Okay, look what I have here," Morillo said, taking his hands to the hips, forgetting he was in his underwear.

"Damn it! Wait here" he said, going into his room in search of his jacket. He came to the door with a police badge in his hand and grabbed the boy by the wrist. The boy paled at the sight of it and tried to pull away, but could not.

"Are we going to get along?"

The boy nodded.

"What's your name?"

"Agustín."

"Listen Agustín, I don't want you to have any problems, on the contrary, I want to help you, but I need to know I can trust you and that you will help me."

The boy kept nodding.

"What do you know about this note?" he asked, showing him the folded paper.

"A gentleman gave me two coins to pass it under your door at exactly two in the morning. I had to stay awake until then to do so. That's all I know."

"Who gave you the job?"

"I don't know, really. A gentleman approached me earlier this afternoon and asked me. I know nothing more," the boy replied, terrified.

"It's all right, I believe you. Don't talk to absolutely anyone about this. In fact, I think I could even appoint you as my secret deputy," Morillo said, slapping him on the shoulder, to which the boy replied with a smile.

"For real?"

"Yes. I trust you to help me in a secret investigation. Do you think you could recognize the gentleman who gave you the note?"

"I don't know him, but I've seen him some nights at the Casino," the boy replied.

"Good, let's leave it for tonight. Do not talk to anyone about this and keep your eyes open. Tomorrow, you and I will have a pleasant talk, okay?"

"Yes, sir. If I ever see the redhead again, I won't tell him anything," the boy replied, turning around and running off down the corridor.

Morillo slowly closed the door and dropped onto the bed with a big smile.

Luck seemed to finally get on his side.

He had found the redhead.

CHAPTER 28

Barcelona. Today.

The interviews Gerard had with friends and contacts of old Casino workers had produced nothing but anecdotal evidence. The majority said they knew about the suicide room legend, but none of their ancestors had verified its true existence or provided any tangible proof.

Gerard thought that, as it was often the case, popular wisdom was right. The room was nothing more than a romantic legend, emerged as a result of the killings that occurred during those turbulent years, but lacking any real foundation.

Gerard wanted to get to the end of the contact list and have the peace of mind he had interviewed them all.

The next on the list was Amancio Cabré, who had worked for years as a shoeshine boy in the Casino.

"My grandfather was one of the most important people in the Casino," Mercedes said proudly, an elderly woman who lived in a nursing home.

They were in a large room with huge windows overlooking a garden, where groups of old men sitting at little round tables played endless games of dominoes or spent hours rereading the same old newspaper.

Several groups of women talked animatedly without looking up from their work, chatting through pieces of linen or lengthy embroidered ribbons they worked on with infinite patience for months.

It amazed Gerard how those women, the youngest of which was nearly eighty, could weave those delicate works with such precision, even wearing bifocal lenses.

The woman was sitting at a table, guarding a teapot and two cups beside her. It was obvious she knew of his arrival and was already waiting for him. She did not get many visitors if any, and she had spent days eagerly looking forward to that visit.

"You don't knit or do needlework, like all the others?" Gerard asked to break the ice.

"That's for old women," she answered, with a sympathetic grimace.

They poured themselves tea and talked about the day-to-day life in the nursing home, and how all of them longed to get out.

"We are not imprisoned here," she explained" we are free to go if we so wish, but, whom will I share my walks with? You cannot enjoy the little things in life if you don't have anyone to share them with, don't you think?"

Gerard nodded, acknowledging how much wisdom and common sense her words exuded. There was so much we could learn and improve as a society if we were humble and listened more to our elders.

The conversation with Mercedes was very pleasant, she knew many funny stories, had lived long and had all the time in the world to rummage in the attic of her mind and distill her memories gradually, until she had prepared an excellent liquor.

Two cups of tea and lots of laughs later, Gerard started driving the conversation toward Amancio's figure. Mercedes told him that in those years, shoeshines were an institution, and there were thousands of them all over the city.

"They had their own room at the entrance of the Casino, with a big sign on the door. There they shined the shoes of customers arriving from Barcelona by tram or car. Dirt roads made shoes dirty with road dust. They could not handle the amount of work they had."

"How many were there?"

"At least two or three worked regularly at the Casino. It was a profession that carried great responsibility. I always say they were like priests, receiving their clients' confidences but not being able to share them with anyone. And they dealt with people from all walks of life, from the rich and powerful, to those who had nothing to eat but sought their fortune in gambling."

"Did you ever hear him comment about any customers who had committed suicide?" Gerard asked casually.

"Sometimes. It was common knowledge such events happened there, it was an open secret. It's only normal that whoever loses his entire fortune and brings shame to his family, may want to end his life, even in such an unchristian way."

"It's not that committing suicide is unchristian, it's just a cowardly way out for the weak" Gerard said, trying to encourage her.

"Yes, for those who have faith in nothing or nobody. Those are always the most dangerous," the old lady sentenced, offering him some biscuits to accompany the tea, which was already cold.

"Do you think there was a special room for them?" Gerard asked.

The old woman looked around and lowered her voice.

"Grandpa had hinted it to us, especially when my late sister and I were little and he wanted to scare us. He told us stories that took place in that creepy room, and it scared us to death. But they were just bedtime stories for little children, to get us to go to sleep."

"Stories of suicides and cursed rooms are not the most appropriate for children to go to sleep, don't you think?" Gerard said, not getting over his amazement.

"Nonsense. Children are very strong, they can endure that and much more. He scared the hell out of us, but we liked it," she said, smiling fondly at the memory.

"Even if the room had existed, my grandfather would have never told us. It was part of his professional secrecy. That's the thing about being always at the feet of people, he saw them all from below, as they really were, don't know if you know what I mean," she said, winking as she spoke.

"I remember he once told us that to reach the room one had to go through tunnels and that only ghosts could get there, but we always believed those were just stories he invented for us, to scare us. In fact, I'm convinced of it. I have a photo album in my room, and my grandfather is in a few of them. Would you like to see them?"

"Of course, I'd love to," he said, suddenly excited at the prospect of seeing graphic material from that era.

"Then finish the cookies while I get the album," she said, disappearing through the door.

Gerard obeyed her and wiped out the entire tray of cookies. When she returned, he took the album from her hands and studied it carefully.

A whole life summarized in just a few pages in a photo album, it was wonderful, but so depressing. It reminded us cruelly of how short life is, and that if we don't pay attention, it may pass us by without us being able to fill a few more pages in the album of our lives.

He found three photographs where grandpa Amancio appeared.

In one of them, he was next to the shoeshine booth. He was thin, very dark-skinned and showed a delicate mustache in the fashion of the best leading men of golden-age Hollywood.

In another one, he was in front of a large window. He stood straight, his right foot resting on the footrest, holding his work tools, his little stool, and his toolbox, with dirty rags, shoe polish cans, and brushes sticking out.

The third was a group photo, showing ten people posing in front of the large terrace from where the semicircular staircases leading down to the gardens started.

"There's grandpa, the third one on the first row. Those were many of his coworkers at the hotel, the other shoeshines, the receptionist, the cleaning ladies, two guards, a few more I don't recognize, and even one of the bellboys, there you have it, he was almost a child," she said, smiling wistfully as she ran her finger deformed by arthritis over the faces of the employees.

She thought they probably took the group photograph on a festive day, since the terrace and the grand staircase were areas usually restricted to staff and reserved only for Casino and hotel guests.

Gerard took the three photos out of their plastic containers to examine them closely. On the back, they all had the date written with a fountain pen in the elegant handwriting the lucky people who could afford an education used to have in that period.

All photographs were taken between 1913 and 1915. Written on the back of the group photograph were the names of all those appearing on it.

"May I make a copy?" Gerard asked, showing his mobile phone. The old woman nodded and Gerard photographed it front and back. He enlarged the image of the back, wrote down the names on it, and recognized a few, having investigated them or interviewed their relatives.

"What do you remember about the bellboy?" Gerard asked, as he was a new character whom so far he did not know.

The old lady smiled when she contemplated the image of the freckled boy, his unruly hair tucked under his cap.

"Yes, little Agustín. Grandfather always said he was everyone's pet, he was like a son to all employees. Apparently, he was an orphan, and no one knew how he arrived at the hotel, but they all loved him. He had a small bed in the hotel storage room and always had his fingers in a dozen different pies."

"What does that mean?"

"That there was nobody he wouldn't know, nor gossip in which he did not take part. He had accompanied all kinds of clients on their arrival or departure from the hotel and had been in all rooms. What that boy must have seen during those years could fill several books," she said, with authority.

Gerard's mind was already moving at breakneck speed. How had it not occurred to him to think of that boy? His job as bellboy gave him access to all the guest rooms and hotel facilities, besides being able to intrude into the privacy of guests arousing no suspicion.

He was only a child back then, he couldn't be more than ten or twelve years old. Could it be possible that he could have known the room he was looking for?

"Do you remember the bellboy's name? Here it says Agustín M."

"Let me think. It was Agustín Medarde, or Medrano, or something like that. My grandfather used to call him only Agustín, Little Agustín."

"Calling him little is kind of relative, isn't it? If he were alive today, he should be over a hundred years old," Gerard calculated.

"More or less but, who cares about age, if the heart is young?" she said, laughing.

"I'll see what I can find out about him."

"That I cannot help you with. After the Civil War, grandpa mentioned nothing about that boy, sorry. But if you find him, tell him I'd love to meet him. If he still is as handsome an adult as he was a kid in that picture, I would not mind if he invited me to dinner or whatever might come after that," she said, laughing and winking at him again.

Deep down, Gerard was amazed at the joy and vital energy conveyed by that woman, who could yearn for someone whom she had only known from a photograph and who, if he were alive, would be over a hundred years old. It was admirable.

He said goodbye affectionately to her, thanking her for her kindness and promised himself and her, to be back soon to visit her again, and if possible, with fresh news about her platonic love of youth.

CHAPTER 29

This was a virgin clue, a new avenue of research no one had followed until then, not even Enriqueta when researching for her book. He had to focus his investigation on tracking the bellboy, look for new photos, and find out where they buried him or if he had left any descendants.

He went through the list of hotel employees and there was his name, Agustín Medarde, but no data about his whereabouts.

How was his life after working at the Casino? If the boy in the photograph was about ten years old, he guessed when the Civil War started the boy should have been around thirty-four years old.

He could check military records to find out if he had enlisted in the army, or search official archives, to find a death certificate or any official document.

It was too much work for one person alone, he needed more hands to help him in those detective tasks and he must resort to his trusted people.

Max showed up at his house with a pizza under his arm.

"Even though you were not explicit about it, I assumed that your call carried an implicit invitation for lunch, but knowing you no longer worked at the magazine and that your financial situation wouldn't leave much room for joy, this pizza is the outcome of my conjectures. Not even Sherlock Holmes would have reached the same conclusion faster," Max said arrogantly, as he noisily dropped the pizza on Gerard's kitchen counter.

"As always, you go too far, but I appreciate the gesture. I have a ravenous hunger," Gerard said, opening the package and throwing the pizza into the microwave oven.

Once seated at the table, Gerard filled his friend in about his research, lingering in what happened in the Casino ruins.

"If I had been there, it would all have been very different," Max said, chewing a big piece of pizza with an open mouth.

"I have no doubt about it," Gerard said. "Probably we would have ended in worst condition than the dog, but it definitely would have been different."

"I will ignore your sarcastic remarks and concentrate on finding the needle in the haystack. It shouldn't be so hard to track down a bellboy, knowing his name and approximate age," Max said, finishing the pizza left-overs."

"Agustín Medarde and one hundred," Gerard said.

"One hundred? It's an unusual name, but it'll make my work easier."

"That's not his name, but his approximate age," Gerard added.

Max frowned and gave his friend a look of incredulity.

"Are you asking me to search for Methuselah and all we know about him is his name and age?"

"More or less, although I may have miscalculated his age and perhaps he's a bit older than that."

"Really? Say no more, I know where to look. In the Guinness Book of Records. It's the only place," Max said, sighing and getting up.

"Thanks, buddy, I knew I could count on you."

"Don't thank me, I do it out of curiosity. This story has all the makings of a Hitchcock thriller, and I won't be the one to miss the ending. Now I must go. Give me a few days and I'll call you when I have news. Chasing ghosts is my specialty," he said, and hugging him, he left.

Gerard spent the following days locating the remaining

names on the list. He found the relatives of the person who had handled the company's administration and accounting, which was particularly interesting since he suspected the Casino finances and some dark financial motive played an important role in that story.

"The accountant had died many years earlier, and his descendants now lived in Switzerland. He spoke with them on the phone, and although they were not cooperative, their attitude was not hostile.

They told him they kept several boxes full of books and documents belonging to their ancestor, and Gerard inferred they would be ledgers the old accountant had kept for years as life insurance. When he asked them to check out the books, they invited him to travel to Switzerland, a trip not in his short-term plans or his budget.

He often wondered how did the books and the trunk get to the attic of the family farmhouse in Argentona. Was that just a coincidence or did a connection exist between his family and the Casino?

It had been more than a week since his meeting with Max and still no news from him. It was clear Max's understanding of space-time differed from his, because when Max said two days, for Gerard it was more than a week.

The phone rang when Gerard was walking into the shower.

"Once more, there won't be enough seafood across the Atlantic to fill the seafood platter I will buy myself on your behalf, with your credit card," was the first thing he heard, Max's voice bluffing over the phone.

"If you have something, let it go now, Max."

"I will get to the point, but the seafood dinner will be historical. I have found your man," he said briefly.

"Really? You're amazing."

"I know, I wish women also saw it that way," Max said.

"What cemetery did they bury him in? Does he have any living relative?"

"Yes, you're in luck, there is one, and very close to him."

"Who? What's his name?"

"His name is Agustín."

"Another Agustin? How original. Where is y

He is not."

"Then, where does the family keep his ashes?"

"Unless you're referring to those from Sunday barbecues, I don't know what other ashes they may keep," Max said, making his friend a little uncomfortable with his black humor.

"Where do they keep him?" Gerard insisted impatiently.

"In a nursing home for people who need significant care," Max said.

"Strange place to store some ashes."

"Strange place to lock up your grandfather. I suppose they no longer knew what to do with him. After all, at this rate, the old man will bury them all.

"What are you trying to say?"

"That the old devil is still raising hell. He is over a hundred years old, and has even received medals and commendations from the City Council and the regional government for his longevity," Max said.

If true, it would be the most wonderful news he could have received, a real godsend. If he could interrogate that old man, that grownup kid, maybe he could find out what really happened at the Casino and know the truth about the room, maybe, maybe.

The only way to clarify so many unknowns was visiting him in person.

CHAPTER 30

Max was sitting in the passenger seat and had not stopped talking since leaving home. Having discovered the old man's whereabouts he believed he had the legitimate right to be present during the meeting, and nobody could have prevented it.

"When I phoned the family to request permission to visit him, they warned me the old man has some degree of dementia and sometimes he forgets things or loses the thread of the conversation," Gerard said.

"Oh really? If I lived to be over a hundred years old, I would gladly give one leg and part of the other so that the worst that happened to me was losing my memory a little. That already happens to me now, that I'm still young and still have all three legs," Max said, glancing at Gerard and expecting a jocular remark from him, which never came.

"I won't dignify your jokes by making judgments about them, sorry," Gerard said, while he parked the car.

"I expected a nursing home for elderly people and yet this looks like an old Mexican pension in Chihuahua, in the Texas border," Max said, standing at the address they had.

"Since when have you been to Chihuahua?"

"There is so much you don't know about me, I Max don't know whether to be offended or happy about it," Max said, slamming the door as he got out of the car.

They were facing a small two-story building, in a quiet residential street parallel to the Paseo Marítimo in Sitges, a picturesque coastal city south of Barcelona.

Huge wooden beams sprouting from its walls like tentacles of a gigantic octopus pierced the whitewashed walls, of dazzling whiteness, shaping terraces and pergolas that evoked the flair of an old Mexican colonial hacienda.

"More than a nursing home, this looks like Pancho Villa's hacienda," Max said, pushing a white metal fence, giving access to a garden.

They followed a path of stone slabs dotted with decorative marine-inspired elements painted in white, an anchor attached to several links of a thick chain, a metal bell, and an old wooden helm.

"Everything is white here. My black soul clashes against such whiteness," Max said, approaching the only element in the garden that showed its natural color, a multicolored plaster dwarf on top of a mushroom and holding a lantern.

Max lifted the figure and cradled it in his arms like a baby.

"They are beings in need of love, and people usually have them imprisoned in their gardens, when what they want is to run free through the forest.

Gerard looked at him stunned, unable to articulate a coherent reply to such an absurdity, when the front door opened and a woman dressed in a dark blue apron came out to meet them. She stopped in front of Max and gave him a disapproving look, to which he responded by returning the little gnome to his place of origin.

"Good afternoon, we were just admiring the garden," Gerard said.

"Since when do they allow you to work here, dressed in blue?" Max asked, smiling at the woman, who maintained her composure.

"Excuse my friend, he's a great comedian in his spare time, although today he seems out of service," Gerard said, looking sideways at his partner.

Gerard explained the reason for their visit, and the woman accompanied them inside and took them to a waiting room on the first floor, decorated like the command bridge of a ship.

"You can see the Mediterranean from this window. I could spend hours watching it, " Gerard said, pointing toward the white beach line, which blurred every time the waves broke on the shore.

"I could detach this room from the house and sail away," Max said, standing behind the giant varnished helm at one end of the room and spinning it like a pinwheel.

An employee dressed in the same color as the walls suddenly appeared and asked them to accompany him to the residential area.

The walls of the rooms were, as expected, completely white.

The employee stopped in front of a door, knocked and opened it, stepping aside. A couple waited inside, and they stepped into the hall to greet them.

"We are Hector and Lucía Medarde, Agustín's grandchildren," said the man, who also seemed the older of the two, reaching out to shake their hands.

"Not to mention his obvious good health," Gerard said.

"Or his good genes," Max pinpointed.

About fifteen years earlier, when their grandfather's longevity started giving him some notoriety in the local media, his grandchildren took him to a specialized nursing home, close to the Mediterranean Sea Agustin loved so much.

"Can we talk to him now?" Gerard asked.

"Yes, but today he is not very lucid. You see, in recent years his cognitive functions experienced a significant deterioration. He has some good days when everything seems normal, but generally, he rambles quite a bit. Alzheimer's progression seems inexorable, although considering his age we can be happy he has made it up to his age keeping so many of his capacities. The treatments he receives have delayed the onset of symptoms, but still, the reality is what it is."

Gerard was eager to talk to the old man, submerge in his memories about the Casino, and dive in those turbulent waters.

As a journalist, he knew that story had all the ingredients of an exciting thriller, deaths, missing people, potential suicides, gambling, millionaires. All that was missing was the villain, but something told him it wouldn't take long for him to appear on stage.

In the center of the room, a man lay in a modern hospital bed, the only discordant element in a room that looked like the ship captain's cabin. Framed marine charts of the Catalan coast decorated the walls.

"Isn't it dizzying to contemplate day and night this gibberish of lines and symbols? If they were abstract paintings they would be priceless," Max said, pointing to one chart on the wall.

Approaching the bed head, Gerard looked at the old man, who was resting peacefully. His face did not look his age. His wrinkles were only those of a person of an eighty-year-old.

Gerard thought of the images he had seen on television, of centenarians in remote villages of Mongolia, those who seemed to feed only on yogurt from goat's milk or some other animal of an exotic name.

Their faces looked like orographic maps of the Himalayas, furrowed by valleys and mountains resulting from very long lives exposed to the elements.

They used to walk hunched over and be of tiny stature, as if their smallness allowed them to go more easily unnoticed when the woman with the scythe and the black cloak came looking for them.

Agustín had a good height and seeing him resting so peacefully one would say he was taking a simple nap.

Lucía walked up to him and touched his shoulder affectionately, talking to his ear.

"Grandfather, you have visitors."

Agustín moved and mumbled a few unintelligible words.

She insisted and stroked his cheek gently.

Agustín opened his eyes and smiled as he recognized his granddaughter. His eyes must have been blue once but age had mutated them into a dull gray, although the spark

Gerard had seen in the sepia eyes of the very young bellboy in the photograph of the Casino employees, was still shining in them.

The same rebellious lock of hair was falling over his forehead and taking his age into account, his hair exuberance would have been the envy of any man.

Considering he could have been born around the turn of the century, Gerard could not stop thinking the man had lived through at least two world wars and several local wars, dozens of presidents of different countries and several Popes, witnessed the fall of countless governments, the disappearance of countries and the birth of new ones.

He had gone from writing with a quill pen and ink to virtual keyboards projected in the air, from the Chinese abacus to supercomputers with processors that would fit within a grain of rice, from traveling riding a mule to supersonic flights and space travel.

Gerard fell into a fit of healthy envy. What he wouldn't give to live as long as Agustín, and to witness what the advances in science and medicine would bring in the coming decades.

"Who are they?" Agustín asked, pointing to his visitors.

"They are friends who have come to see you. They are gathering information on Art Nouveau Barcelona and are interested in talking to you about the Casino de la Rabassada," Lucía said, raising her voice so he could hear her well.

"A lot of water has gone under the bridge since then," Agustín said, and reached out to one side as if searching for something on the mattress.

"Yes, a lot of water," Gerard repeated, approaching to shake his hand.

"Do you like magic?" Agustín asked, taking Gerard's hand in his.

"Yes, very much," Gerard said.

"Then you will like this," Agustín said, and raising both hands, he waved them in the air doing a magic pass, and instantly the bed began to rise.

The old man lowered his arms, and the bed did the same, slowly descending. He moved them to the side, and the bedhead rose, while the feet of the bed stumbled and folded. The cushions and the tray that rested on his legs fell to the floor with a rumble.

"What the hell is this?" Max said in amazement.

"Grandpa, enough," they heard Lucía say.

CHAPTER 31

Gerard looked around, and suspecting what was happening, did not attempt to stop the exhibition.

Agustín repeated the same gesture in the air and the bed movement ceased, while he smiled with delight, with the satisfaction of someone who felt superior to all.

"Grandfather, how many times have we told you to stop playing with that?" Hector reproached him.

The old man put his hand under his body and, unable to contain his laughter, pulled out a huge remote control connected to the bed by a cable.

"Can someone tell me what did he use to push the buttons?" Max said.

"Please, Max, don't ask. A magician never reveals his tricks, doesn't he? Gerard said, winking at the old man.

"Oh my God. It can't be true," Max said, frowning after his sudden clairvoyance.

"Excuse him. Grandpa loves to play with that," Lucia said.

Agustín was still laughing in silence.

"Some toy you have here," Gerard said, approaching the old man again.

"Yes, I like a little wiggling from time to time. The days don't feel so boring," he said.

"Things have changed a lot since you worked at the Casino, haven't they?" Gerard asked, trying to steer the conversation.

"It's all very far away, in a former life."

"You were very young, weren't you?"

"I was just a kid, but I've lived a lot since then. I have lived experiences to fill four or more lives, but I also learned that the past is past. What counts is always the most recent, what we have at hand at that moment. Life is the present, tomorrow does not exist yet, and the past is just that, what could have been and was not," the old man said, puffing and with a straight face.

"Do you remember what life was like in the Casino, the type of customers you met? I'm sure you rubbed shoulders with the cream of Barcelona's society of that period," Gerard said.

The old man did not answer; he seemed to be walking his memory halls, opening and closing doors or rather checking which were still open.

"I met them all, politicians, businessmen, princes, aristocrats, the best of society," he said staring into space. "But also the worst," he blurted.

"Tell me about that. Whom do you mean?" Gerard asked, unable to hide his interest.

"Nobody in particular. In the Casino abounded the scoundrels, card sharks, professional gamblers, swindlers, flatterers, and those who sought to make easy money at the expense of the unwary, you know. Ah, and there were also the easy women, although I was very young and not supposed to know anything about that, but the things I could tell you..." and he stopped, leering at his grandchildren and gesturing with his finger for Gerard to come closer.

"You don't expect me to tell you stuff about women in front of my grandchildren, do you? I have a reputation to maintain," Agustín said, winking, although everyone in the room heard him.

Gerard knew they would not allow them to stay with the old man for very long, so he took a more direct shortcut.

"Apparently there were many deaths in those surroundings. Is it true? Do you remember that?"

"Those were different times, there was not much

control, and the police back then was not the police we have today. It was like the Wild West, but you got used to it. Nothing that would not happen elsewhere. Money and gambling attract all kinds of thugs and criminals."

"Rumor has it that some committed suicide after losin their entire fortune. Was it true?"

"Yes, that has always happened, but not only in the Casino, in real life it happens every day. Life can sometimes be a piece of shit," Agustín said, taking a sad and pessimistic tone.

"What is it exactly you are researching about?" he asked immediately afterward.

"I am researching the Art Nouveau period, specifically about the pillaging that took place over large Art Nouveau buildings that were eventually demolished, prey to urban speculation, political corruption and the ignorance and neglect of some city mayors and their teams. The Casino de la Rabassada is one of them, and although architecturally was nothing special, it was a symbol of the growing power of the bourgeoisie," he said, taking a short breadth before continuing.

"I'm very interested in researching how was the life between its walls, who went there to show off, who was the biggest spender in its gambling halls, who controlled the gambling business, in short, the social impact the Casino had on early last century Barcelona. My interest is purely personal, I don't intend to make any profit from this project, but I'm fascinated by that period and I just want for the truth to come out."

"Some speech you have just given me. Had I known, I wouldn't have asked you," the old man said, commanding everyone's laughter.

"Did you ever hear about the suicide room?" Gerard asked bluntly.

The old man did not answer. He seemed not to have heard the question, but Gerard was sure he had and waited.

"We've all heard those stories," he said, letting out a deep sigh, to show he was exhausted. His granddaughter

161

came to him right away.

"Do you need anything, grandpa?"

"I want to get some rest."

"Did you ever get to see the room?" Gerard insisted.

"Grandpa has to rest, better if we finish the interview here," Lucía said.

"I never saw it, nor was it known by that name. It's likely to be only a legend created by the press years later," he muttered lamely and staring blankly at the ceiling.

The grandchildren approached the bed, a clear sign they wanted them to leave the room. Max nodded and started for the door, but Gerard remained at the bedhead. He sensed the man was hiding something, and could not miss that opportunity.

"If it had another name, what was it? Do you know someone who ever saw the room? Did you know where it was or how to get to it?"

The granddaughter walked to the bedhead, to stand between Gerard and her grandfather, but he raised a finger to ask her to stop.

"You ask too many questions. There were many rooms in that hotel, but none was cursed, I can assure you because I knew them all," he said, his voice choked by fatigue.

"You should start saying goodbye, please," the granddaughter begged them.

With a nod, Gerard brought his head closer to the old man's as if to say goodbye to him. Agustín reached out and shook his hand, and pulled it to bring Gerard even closer, and whispered something in his ear.

Gerard looked up slowly and patted Agustín's shoulder, then he turned to the grandchildren and thanked them for their kindness letting them share a few minutes with that exceptional man.

Once on the street, they stopped for a moment to take a last look at the peculiar building.

"I feel like I just sailed on the Nautilus," Max said, pointing to the seafaring shapes of the construction.

"Yes, and we may be on our way to discover some

162

unknown and mysterious island," Gerard added, walking toward their car.

"I always wanted to be a ship commander, but I let it go because they would not have taken me because I'm two or three centimeters short," Max said.

"Is that all?"

"Well, that and because I hate science and math with all my heart, but that wouldn't have been a problem, because in the Navy they also need poets."

"And do you happen to know any?" Gerard said, getting a nudge from Max.

Once they merged into the heavy late afternoon traffic, they chatted as they rolled at speeds closer to those of Christopher Columbus' ships than to Captain Nemo's submarine's.

"It's amazing how great that old man looks after so many years, although I suspect in that nursing home they must administer him some secret seaweed-based treatment or ice preservation procedure like they did with Walt Disney. Too bad he couldn't tell us anything about the room," Max complained.

"Don't be so sure of about that," Gerard said, to which Max replied with an inquisitive look.

"The old man told you something?"

Gerard only smiled.

"He said he had not seen it, that the room was a legend," Max insisted.

"To be precise, he said that back then it was not known by that name, that's why he did not know it."

"Yes, I heard that myself. If he told you anything else, when did he do it?"

"When I bent down to say goodbye he talked to my ear."

"Great, did he tell you where the room was?"

"Not exactly, no."

"I don't understand a thing."

"*To hell you must get through water, for it is the fountain of all evil. The black lady guards the entrance.*"

163

"Hey, am I not supposed to be the poet here? What is that?" Max asked.

"That's what the old man told me."

"And what does it mean? Is it a quote from the Divine Comedy, perhaps?"

"I don't know, but I'm convinced it's a clue. There lays the key to everything."

"*To hell you must get through water, for it is the fountain of all evil,*" Max repeated.

"If that is a clue, I'm the queen of Egypt, but I have more than one friend who would fit into that saying, because they're allergic to water and getting close to them is like living in hell, or at least they smell like it."

CHAPTER 32

"Having chosen a public holiday for this hiking trip is almost a sin," Max said, while Gerard drove his old wreck along the road that went up to the Collserola forest.

"You will like the place, believe me. Taking a walk through the woods on a Sunday morning, what could be nicer than that?"

"Staying in bed until noon, for example. Or taking a stroll visiting the Barceloneta bars, also another option."

Gerard parked the car in the ditch, exactly in the same spot he had parked it on his previous visit. The morning was sunny and the road traffic was dense with families spending the day at the nearby Tibidabo amusement park.

Revisiting the Casino ruins in broad daylight, was quite reassuring for him.

He had promised himself he would return with reinforcements, and although being accompanied by Max hardly fell within the definition of reinforcements, having a friend next to him was more than enough to give him courage.

"You were right, an army of ants has swarmed over here, there's only one wall left standing," Max said, after walking through the front door and seeing there was only forest behind it.

"Follow me, and be careful, the path is narrow and slippery," Gerard said, walking down the mountain until he reached the tower ruins.

"It's amazing, is still standing. And look, there's even a woman's face over there, like a gargoyle," Max said, pointing to an Art Nouveau sculpture showing the delicate face of a woman.

Max abandoned the path, phone in hand, and delved into the brush to approach the tower and take photos more closely, while Gerard walked down the path until he reached the tower's open door.

A vague sense of danger prickled the hairs on his legs, putting his body on a tense alert. To his right, several pieces of clothing of an undefined color, hanged in the sun to dry, from a line in the bushes.

His first intention was to go inside to inspect the tower, but he preferred to wait for Max first. Where was his partner?

"Max, are you out there?" he shouted but got no response. He retraced his steps and returned to the point in the path where they had separated. He looked at the tower but his friend was no longer there.

Thinking he might have gone around, he went back to the door to wait for him there. The sound of footsteps on the gravel, coming from that direction, reinforced his conviction.

"Where were you hiding, damn coward? Or did you make a stop to take a leak behind a tree?" Gerard shouted. He could not keep joking. He stopped short when he saw a huge black dog running up the path at full speed, blowing the gravel with its legs with each stride.

"Noooo, not again, nooooo!" Gerard shouted, running toward the tower, jumping over bushes and dodging trees. It was hard to break through the thick vegetation, but listening to the rhythmic cadence from the steps of the beast running after him was enough encouragement for him to even fly over the trees if it had been necessary.

When he finally reached the esplanade, there was no one there, no sign of Max.

The barking was getting louder, so he did the only thing he could do in that situation. The unhinged open door to the tower showed him the only safe place to hide, so he ran inside and pushed hard to close the door behind him.

Darkness was complete, but he kept his feet anchored to the floor, and his two arms leaning against the door. Outside, the dog was banging against the door with its snout and clawing with its powerful paws, trying to break through the wood.

There was no lock, so Gerard could not stop pushing with all his might. He didn't know how long he could resist, but the answer to that question came in the form of a large wooden stake coming down at cruising speed against his neck, causing him to collapse and leaving him unconscious. All his worries ended right there.

Someone was hitting him in the face, trying to disfigure his face. He wanted to fight his attacker, but strength was abandoning him and his lack of coordination prevented him from putting up an effective fight.

He felt dizzy, but concentrating all his strength in his hands he managed to hold his attacker's wrists and stop one blow. Immediately he launched blindly one fist in the direction from which the attack came and landed a blow against his jaw.

"What the hell are you doing, you animal?" he heard someone shouting in front of him. The blows stopped for a moment. That voice was oddly familiar, it wasn't the voice of a murderer.

The shower of blows to the face resumed, but his greater state of consciousness allowed him to recognize them as mere slaps and no punches. Someone was trying to wake him. He relaxed and focused his energy in opening his eyes and focus.

Max's plump smiling face revealed itself before him as if appearing through the misty haze of a swamp. After the initial shock, Gerard leaned back after having such a disturbing vision, but soon relaxed and realized where he was.

To his surprise, he was not inside the tower but far away from it, stretched between the vegetation next to the path.

Max was kneeling beside him, trying to revive him.

When he could stand, they went back into the tower, but they found it deserted, except for the flea-ridden mattress.

Gerard decided that was the end of his expedition. He did not want to go through that experience again, although he had already done it.

This time he had to report it to the police, and he would hold nothing back. A madman was on the loose out there and it was necessary to put an end to such madness. They went back to the car and drove to the police station.

The officer on duty who spoke to them through the window tried in vain to write the complaint coherently, given Max's verbal incontinence and his constant interrupting Gerard to, in his own words, present data of vital importance.

After that first statement, Gerard had insisted on talking to a higher-ranked officer. That he identified himself as a journalist, and also being accompanied by such a peculiar character as Max, forced the young officer to agree to consult with his superiors.

Lieutenant Elias Botell, from the Mossos d'Esquadra police station in Sant Cugat, the town where the Casino grounds were located, welcomed them with the cold courtesy that came from years of experience.

It surprised Gerard to note the officer had used a computer to write the complaint.

In his years of journalistic experience visiting court rooms and police stations, he had identified two eras, the classical period, defined by the manual typewriter and carbon paper, and the contemporary-digital period, in which they used fingers after introducing the electric typewriter and the correction fluid.

Now he added a reduced and select third group, clearly at the forefront of technology, which had gone beyond the Olivetti typewriters' stage and had fully entered the computer age. While computers might have been already in use in those institutions, the devices they used were contemporary to those Steve Jobs and his colleagues assembled in the mythical garage of his California home.

Lieutenant Botell was a man in his forties, with prematurely gray hair and a diplomatic smile he had polished after thousands of interviews like that one.

He thanked Gerard for sharing with him his expert opinion about the Spanish judicial system and listened with attention his explanations about both incidents.

"Why would you continue visiting that place if you already know how each visit ends?" the lieutenant asked. Gerard did not know whether it was a legitimate question or he was joking.

"Don't you think you should ask yourself who is on the loose in that damn place?" Max interrupted, whom Gerard tried to appease with a disapproving look.

"I believe you were not present in any of the two occasions when Mr. Bach was allegedly attacked, were you?" the policeman asked, staring intently into Max's eyes.

"He was not, but I was," Gerard said, lifting his shirt and showing him the bruises on his side and the wounds and scars on his head.

"I understand your position, but you must also understand mine. You did not file a complaint when you claim they attacked you the first time, nor have you provided any medical certificate. Those injuries could have occurred anywhere, or even be self-inflicted."

"Excuse me?" Max said, standing up in a flash, until Gerard forced him to sit down again taking him by the belt, fearing a confrontation with the policeman.

"I did not file a complaint because I thought it had been a combination of carelessness on my part, bad luck to meet a wild dog, and doom by finding a violent drifter living in the ruins. But this second time it was different. There's something else there, what happens there is not normal, and you should at least investigate. That's all I ask for now, before going public through the media," Gerard said, in what sounded like a veiled threat.

The lieutenant stood, visibly upset by that last comment

and wanting to end the meeting.

"I'll take your words as the consequence of a stressful situation that has put your nerves to the test. I assure you I will devote the necessary means to investigate your complaint and I will soon send a patrol to inspect the area. Until then, I would appreciate if you... if both of you refrain from going back to that place and leave the investigation to the professionals. I'll call you if we need to take your statement again," he said, heading for the door.

Gerard and Max stood up and followed him. Gerard shook his hand, but it was clear he considered that meeting a waste of time, although he did not want to unnecessarily antagonize a senior police officer.

Not all agreed.

"I hope we will soon get your call asking us to identify the suspect in a police lineup or to witness his interrogation behind one of those glass mirrors," Max said, pointing his finger at the lieutenant.

"Rest assured you will be the first one we notify. In fact, we will send you a patrol car to pick you up, so you can travel to the station in comfort," the lieutenant said, with diplomatic irony.

"I hope so. Goodbye," Max said as he walked out the door, holding his gaze in a look intended to be intimidating.

When they were back on the street, Max turned to Gerard and smiled.

"I think it was necessary for me to intervene in the conversation and set the record straight. Look how he is now eating out of our hands," he said, showing the palm of his hand.

Gerard sighed, rolling his eyes and starting to walk.

"What? What do you mean? That he won't listen to us? That he's not taking us seriously?" Max said as Gerard walked a few steps ahead of him, ignoring him.

"Tell me something, do you think she was kidding me?" Max insisted, to no response.

CHAPTER 33

Casino de la Rabassada. 1912

Morillo woke up early. Standing on the bed, he managed to peek through the tiny window of his room, which looked more like a vent, and the sun reflecting on the whiteness of the Casino walls forced him to squint.

He took a deep breath and the fresh air of the Collserola mountains filled his lungs with energy. Now he understood why the place was being advertised as a recovery center for people in need of fresh air and medicinal waters.

What he still found jarring was the peculiar combination of a health center with a den of vice and gambling like the Casino. The desire of businessmen and politicians to do business was understandable, but it was a mixture whose logic escaped him.

He looked down, attracted by the noise coming from the street. The tram driver was almost done pushing the car on the rotating platform, to leave it facing the opposite direction for the return trip to Barcelona. With almost no passengers on board at those early hours, soon the tram was on its way, clattering away as it climbed the hill.

An unusually large group of people gathered in front of the main Casino entrance. They argued and gesticulated, pointing to the mountain. His police instinct told him they were not discussing politics or sports, and he dressed quickly to go down to take a look.

A few minutes later, and without taking his usual morning latte, he was already on the street, mingling with the bystanders which were quarreling.

"It's not the first time it happens, nor will it be the last. An establishment like this cannot afford such events to occur in its vicinity," argued a skinny man already dressed in a tuxedo that early in the morning. Morillo wondered whether it was part of his everyday wardrobe or he was a night owl that yet to go to bed.

"What happened?" Morillo asked, talking to no one in particular.

"They have found another body in a nearby farmhouse," said a man in a white uniform, who seemed to work in the hotel kitchen.

"Another? Have there been more?"

"You're not from around here, are you?" said an elderly gentleman who walked with a cane and held a newspaper under his arm. Morillo shook his head.

"For some time now, this mountain seems to be cursed. They have already found several dead bodies in these forests. Too many. The opening of the Casino here has only attracted more criminals and thugs to this area. We cannot live in peace, and it is dangerous to leave the Casino premises alone, you risk your life," the gentleman added.

"Has anyone called the police?" Morillo asked, and the old man spoke again.

"Believe me, it would do no good. Before the Casino established here, this area was peaceful and quiet, but the few times we needed them to come, they never did, or they were late and useless. We have never been a priority for them. It is clear there are not enough mansions from wealthy people here to make it worth their time. After the Casino opening, is getting even worse," the man said, jabbing with his cane on the dirt road and lifting a small cloud of dust.

"Where did they find the body?" Morillo asked.

"In the woods, near Can Cortés farmhouse, up that path over there," he said, pointing to an uphill path to his right climbing into the forest.

Morillo said no more and started walking in that direction.

"These nosey tourists, they don't stop at anything; it seems all they want is to look for trouble," the old man said, shaking his head from side to side, as he watched Morillo walk away into the forest.

He walked for ten minutes following the dirt road. There were visible tracks, indicating some kind of vehicle had traveled along that road recently.

He ventured to guess with all certainty it had animal traction, given every ten-meter intervals the road center was dotted with small shit cakes hidden in the grass, one of which he could not dodge in time, leaving an aromatic memory stuck to the sole of his shoes.

Soon he saw a building in the distance through the trees, and a small detour leading down to the house, a traditional Catalan farmhouse, a double gable roof, and a large front courtyard.

Several people gathered outside the front door, but Morillo headed toward two figures he saw coming out of the trees. They dressed as peasants, and appeared to be father and son, but carried no tools in their hands. He stopped before them.

"Good morning, gentlemen."

The men greeted him with a nod but did not stop.

"Excuse me, I would like to talk to you," Morillo told them.

"We don't have time."

"What happened?" Morillo asked, stopping beside them.

The men looked at each other and one of them replied.

"A man has died. But go away, it's none of your business, the police will come soon," one of them said.

"You're wrong. It's already here," he said, showing them his badge.

"How is it possible? We have not even called yet," the younger of the two exclaimed.

"We have our sources, and we try to always be one step

ahead of evil, whenever possible," Morillo said with a smile, unable to not brag a bit.

"Well, this time evil was one step ahead of you again," the oldest said. "Come and we'll show you where the body is."

After walking about fifty meters through the forest, they came to a small clearing among the pine trees, and Morillo saw a pair of legs sticking out between the brambles.

"Did you discover it?" he asked.

"No, it was Petit," said the young man.

"What was he doing in this area?"

"Hunting rabbits."

"Can I talk to him?"

"Yes, you can talk to him, but I don't think he'll answer you," the father replied.

"Why? Is he still in shock?"

"No, because it's a dog," the father said laughing, pleased to show his air of superiority over that city cop in front of his son.

Morillo ignored the comedian side of the peasant and concentrate on what he had at hand, which in this case was a pair of legs, the corpse's.

The corpse was lying face down inside a huge bush, and all that was visible were his legs sticking out. Morillo lifted one leg grabbing it by the shoe, an expensive black leather model. The soft-touch on the fabric of his trousers indicated it was a quality suit, probably custom made.

He lifted and pulled the other leg to reach the pockets of the pants and almost fell backward as the leg unhooked from the rest of the body and Morillo flashed an awkward smile standing there, holding the leg in his arms.

"What the hell is this?" he exclaimed, as surprised as the two peasants, who came to help.

Several hours later, the corpse had not yet been removed from the site, but two police officers already controlled it, having come to the site after receiving the alarm given from the Casino premises.

Beyond the parts already devoured and disfigured by the

dog, the body was completely dismembered.

Morillo concluded the man had been killed and dismembered elsewhere and his remains placed there on purpose. Had they had quartered him on that spot, there should have been more blood than in a municipal slaughterhouse and all brambles and grass around him were practically dry.

What could have been the motive for such cruelty? A Satanic sect ritual? Revenge? It was imperative to identify the body and thus determine whether if it could be the work of a serial murderer. And the most important question for Morillo, if there could be a relationship to the murders he was investigating.

After interrogating the inhabitants of the farmhouse, he did not find out much. Regarding the other murders in the Collserola mountains, they told him those were not murders committed by common criminals in search of booty but very violent deaths.

The victims were not locals and their bodies used to appear in the most inaccessible places in the mountains, indicating someone had placed them there on purpose.

If he were to return now to the Casino he risked being recognized by someone as a cop, so he decided to go back to the station. Later he would call "Bicycle man" and would give him the pleasant task to pedal up the mountain and go to the Casino to pick up his suitcase and his belongings from his hotel room and pay the bill for his accommodation.

He was sure the kid would greatly appreciate that assignment, which would make him sweat to death.

CHAPTER 34

Two days had gone by since the discovery of the body near the Casino. Captain Botell had given explicit instructions to the agents involved, to maintain a discreet silence about the case details, to avoid alarming the Casino clientele, and to avoid unnecessary panic.

"The mayor has personally asked me to treat this incident as what it is, an unfortunate accident, an assault committed by a criminal looking for easy money," the captain told them during an informal meeting in the common room.

"But if we could find out the identity of the victim, we could at least inquire within his family circle, friends and contacts, to try to identify who could benefit from his death," Morillo replied.

"The meeting is over. Get to work. SubInspector Morillo, come to my office, I want to talk to you in private," the captain said, leaving the room.

"Morillo, you are indeed testing my patience," he said, as he closed the door behind him.

"What do you mean, sir?"

"I believe that until today I have been clear in the instructions I have given you, always trying to steer you in the right direction," he said, as Morillo watched him with an expression of not knowing what he meant.

"My instructions, or should I better say, my orders, have

been as clear as the water coming out of the tap in the toilette, don't you agree?"

Morillo did not know how to respond, impressed as he was by the enormous poetic sensibility his boss showed.

"I clearly told you not to devote more time to investigating cases that have no relevance, and not to waste time or police resources chasing ghosts. Not only have you not obeyed me but you even had the audacity to conduct investigations to which you had not even been assigned, like that of two days ago near the Casino."

Morillo kept silent, waiting to see where the captain wanted to take the conversation.

"By the way, please explain how the hell you showed up so quickly in Collserola, when the call from the Casino letting us know about the finding of the body took place at ten o'clock in the morning. According to the agents sent to the place, you had already been there for several hours, interfering with the investigation," Botell said, giving a strong blow on the table.

"Sir, I was in the area by chance, in the tram heading toward the town of Sant Cugat, where I wanted to meet with a potential witness. When we passed the Casino, seeing the crowd's excitement, I was compelled to fulfill my police duty," Morillo said, in a watered-down version that neglected to mention his overnight stay at the Casino.

"Nonsense. Your duty is to obey me and not making your life even more difficult engaging in banal investigations leading nowhere. This is my last warning to you. If you want to make a career in the force, stick to following my orders to the letter and do not deviate one iota of what I command of you. Only in this way will you avoid getting into trouble because you don't know whom you're playing with," he said, frowning and turning around.

"Whom are you referring to, sir?" Morillo asked, intrigued by the veiled threat, which seemed to indicate the captain knew more than he admitted.

"To me, of course, because you don't want to play with me," he said with a trembling voice, sitting on his desk and taking a few folders in his hands, a sure sign the meeting was over.

For Morillo, the captain's repeated warnings did nothing but increase his suspicions and the feeling some murky motivation lay behind his orders.

Spurred by that conviction, Morillo redoubled his efforts and spent many hours delving into police files on missing persons.

He was convinced there was a connection between the death of the man and the prostitute, and the death and subsequent unexplained disappearance of the coroner, the manipulation of the autopsy report and also with the murders in Collserola, but he had yet to find what was the link they shared.

It was midafternoon, and he went out for coffee at a nearby tavern. The bitter taste of strong coffee kept him alert, and although he was convinced it was purely psychological, hardly an afternoon went by without him having at least one or two cups.

A little boy came in carrying several copies of the evening newspaper "El Noticiero Universal" and Morillo raised his arm to get his attention and ask him to leave one with him.

He glanced at the headlines only, as he liked to do, reading no particular article. This time his gaze fell on the headline of a small article hidden on the inside pages, in the section "Random notes".

"*CORPSES KEEP POPPING UP IN COLLSEROLA,*" was the headline of the short article, in which the journalist reported the discovery of the mutilated body near the Casino.

He avoided the gory details, but what caught his attention was a paragraph that stated: "*the account of chilling discoveries in our formerly peaceful old forests keeps growing, over twenty and counting. A coincidence? Crimes against homeless people? Simple thefts? Official statements are released, each more disparate and lacking any coherence. There is nothing simple and conventional*

*about the crimes, but it will probably be necessary to reach
a count of a hundred or that one of our glorious politicians
becomes the next victim, for our police force to give the
case the attention it surely deserves. Collserola Mountain
has become Death Mountain. J.P."*.

Morillo reread the article several times. That confirmed
his suspicions and reinforced his intuition that this matter
went far beyond a few simple robberies with murder as a
dessert.

He got up and left the tavern in a hurry. He had to
contact the author of the article and find out more details
about the other murders, but first, he returned to the police
station to squeeze the archives for the umpteenth time
looking for data on deaths or bodies found in the Collserola
Mountain in the last two years.

CHAPTER 35

"El Noticiero Universal" Newsroom. 1912

The newspaper newsroom was in a centric building in Lauria Street. Morillo entered through the front door pushing his bicycle, and after identifying himself as a policeman before the doorman, he charged him with the custody of his prized vehicle.

He climbed the stairs to the floor the doorman had indicated and walked into the reception area, heading toward a small wooden counter.

Morillo could hear the hammering of a typewriter but saw no one, and when he peered over the counter, he faced a huge black Underwood machine, which seemed to write by itself. That was a true novelty.

He coughed hard, trying to beat the sound of the machine, and wisps of wavy brown hair appeared behind it, followed by the serene face of a middle-aged staffer who smiled at him.

"Good morning, miss. I'm looking for the journalist who wrote this article," he said, showing her the newspaper folded by that page, together with his police badge, to pressure to expedite the procedures.

"Oh, gosh. You don't look like a policeman, if you don't mind my observation. I always imagined you guys to be older, stouter, with an air of..."

Morillo had no choice but to interrupt her. "I'm sorry if

my appearance has disappointed you, but I don't have another, and what I also don't have is time to keep debating this fascinating subject with you. This is official business and I have to speak to him urgently. Can you help me?"

"Of course, officer. I'll better check in the newsroom. Give me a couple of minutes," she said, somewhat flustered, taking the newspaper from his hands as she ran into the newsroom.

In less than three minutes, the door opened again, and she showed up accompanied by an individual of about forty, his hair prematurely gray, with a thin mustache and wire-rimmed glasses. Morillo took a step forward and reached out to him.

"I am subinspector Morillo, Simeón Morillo," he said, shaking his hand.

"Glad to meet you. I am J.P., a local news editor. I wrote this article," he said, pointing to the newspaper headline he held in his hands. "I am Joseph Parrot."

Morillo could not help diverting his gaze for a second and when he looked at the receptionist, who was trying to suppress a laugh, she lowered her head and immediately hid behind the counter.

Now he understood why the journalist signed with initials and not with his full name. He could only imagine how they would have treated him at the police station had his name been that.

The jocular comments he had to endure for being named Morillo were still ringing in his ears, but that man far exceeded him.

"How can I help you?"

The question took him out of his reverie and brought him back to the urgent reality.

"Can we talk privately?"

The reporter showed him the way to a small room furnished with only two chairs, a small table with a green vase on it and a magazine rack displaying several back issues of the newspaper.

He closed the door, and they sat.

Morillo told him in broad strokes about his investigation into the killings of unknown people and his interest in everything having to do with unexplained deaths in the Collserola mountain range.

The journalist was very pleased to meet a member of the police who showed an interest in his work and who tried to clarify those mysteries, which he considered a success and a consequence of his repeated accusations.

"I'm afraid it's not the case. I'm here in a private capacity, it is not an official visit," Morillo said with sincerity because something about the man felt reassuring.

The journalist decided that, whether or not on an official mission, it was better to have the attention of a police subinspector than to have nothing at all, so he acknowledged his trust by sharing with Morillo all the information he had.

He told him he had spent years researching and writing about deaths and gruesome events in Barcelona. In February of that same year, he had written a series of articles on the occasion of the arrest of the famous Enriqueta Martí, known as "the vampire of the Raval".

They accused the sinister woman of having killed and dismembered dozens of children, whom she kidnapped and enslaved, offering them to pedophiles in the city, and after having exploited them she butchered them and used their body parts to prepare potions, concoctions and ointments she sold to her ghoulish clientele.

It was rumored that among her belongings the police had found a notebook in which the woman wrote the names of all her clients, which included politicians, bankers and public figures whom Enriqueta provided children, acting as their pimp.

Sensing a possibility of drinking only from official sources, the reporter showed an enormous interest in Morillo confirming the existence of such a notebook and in having access to it and offered Morillo all his help in exchange for being allowed to look at it.

Morillo knew of the case but had not handled it directly.

He confirmed the existence of the notebook, which was in the custody of captain Botell, his immediate superior, which resulted in a strange coincidence, for he was not aware of any ongoing investigation on people whose names appeared on the notebook.

Parrot explained he knew about at least ten or twelve bodies found in different parts of the Collserola mountain range in the last year and a half.

None of them had been identified nor claimed by relatives, which although not unusual in a big city like Barcelona, for Morillo it was like throwing gasoline on the fire of his imagination, leading him into thinking once again about some secret conspiracy.

The journalist showed him the personal notes he kept about those cases and Morillo found several of them matched those he had found in the police archives, all of them labeled as unsolved cases, but no active investigation was being followed on them.

"Don't you think all those deaths could be related to each other?" Parrot asked him.

"If that were so, we would face a possible serial murderer or a conspiracy at the highest level," Morillo said. "Do you have any photographs of those cases?"

"I'm afraid only of three of them, those in which we could get to the scene before the police showed up and removed the bodies. Pardon me but, your colleagues are quick to show up and remove evidence, but painfully slow to investigate. That's the reality."

Morillo was not taking the hint. He was increasingly surprised and determined to get to the bottom of that matter. Parrot put on the table several photographs showing bodies found in the mountains.

"You can barely recognize the faces, they are shattered," Morillo said.

"Yes, most bodies were dismembered, and had their faces disfigured, usually as a result of a frontal gunshot, point blank," Parrot said.

"All of them?"

"Yes, without exception. Identifying them is virtually impossible. The victim could either be a tramp or the Prime Minister himself, there's no way of knowing" Parrot said, closing the folder.

"Who do you think can benefit from those deaths?" Morillo asked.

"It's hard to answer this without knowing who they are. I've given it a lot of thought, and even though it seems crazy, my theory is they must be important people, businessmen, or at least wealthy people."

"Why do you think so?"

"Think about it. If they were simple robbery murders, why so much violence? Why such cruelty with the bodies? In my modest opinion, it's clear the murderer is trying to erase any clues."

The gears in Morillo's mind were spinning at full speed, assessing options and asking himself a million questions.

"Maybe leaving witnesses is not what bothered him, but to prevent the family or friends from recognizing the bodies," Morillo said, thinking aloud.

"Perhaps because the victim knew the murderer," Parrot added.

"Yes, but why? What did he have to win or lose if the families recognized the bodies?" Morillo said. "The only explanation has to be financial. If they were not identified, no one could claim their assets," he added, very excited.

"A little twisted, but it makes sense," the journalist said.

"Can you or your newspaper find out if there have been businessmen who disappeared under strange circumstances?"

The veteran journalist smiled. "I'm ahead of you. I'll give you a list of the names we have here in the newsroom. I put it together a few weeks ago with the help of my colleagues from the society pages," Parrot said, unable to contain a smile.

"What's all the commotion? What's going on?" Morillo asked, getting up and walking to the door. The shouting was considerable, and although a newsroom was not exactly a cloistered convent, the scandal was most unusual.

They both ran toward the newsroom. Nobody was sitting, people ran all over the place, talking loudly and huddling together. Parrot approached one group and when he came back to Morillo, his expression told him something serious was going on.

"Something terrible happened, we have just received a communication from our foreign correspondents," he said, slurring his words as if he had difficulty speaking.

"What happened?"

"Hundreds have died, maybe even thousands," the journalist said.

"But what you're talking about? Where?" Morillo insisted.

"Excuse me, but I have to go, it's an emergency. We'll talk tomorrow about the other issue, if it's okay with you," Parrot said, turning around and running to the group of journalists waiting for him, and they disappeared into a meeting room.

Morillo turned to the receptionist behind the counter, who stood there, following the action.

"What's going on? Do you know?" Morillo asked.

"Wait here just a minute," the woman said, and abandoning her desk she disappeared behind the newsroom doors.

A few minutes later she returned holding several large uncut paper sheets, which looked like print proofs for some of the newspaper pages, probably the cover of the next afternoon edition.

As she approached, Morillo saw the big black lettering from the headline and could read it from afar.

He just had to read one word to understand what it was all about. TITANIC.

CHAPTER 36

The sinking of the Titanic, after hitting an iceberg during her maiden voyage caused a monumental stir in society. The magnitude of the tragedy and the social relevance of many of the illustrious passengers overshadowed by far any other news, and for several days they monopolized the international media.

Morillo had great difficulty to meet with his new collaborator, Parrot, for all journalists intuited during those days history was being written in capital letters, and nobody wanted to get distracted or miss their chance to seize the opportunity to write it themselves.

In the two brief meetings they held, they concluded the number of missing industrialists and entrepreneurs surpassed ordinary crime rates of any big city. It was clear something sinister was happening.

"Can we identify a pattern in all these cases? Do they have any other point in common besides the fact they were all disfigured, that they were potential entrepreneurs and that they were found in the Collserola mountain range?" Morillo said aloud.

"Most likely they all owned substantial wealth or properties," Parrot said.

"Yes, that gives us a good motive for murder in all cases."

"Age does not appear to be a factor to consider, although they generally were middle-aged or elderly," Parrot added.

"Yes. Nor can we pay attention to whether they had company, as three of them appeared next to the bodies of murdered women, probably prostitutes, but the rest were alone."

"Sometimes it's better to die alone than in bad company, but only sometimes," Parrot sentenced.

Morillo was not listening. He had one idea in the back of his mind, and he wanted to give it shape before sharing it.

"Money is important," Morillo said.

"Of course, anyone who says otherwise is lying."

"No, I mean it seems to be important in all these cases. Maybe the apparent motive was robbery, either whatever belongings they carried on them, or their assets and properties, but they sure were after the money."

"Yes, but... what are you getting at?" Parrot asked, not fully understanding that reasoning.

"Only as a hypothesis, what social class have we always assumed most of them belonged to?" Morillo asked.

"Businessmen, wealthy people."

"Exactly. Tell me, did anyone carry any money on them when they were found?"

"No, nobody. Neither money nor documents."

"And where were they all found?"

"Abandoned in the Collserola Mountains."

"What in Collserola can attract so many greedy businessmen, apart from boars and medicinal water springs?"

Parrot pondered his answer for a few seconds.

"Pensions, restaurants, hotels... and even a casino."

"Exactly, a casino of international fame, where people win and lose large sums of money daily."

"Mostly lose, I'd say," Parrot pointed out.

"Yes, and don't you think it's an odd coincidence? When did the Casino de la Rabassada open?"

"Construction started in 1910 and it opened in July last year, in 1911."

"When did you start noticing an unusual increase in the

number of corpses appearing in Collserola?" Morillo asked.

Parrot approached him, speaking slowly as he considered the possibility.

"It wouldn't be more than a year ago, since early last year. My God, it's true!"

Morillo filled him in on the outcome of his recent and unsuccessful investigations at the Casino, including the mysterious note he received during the night.

Parrot corresponded by telling him about one of his sources at the Casino, a former employee that had worked as an accountant for the company operating the facilities. They fired him at the end of the year for unknown reasons. He was currently working in an insurance company, and Parrot gave him the address.

Morillo showed his badge to the receptionist and asked for Mr. Rodolfo Calvet. After waiting a few minutes sitting on a red velvet sofa, the girl led him to an aseptic waiting room with only one table and two chairs, and an uninspiring glass of water next to an almost empty pitcher.

"Sorry, I cannot offer anything stronger than this."

Morillo turned and faced an extremely thin man, with tiny glasses over an aquiline nose, who came in and poured himself a glass of water.

Upon seeing him, Morillo smiled inside, thinking he was before the universal prototype of an accountant, who only had to rub his hands and smile sideways to complete the picture. His shrill voice broke all of his character's charm.

"I appreciate it, but even if you offered me good liquor I could not drink, I'm on duty."

"Of course. How can I be of help?"

Morillo briefly summarized his interest in knowing his views on the Casino's financial situation, how did they handle customer's profits and losses and any other information he might consider relevant.

Mr. Calvet explained the basic cash inflow and outflow operation of the Casino and how they accounted for and registered revenue.

"But what you are telling me is the normal operation of any casino," Morillo objected.

"What do you want me to explain, then?"

"Did you notice any irregularity, any maneuver out of the established practices? Did you ever receive any request out of the ordinary?"

The accountant squirmed in his chair, and Morillo perceived it clearly.

"I wouldn't know... we all have received strange requests every once in a while," he responded, with a trembling voice.

"Tell me, why did they fire you? Do you think there was a valid reason for it?" Morillo attacked, without giving him a rest.

"It was a bit unfair, yes, I won't deny it."

Morillo had the feeling if he kept pulling the thread, he would get the man to come clean, he just had to get him to trust him.

"If you don't mind my asking, why is the police department so interested in my personal situation?"

"I'm not here as a policeman, but in a personal capacity. This is a private investigation," Morillo said, in the most conciliatory tone he could convey.

The accountant seemed to relax and after chatting more with Morillo and knowing his friend Parrot had sent him; he was more willing to share information.

"The continuing claims and gambling prohibitions dictated from the Central Government in Madrid badly affected the Casino. They all had to be resolved through bribes and alleged donations to the municipality. I was in charge of managing them, and making sure no record of them was kept," he said, swallowing before proceeding.

"Many loan shark businesses and moneylenders have emerged under the umbrella of the Casino, and very influential citizens are stakeholders in all that dark and dirty business. I did not feel comfortable in that environment, and at one point expressed my disagreement with what they asked me to do," the accountant said, and shut up, quietly watching Morillo.

"I can guess what happened next, they invited you to leave."

"Not exactly. I left because I couldn't take it anymore," Calvet said.

"Our conscience is a burden none of us can cope with," Morillo sentenced.

"It wasn't my conscience, it was my survival instinct. I was scared shitless," the accountant said, with trembling hands.

"What do you mean?" Morillo asked, his interest growing by the minute.

"I witnessed people losing great fortunes in just a few hours. Well-known public characters of high society and politics. I'm not proud of what I did, although I simply fulfilled my professional obligations and never had an active part in that business nor did I ever benefit from it, beyond the salary I received. I do not consider myself to be one of them.

"What do you mean?"

"I had to quit. I suspect in that place worse things than simple financial tampering or accounting hustle occur. They asked me to investigate on the financial status and heritage of some of our customers, but I suspected the real reason was not to assess their solvency to grant them a line of credit for gambling, the real purpose was much darker. They asked me to manage powers of attorney of doubtful origin, to order blind money transfers without knowing who the recipients were, in short, the word *ethics* had completely vanished from my dictionary."

"Speak clearly, please."

"I have received threats and my family is the most thing important to me. I hope you understand," he said, while the leg of his chair creaked under his trembling legs.

Morillo was sorry for him, but he could not let go of his prey at that moment.

"Did you ever see or had any dealings with a big, red-haired man?" he asked directly and by surprise.

The expression on the accountant's face and his sudden pallor gave him the answer, but he still waited to see what he had to say. The accountant began to move his head from side to side as if he had a nervous tic.

"Sorry, I have already said too much. I trust you, but I can only accompany you to the curtain and show it to you. If you want to see what's behind the curtain, you must raise it yourself," the little man said, standing up and leaving the room without even saying goodbye.

CHAPTER 37

Barcelona. Today.

T he week had elapsed with a slowness directly proportional to Gerard's desire to make further progress in the investigation.

One of Lieutenant Botell's warnings was to refrain from going back to the Casino ruins until they could conduct a police investigation. What he had not specified was how long would the involuntary quarantine last.

Gerard agreed, for now, to leave it to the police, albeit their slowness and little interest in the case. It was the same everywhere, someone had to die quartered or mummified corpses had to appear for the police to truly get involved.

He was convinced Lieutenant Botell had mistaken him by a paranoid, injured while exploring ruins of abandoned buildings. He did not expect much from the police investigation, if they ever came to set it up, but decided to be cautious and stay away from the Casino for a while.

The police could keep saying he had imagined everything, but the bruises and wounds decorating his whole anatomy were the palpable and painful proof that it was all true. Resting a few days would allow him to recover and face the next phases of his research full of energy.

He spent the next few days reviving old contacts in search of a job opportunity that still did not materialize and deepening in his documentation task about the Art Nouveau period and the architectural jewels disappeared under the pickaxe of the builders.

The structure of his exposé on political corruption and connivance with urbanistic interests of builders, businessmen, and politicians of the time was gradually taking shape. He had already accumulated enough information and evidence to produce not one but a series of reports, maybe even a book.

It would not be a best-seller, but a good and well documented critical report would always have its audience, and with a little luck and the proper promotion, it could even become a reference work for scholars interested in that period.

Nothing he could do would bring back the buildings already destroyed and lost forever. But he could do everything in his power to raise public awareness about the importance of keeping their memory alive and to publicize the existing photographic archive so that new generations would know the great treasure their forefathers placed in their hands and the need to safeguard it.

Gerard suffered painfully whenever he saw images of ancient temples and historic monuments anywhere in the world, destroyed by religious fanaticism, radical terrorism, ignorance, greed, speculation or other equally reprehensible extremisms.

To watch ancient sculptures being blown up in pieces tore his heart apart, it was as if they ripped a part of his being with each fragment that went flying.

To him, art was the ultimate expression of what differentiates man from other animals, which gave us a unique and wonderful quality, the capacity to be thrilled and enjoy the beauty and share it with our fellow human beings.

Gerard thought every work of art destroyed, every piece of stone that fell to the ground brought us closer to the Stone Age.

He believed barbarism took humanity back in time,

back to the darkest stages in the history of man, to the point mankind would lose its identity, and human beings would cease to exist, being what they really were, an insignificant speck of dust in the evolution of living beings, a mere evolutionary accident that would self-correct over time.

He could then summarize the sad culmination of man's presence in this world with one word, containing the essence of what humanity had achieved after thousands of years of evolution. Self-destruction.

Condemning the political corruption of the period was another objective of his work, to prove that, one century later, it was still present and rooted throughout the country, especially in the central government.

It would take several generations to get to root out the scourge of corruption, after too many centuries of little kings, intrigues, fratricidal wars, imperialist ambitions, absolutism, and so many classic manifestations of the worst that old Europe understood as progress.

History always repeated itself, therefore exposing the abuses by politicians and businessmen of the period would bring out those who were doing the same thing today, and Gerard hoped the social pressure and the unstoppable force of a society well informed and eager for change would do the rest.

Max was out of the country on a business trip that week, and taking advantage of the relative quiet, Gerard had started writing the first draft of his report, which at least soothed his conscience.

He entered his apartment carrying a bag full of groceries to survive a couple of days, his usual purchase, and followed his routine of walking to his phone answering machine to listen to the messages.

In the era of mobile phones and nanotechnology, he probably was one of the three or four human beings in the entire world still using those devices to record their messages in a tape.

He had tried to get used to the voice mail on his cell phone but lacked the patience to spend several minutes navigating through auditory menus and infernal key combinations to access his mailbox.

There was something about the elegant simplicity of those machines that attracted and reassured him. The almost prehistoric cassette tapes never broke down, they could record more than an hour of messages, and when they were full, one was only to extract them, turn them over and continue recording.

Coming home and turning his gaze to the flashing red button that told him he had messages waiting, had become not only a routine but also an exciting habit, and he often caught himself trying to guess, from the elevator, if he would find messages or not when he entered the apartment.

Either he was getting old, or he desperately needed to go on a date, since it was clear living alone was taking its toll on him.

The red light was blinking next to a number three on the screen. He pressed the button eagerly and listened to two messages from his phone company rewarding his loyalty, offering him the possibility of buying new services and end up paying twice as much on his monthly bill, deals that would expire in just a few hours, so they urged him to make a quick decision.

He ignored such siren songs and when he was listening to the third message, he dropped the bag on the kitchen table and ran to the phone.

"Mr. Bach, this is Eva, Juana Caballero's granddaughter. I have something that might interest you, but it will cost you at least a coffee, or better yet, a snack. I hope to hear from you soon, Mr...., well... I mean, Gerard."

Gerard smiled at the comment. It was she who had insisted they went on a first-name basis. She was a strange woman, but something in her attracted him, although it was a somewhat contradictory feeling, attraction, and prevention at the same time.

He wanted to explore that mystery more in-depth. What could it be she wanted to show him now? Would it be just a ruse to see him again? There was only one way to find out.

Gerard was already on his second latte that afternoon, and regarding the total number for the day, he had lost count.

He called Eva twice on her mobile phone but he could not reach her, so he left her a message asking her to meet him by mid-afternoon in a central coffee shop in the Eixample, Barcelona's Art Nouveau quarter par excellence.

He did not know whether she would show up, he could not even be sure she heard his message. He called again her mobile phone twice from the cafeteria, with the same luck. He would wait for another half hour and then return home.

From the next table he grabbed a newspaper, so wrinkled and stained with oil and coffee it seemed someone had been practicing how to wrap a ham sandwich with that issue.

He flipped through the first sections, turning the pages with only his fingertips, but he did not go beyond the international section, whose pages were glued together with a sticky substance of unknown origin.

"I dare not ask you what you've been doing with that newspaper," a female voice said behind him.

He turned and faced a smiling Eva, who sat opposite him without waiting for his answer. She wore an old-fashioned dress, with ruffles at the collar and cuffs, and a light pale gray jacket.

"I won't talk unless my attorney is present," Gerard said, raising his hands.

They asked for more coffee and several pastries and chatted for a few minutes on insubstantial issues.

He found that woman intriguing. She was beautiful, but hers was an inner beauty. Her big blue eyes gave her a feline expression he found disturbing and appealing at once.

He had to admit he was nervous being in front of her, which made him even more nervous, in an impossible vicious circle leading to nothing.

On the other hand, he suspected she was hiding something, or at least she was not being completely honest with him but decided not to anticipate events and give her a chance.

We must live life step by step, in small doses. That had always been one of his mottos, and he would not stop applying it now.

"Your message said you had something to show me," Gerard said, being direct.

"No, I told you I had something that would interest you, is not the same," she said, suddenly adopting a serious attitude, which surprised Gerard, not knowing whether she was joking. Her sudden mood changes baffled him.

"Thank you for pointing it out. What is it about?"

"My great-grandmother came to work in the city from a small farmer's village in the province of Navarra. She was a woman of few words. I barely met her, but in the short time I shared with her I never heard her speak more than five minutes at a time. However, she was an exceptional woman, a hard worker, dedicated to her family and educated from childhood in the value of hard work and responsibility."

Gerard did not see where she was going with her dissertation but did not interrupt her.

"That's why I was so surprised to find this among her belongings. When I was cleaning her house, inside some boxes full of books and papers I found this," and she opened her bag and pulled out an object wrapped in brown paper.

"You have me intrigued."

"Now I will show you something," she said with a smile, and unwrapped the package, inside of which there was a small notebook with soft leather covers, very worn and scratched.

"Is it a Bible?"

"It looks like it, but no, it isn't. It's a diary," she said, letting the pages run between her fingers.

"I never thought my great-grandmother could keep a journal, so uncommunicative as she was, but she did, at least for a while. The entries are sporadic and sometimes

197

many months go by between them, and rarely are they more than four or five sentences, but there they are," she said, leaving it on the table.

Gerard took it as an invitation to leaf through it, but before taking it he requested permission from Eva with a look, to which she responded with a nod.

He flipped through the first few pages. For a peasant woman, her handwriting was tiny and balanced, with strong and very rounded strokes. The handwriting lines seemed like rows of small snails creeping through the page.

It was obvious the woman had received a certain level of education. Each entry was preceded by the date, written in larger print.

"What topics does she write about?" Gerard asked.

"Mainly family issues, but there are also parts where she talks about her work, her aspirations, her dreams. They made me discover a side of my great-grandmother I never suspected existed; it turns out she was a woman of great sensitivity. What caught my attention was this," Eva said, taking the book from his hands and turning pages until she stopped at a certain spot, pointing at with her finger.

"When you left the other day, I remembered the diary had some entries related to the Casino, specifically three of them. I reread them all and one struck me specially."

"*I cannot stay here any longer, they cannot force me. Agus says that the devil dwells in MM and I don't want to end up like the others.*"

She wrote the sentence with a trembling hand, and next to the lines, there were two small drawings in coarse and simple strokes. One of them represented a mountain, pierced by a dark hole in the shape of a door. The other could be anything, but Gerard thought he saw a creature with its mouth open, with what looked like fangs, an undulating body, and two wings. What did she try to portray with that picture?.

"You're wondering what that drawing means, aren't you?" Eva said.

"Are you also a mind reader?" Gerard said, smiling.

"Yes, it's an interesting drawing. Do you think it refers to the devil she mentions in her text?"

"I've often thought about it. It's highly likely. I think she was a very religious woman."

"Everyone was at that period," Gerard said.

"Yes, I guess so. I suppose she was speaking figuratively, as if joking. She probably meant she was tired of her job, and I don't blame her, because being responsible for all the hotel room services must have been exhausting for her."

"But that's what she would say during a conversation. She would mention the devil referring to a mischievous or daring person. It's strange to think when writing her intimate confessions in her diary she would express it in the same way, unless she was serious about it, which is what people do when they confess," Gerard said.

"Do you mean she believed the devil existed and lived in MM, whatever that place was?"

Gerard ran his hand through his hair and sighed. "No, is not that. But it sounds as if she was very concerned about something, and someone terrified her. Perhaps she refers to one of her bosses at the Casino, or an especially demanding or capricious customer. Who knows?"

"I have always felt so sorry for her after reading that sentence. It gives the impression she was suffering a lot, especially when she says she doesn't want to end up like the others. I guess she means not ending deranged, or exhausted, or perhaps she was afraid of being fired. We will never know the truth; it's a pity there's no one left alive to tell us what happened," Eva lamented.

"Don't be so sure. Perhaps there is still a possibility," Gerard said, smiling enigmatically.

CHAPTER 38

Gerard walked across Balmes street and looked for the address they had given him on the phone, a modern office building, wedged between two old buildings from the last century.

Another attack on good taste and a new stab to the city's Art Nouveau tradition. And it was ironic it all happened just a few blocks from Barcelona's Art Nouveau Museum.

He skimmed the business directory in the lobby until he found the name of the law firm where Agustín's granddaughter worked.

After reading in Juana's diary her allusion to "*Agus says that the devil dwells in MM*", he knew Agus had to be Agustín, and only he could clarify whom Juana meant when she spoke of the devil.

When he called her granddaughter to ask for permission to visit her grandfather again, Lucía replied with sobs and summoned him that afternoon at the office where she worked.

The young receptionist took him into a private meeting room and offered him a glass of water. Gerard wondered what criteria the big law firms used to select those young girls to be receptionists.

It could not be a coincidence that all of them were so spectacularly beautiful and conveyed such understated elegance.

In his job, he had visited major law firms, and that type

of elegant yet explosive woman was a constant in all of them.

Was it a strategy to attract clients? The select clientele frequenting those law firms did not strike him as the kind that could be lured in by a few centimeters of more cleavage or less skirt.

He assumed it was not due to commercial reasons. They were there to satisfy the impulses of the partners, to act as eye candy and feed their fantasies.

The door opened but instead of the spectacular receptionist, it was Lucía, whose bloodshot eyes betrayed she must have been crying all afternoon.

"I'm very sorry for your loss. Please extend my condolences to your brother and the rest of the family," he said, shaking her hand warmly as if trying to convey warmth and affection through his fingers.

Lucía nodded and sat next to Gerard at the table.

"I cannot believe your grandfather is dead. We were with him just a couple of days ago and he looked so fresh and in such good health."

"We thought so, too. Doctors cannot explain it. After your visit, grandpa was in a good mood; it seemed that remembering the old times with you and talking about the Casino, his childhood, after all, had rejuvenated him. But the next day something changed. In the afternoon he suddenly began to feel sick but could not explain what happened to him. We didn't understand what he was saying, and he came to the point of raving, of not recognizing anyone, and finally, around midnight, he died. Cardiac arrest," she said, between sobs.

"The autopsy will determine the cause," Gerard said.

"Not in his case. Perhaps there won't be an autopsy."

"What do you mean?"

"For the love of God, he was an old man over a hundred years old. There are millions of possible causes, all of them reasonable, don't you think? Why make him suffer after death? It's better to incinerate him and keep his memory."

Gerard questioned the legality or at least the ethical

framework of such a position, but chose not to argue with her in those difficult times.

"I suppose if life were a football match, when one becomes centenary, all the time lived from there on becomes part of the extra time, and there's little we can claim the referee about," Gerard said, ashamed he couldn't come up with a less trivial cliché than football.

"He enjoyed living and lived a long and happy life. That's the only comfort we have," Lucía said. "We have received calls from the City Council and the local television station. They want to interview us today or tomorrow. He was the longest-lived person in the country, did you know that? At least he will now have his fifteen minutes of glory, even if it's after death."

"I think he had much more than that. And although I barely knew him, I have the impression that with grandchildren like you and your brother, Agustín felt that true glory was to be with you and feel so loved and protected," Gerard said, taking her hand.

"Do you think so?" she said, with tears in her eyes.

"Do not doubt it."

A soft knock on the door preceded the appearance of a daring cleavage, accompanied by the receptionist's beautiful face.

"The TV3 film crew is here," she said, and Gerard liked to think she was solely addressing him.

"I'll be right there, ask them to wait in another room," Lucía said, and the cleavage disappeared just the same way it had appeared.

"I don't want to bother you; I called you because I would have liked to talk to your grandfather again, and ask him a few more things, but it has not been possible. That's life," Gerard said, rising and getting ready to leave.

"He liked you."

Gerard stopped and turned to her.

"How do you know that?"

"I know. I knew my grandfather well. I know he was very excited someone took that period seriously and investigated on the Casino and its history."

"Your grandfather was part of that history, the Casino was a part of his life," Gerard said.

"Yes, and a very important one. We always felt there was much that Grandpa hid from us about those years. We thought maybe there might have been some woman, or something happened he did not want to explain, perhaps a messy affair, or he saw something he shouldn't have, which is possible because his work as bellboy gave him access to everything and everyone," Lucía said, speaking as she wiped her tears with a tissue.

With his gaze, Gerard encouraged her to keep talking.

"Did he ever talk about MM?" he asked directly.

"MM? What are they, initials?"

Gerard didn't know, but maybe they were. He would have to review again the hotel staff and clients' listings to see if he found out something.

"I don't know. Someone or somewhere. A person who had worked with Agustín mentioned it, and I thought maybe he'd know what it was."

"I'm sorry, it doesn't ring a bell. Well, I have to meet the television crew. I should have stayed home and not come to work today, but I need to be busy, and I know that coming to the office will keep me distracted for a few hours. My brother takes care of all the preparations for the funeral, mass, service, whatever. And thanks for coming. I really appreciate it," she said, shaking hands with him, and headed for the door.

Upon reaching it she turned.

"I almost forgot it. My grandfather left these written notes after you came to visit him. He asked us to get them to you, but the truth is we had almost no time to think about it because he died the very next day," she said, handing him an envelope as she went out to the corridor.

Gerard put the envelope in his pocket and followed her. She said goodbye and turned to shake hands again. Gerard came over and kissed her on the cheek, which she appreciated, since she closed her eyes and sobbed again.

"I'll find my way out, don't worry," he said.

"Thanks, thanks again."

She walked down the hall. After several steps, she stopped, turned and spoke through tears and sobs.

"Please, say nice things about my grandfather in your book. He deserves it," she said, and Gerard nodded shaking his head and smiling at her from afar.

Once he was out on the street, he went into the first decent and discreet coffee house he could find, and ordered a vanilla-flavored cup of coffee, although he positively knew the chances they would have it were minimal, but he never got tired of trying.

He settled for a regular latte and opened the envelope. Inside he found a single sheet torn from a spiral-bound notebook, written only on one side with shaky handwriting and very hard to read.

At the bottom of the page, he could see a signature, a large letter A followed by some scribbles that probably represented his name. At the top of the sheet, he could read a word followed by "Rabassada", but the word was crossed out.

Underneath there were some child-like drawings. There was a house drawn with straight lines, with windows on two floors and a smoking chimney. It was exactly the same house any five-year-old child anywhere in the world would have drawn.

Beside it, a drawing made with rounded lines showed an eagle or a large bird that seemed to have horns and a very elongated body.

At one end of the page footer he had drawn a tap with a large water spurt coming out of it, and next to it, a ship the same child who drew the house could have drawn.

At the other end of the footer he had drawn a square with very thin, barely visible stroke, and inside what looked like a small flame rising from a straight line, as if it were a candle placed horizontally.

That was all. Gerard contemplated it. What the hell was that? What was Agustín trying to tell him with those drawings?

He didn't know if the old man couldn't draw better, or perhaps his senile dementia was taking him back in time and his intelligence was losing faculties, closing the circle of life that made him return to his childhood. Or maybe he had done it on purpose and had used simple and easy to decode symbols.

Whatever the explanation, it was clear Agustín was trying to tell him something he did not want or did not dare to write with words and hid it disguised behind the falsely childish strokes of those drawings.

During his conversation with Agustín, the lucidity and mental agility of the old man had impressed him. He could not understand how on that same night he could only make such basic drawings, unless he would have done them consciously.

Plus, there was something strange about his death. The old man had lived over a hundred years in good health and he died just hours after Gerard and Max visited him and asked him questions about the Casino.

Too many coincidences and Gerard had never believed in them.

Lucía had asked him to say nice things about Agustín in his work, and he would do it.

He owed it to that mysterious and remarkable man, who seemed eager to help him even from beyond the grave.

CHAPTER 39

S everal days had gone by since Gerard had been with Agustín's granddaughter. He had not heard from her, nor did he know whether they had conducted an autopsy. So many questions hovered over the matter, Gerard was confused.

He needed to take some distance and look at things from a different perspective.

He sensed the key to it all had to be in the Casino ruins, but so far all his experiences there had ended up with his bones crashing against the ground, with bruises and visits to the police station.

Max had left him a message on his answering machine, letting him know he would return from his trip in two days. He was sure he could convince Max to accompany him for another tour of the ruins. After all, the mountain belonged to everyone, nobody could prevent them from going out for a walk in a natural Park like Collserola.

He spent the day rereading several huge volumes of bound copies of the newspapers "El Noticiero Universal" and "La Vanguardia" for the period from 1910 to 1915 he took from the library.

Putting to practice what he learned in a speed-reading course, he scanned the pages diagonally, retaining only headlines and keywords. Even so, those readings felt as soporific as if he was reading four hundred telephone guides.

The newspapers of that period were much denser than today's.

To the scarcity of images, one had to add the tediousness of the texts and the maximum utilization of every millimeter on the page, which resulted in pages packed with information, in which news about different issues mingled indiscriminately with many advertisements.

Could it be that journalists from the last century didn't know what newspaper sections were? Those newspaper issues were the news equivalent to the current low-cost bazaars, so common in modern cities.

He found several articles reporting on the inauguration of the Casino de la Rabassada, advertising with the pompous and descriptive language of the period the wonders offered by that gambling and leisure complex. They described the hotel and Casino, reveling in the luxury and sophistication, and encouraged the public to visit the fabulous amusements.

He also found articles criticizing gambling and the pernicious effects it could have on those who practiced it in excess.

Scattered among so many pages of information, he found some articles explaining the discovery of corpses in the Collserola mountains, and some establishing a relationship with the Casino.

They were all written from the perspective of the pernicious influence of gambling, acting as a magnet for crooks and thieves and about the backdrop of vice and corruption that eventually grew around such establishments.

A name caught his attention. An article mentioned a police captain, a certain Casimiro Botell, whose team had investigated anarchist cells planning to carry out attacks in the city.

He found other similar articles, and from the tone used by reporters when referring to him, captain Botell seemed to be an influential person.

Gerard took a mental note to investigate whether the

captain could be a relative of the current Lieutenant Elías Botell, whom Gerard recently had the pleasure to discuss with.

He put aside the old newspapers' volumes, since his eyes needed some rest and fixed himself some vanilla coffee. Without knowing why, he examined the drawings he had copied from Juana Caballero's diary and the ones that Agustín the bellboy let him in his letter before he died.

Placing them side by side, he compared them. The style was very different, but they had elements in common, especially that strange animal, a mixture of a bird, snake, beast, lizard, it could be anything. The two had tried to draw the same, and it felt oddly familiar.

Juana had drawn a mountain with a hole that looked like a black door, while Agustín had drawn a house and a squirting water spurt.

Gerard spent over an hour searching for old Casino photographs on the internet, fascinated by them, imagining himself wandering around those sites, as Juana and Agustín had done, and wondering how life would have been like in that period.

He scrolled back to look again at some sepia photographs from the amusement park. He could see women wearing the bulky skirts and hats of the period, crammed into small roller coaster cars, along with their partners, wearing bowler hats and walking sticks, ready to experience the thrills of those descents and dizzying curves, and the journey through the dark bowels of the mountain through the tunnels.

In some photographs of the lowest part of the valley, he noticed a cement reproduction of the characteristic sawtooth-shaped silhouette of the Montserrat mountains, built next to a natural water spring, in a picnic area close to the Casino.

The mouths of those tunnels bore a strong resemblance to Juana's drawing. What if she had tried to represent the entrance to one of those tunnels in her drawing?

From the articles he read, he knew the tunnels were

short, and most of them still existed, because being inside the mountain kept them from being demolished as the rest of the enclosure was.

He had to go back to that place. Nothing could stop him, although the wise thing to do was not to go alone. He needed a companion, but Max would not be back until the next morning.

"I should say I'm excited by the prospect of this adventure, but the truth is I'm a little frightened," Eva said as they climbed the road leading towards the Casino ruins.

"And I don't mean the ruins, nor the ghosts that may live in them, but the experience of riding pillion on your motorcycle," she said, holding tightly to Gerard's waist while he negotiated the many sharp curves, which seemed more twisted since the last time he drove there.

The city slowly faded away behind them, and soon Eva succumbed to the charm of the wonderful views that unfolded before her.

Gerard stopped briefly at a small viewpoint cleared on the side of the road behind a more than 180° curve, from which they could admire a spectacular view of Barcelona city, surrounded by the immense Mediterranean sea that affectionately embraced her and did not let her escape, reflecting the sun like a giant golden foil.

It was a popular place for tourists, who stopped there at any time of day to take pictures of the city, and for couples, who stopped there at night, to enjoy the views from outside and inside their cars, neatly parked, with their rolled-up windows all fogged up.

They soon reached the summit and began the descent, up to the straight stretch of road where the only left standing Casino wall surprised Eva.

Gerard grabbed her hand as they descended the slippery path leading to the tower and the terrace, places he wanted to avoid at all costs. He planned to go straight to the bottom of the mountain, where he hoped to find some tunnel entrances to check them out.

"I see a building down there, between the trees," Eva said, pulling him and pointing toward the tower.

"Yes, I know. It's nothing more than an old crumbling Casino tower, there is nothing of interest there," he said, trying to get away from the path.

Gerard had chosen not to tell her any details about his past experiences because he didn't know yet if he could trust her and preferred not to scare her in advance.

"I would love to see it. My great-grandmother must have worked there. If it was part of the hotel, I'm sure she had stepped on those floors. Let's go see it, please. Look, I see more people there," she said, pointing toward the path.

Gerard saw a group of tourists, dressed in trekking attire, standing at the end of the path, next to the tower. He pricked up his ear, and it reassured him not to hear any barking. To satisfy Eva, he nodded and started walking in that direction.

"Good morning," Gerard said, addressing the one who looked like the group leader, a heavyset man with thick sideburns and thick glasses, who must have been about sixty years old. Three women who seemed to surpass him in age, but not in size, accompanied him.

"Good morning," the man replied.

"Anything of interest in that tower? Have you met anyone?" Gerard asked, innocently.

"If you consider interesting to see piles of garbage, the smell of piss and shit, and the risk of being crushed by the roof falling down on you, you will find it fascinating," the man replied wryly, wiping his forehead with a handkerchief. "Well girls, shall we get going? I want to reach the car and go have lunch at the farmhouse restaurant one kilometer from here. We deserve it, don't we?"

Gerard wondered what could they have possibly done to deserve a sumptuous feast such as the one they would surely regale themselves with when they got to the restaurant, but he chose not to ask. The group walked away, following its rotund leader, and Gerard went around the tower to look inside.

Eva went in with him and immediately stopped, stalled by a fetid wave threatening to end her life in just a few seconds. It smelled as if they had killed there someone and left the corpse to decompose, macerated in his own feces, such was the unbearable stench emanating from the room.

"Those people have fallen short in their description, this doesn't just smell of urine, it's as if we were floating in a filthy and fetid sewer, paddling with our own hands toward..." Eva said.

"Enough, please," Gerard interrupted her. "I think the analogy is more than clear. Can we abandon the subject, please? I told you there was only trash here, there's nothing of interest," Gerard added.

"I hope when my great-grandmother worked here, the clientele, and the establishment were of a higher profile," she said, covering her nose with one hand and pointing with the other to the old mattress and the remains of old clothes and junk piling everywhere.

They ran back to the path and Gerard made his way through the thicket to head down to the bottom of the valley, to the area where the attractions used to be.

CHAPTER 40

I t was hard to believe there had been a modern amusement park in that place a hundred years earlier.

They were amid what was now a thick forest, yet a century ago, thousands of citizens walked through that area, eager to feel the excitement of going down at breakneck speed along narrow rails in a wagon, to the delight of its idle occupants.

Nature, eternally patient, always ends up claiming what is hers.

The vegetation was very thick, but some visible trails crossed the area, probably made by hikers who often crossed those woods walking towards the Tibidabo.

Through the weeds, Gerard saw the remains of an arch, giving access to a small tunnel a few meters long, on a steep slope. He identified it as one of the roller coaster tunnels, although there were no rails left or any other sign of what it had once been.

He knew the total length of the original roller coaster circuit was two kilometers, but considering there were several straight stretches and curves of almost 360º, the maximum extension of the circuit must have been around three hundred meters. The remaining tunnels could not be far from that one, but finding them among the thick vegetation would not be easy.

They separated to keep searching, although they agreed

to always maintain eye contact. It didn't take long for them to find what they were looking for.

"Here," Eva shouted, unable to hide her excitement.

Gerard saw an archway entrance to a brick-built tunnel over four meters high, and surprisingly well preserved. Its stone and cement floor had prevented the vegetation from invading and hiding it completely.

"Let there be light," Gerard said, proudly pulling from his pocket a small LED flashlight he bought in a bazaar.

"Is this all the lighting equipment you brought?" Eva asked incredulously.

"It's brighter than it seems, don't let its small size fool you," Gerard said, refraining from making the obvious joke her question had prompted, an opportunity his friend Max would have seized.

Gerard entered the passage followed by Eva, who walked with her hand on his shoulder. The long tunnel described a very open curve, so the cars would not gain too much acceleration inside.

The trajectory was barely twenty meters, and Gerard hoped the bright light at the end of the tunnel would be the exit into the forest and not the entrance to eternal life.

Judging from the graffiti decorating the walls, they were not the first to visit the tunnel, which seemed to have received more visits than the Cathedral in Barcelona.

Once outside, they continued searching the mountain, and half an hour later Eva found the entrance to another tunnel, similar to the previous one, but bricked up, with a door that had volatilized many years ago.

The weak beam of the small flashlight could barely break into the darkness. This time Eva grabbed Gerard's arm, in a display of a familiarity that grew as time went by and they went deeper into those murky tunnels.

They meandered among the rubble, debris and the occasional remains of nocturnal sprees, empty bottles, beer cans and other waste of a less identifiable nature.

"Why was this tunnel bricked up?" Eva asked.

"After the Civil War, they used some of these tunnels as

warehouses and cellars, that's why they bricked them up. They have great storage capacity and the temperature inside is several degrees lower than outside," Gerard said.

"Yes, I can feel it. My blood froze in my veins, this place gives me the creeps," Eva said, clutching Gerard's jacket sleeve.

They reached the other end of the tunnel, also bricked up, but they reach the forest through a narrow opening in the wall.

"Ahhh, what a pleasure to feel the warmth of the sun, even if it's through the trees," Eva said, looking up to the sky." Where are we?"

"I don't know exactly. I think we have come out in one of the farthest edges of the amusement park area. Here begins what has always been the forest, and the slope gets steeper until it reaches the bottom of the valley."

"So, what do we do now? We have found nothing of what you expected to find, whatever it was. Although it has been very exciting to walk through these sites, knowing my great-grandmother spent part of her life here," Eva said, sitting on a fallen log.

Gerard looked around. Some three hundred meters above and behind them, they should find the Casino ruins, and in front, the wild forest.

They went back to the main ruins, but instead of following the same path, this time they would take the West route, walking around what had once been the perimeter of the Casino grounds.

The climb proved difficult, given the steep terrain and thick vegetation. Gerard helped Eva taking her hand as often as he could, which he found a more pleasant task than he had initially envisioned. He held and pulled her even in sections where the terrain offered no difficulty.

"There is something there," Eva said, showing how good she was at identifying structures through the vegetation. She was pointing to a small rise in the ground near a huge tree, covered with moss and fallen branches.

"It's only a buried rock," Gerard said, walking there and

kicking it with his foot.

"Yes, but its shape is too rectilinear, I think there's something down there, and it seems man-made," she insisted.

Gerard was not convinced, but he picked up a large dry branch and stuck it underneath, poking and prying until he lifted a large plate of earth and moss. He kept digging and pushing dirt away and he soon reached what looked like a flat concrete slab.

"You were right," he said, very excited. "It can be a fallen cement block, or maybe a slab covering a pit. We have to keep clearing it."

The slab turned out to be the top of a cement structure, under which there was a small thick wooden door locked with a rusty lock. It looked like an air vent or the entrance to a coal bunker. Even if they could open the door, space barely allowed the passage of an adult.

"Judging by the condition of the door, this must have been here since last century, buried and protected from prying eyes. With the number of people who have been here all these years, it's amazing nobody has discovered it," Gerard said.

"What do you think there is inside? Perhaps the Casino's secret treasure? Its vault? Its safe?" Eva said, laughing.

"I don't think so. It's quite far from the Casino, and I have no evidence there ever was a vault. It must be some storage room. I'll try to open it."

"Did you buy a set of lock picks in that bazaar you seem to be so fond of?" Eva joked.

"No, in this case, there's nothing like our national technology," Gerard said, unearthing a large rock and approaching the little wooden door.

He unloaded several heavy blows, throwing the rock hard against the lock, which started bending and disengaging from the wood, weakened by moisture and the passage of time. A loud crack indicated the door had given way and Gerard threw the rock aside and introduced his

215

flashlight through the hole.

A stretch of five stone steps disappearing into the dark was all he could see. Beyond the steps, the passage turned left and went deep into the mountain. Eva and Gerard looked at each other, and there was no need to exchange a word, their gaze carried implicit both the question and the answer.

Gerard was first through the hole and once inside he helped Eva. The passageway was a little over one meter high and they had to crawl on their hands and knees for about five meters until they could stand. They were inside a tunnel that seemed to tap into a natural cave, and from there it penetrated the mountain.

They could be in an uncharted place, in a part of the Casino enclosure that had been closed for more than a century. The prudent thing to do would be to come back another day better equipped.

Gerard thought about calling Max and return to explore it all with good lighting and tools. It was reckless to do it now, with a cheap flashlight and accompanied by a woman he had just met.

Whom was he kidding? The adrenaline rush was so strong he suspected it had to also contain pheromones, since both of them had the firm resolve to move forward.

"It looks like a cave," Eva said, running her hands over the rock walls.

"The floor is a natural rock, but notice there are cement parts, and there are areas that have been artificially widened," Gerard said, pointing forward.

The atmosphere was stuffy, humidity very high, and it was hard to breathe. The air had a sweet smell of mold and rotting vegetation, which, although annoying, it wasn't unpleasant and they soon got used to it.

They walked for about ten minutes, following the gently upward sloping cave floor until they reached a fork in the path.

"Now where to? Where must we be?" Eva asked.

"Considering how far we have walked and going

eastbound, more or less, I think we must be near the Casino, well above the amusement park area," Gerard replied, not quite convinced of what he was saying.

He walked a few meters along the wider tunnel and noted the passage kept going uphill and the ground seemed more traveled. He turned back and briefly explored the other passage, much narrower, extending along two curves and ending in a stone wall.

Gerard approached the wall and bent over.

"What's going on?" Eva asked, startled.

"Here's an entry. Look," Gerard said, pointing to a small wooden hatch, hidden behind a rock outcropping.

"It's another wooden door, but I see no lock. There's only this ring. Let's see," Gerard said, pulling hard on a thick rusty iron ring attached to the door.

After several attempts, the small door gave way and opened out. It was a lid more than a door; it lacked hinges and was loose. Gerard placed it on the ground, bent down and put his head through the hole to illuminate the interior.

Eva saw Gerard contort and disappear through the narrow opening.

"I hope you're not claustrophobic," Gerard said, seeing Eva followed his footsteps to avoid being left alone in that dark passageway.

Once inside, they could stand with no difficulty and this time Eva embraced Gerard's back unabashedly, putting her arms around him, her hands resting on his chest, raising no complaints from him.

The flashlight beam showed a not too wide space, with smooth and slightly curved walls.

Gerard wondered if he had finally discovered the famous suicide room. It was a gloomy chamber with a smooth concrete floor. The ceiling was... there was no ceiling, the walls formed the ceiling, like a large cylinder.

When they moved their feet, they heard the splash of water, and when he aimed down the flashlight, the light bounced in about ten centimeters of still water. Gerard turned off the flashlight, and he automatically felt the pleasant sensation of Eva's nails digging into his chest again.

"Can you hear it?" Gerard asked.

"I hear water drops falling," she said, listening to the rhythmic sound of several out of step drops falling on the water surface.

"Exactly."

"But I can assure you I can hear them equally well with the light on; even better, in fact," she added.

Gerard turned on the flashlight and pointed it at the ceiling, where several tree roots had penetrated through cracks in the cement layer, floating in the inner space like the sinister tentacles of a threatening being.

Water slowly dripped from the tip of several of its branches, and in the gloom of that space, it seemed like blood drops from the limbs of a wounded animal bleeding out to death.

"This is only a cistern, probably used to collect rainwater. There must be a drain at the bottom to empty it," Gerard said. "Let's get out of here."

Gerard bent and was again the first to go through the narrow opening out into the passage. Eva crouched behind him, reached out and put her head through the hole for him to help her out, but to her surprise, Gerard's hand pushed her head in.

"What's going on?" she shouted.

"Stay there. Don't move. I heard something, like the sound of footsteps in the wide passage, after the fork. I'll go take a look."

"Don't leave me here, I'm coming with you," Eva cried, in what looked more like a whimper than a request.

"No, you'll be safer in there. Don't go out. I'll be back soon to get you out," he said, and Eva felt Gerard's hand disappearing through the hole, leaving her into the tank.

"But I have no light..." was all she managed to say, and everything went dark and silent.

She looked up, and even though she could see nothing, she felt the tentacles of the bleeding roots still over her head, she could hear them slowly bleeding out.

She tried to take that image from her head. What was the song her great-grandmother used to sing her to get her to sleep?

Endearing images of her great-grandmother began parading through her mind; she could see her smiling, right there in front of her, dressed in her shiny Casino employee uniform, extending her welcoming arms and reaching out to her.

CHAPTER 41

Barcelona. 1912

The walk with Agnes was proving to be very pleasant.

Morillo had asked her to meet at the end of the elegant Paseo de Gracia. Since they started dating, he tried to get her away from the modest neighborhoods he normally frequented, not because he was ashamed of it, but to make her feel special.

They walked through Plaza Catalunya, dodging some of its many trams, both of animal traction and electrical.

The square was a sea of recently planted palm trees, which gave it a fake tropical appearance, in contrast to the classic elegance of the buildings surrounding it.

They continued up to the bustling Rambla de Canaletas, and Morillo walked to the popular refreshment kiosk that stood near the fountain that gave the avenue its name.

The kiosk was a beautiful Art Nouveau construction open on all four sides, with an inclined marquee from which several round glass lanterns hung, and where a giddy group of waiters hampered each other trying to serve the many customers asking for refreshments at the top of their voices.

Morillo pondered the possibility of flashing his police badge to ask for the lemonade he wanted to offer Agnes but decided not to abuse his authority.

"To hell with them," he said to himself, and offering Agnes his arm he dragged her out of the commotion and they walked toward Pelayo Street.

"I have an idea," Morillo said. "There's a place that just opened and is just around the corner. We'll be more comfortable there, and with a little luck we may even find a place to sit."

Soon they were at the gates of the newly opened American Bar. Inside it was very crowded and Morillo had to dismiss his idea to find a free table.

He left Agnes waiting at the entrance and had to withstand shoving and jostling, but managed to reach the front line of the bar. From there, his struggle focused on capturing the attention of the waiters behind it.

Once he achieved his goal, and when he was swimming back across the sea of customers, he had a strong run-in with a guy who hit him on the side. Morillo stumbled and had to juggle to prevent the two glasses of lemonade from spilling. When he regained verticality, he went to Agnes and handed her a glass, while looking around with a furious expression, trying to locate the impetuous client.

"What happened? Who did you see?" Agnes asked, surprised.

"An animal hit me and almost made me spill the drinks," he complained, running in circles and standing on tiptoe to look over the sea of hats and heads.

"Forget it and let's enjoy the refreshment while taking a stroll. Come on, let's get out of here," she said reassuringly, taking his hand and taking to the streets.

They walked for about twenty minutes, sipping their drinks, laughing and enjoying the inexhaustible display of life in the city. They strolled down Pelayo Street to the main University of Barcelona building. There they sat on a bench in the Gran Via, under the trees, and chatted, watching the afternoon pass.

Agnes sneezed a few times and Morillo reached into the outside pocket of his jacket to offer her a relatively clean handkerchief.

When he removed it, something fell from his pocket. He bent down and picked it up. It was a folded piece of cardboard, torn from a box. As he unfolded it, he saw there was a note faintly written in pencil, *"Palau de B. Arts. 11 Thursday night. Calvet."*

"What the hell is this?" he wondered aloud.

Agnes turned and looked at him in puzzlement.

"This is not mine. Someone put it in my pocket. Probably the guy who hit me in the bar."

"What does the note say?" Agnes asked, somewhat uneasy.

"Nothing important, it makes little sense. He must have put it there by mistake," he said, diverting her attention not to worry her.

"Well, it's getting late, and it's time for the police to escort you home, don't you think?" Morillo said, with a smile.

"You indulge me in excess. There's no need for such surveillance, I feel as if I was the queen of Spain."

"No, not the queen. Better a princess. Yes, a beautiful princess," he said, taking her hand and squeezing it.

"I'll walk you home and we'll wait there until the agent that will keep an all-night watch on the street arrives. I will not rest easy until we catch that lunatic," he said, walking with her to one of the tram stops.

An hour later, Morillo was walking towards the Palau de Belles Arts. The note was clear, Calvet the accountant wanted to meet him there on Thursday at 11 at night.

He hoped he would have reconsidered and this time would keep talking. He sensed that man's testimony would help him clarify what was happening in the Casino.

The Palau de Belles Arts was a spectacular building, and like many others in Barcelona, built for the Universal Exhibition of 1888. With a height of about fifteen floors, it was flanked by two quadrangular towers topped by pyramidal domes and at each apex, gigantic stone angels balanced with their wings upright pointing to the celestial vault from which they came.

It was a sparsely populated area of the city, with wide-open spaces, mainly the Ciudadela Park nearby. At that time of night, traffic was almost nonexistent, just some horse-drawn carriages returning illustrious people to their homes, some merchants pushing their wagons and the occasional motor vehicle.

The street lighting was very poor, only a few streetlights placed along the sidewalk surrounding the building. Morillo waited in the shadows, a few hundred meters away from the main facade.

He checked for the umpteenth time his pocket watch. Ten minutes to eleven at night. He ran his sweaty hand through his slicked hair, which had lost its stiffness with the passing of the hours and his growing nervousness.

He didn't know what to do or where he had to meet Calvet, since the note did not specify the exact meeting point, and that was a very wide area.

During the last hour, he had walked twice around the building, meandering and keeping a good distance, watching all the entrances, the windows on the upper floors and controlling any activity that took place nearby.

Everything seemed quiet. He saw employees entering and leaving the building, but apparently no events or activities were scheduled for that night, thus it would soon be empty, except for a night watchman.

It was almost eleven o'clock, and he decided to approach the building and find a discreet entrance. When he was about to cross the street, he saw movement between the trees adorning the side street. He stopped and thought he saw a man gesturing with his arm from behind the fence bordering the building.

Morillo crossed the street in a hurry and headed there, taking a detour to avoid passing under the streetlight.

A small iron gate gave way to a small interior garden bordering the building. The door was unlocked and Morillo quickly got in.

He reached a side door leading inside, where he had seen the figure disappear, not before beckoning him again to follow him inside.

CHAPTER 42

He was in a very long corridor that ran all along the side of the building, and when he heard one of the doors closing on the other end, he ran in that direction.

There was a staircase, and although it was dark and he could barely make out the steps, he could hear clearly footsteps climbing ahead of him.

He went up to the first floor and found a closed door, so he kept climbing until he reached the door to the second and top floor. He opened it slowly and the beauty and magic of the scene left him momentarily speechless.

It was a huge rectangular room, with very high walls, topped by a glass roof through which the soft moonlight glow spilled like a silver waterfall. The carpet drowned out his footsteps, so thick he felt as if his feet sank in wet sand on the beach.

A large white statue of a graceful female figure whose face he could not distinguish guarded each end of the room. The walls were cluttered with paintings of all shapes and sizes, hanging next to each other, with no possibility of breathing, choking each other.

There were so many paintings that Morillo thought maybe they bred at night and grew during the day to keep invading the free surface of the walls.

He passed by a huge painting over ten meters long, which seemed to mock his fellow paintings in the opposite wall, a myriad of small paintings cramming the wall and threatening to engulf the door through which he had come in.

The scene was of singular beauty; strolling along that gallery to the blue and ghostly light of an almost full moon, leering all those faces watching him from their canvases, windows to a parallel world that only could be accessed from there.

He lost track of time and almost forgot why he was there. He had to make an effort to concentrate and head toward a double door at the end of the corridor, which he guessed should lead to the great central nave of the palace.

Morillo strolled, intoxicated by the beauty and serenity conveyed by those works of art, and finally came to the door, which was locked. He had seen no other way out, so Calvet should be behind it.

He walked to the great white statue he had seen from afar and stopped to admire it. It was the figure of a slender woman, probably a nymph, with her outstretched arm pointing toward infinity and wearing airy robes, as if lifted by an invisible gust of wind.

She was very beautiful, and Morillo could not help but touch it with his fingertips. The stone's rough surface conveyed a strange feeling, and he felt an absurd mixture of embarrassment and shame to be touching a woman's leg that way, even if she was a simple statue.

Terror paralyzed him when suddenly the statue seemingly came alive and moved toward him. In the room's dimness, he could not distinguish it well, but the statue was moving.

In just a split second, the statue kept moving and fell on him, giving him just enough time to jump to the side to avoid being crushed by the heavy stone mass, however graceful and feminine the model could be.

It couldn't be magic, nor that the statue had come to life. Someone must have pushed it. He looked up and could briefly glimpse a glow through the crack of the door closing before him. Calvet had attacked him and fled into the palace.

His leg hurt, but before proceeding he felt it to check its integrity, trying not to trip over the shattered statue fragments scattered on the floor.

Before opening the door, he drew his gun and took a deep breath. Things had become complicated, and he was alone, and no one at the precinct knew where he was, so he should be particularly cautious.

He lowered the handle and pushed the door hard. The impression he received was similar to the previous one but elevated to full power. He had accessed the large main hall of the palace and was standing on a balustrade going around the perimeter of the gigantic hall at a height of several floors above ground.

The moonlight seeped through huge windows covering the entire hall front and floated down to the floor in a beautiful inclined beam, a slide of light tinging the atmosphere with a blue mantle in which he even thought he saw floating stars, although they probably were only floating dust specks.

It was a huge, open space with no columns impeding visibility. From the ceiling hung an immense fabric tapestry decorated with stripes and floral motifs, lining the inside of the hall like a gigantic tent built inside the building.

In the exact hall center, a gigantic crystal chandelier with hundreds of electric bulbs hung from the ceiling by a thick cable, like a monstrous spider waiting for the right time to jump on the public.

He walked along the balustrade looking in all directions, distracted by the walls filled with small paintings. The passage was clear, there was no one there, just chairs and empty seats scattered throughout the way. He walked to the railing and looked down. The view was overwhelming, he had never been in a space of such giant dimensions.

Even not being a religious building, it was a true cathedral devoted to beauty and art, given both its content and its structure. As if to compete with a cathedral, it even had its own pipe organ.

Morillo remembered having read they built it in 1888,

the first electric organ installed in the country, which now occupied most of the front wall, right under the huge stained glass window.

Dozens of metal pipes of different thicknesses and lengths shone and rose into the light, ready to offer solemn musical accompaniment to the great events and concerts organized in such majestic grounds.

On the main floor, right under the organ, a large white stage evoked the glory of ancient Greece, flanked by caryatids supporting the roof, from which a heavy red velvet curtain hung, resting while waiting for the next show.

Down on the main hall, hundreds, if not thousands of wooden chairs slept in a chaotic formation, waiting to be placed in orderly rows to accommodate the public when need be.

Black statues dotted the entire hall perimeter, naked bodies of men and women in different poses, which distracted Morillo's attention, although after his recent experience he resisted going down to check if they were made of stone.

A staircase went down from the balustrade to the main floor, from behind the stage, and he walked in that direction. He concluded that Calvet must have gone down that way, and since the center of the floor was clear, it was likely he would hide inside the stage.

Gun in hand, he descended the steps to the main floor and approached the stage from the front. With the barrel of his gun, he lifted the velvet curtain and bent down to look underneath, as if peering under a woman's skirt. Behind the curtain, there was total darkness and he could see nothing, so he did not venture to go further.

A distant noise made him turn. He clearly heard it, the sound of a wooden chair being dragged against the tile flooring.

He ambled with his gun in front, walking among the endless rows of jumbled and disorganized chairs, looking in all directions. They were light chairs with a wooden structure and latticed seats and backs, and he guessed there must have been more than a thousand.

He was reaching the back of the room but could see no one. He could not be far away from the place the noise had come from, but it was impossible to know which chair had moved, although there was no place to hide, anyway.

The surrounding statues made him uneasy. Not by their nakedness, but perhaps because of their being black, which carried sinister connotations, against the peace and beauty conveyed by the more traditional white statues.

He had reached the end of the hall and had found no one. In front of him, there was a statue of a muscular man and a woman, both naked, holding a child in their arms, or at least that's what it appeared to him, because that part of the hall was the darkest, being far away from the windows.

It surprised him to see the child was not a newborn, but given his size, he seemed pretty well fed.

He approached the statue and confirmed the child was not normal, it looked as if he had two heads… or perhaps there were two children. Morillo was confused, it was not possible for a classical statue to portray an aberration of nature and exhibit it in the Palace of Fine Arts in plain view.

Reaching out to touch the statue, his fingers brushed against one of the child's heads. Morillo's heart almost came out through his mouth when he noticed the child's head moved and fell, bouncing off his parents' body and rolling on the floor.

Morillo jumped back, and in doing so he dropped his gun, which he heard sliding across the floor.

As he got up quickly, he approached the rolling head, stooping to pick it up. He could not suppress an exclamation of surprise and disgust to note this was not a head made of stone or plaster, but it seemed real.

He lifted it, horrified to find it was a human head. The half-open glassy eyes of a man of about sixty with a thick mustache watched him from that mass, still warm and dripping what must be fresh blood.

CHAPTER 43

Morillo laid the head at the base of the statue. He suspected it belonged to the night watchman, savagely mutilated.

Now his priority was to find his gun. He squatted down and frantically searched the entire area around the statue, his hands sweeping the floor in circles and banging and knocking down all the chairs in his wake. All was in vain, it was like looking for a gun in a dark haystack.

In full despair, it was a relief to see someone finally coming to his aid, as the lights of the hall started turning on gradually, first the lamps on the sidewalls, one by one, and finally, the great central chandelier with its hundreds of light bulbs.

Morillo took advantage of the better lighting and finally found the gun, buried under a mountain of chairs. When he stretched out on the floor and reached out to get it, he heard a voice calling him from the stage.

He got up and looked out there. The curtain was slowly rising, and a figure came down the stage and stumbled down the aisle, between the fallen chairs.

Morillo made room, kicking chairs aside and raised the gun pointing it directly at the figure that stumbled toward him.

"Freeze, don't move! Do not take another step or I'll shoot! I'm a cop!"

The figure kept walking. Morillo found it somewhat familiar, and soon recognized the features of the accountant

Calvet, walking straight toward him.

"Freeze or I'll shoot, I won't say it again!" he shouted.

He couldn't take risks, he was facing a serial murderer and didn't know whether he also carried weapons, so he fired, aiming at his shoulder. Calvet took the hit and stumbled, but kept going. Morillo aimed again, this time to the legs, and made two more shots that knocked him down instantly.

He approached and kept aiming at him. He had no weapons. In fact, he looked badly hurt and had... his mouth gagged, and his hands tied together and secured to his belt with a rope.

He could not believe he had shot a helpless handcuffed man. Now he could only think of releasing him and finding the real maniac. He lowered his gun and got close to Calvet's mouth, loosening the clamp so he could breathe.

"Watch out, it's a trap," the accountant muttered, and in his eyes, Morillo could see pure terror reflected.

Then he heard it, it was like the buzz of many bee swarms hovering over him. The light all around them blinked, and the sound of thousands of bells and jingles made him raise his head and look up.

The gigantic chandelier was falling on their heads, hundreds of kilos of iron and glass bulbs bumping and hitting each other, collapsing on them. Morillo closed his eyes and rolled to the side, knocking down a few chairs.

The roar that followed was impressive, a burst of glass and iron, with thousands of pieces of glass and wood from chairs flying in all directions.

A few seconds later, Morillo tried to get up but his foot was trapped and he feared it was under the chandelier. He tried to move it, but the pain was considerable, although he finally bent his leg and got it out from under a pile of crashed chairs.

He lifted his head and saw a mass of twisted iron arms, glass shards and legs, and backs from broken chairs everywhere. The few light bulbs that survived, flickered before going extinct one at a time. The giant spider was dying.

Morillo sat up and crawled, cutting his hands with pieces of glass and wood splinters, getting as close as possible to the debris to help Calvet. He could only recognize one of his legs and part of the other, which had fallen close to where he was, separated from the accountant's body, guillotined by the giant heaven-sent mass.

He knew there was nothing he could do to save him and concentrated on locating the true murderer. Trying to find his gun amidst all that chaos was a mission not even worth trying, so he stood up and looked around while the remaining hall lights were still on.

And then he saw him, inside the stage, leaning out on one side. A burly man, wearing a black coat, with that lifeless piercing gaze, which conveyed nothing but horror. In a show of overconfidence, he was bareheaded, and his red hair shone under the light from the footlights that lit him close-up.

Morillo would not have more opportunities, so without thinking, he bent down and picked up a curved piece of wood, taken from the back of a chair. Pushing aside glass and debris with his feet, he started walking toward the stage. He had lost his gun, but the murderer didn't know, so he raised his arm, aiming at him from afar with the piece of wood.

The murderer saw him coming and disappeared through the side of the stage, jumping from there to the stairs going up to the balustrade. Morillo went around the stage and ran behind him, although one of his ankles seemed about to dislocate at every step.

"Freeze, police. I'm armed!" Morillo shouted several times, running up the stairs behind him. When he reached the top corridor, he stopped at the great pipe organ. He had not seen him fleeing to the right, nor had he entered the picture gallery, so he had to be hiding nearby.

He walked to the end of the balustrade. Large potted plants and a fence decorated with huge fabric ribbons obstructed the way. From there, another flight of stairs symmetrical to the one he had come up from, descended on the other side of the stage.

The killer couldn't have gone down that way either, or he would have heard him. He turned and retraced his steps. When he reached the organ, he stopped and examined it carefully.

The mammoth instrument was made of seven blocks of metal pipes of different sizes, all supported on a base of wooden panels. He couldn't help approaching and knocking on them to check if they were solid or if any of them hid a trapdoor or a fake panel. He bent down and examined them all, but found no opening.

In the center, there was a small wooden table holding a musical keyboard made of ivory and mother-of-pearl keys, and a bench for the organist.

On one side he found a panel with several switches. He pressed the one bearing the inscription "On" and a deep buzz started to sound, gaining in intensity, accompanied by a multi-tonal murmur, as if the metal pipes were waking up and gargled, preparing for an imminent performance.

He went around the structure and checked the space between the pipes and the back wall, but it was too narrow for anyone to hide there. He seemed to have vanished.

He looked around and walked to the railing to look out from there, and saw the stage roof. As soon as his head leaned out of the railing, a pair of arms appeared out of nowhere, rising from the outside of the railing and grabbed him hard by the neck.

Morillo grabbed the pole with both hands and held on. The murderer was literally hanging from his neck and pulling hard to make him lose his balance and fall over the railing, onto the stage roof.

He pulled back with all his strength, and the redhead took advantage of it to put his foot on the railing and help himself up.

Fighting continued on the balcony floor, both struggling and beating each other savagely launching blind punches that half the time barely reached their target.

Morillo knew he could not resist much longer because that guy was much stronger than him. The redhead turned around and stood behind him, holding Morillo's arms while he grabbed him by the neck and pressed tightly to strangle him.

"Is there anybody there?" someone shouted in the distance.

"If there's anybody there, come out immediately. We are municipal police agents!"

Attracted by the unusual lighting of the Palace at night, clearly visible from the outside, two municipal police officers had entered the building and were at the other end of the hall, near the statue of the couple and the supposedly bicephalous child.

They soon found the watchman's head at the feet of the statue, which put them on high alert.

Morillo squirmed trying to free himself from the man's deadly embrace and come to the railing to let the officers know where he was, but the redhead held him tight, keeping him on the floor, hidden behind the balustrade railing.

He felt his strength abandoning him; he had no gun and his hands were busy trying to loosen the clamp the savage applied on him. All he had left were... his feet.

Taking advantage of the last life beats remaining in him, he had only one option. He held on tight to the arms that were choking him, and hung from them, stretching his legs to the maximum until his feet touched the wooden panels of the base of the organ.

Leaning against the panels, he raised his feet step by step while he was still hanging from the arms of that gorilla until one of his feet could merely brush the organ keyboard.

He could barely breathe, unable to catch his breath, but he used his last ounce of energy to lift a foot and drop it hard on the keys.

Instantly, the pipes responded by delivering a mix of deep and metallic notes that caused the whole balustrade structure to vibrate. Morillo hit the keyboard several times, playing a cacophonous melody that resounded throughout the gigantic hall.

The notes traveled through the hall and reached the two officers who, alerted by the sudden organ concert were already running between the chairs, dodging the fallen chandelier and up the stairs.

The murderer, seeing the police officers come close, knew he had clearly lost the battle, but still had the strength to try to kill Morillo, holding his head and giving him several blows against the floor.

The officers were already climbing the stairs, one on each side, and finding himself surrounded, the redhead leaned and jumped over the railing, landing on the stage roof and disappearing through the trapdoors and stage machinery.

One officer pointed his weapon at Morillo.

"Do not move, you are under arrest!" he shouted.

Morillo had not lost consciousness, but was stunned by the blows, and did not respond.

The officers pointed their weapons at him, while he gestured them to look over the railing, but they ignored him. He sat up slowly and leaned on the organ keyboard to help himself up, and the tubes spat their powerful notes again, a true hymn to fatality.

One officer approached him and held both his hands against his back.

"Police... police," Morillo said, with great difficulty.

"Yes, we are the police, unfortunately for you," the officer shouted in his ear.

"I'm... police and..." he finally managed to say, "my badge is in my pocket..."

He finished the sentence, which cast doubt in the face of the agents, who looked at each other, while one of them reached into the pocket of Morillo's jacket.

When the subinspector badge came to the light, the agents didn't know how to behave, fearing reprisals from their superiors.

"Sorry sir, we believed that... I mean, we saw the lights, and we found a head down there... and when we heard the music, we thought..."

"It doesn't matter, and I thank you because I probably owe you my life," Morillo said, interrupting their string of apologies.

"The murderer is still at large, and that's what is regrettable," he said, by way of consolation, while they stared at each other not knowing how to act.

"Although now there is a serious question that is tormenting me," he told them, and the officers looked at him with concern.

"Tell us, sir," they replied in unison.

"The murderer has fled, but I don't know if what scared him was your arrival or if it was my musical performance that terrified him.

Gentlemen, what do you think?"

CHAPTER 44

Morillo would have to spend all day in the infirmary. His injuries were not serious, but the doctor wanted to run some tests and ordered him to rest. To make sure he obeyed, he put him under the care of a veteran nurse who did not take her eyes off him.

It wasn't long before he simulated a deep sleep, spiced with convincing snoring, which made his jealous caretaker lower her guard. During a brief oversight of his nurse, he picked up his clothes, and faking a physiological emergency he locked himself into the bathroom, from where he escaped through a window.

He had no time to waste; his life, Agnes' and that of many others was at stake. He headed for the police station and went straight to the storage room where they kept all belongings from detainees and victims.

He requested the personal effects of the accountant Calvet, whose body should already be on his way to the Laboratory of Forensic Medicine.

The contents of his pockets were rather scarce, only one key, a few blank folded sheets of paper, a watch, and a handkerchief.

Why would he carry blank sheets of paper? Did he mean to write a letter? He unfolded the sheets, two blank pages showing the letterhead of the insurance company where he worked. One had something written on the back, words carelessly scrawled in pencil, hard to read because the strokes were weak.

He approached the lamp to take a better look. It seemed to read *"Morillo Maison"*. What could that mean? It was obvious it was a message to him, but what?

Presumably, Calvet had asked him to meet at the Palace of Fine Arts to give him some clue, when the murderer caught him and blackmailed him to act as bait to lure Morillo into the building. That Calvet had been gagged, supported this second hypothesis.

He went in search of subinspector Aromí. He needed to have someone he could trust minimally, and Aromí fit the profile, albeit also minimally.

He found him sitting at his desk and waved at him from the lobby for him to join him on the street.

Once outside the police station, they went to a coffee shop in a discreet alley nearby and sat at a table.

"Morillo, I thought you were still in the infirmary. I don't want to ask you why the secrecy but, why the secrecy?" Aromí asked, firing first.

"Please don't ask me questions. I'm on to something and is much bigger than it looks."

"It must be, for Lieutenant Botell to be so hysterical. He has been asking about you non-stop for the last few days."

"I can imagine. I cannot talk to him now. I'm sorry but I cannot explain why, although I'm almost certain he is involved in all this somehow."

"Involved in what? What are you talking about?"

"About the serial murderer running loose in Collserola since almost a year ago. About an organized plot to cover up his murders, which involves very important people in Barcelona. Many entrepreneurs have disappeared under mysterious circumstances, and no one is claiming for it; in fact, we cannot even prove they have disappeared," Morillo complained.

Aromí, whose verbal incontinence was mythical, was speechless.

"Are you familiar with the word *Maison*?" Morillo

asked, suddenly.

"With my French skills, I would be embarrassed just to get close to the French border, but I know it means home, that much I know."

"Me too. What I mean is if it does ring a bell; maybe it's someone's name, a restaurant, a shop, I don't know, something that may connect it to Collserola, or perhaps to the Casino."

Aromí remained pensive for a moment and suddenly a mischievous smile crossed his lips.

"Maybe I can help you," he said smiling. "I have a friend who once told me he knew someone, whose brother-in-law was once in a place called something like that."

Morillo came over and leaned with both arms on the table.

"What do you mean?"

"You see... always according to my friend, I mean, to his brother-in-law, that is, well, you know what I mean. There's this house in the Collserola mountains, where wealthy people go to... let's say, get healthy.

"A sanatorium for the spirit?"

"For the spirit and more, you know what I mean. It's popularly known as the "Maison", or at least that's what I've heard out there."

"That's what you've heard," Morillo repeated slowly.

Aromí nodded in silence.

"Out there," Morillo whispered.

Aromí kept nodding.

"To your brother-in-law".

"No, a friend's."

"I see. And where might that miraculous sanatorium be?"

"In fact, it is near the Casino, about a kilometer and a half I would say, following the same road coming from Barcelona, to the left. The building is somewhat unique, I would even say it's a bit sinister".

"Your friend's brother-in-law gave you very precise directions, from what I can see."

"Well, he has an eye for detail, yes."

That very afternoon Morillo was enjoying again the views of Barcelona from the window of the tram climbing the Collserola Mountain. It was not as crowded as on his previous visit and he could breathe and spend much of the trip meditating about everything that happened and planning his next steps.

He had talked with the officers watching Agnes' home, to reiterate the seriousness of the situation, and not comfortable with that, he had sent "Bicycle Man" with a message for her.

In his note, he asked Agnes not to leave her house until he arrived, showing her his affection in writing, at the end of the note, as he was incapable of doing it in person.

When the tram reached the mountain summit, it seemed as if it paused a few seconds to catch its breath before starting the descent, which passengers always greeted with an uproar, cheering and smiling when they felt in their stomachs the effects of going downhill.

Since the descent had begun, Morillo paid attention to all the houses he saw along the way, trying to second guess which would be the one he was looking for.

It was late afternoon, the sun had already started its way to retirement, and it would soon disappear behind the mountains.

The tram driver, from his open position in front of the car, pulled the lever hard and a sharp screech of metal against metal accompanied the braking, which stopped the tram opposite the main Casino entrance.

Once on the ground, Morillo was tempted to get in and walk around its halls and the bar, but the finding of the body in the woods was still very recent and he preferred to stay away from the Casino before someone recognized him.

He retreated down the same road, and walked for about fifteen minutes, stopping to study all the houses he saw through the trees.

If he had to trust the brother-in-law of the acquaintance of Aromí's friend, the building should be on his right.

241

When he estimated he had walked a little more than a kilometer, he stopped in the middle of the road and looked around.

A few hundred meters from where he was, he saw two buildings on a hill, hidden into the forest and sufficiently elevated and separated from the road as to enjoy utmost discretion.

The main building was a beautiful quadrangular construction in garnet color, with pointed double gable roofs. The structure had a small tower on top, rising in the center of the roof and making it stand out like a beacon on the mountain.

Inside the same property, about twenty meters below the main building, a more conventional building seemed to be there as the first line of defense. It was a rectangular three-story building with a cream-colored facade.

Morillo had the feeling this had to be the place he was looking for. He stepped aside to let the tram on his return trip to Barcelona go by, and he walked until he reached a fork in the road.

He walked up a narrow path and soon arrived at something that could fit Aromí's definition of sinister.

He followed the curved wall surrounding the property, which must have been over three meters high.

When he reached the front door and was shocked to find an imposing iron gate, supported by soaring columns, on top of which two large winged stone beings stood guard.

They looked like dragons, with the body and head of a lion, their wings spread, stationed on their pedestal in perpetual vigilance. It was a most disturbing sight, which for a moment put his conviction to the test and made him wonder what he hell was he doing there.

The memory of the murderer, savagely beating poor Isabel Xamot on her deathbed, encouraged him to keep going.

That heartless killer had made Agnes and many more people suffer, and he was determined not let him roam free.

CHAPTER 45

The iron gate was locked and there was nobody around. Morillo retraced his steps and walked along the wall until he reached a small iron door, behind which he could see steps carved into the rock.

He knocked on the door to call the attention of whoever might be behind it and was about to give up when a peephole opened and he saw some male eyes watching him intently.

"What do you want?" someone asked from the other side.

Morillo had to decide in a split second whether he identified himself as a policeman or posed as a client. He regretted not having foreseen that earlier, but now he had to improvise, hoping they would not ask him for a secret code.

If the revitalizing treatments offered in that establishment were of the kind he imagined, he would better leave his police badge into his pocket.

"I've come to... visit this establishment," he said haltingly. "My business partners recommended it. I'm staying at the Casino de la Rabassada," he lied, gaining confidence by the minute, once he decided to hide his badge.

The peephole closed, and after a few seconds of waiting, the sound of locks unlatching announced he was allowed access. Once he crossed the threshold, the door closed again and the man who had opened it mysteriously disappeared.

Morillo strolled up the stairs, toward the smallest of the two buildings. The thick hedges on both sides, neatly trimmed and well maintained, hid the rest of the garden from view.

When he reached the top, he walked to the front door of the mansion. As if someone had been waiting for him, the door opened without him touching it, and a middle-aged woman invited him to come in and sit on a chaise lounge beside the wall.

He was in a long, narrow hall, with walls painted dark green, which reinforced the feeling the room was an extension of the lush vegetation outside.

Opposite him, a wooden counter so small it could conceal no one, next to an enormous vase decorated with Chinese motifs from which long-languishing white pampas grass plumes dropped their hairy tears on a rug.

The woman had disappeared through a side door, and for a moment Morillo did not know how to behave or what he was supposed to do in that situation.

He considered himself a man of the world or at least liked to brag about it to his colleagues, but the truth is he found that place both disturbing and sinfully appealing, but above all, it bewildered him.

A door opened and a plump woman appeared before him, stuffed with obvious effort in a dark maroon dress adorned with golden trim. Her hair was tied in a big bow and her oily skin glowed under the light of the lamp hanging from the ceiling.

"Good morning, how are we?" she said, heading straight for him and offering her hand as she smiled at him excessively.

Morillo shook it gently, surprised by the energy with which she crushed his fingers.

"Have we come alone today?" the woman continued.

Morillo could not stand people who referred to themselves always speaking in the plural, and that case was one of the most clamorous he had known.

"Yes, that's right, we have come alone, me, myself and I; that is, from us, it's me alone," he said, aware he was making a fool of himself.

"Perfect, that way we'll have more privacy. I understand that we're staying at the Casino, aren't we?" she said, turning around and rummaging through the papers behind the counter.

"Yes, it's true. My business partners spoke highly of your establishment, therefore, we wouldn't be disregarding the truth if we said it's my first time," Morillo said, trying to convey an innocence he did not have to fake.

"There's always a first time for everything, isn't it? I will not ask you who your business partners are, because, above all, we respect discretion. We love getting first visits. We understand what it means to be a first-timer," she said without turning.

"Yes. For this reason, I have to trust your judgment and let you guide me," he said, testing the waters, not knowing exactly what he was talking about.

"It's quite all right, sir. We take care of everything, you are in good hands," and with a smile on her face, she opened the hatch to a small wooden panel on the wall.

Several silk strings of different colors hung inside, ending in large tassels. She gave several hard pulls on one of them and closed the hatch.

"Make yourself comfortable, but the wait won't be long," she said, turning toward the counter to continue scribbling on some papers.

Morillo didn't know what to do, but he was obedient and waited sitting there and barely moving. No more than three minutes had gone by and the sound of soft footsteps coming down a staircase lined with Art Nouveau mosaics made him turn.

A young girl in her early twenties approached him slowly. She wore a silk violet gown, through which he could glimpse at a corset so tight Morillo suffered and puffed just from seeing it.

The girl turned around and went up the stairs,

occasionally turning her head to look if Morillo was following her, smiling mischievously.

They walked down a dark narrow carpeted corridor, with doors on both sides.

The place was just as Morillo had always imagined those places should be; it met all the requirements in terms of clichés, the Madame at the entrance, the girl in the negligee meeting the client and accompanying him to the room, the dark hallways, dingy rooms, silence, loneliness, sadness.

Without stopping or turning, the girl disappeared into one room facing the back of the mansion.

It was a small room, but decorated with exaggerated theatrical sense, with large velvet curtains covering the window, thick carpets, walls lined with fabric, and a lamp next to the bed with a screen that tinted the atmosphere with a dramatic and passionate red color, which to Morillo was more reminiscent of blood than passion.

When Morillo finished inspecting the room, the girl was already in front of him, offering him a glass of liquor and a smile.

"No... thank you Miss, I don't drink when I'm..." but he stopped before giving away his identity, "when I'm... in mourning," he skillfully added.

"Oh, I'm so sorry," the girl said, in a tone that oozed sincerity.

"Yes, my wife died a few months ago."

"That's terrible. Then you better take a sip, it will help you relax. Believe me, I have lost many friends and family, I know what I'm talking about," she said reassuringly.

Morillo decided that staying in character was more important than respecting the rule of not drinking during service. It was an ongoing investigation, and the end justified the means. He reached out and took the glass and sat in an armchair beside the curtains.

The girl sat on the edge of the bed, letting her robe open intentionally, and kept smiling at him.

Was it his imagination or that poor girl was missing a

tooth? From his position, Morillo thought he saw several dark shadows uglying up the smile on a face that must have been beautiful in her youth, a very relative term in those sordid environments.

"Please don't take it as a rejection, but I think what I would really like is to talk," Morillo said, trying to get the young girl to abandon her tried and trite flirting tactics.

He played the role of the contrite widower who wants to be with a woman but is suffering from remorse, and all he needs is someone to listen and to pity him for his misfortunes.

She had no problem playing along. Those kinds of insecure clients were the best, since they allowed her to earn money comfortably without working for it.

CHAPTER 46

T hey chatted for nearly two hours, Morillo asking about her personal life and her family, and she, being honest with him more than she had been with any other man.

She came from a family that moved from the countryside to the city in search of a prosperity that never came. Her father died after working several years under precarious conditions in a textile factory and her mother had to do miracles to raise three children in the grueling early century Barcelona.

Her ending up in prostitution was nothing but the usual consequence of the deconstructed environment in which she had to live. Morillo's conversation drifted to her experience working there. He asked her about client types, her relationship with the nearby Casino, her partners, her fears, her joys.

She told him strange things happened in that establishment. They treated some customers different from the rest, in utmost secrecy, with total discretion.

"A colleague told me that sometimes they hear screams, and that scares me."

"But that should not be strange in an establishment like this. They must come from every room, am I right?"

"I don't mean screams of pleasure, but of another kind, the really scary kind."

"And where did they come from?"

"I don't know, I really don't know. There's a man in the

other house who is very bad to us, he brutalizes us," she said pointing to the curtain.

Morillo walked over there and lifted the red velvet curtain that covered the window and looked out. In front of him, he saw the garnet mansion facade that presided over this land. It must be the house of the owner of that establishment.

"Who lives there?" he asked while spying behind the curtain.

"I don't know, I think they use it to entertain important clients. I have never been inside, but I know some girls who have."

"Could I talk to any of them?" Morillo asked, very solicitous.

"I don't understand what is your interest, but it won't be possible. I have seen none of those girls in months."

"It's weird, isn't it?"

"Yes, I would say so. The redheaded man keeps a close watch on us and we are not free to do what we want," she added.

"What did you say? What man?" Morillo asked, jumping at the mention of the name.

"The redhead. A man that rarely comes, but when he docs, we all fear him. He seems to be one of the owners of this business, but I am terrified of him. Luckily he has never been with me, but he has laid down with other girls and I know how he abuses them."

Morillo insisted on speaking to any of those girls, but he could get nothing out of that young lady, not even incentivizing her will with the promise of money, because Morillo's meager economy did not allow him to give away anything but promises.

"I really have heard nothing from them again. If I knew anything I would tell you, believe me," she said, in a tone that left no doubts about her sincerity.

"There is really nothing you can tell me about the red-haired man? Do you know if he lives in that house?" Morillo said, pointing to the garnet house behind the window.

"I don't know, but I don't think so, because if he lived there we would see him more often, I think."

Morillo was desperate, he had clarified nothing during the long time he had been in there, but he could feel in his neck the cold breath of that redheaded maniac, he was getting closer every time.

"Although now I remember something," the girl blurted.

"Yes? What is it?"

"The girls said he's a very rich man, one of those who have a box at the Liceu or the Palau de la Música, I don't know. In one of those places where people sing serious stuff and shout a lot," the girl said, showing a musical culture of the highest level.

For Morillo, the Liceu and the Palau de la Música were not the same. One was one of the oldest opera theaters in Europe, and for centuries considered the biggest.

The other was a spectacular Art Nouveau building opened in 1908, which used to house classical music concerts and performances by prestigious choral groups.

Since the girl had mentioned there was much shouting, he opted for the Gran Teatre del Liceu, an operatic temple of the first magnitude.

Also, at the Liceu there were plenty of boxes, many of which were held in property by royalty, the bourgeoisie and personalities, and politicians of relevance in the city. It was quite possible the redhead was one of them, and that could be the clue he was expecting.

"Is there anything else you remember or can tell me about this man?"

"I don't know why all the interest in him when you can have me. It's not as if you were a cop, asking so many questions," she said, laughing at her own joke.

Morillo was not laughing and kept staring at her, waiting for an answer.

"I think I've heard the girls refer to him as Gisbert or something," she said, attempting to remember.

"Gisbert? Are you sure?"

"Yes, I am. They say he's a man of great wealth, who owns factories and all that," she added.

Morillo was very excited and not only due to the presence of a woman in her lingerie in front of him. Could he be the industrialist Mauricio Gisbert? He had one of the biggest fortunes in the country, although the origin of his fortune had generated much debate given the opacity of his activities.

Despite his social relevance, he was a great unknown, because he hardly appeared in public, and attended very few social events, avoiding any notoriety in the press.

If it were he, Morillo would have scored big, although getting to him would not be an easy task. He lacked evidence to incriminate him, and given his status as a successful industrialist, he operated in circles of the high bourgeoisie and had connections in the highest political circles, just the opposite of Morillo.

If his love of opera was true, the Gran Teatre del Liceu was the ideal place for a casual encounter. Morillo rose, thanked the young girl and reached into his wallet to look for some banknotes to reward her, but found nothing but cobwebs.

Cursing his poverty, he had no choice but to reveal his identity.

"So you're a cop, sir? I knew it" she shouted, not knowing whether to show anger or fear.

"Now you call me sir, after all we've been through together?" Morillo said smiling.

"Together? But we did nothing," she complained.

Morillo's laugh contributed to lowering the tension a little.

"Relax, you're very beautiful, and I assure you that under different circumstances... I mean, you don't have to worry. If you can keep my secret, you have a friend in me. And I can assure you there are worst things than having a cop as a friend, don't you think?"

She seemed to consider it for a moment and soon she flashed a big smile. No more words were needed. Morillo approached her, kissed her on the cheek and rushed out the door.

He had to meet with Agnes as soon as possible. He only hoped she liked opera more than he did, because the closest he had been to the Gran Teatre del Liceu was when he apprehended a group of drunks who were urinating on one of its portals during the intermission of "Turandot".

This time he hoped his visit would be of a higher standard and he could indulge in enjoying the surroundings.

One thing was clear, with Agnes he would be in much better company.

CHAPTER 47

Casino de la Rabassada ruins. Today.

Gerard didn't know how long had he walked through the passageway since he separated from Eva, but it couldn't be more than ten minutes. He was positive he heard footsteps coming from that direction, but there seemed to be nobody there. Could have been just an animal? He was no longer sure of anything.

The flashlight languished, and despite giving it a thud against his leg it barely revived. The passage kept climbing up the mountain, but being underground it was very difficult to find reference points for orientation.

He had to go back. Eva probably was terrified, alone in the dark and in an underground cistern. What was he thinking?

The flashlight had gone from dazzling white to flickering jaundiced yellow. He had to quicken the pace, otherwise, he would soon be in complete darkness inside that maze.

He came to the fork and ran to the cistern. He could swear he had replaced the lid when he left Eva, but he was not certain. Perhaps Eva was scared and had replaced it herself.

In any case, he had to get her out of there.

"Eva, I'm here," he said, removing the board and putting it at his feet.

Before getting in, he lit the inside of the cistern with the flashlight. The faint light beam couldn't beat the darkness and only lit a one-meter semicircle in front of him. Eva was nowhere to be seen.

"Eva, are you there?" he whispered, not knowing why.

Once inside, he lit up every corner of the tank. He saw her in one of the farthest ends, curled up like a frightened child hiding from something lurking her.

"Eva, it's me. I'm here," he said, and his feet splashed in the water puddles as he approached her. He had the uneasy feeling something was not right.

When he reached her, it surprised him she did not reach out upon seeing him. He raised his flashlight to her face and dropped it in the water in shock when he faced her blank eyes staring into space.

He reached into the water to pick up the flashlight before it went out completely and shone her face again. Her expression conveyed the horror she had suffered, making words unnecessary.

Gerard took a step back, scared when he saw Eva's body moving and slowly sliding into the water. He tried to hold her, but could not avoid her ending up lying on her side, half-submerged in the muddy bottom of the tank. He felt her jugular but found no pulse. She was dead.

Damn it, how was that possible? What happened? An accident, or was there someone else there?

He pointed the light beam in all directions, but there was no one else. The flashlight flickers announced its imminent death, there was no time to waste. He crawled through the hole and ran down the mountain passage.

The flashlight died suddenly and Gerard hit his head against the rock ceiling and fell. He felt the wound in his scalp and noticed it was bleeding. One more scar for his extensive collection, he thought.

He put a handkerchief over the wound and pushed hard. He could not be far from the exit, so he started to walk, feeling the surface of the rock wall with his hands while keeping his foot in contact with the angle between the wall and the passage floor, just as a blind person would do.

His mobile phone did not help much to light the way. Seeing the ridiculous faint glow the tiny display emitted, he cursed himself for not having invested in a giant screen smartphone instead of the antediluvian apparatus he carried, one that must have been a contemporary of Graham Bell's.

He made slow progress but finally, he glimpsed a distant hazy light that showed him the way forward until he reached the last corner and climbed the stairs to the exit.

Once outside, he collapsed and sat on a rock, next to the tree trunk under which they had found the passage entrance. He needed to think.

The most urgent thing was to get help, although it was too late for Eva. What had happened? How did Eva die?

He had to go back inside and find out; he needed to know if there were signs of a struggle, if she was scared to death or had been killed. If so, the murderer could still be there, lurking in the dark waiting for him.

He had to report it to the police as soon as possible. That would not be easy to explain, and Lieutenant Botell surely would enjoy the opportunity to put him away.

There would be time for that later, but first, he had to talk to Max. Now he needed more time to investigate on his own and Max would help him.

He checked his mobile phone and left him several voice messages, hoping he would listen to them when his flight landed.

Two hours later Max asked the astonished taxi driver to stop the vehicle on a straight stretch of the road from Vallvidrera to Sant Cugat, facing some ruined walls, with no house in sight.

"Are you sure you want me to drop you here?" the surprised cabbie asked.

"Yes, right here."

"I'll help you with your suitcase."

"Thank you," Max said, paying the fare and getting off

the vehicle.

"Do you want me to wait for you and take you back to town?" the driver insisted.

"It won't be necessary. They are expecting me at this hotel," Max said, taking the suitcase from the driver's hands, heading for the only wall left standing and stopping at the crumbling entrance door to what had once been the casino hotel. He pulled out his cell phone and began talking to someone.

The taxi driver followed Max with his gaze and saw him disappear dragging his suitcase through a door behind which there was only forest. Incredulous, he walked to the door, as Max disappeared through the undergrowth.

He returned to his car, shaking his head and wondering if he was dreaming. He now had a new story to tell his taxi driver colleagues at lunchtime.

"Where the hell are you going with that suitcase? If you want to check-in at the hotel, I'm afraid you're a hundred years late," Gerard said when he saw him dragging the heavy suitcase through the bushes.

"They told me they offer a special weekend package with a buffet breakfast included. You know I cannot resist any proposal carrying the word buffet in it," Max said, puffing and flopping down on a log to rest.

"Yes, I don't know which of the two words attracts you more, buffet or free."

"Which came first, the chicken or the egg?" Max said.

Gerard filled him in on the details of the situation and both agreed it was best to re-inspect the crime scene so they could provide more details when they called the police.

"Follow me. Did you bring the flashlights I asked you?" Gerard asked.

Max smiled and took out a keyring in the shape of a Star Wars character, whose eyes lit with two LEDs when he squeezed his head.

"What is this?"

"What? It's the only thing I could find in the souvenir shop at the airport. But don't worry, I brought one for you too," he said, throwing another keyring in the shape of one robot in the movie.

Gerard grimaced and disappeared through the hole next to the tree. Max put down his suitcase and followed him.

"When we get out, give me back the keyring, these are collector's items," Max said.

"I can't believe it," Gerard muttered as he kept walking.

They soon reached the fork and Gerard stopped.

"If you keep going along that wider passage, it keeps going up. I have not gotten to the end, but it must lead to some room in what used to be the Casino, I don't know. The cistern is that way, about twenty meters from here, on the left. You enter through an opening almost at ground level," Gerard said.

"Let me go first," Max said, starting to walk down the narrow passage.

"I don't know if you will fit through the opening," Gerard shouted with a smile, while his friend disappeared around a corner.

Gerard shone his robot flashlight on the passageway to his right, wondering how far it would go. He thought he heard noises, but he was not sure of anything. They were underground, and there could be rabbits, rats, any creature capable of making noise, it didn't have to be a murderer necessarily.

He went back to the corridor where he had left Max. When he arrived, his friend was trying to get out, slithering through the opening of the tank. Gerard pulled him to help unclog his waist.

"What do you think?" he asked, staring at him.

"I think the entrance to the damn tank is narrower than what you told me," Max said, lifting his shirt and rubbing his waist to relieve the pain of chafing.

"I mean the girl. It's horrible," Gerard said.

"I don't know, I cannot judge whether she is horrible if I can't see her."

"I don't mean that she's horrible, I mean the situation," Gerard said. "What do you mean with "if I can't see her"?"

"Didn't you say that she was inside? There was nobody there," Max said.

Gerard gestured for him to step aside, kneeled and put half his body through the opening, moving his arm in all directions.

"Did your galactic robot find anything?" Max asked, mockingly.

"It cannot be, I swear her body was inside, leaning against the wall. I saw it myself," Gerard said, standing up.

"Well, either she was less dead than you thought, or someone has taken her," Max said.

Gerard bent down and examined the passage floor. For the most part, it was the cave's natural rock bed, but there were parts covered by a thin layer of soil, which had been falling over the years through cracks in the ceiling.

"This has been too trampled by all of us, I cannot see clear footsteps," Gerard said. "Maybe in the wider passage," he said, and ran to examine the floor on the other corridor.

He could clearly distinguish their own footprints by the mark left by the soles, but there were areas where other marks were visible, smoother, as if they pertained to leather soles without engraving.

In a Hollywood movie, someone would immediately tell him the size of the murderer's underwear just by looking at one of those tracks. But this was real life, and he could not reach any conclusion.

Back in the cistern, he kneeled and looked inside once more, shining his flashlight at the walls. In the area where the corpse had been leaning, he noticed spots on the wall that could be blood, although he could not guarantee they belonged to the body, because he had been bleeding from the blow to his head.

He lighted the thin sheet of water that covered the bottom of the tank. He ran the light beam along the mud layer until he stopped when he caught a small glimmer.

"Hold me by the feet, please," he shouted at Max, as he lunged with almost his whole body into the tank, while

Max held him by the ankles. He reached out and put his hand under the water, poking around in the mud until he rapped on the wall to tell Max to pull him out.

"Shine your light on here," he asked him, and Max pointed the beam of his galactic soldier to his hands. In his muddy fingers, he had a small shining earring, a silver cross on what looked like the head of an animal.

"Are those your friend's earrings?" Max asked

"I don't know, I think so. I didn't pay attention."

"What a shame. Since when one does not pay attention to a woman? The only possible excuse for your distraction is if you were staring into an area of greater interest than her ears," Max said, lecturing. "Was that the case?"

Gerard had no time to answer him, a distant thunder rumbled through the passageway walls, muffled but audible.

"What was that? Did someone close a door?" Max asked.

"There are no doors here. It sounded like a gunshot."

Max looked at him in disbelief, but his expression changed as he took in the situation.

"Where do you carry your gun? Now it would be a good time to use it," Max muttered.

"What gun? You know I haven't seen one since I played cowboys and Indians with my brother twenty-five years ago," Gerard said.

"Might as well be twenty-five thousand. My vote is we get the hell out of here," Max said.

Gerard turned in all directions. They were in imminent danger. The time to play detectives was over, they had to involve the police as soon as possible.

"Let's get out of here right away," he said and started running down the corridor, followed closely by Max.

CHAPTER 48

"Don't you have cell service yet?" Gerard asked as they walked along the side of the road. Max dragged his suitcase, which rattled as its small wheels got stuck in the roadside gravel while he held his mobile phone with one hand.

"As soon as I get one bar of service, I'll call my friend the taxi driver who brought me here, and he'll come to pick us up."

"My motorcycle cannot take the two of us, especially not with that monster suitcase of yours. The other option is to hitchhike, but the way we look, only the garbage truck would pick us up," Gerard said.

About twenty minutes later they descended toward Barcelona comfortably seated in the same taxi that had brought Max. The taxi driver, who could not get out of his astonishment, had to extend a plastic sheet over the rear seats, seeing the sorry state they were in, wet and muddy.

"I see you've found your friend," the taxi driver told Max.

"You're very observant."

"Did you enjoy your stay in that hotel? I'm asking because if you recommend it, maybe I'll take my wife to spend a romantic weekend there," the taxi driver said wryly, staring at the rearview mirror.

"Highly recommendable, yes, be sure to take her. And make sure they give you the tower room. Guaranteed success. There's even aromatherapy included in the room rate. There isn't a more romantic place in Barcelona," Max said and turned to Gerard to let the driver know the conversation was over.

Finally, the taxi stopped at the address Gerard had indicated.

"But this is a police station," the taxi driver said.

"You keep amazing me with your exceptional observation skills," Max told the driver, throwing a banknote over the seatback.

"You should quit your job and become a detective," Max added, mockingly.

"Let's see if you stay longer in this hotel than on the previous one," the driver shouted out the window, seeing Max headed for the door to the police station, dragging his suitcase.

"Want to come along?" Max replied, making a rude gesture lifting his forearm and taking his hand to his bent elbow, to which the driver responded by showing him the finger he didn't use to wear his wedding ring.

Max turned and stopped in front of Gerard, before entering the precinct.

"Gerard, I don't think this is a good idea."

"What?"

"Get the police involved."

"Max, someone has been murdered."

"Who? We don't even have a body. Plus, even if we did, think who would be the prime suspect," Max said, staring intently at him, raising his eyebrows in a questioning gesture.

"Exactly, you," Max exclaimed forcefully. "How do you explain your presence in those tunnels with a woman you barely knew? How do you explain you didn't obey the lieutenant's request for you to stay away from the Casino? Don't you realize you're only asking for trouble? And you will drag me along too."

"If you want, I can keep you out of this. They need not know you were also there with me, this is just my business," Gerard said.

"If you think you'll make me feel guilty that way, you're mistaken. When have I shied away from a fight or hidden from anyone, especially from the police? I won't leave you alone in this mess, not if there's also a beautiful woman involved, even though I haven't met her yet," Max said, stepping aside to let him pass. Gerard smiled and walked into the police station lobby.

"I don't know why, but something tells me I have let myself be manipulated again, and he's getting me straight into a new mess," Max mumbled as he entered the building resignedly, following in the footsteps of his friend.

"Lieutenant Botell is in a meeting right now," the officer behind the counter told them when they asked to see him.

"It's very important we see him right away," Gerard insisted.

"Did you tell him our names?" Max asked as if he were a celebrity, surprised that the paparazzi would not recognize him.

"Yes, and that's when he told me he cannot see you right now," the officer said. "If you follow me to a waiting room, the officer on duty will take your statement. Lieutenant Botell will be promptly informed of everything, don't worry."

"It's a murder case," Gerard said, dropping the news.

"A possible murder," Max interrupted.

"You are not sure? Who is dead?" the officer asked.

"A friend of mine. Well, I think she's dead, but the body has disappeared," Gerard tried to explain.

"Are you a witness?" he asked Max.

"I could say I am, but I would be lying. The truth is I would have loved to have met the young woman, but when I got there she was already gone," Max said.

"Then it was just attempted murder," the officer said, trying to clarify the matter.

"An attempt with a happy ending," Gerard said, trying to ease the tension.

"You didn't tell me that part. Well, well, so there was a happy ending. Now I understand everything," Max said making faces, his eyes wide open and shaking his hands up and down.

"Shut up, asshole, I mean the happy ending of the attempted murder, which is the murder itself, isn't it?" Gerard said, staring at the officer.

"Don't look at me, I have enough just by trying not to lose the thread of this story. You know what? Please wait in room number three, and one of my partners will be right with you. Now if you'll excuse me, I have other citizens waiting," the officer said, motioning to the next person in line to move forward to the window.

Two hours later, they signed two copies of their complaint forms. The officer in charge of taking their statements had to leave the room twice to grab a strong coffee, to withstand the whole session.

To the officer, that case had all the ingredients of the stories that used to fall into the category of a tall tale; the kind of complaints that showed so many inconsistencies and contradictions it relegated them to a second or third level of interest and urgency.

However, it had traces of seriousness which, if proven, would require to start an immediate investigation.

The officer assured them he would inform Lieutenant Botell personally, and they would assign all the necessary resources to the case.

Despite Gerard's insistence to accompany and guide them to the place of the alleged crime, the officer declined his offer but said they would call him should his cooperation be necessary.

"They didn't say all that crap about you not leaving the city or the country," Max told Gerard as they left the police station and walked down the street toward the subway.

"They take it for granted I shouldn't do it. Nor have they asked me in which zoo did I find you, and they could have done it," Gerard said, with a straight face.

"Don't get so upset, she was just one more girl," Max

said.

"It's not the girl. Well, a little bit maybe, but that's all. I don't think the police will do anything, they didn't take us seriously," Gerard complained.

"And does that surprise you? Unless it involves unless someone of a certain substance, they will not move a finger. Sure they will investigate, but it will only be on the surface; they'll send a rookie, just enough to cover the bases."

CHAPTER 49

The patrol car drove down the road that went by the Casino ruins. Young officer Iolanda Vehils had never worked that area, although it should not be surprising, since she had only been three months on active duty as an officer.

Since leaving the police academy, one of her dreams was to be assigned to a modern police station, in a good part of town, and she had fully achieved it.

Her station was in the upper part of Barcelona and the building had been completely renovated less than a year earlier, with spacious offices, natural light, modern equipment, just what she had always dreamed of.

Another dream of hers had been to soon be allowed to patrol the streets in a patrol car, and it had also been fulfilled, and not only that, but she was also usually in charge of getting behind the wheel, which added an extra incentive to her work.

The last of her dreams had been to work on exciting cases and to partner with an experienced officer, respected and admired by everyone in the force, and who looked like George Clooney. That dream was also fulfilled... halfway.

Good old George must not have been available the day they put together the teams, and she ended up partnering with Horacio Guzmán, an experienced officer, respected and admired by all, but one whom some would gladly give up their paychecks not to work with.

She always drove the vehicle, but not thanks to her

merits but Horacio's wishes, since he liked to brag in front of his fellow officers he patrolled with a private chauffeur.

Horacio also delegated many tasks in her, but not because he valued her work ability or insights, but out of sheer laziness, leaving in her female hands the ever tedious task of writing all kinds of reports and the summary of the preliminaries of each new and exciting case that fell into his hands.

The old Casino ruins must be nearby, Iolanda thought, checking the coordinates she had entered into the vehicle's GPS. Until just a few hours ago she did not even know a Casino had existed in Barcelona a hundred years earlier, let alone where its ruins could be.

She stopped the vehicle at the exact spot marked by the GPS and turned to his partner.

"Here we are."

The officer turned and rolled down the window.

"Are you sure? There's nothing here, just a wall full of graffiti and the mountain."

"It's what the GPS shows. What did you expect to find, a Roman temple with a marble colonnade? A promenade lined with palm trees, fountains and water spouts?" she said.

"I don't know, but to me, a casino must have a driveway, and it must be in an attractive location, breathing luxury and elegance, not here in the middle of this road lost in the mountains," Horacio said, getting off the car.

"We're looking for ruins, the remains of what once were luxurious buildings. These are ruins, aren't they?. I suggest we get in to explore. That's what we have come here for, right?" she insisted, walking under the old hotel door's empty arch.

"If there's no alternative. After all, it is you who will write the report," the officer said, reluctantly following her, trying to find his way in the thick forest.

Iolanda found the path leading to the tower and walked down, motioning to her partner to follow her. Horacio had been tired almost since birth and was puffing hard with every step he took through a forest which so overwhelmed him.

"Is this all that remains of the Casino?" Horacio shouted when he made out in the distance the tower ruins.

Iolanda stopped and waited until he caught up with her.

"Lower your voice, sir, there might be someone inside. Do we split here?" she suggested.

Since they began working together, she never treated him on a first-name basis. Not because her partner intimidated her, but because of her good Catholic education, to keep some distance between them and out of respect for her elders, although that last point she would never admit in front of him.

"The entry must be just around that corner of the building," she whispered. "One of us can enter from there and the other could go around the tower through the undergrowth and appear on the other side."

They both looked at each other and took the guns from their holsters.

"Okay, see you at the entrance," Horacio said, taking the wider path and leaving to Iolanda the honor of going around the building through the brambles and weeds. As always, Horacio had chosen for both of them.

Iolanda kept her gun raised, while her other hand cleared away the branches blocking her way as she circled the tower. The ground sloped down steeply and then went back up, so she should run if she wanted to reach the door at the same time as her partner since she had a longer way to go.

When she finally got out of the bushes and reached the clearing opposite the tower entrance, Horacio was already at the door, waiting with the expression of one who had been waiting for three hours. Iolanda showed him the palm of her hands as if trying to justify herself. Her face was full of scratches and she was bleeding from several wounds in arms and neck.

The wooden door was ajar, and Horacio motioned with his hands to indicate they entered together at the count of three. Fingers appeared and after the countdown both stormed in, in a more theatrical than effective entrance.

Iolanda immediately turned on her flashlight and walked around the perimeter of the room. She had to cover her nose with her hand because the stench was unbearable.

"It wasn't me, don't look at me," Horacio said, laughing, the only one enjoying his rude humor, which only provoked self-hilarity.

"There doesn't seem to be anyone here," she said, taking a few steps forward.

"I don't think anyone could put up with this stench, it smells like a dead dog," Horacio said.

"I don't know which neighborhoods do you hang on, but this time you guessed it right," Iolanda said, stooping to pick up from the ground the metal rods from a broken umbrella, with which she pushed a lump beside her feet.

"Yuck, looks like a dead animal, the body of a rather large dog," she said, "and it's quite decomposed; it must have been here for days."

She pushed it with the rods to turn the body around and the dog's head broke off and tumbled toward her, as she jumped back and quickly pulled away.

"Shit, it almost fell on me."

"Perhaps the pooch is still alive, and it likes you," Horacio said, letting out a laugh.

Iolanda bent down to examine the dog's head, from a giant specimen with very dark black hair. Its eyes were hanging and seemed half-eaten by some other animal, probably rats.

"Look at its neck," Iolanda said, approaching the head and touching the neck with the metal rod.

"Yes, a beautiful animal. If you want to take the head home, you can have it stuffed and hang it over your fireplace, or better yet, in your bedroom," Horacio said, again laughing solo at his own jokes.

"It's a disgusting comment, you know? I meant to look at the cut through its neck; it seems they cut the head with a sharp object, or perhaps an ax. They have cut off the head."

"Maybe there's a guillotine around here, let's search for it. Perhaps this is the tower of the Bastille and the heads of those who dare enter it still keep rolling," Horacio said, putting his hands around his own neck in an unpleasant grimace.

As much as it disgusted her having to endure his patrol partner's sexist, rude and misogynist comments, his spontaneous allusion to the Bastille surprised her because she believed his ignorance threshold was at an even lower level.

"Forget about the dog and let's focus on what we have come to check. I want to get out of here as soon as possible," Horacio said, turning around.

"Clearly, the tramp that crazy Gerard Bach and his sidekick say they saw living here, either has moved recently, or his nose must be atrophied, because I don't think anyone in his right mind can live in this dump with such a rotten stench," Horacio said, not without some reason.

"We should search this room and look for evidence," Iolanda said.

"And what do you expect to find out? That a beggar lived here? We already know that; there was no need to come here to learn that. All abandoned buildings in this country, either have a bum living inside, or a squatter, or even a ghost and sometimes they have the three together. Let's look around the area, to cover the bases, and let's get out of here, I can't stand this smell," he said, and they went outside to breathe the moist and fresh mountain air.

"Let's search at least for the entrance to the passageways where they said they found the girl's body. According to them, it was in that direction, about two hundred meters into the valley," she suggested.

"Please, don't tell me you have given credit to that absurd story. It seemed like a radio program from the forties. I'll tell you what happened here. Those two have come to the mountain to smoke a few joints in secret, or maybe even to buy drugs from some of the dealers that often mill around this beautiful surroundings, like the one that must live in the luxury tower we just visited. They were doped out in cocaine and then the girl appeared in front of them alive and kicking, then dead, then alive again, the same way the very same angels from Heaven could appear in front of me right now, dressed in mariachi costumes and singing Mexican songs," Horacio said, starting to walk up the path.

"I want to check it if you don't mind, sir," Iolanda insisted, undeterred.

"OK, do as you like. I'll wait in the car. Don't take too long," he said and disappeared up the mountain.

The agent went down through the forest, drawing an imaginary diagonal line from where she was, toward the lowest point at the bottom of the valley and tracked down the area delimiting a perimeter and establishing quadrants she swept thoroughly in search of the benchmarks Gerard had given them.

Over thirty minutes had gone by when she saw a thick and twisted tree trunk, and next to it a small quadrangular structure.

She ran there and smiled when she saw that it was a vent or an entry on the ground, covered by a wooden trapdoor. The ground around had been very disturbed, and it was clear the entrance remained hidden and buried until recently. It was definitely the place they had described.

She turned the walkie-talkie on to communicate with the patrol car.

"Horacio, can you hear me, sir?"

A crackle of interference accompanied the sound of her partner's tired voice.

"Yeah, what's up?"

"I've located the entrance to the passageway. I'm going in and I'll try to get to the tank to check whether the witnesses' statements have plausibility or lack veracity," Iolanda said.

"Translate it into my language, please," Horacio said.

"I'm getting into the cave to see if I find the stiff."

"Got you. I'll be here. Over and out," Horacio said, and the line went dead.

Iolanda heaved a sigh of resignation, removed the wooden lid and walked down the stone stairs.

CHAPTER 50

Gran Teatre del Liceu. Barcelona. 1912

He almost had to pawn the collection of meerschaum pipes he had inherited from his father to pay for the tickets to the opera. He would have never thought opera tickets could be so expensive.

For that price, they must include at least a grilled meat and barbecue dinner in addition to the show, Morillo thought naively.

He had inquired discreetly about Gisbert and the little he had learned, confirmed him as a good candidate to be a suspect.

Mauricio de Gisbert came not from a wealthy family, rather the opposite, but he had made his fortune in the textile industry. He started selling fabrics in small village markets, a business he soon expanded to cater to small shops in the city.

He soon leaped into manufacturing, aided by his good looks and his way with words, with which he conquered the hearts of more than a lady of the Catalan bourgeoisie and the checkbooks of their wealthy husbands.

In partnership with several investors, he started a textile factory and had the vision to focus on the development of resistant fabrics to manufacture gowns, aprons, work trousers and other garments used to equip the growing workforce of the many factories the industrial revolution was spreading throughout the geography of the country.

From there, the classic story of self-improvement and industrial vision twisted and gained darker tones. At odds with most of his partners, they started vanishing from the map, both the industrial and the mundane, disappearing under circumstances never fully clarified.

Gisbert ended up alone and began a period of dizzying growth that took him to build a textile empire, with the connivance of unethical politicians. The rumors said even the mayor of the city was on his payroll, plus many officials both local and from the central government in Madrid, also within range of his far-reaching tentacles.

Always staying in the shadows, his figure had gained a legendary status. There were all kinds of rumors about him, from the most cautious and probably accurate, picturing him as a greedy industrialist who did not hesitate to use illegal practices to achieve his aims, to the riskiest, claiming he was a white (or not so white)-collar criminal.

In the more sensationalistic end, there were plenty who claimed he was a maniac who carried out vampiric practices and those who swore he was the leader of a network abducting children for wealthy families to adopt. Formally accused of it, charges quickly vanished as they hit the legal protection wall raised by his army of well-paid lawyers.

Apparently, one of his few hobbies was going to the Gran Teatre del Liceu on opening nights of the most celebrated operas.

Morillo suspected those attendances did not obey to his melomania or his extreme sensitivity and love for opera. Premieres were an excellent opportunity to maintain a certain public presence but in the darkness of a great concert hall, in the privacy of his own box, away from prying eyes.

He often left the theater before the end of the play, to avoid mingling with the rest of spectators at the end of the show and disappeared into his carriage, waiting for him at the front door, overlooking the Ramblas.

Agnes was beaming. Morillo could not help but admire her serene beauty and elegance when she walked down the stairs and out the door of her house, where Morillo was waiting.

For obvious reasons, he had to discard the bicycle as their means of transportation, but he could not afford a carriage either, nor paid out of his own pocket, much less with police department funds, since in that investigation everything fell on his own account.

Agnes had found an empty seat on the tram and Morillo traveled standing beside her as the tram descended with plenty of rattling and sudden braking, to Plaza Catalunya, and then started down the Ramblas.

They got off the tram two blocks before reaching the Gran Teatre del Liceu, since Morillo wanted to stroll along the Ramblas taking Agnes by the arm, and approach the Gran Teatre slowly, enjoying every second they could feel as bourgeois for a few hours.

Morillo had gained ten kilos just from the satisfaction to be seen with a girl as beautiful as Agnes in his arm.

They approached the main entrance to the theater, which was already swarming with people, and mingled with the hundreds of dressed-up couples slowly coming in, showing off, while a long line of horse-drawn carriages waited their turn to discharge their passengers in front of the main gate.

Despite having the opportunity to descend from the carriages several blocks before reaching the theater or on adjacent streets, almost nobody did. The important thing was to get to the main front door and descend from the carriage in a triumphal entry, the ladies flaunting their spectacular dresses, skirts, and hats, and the gentlemen their cloaks, coats and top hats.

Among the line of carriages, some motor vehicles waited their turn, their drivers gunning the engines and honking their horns to catch the eyes of the hundreds of onlookers who crowded outside the gates. It was all part of the ritual. An opera premiere, a chance to gossip and be seen.

Morillo wondered how many of those toffs really understood anything about music or could discuss knowledgeably the works they were about to enjoy.

Surely there was a group who loved opera and went there to enjoy the music, but he suspected a large majority did so only to be seen. They would have been equally happy parading between cornfields, provided there was public. Morillo even thought he could identify them by their expression.

Morillo thought the exterior facade of the theater was rather dull and vulgar, of great sobriety that did nothing to prepare them for the lavishness and obscene luxury of the great room waiting for them inside.

Rarely had he felt that way, so happy and proud of himself for having captured the attention of a woman as beautiful and intelligent as Agnes. He was floating on a cloud; he felt like one more in that privileged group, entering through the front door, walking on the red carpet and ascending the grand staircase to the third floor, where their seats were.

They walked down a hallway that led them through a hemicycle to a big door. Nothing had prepared them for the impression they received when they crossed the threshold and went into the great main room.

The vastness of that space overwhelmed them. There must be hundreds if not thousands of lamps lit on all floors. A gigantic chandelier hung from the cciling and it was so large it seemed it could fall at any time, ripping the moldings in the ceiling along with it.

The horseshoe-shaped enclosure was a gigantic golden hive, full of small cells in which hundreds of people moved. The shine from the jewels and the lenses in the binoculars betrayed their presence and gave life to that immense operatic cathedral.

An usher accompanied them to their seats, and Morillo pretended not to see his outstretched hand expecting a tip

275

that never came.

"Do you like it?" he asked Agnes.

"It's amazing," was all she could say.

"I had never seen so much gold, and look at that huge piece of red velvet, is immense," he said, with undisguised admiration.

"It's the curtain, and it will soon rise to start the play. First, we will hear the overture and when the orchestra finishes, the curtain will rise, the singers will appear and interpret their arias," she said.

"How do you know so much? Had you already been here before?"

"Yes, I came with Mrs. Xamot a few times, but then we were in one of those boxes," she said, pointing to the right and one of the lower floors.

"I loved it, the music is wonderful," she added, closing her eyes and smiling.

Morillo was in heaven. He could not help but admire Agnes, with her brown hair up in a beautiful headdress, her red lips, her delicate white skin, her bare shoulders in a beautiful deep navy blue dress that ended in a spectacular skirt dotted with delicate embroidery.

He wondered how Agnes had been able to sit in those narrow seats with such a skirt, but women always had resources, he thought, as he held her delicate hand between his and pressed it affectionately.

"What play have we come to see?" Morillo asked.

"Wagner's *The Valkyrie,*" Agnes said.

After long years of absolute domination in audience preferences by Italian opera, Barcelona was becoming the world capital of Wagnerian opera after Bayreuth, specializing in the German composer and attracting the best directors and singers, who performed Wagner's works in the Liceu in its original German version.

"If this is the first time you come to the opera, it would have been preferable you started with something from Puccini, such as *Tosca* or the fabulous *La Bohème*, because they are more melodic and accessible to the ear, and demand less of the spectator," Agnes said in an academic tone.

"What are you implying, that I'm a musical illiterate?" he said with a frown, to what she did not respond, preferring to ignore him. "If that's the case, you're right, I wouldn't distinguish Pagner from Puccino if I crossed them on the street."

Agnes looked at him tenderly, and taking his hand she led it to her lips and planted a gentle kiss.

Morillo had almost forgotten the reason they were there, and felt bad for having kept it from Agnes.

He would have preferred to be there to enjoy the opera with her and forget about following the trail of a bloody psychopath, but he knew that in life, like in the theater, happy endings are not very common.

CHAPTER 51

Morillo was aware they were living in times of great social tension and the Liceu was not alien to it. The echoes of the bomb an anarchist threw at the stalls in 1893 causing a bloodbath between the audience still resonated among those majestic walls.

He was secretly glad to be on a higher floor, although the probability of a similar attack taking place again was very low.

While spectators were taking their seats, those already seated devoted their time to look around and contemplate each other.

All kinds of monocles and pocket binoculars appeared, and although their main purpose was to facilitate following the action on the stage, before the start of the show they were the ideal weapon for gossip and social espionage.

The main target for most of them used to be the theater boxes, always on the lookout for a famous politician or a successful entrepreneur, many of whom were often in the company of women who were not their wives but their official mistresses, whose sighting was a popular pastime among spectators.

Morillo borrowed the binoculars from Agnes and made a systematic sweep of all the boxes, starting with the lower floor and gradually moving up. He didn't have much time because soon they would turn off the lights and his chances of finding Gisbert would vanish at the drop of a hat.

When he started a second and faster round, he discarded the clearly empty boxes or those where he could get a good view of its occupants. That was when he saw him, after passing twice over the same spot, in a box on the second floor, the one closest to the stage on its right side.

At first, he thought it was empty until he saw a woman's arm leaning on the velvet railing. He went back with the binoculars and paused for a moment, waiting to detect any other movement and was about to move on when it happened.

It was just a glimpse, but he saw him. The hall lights began to fade, but he could see clearly a burly man coming to the railing, and taking a quick look in all directions before sitting down and disappearing, hidden behind the dividing screen between boxes.

It had to be him, his appearance just at the last moment, his build, and especially his red hair, which he could distinguish perfectly since the man was close to the stage lights.

The majestic overture notes suddenly began to fly, startling Morillo as if he were on the street in front of a tram. Immediately the audience went quiet, and darkness was almost complete.

Morillo didn't know what to do. For a few minutes, he was spellbound and let the notes of the majestic piece carry him away. He had no operatic culture, but he had sensitivity, and the combination of the solemnity of the music, the spectacularity of the orchestra, the magnificence of the environment, all allied to create magic from which he didn't want to escape.

When the curtain rose slowly and the blue stage lights breathed life to the first scene set, Morillo was as excited as a child before a candy store window, eager to see what would happen and to enjoy it to the fullest.

But he could not forget his mission, and his police conscience kicked in and brought him back to reality.

"When will the first break come?" he asked Agnes

whispering in her ear.

"The play has just begun and you're already asking about the intermission?" Agnes said, somewhat angrily.

"I'm just curious."

"There are three acts, but I don't know where the break will be, perhaps between the second and the third," she said, taking her finger to her lips gesturing for him to keep silence.

He thought the music was spectacular. The play was part of Wagner's tetralogy about the story of Siegfried and the Ring of the Nibelung. It was a dense work, which required a larger orchestra than usual, and had great technical complexity for both musicians and singers.

Morillo was captivated by a storm of unleashed emotions, trapped by a raging sea of musical sensations that took him to the heights and down to the abyss, riding dark and giant waves as did the brave Valkyrie warriors, protagonists of the play, riding their powerful stallions.

Unable to resist, toward the end of the first act he stood up, under the pretext of an irrepressible physiological urge, which earned him a withering look from Agnes.

He returned to the main staircase and went down to the second floor, intending to get as close as possible to Gisbert's box. Several theater employees guarded the access to the semi-circular corridor that ran all along the floor, to which all the box doors opened.

Pretending to be a bored husband stretching his legs while his wife was still inside, he observed the evolutions of the employees, who never abandoned their post.

The solution was to wait for the intermission and mingle with the crowd that would probably fill the corridors heading toward the cafeteria or to the bathrooms. He decided to ask a young employee who walked past him.

"No sir, there is no intermission. Today they will play the whole opera in one go, to enhance the audience experience," the boy said.

Morillo's face could not hide his surprise and disappointment at the same time. Several hours without a break, that was unthinkable. He didn't have that much time nor could he wait that long.

Desperate situations called for desperate measures, he thought. He walked resolutely up to the two employees who guarded the access to the corridors, behind a barrier of thick red velvet cord.

He walked past them without stopping and went into the corridor on the right.

"One moment, sir, please. May we see your ticket?" one of them asked, running after him.

Morillo rolled his eyes, with a weary expression, producing his police badge from his pocket.

"I'm a subinspector of the secret police, here on official police business, on orders by Commissioner Pizcueta," he lied, vaguely remembering the Commissioner used to frequent those circles, where he often met with the mayor and other city officials. It was more than likely he would even own a box, thus Morillo took the risk. The ploy seemed to work.

"Excuse us. We had not seen you arrive with the Commissioner. I hope you won't hold it against us, and apologies for any inconvenience, we were just doing our job," the employee apologized.

"Of course, young man, you don't have to apologize. We're all working here, aren't we?" He said, and everyone relaxed and laughed.

Morillo started walking down the corridor on the right.

"Subinspector, the Commissioner's box is in the corridor on the left, box number 17," the employee reminded him, pointing toward the opposite end. Morillo stopped, disgruntled, and turned around.

"Yes, of course. I always get lost in these places. All hallways look the same to me," he said, retracing his steps and disappearing down the left corridor, just on the opposite side of where Gisbert's box was.

The corridor described a sharp curve and was covered with thick maroon carpeting that muffled all sound completely, giving him the feeling of walking in an absolute vacuum. Only the thundering orchestra in the distance, filtering through some box doors ajar brought him back to reality.

Morillo came across a gentleman with a tilted top hat, who had evidently paid tribute to the Valkyries over more than one glass of champagne and was sailing down the corridor toward the bathroom, dodging imaginary sea monsters that forced him to walk zigzagging.

When he was coming to the end of the corridor, he knew the boxes there had to be on the diametrically opposite end of Gisbert's box. He saw one of them had the door ajar, and without thinking it twice he got inside.

The small anteroom, stylishly decorated, had a small table with several bottles of liquor and glasses, a comfortable green velvet couch and a small folding table attached to the wall.

You didn't have to be a fortune teller to imagine the incredible stories those anterooms could tell, the business deals sealed toasting with those glasses, the marriages broken or maybe saved in the darkness of the room and the comfort of those divans.

In front of him, a dark garnet curtain blocked the view behind it. He reached out his hand and when he dragged the curtain, he stood still, amazed by the impressive sight unveiling before his eyes.

The box was on an inclined plane, oriented toward the stage, only a few meters away from where he stood. He counted six empty wooden chairs, and beyond them, the imposing majesty of the main hall unfolded. Darkness was considerable because on stage the actors were playing a night scene in a forest, to the light of a bonfire.

Under the cover of darkness, Morillo slipped against the wall and sat in one of the rear seats, took Agnes' binoculars from his pocket and searched for Gisbert's box until he found it.

A faint sound made him turn. He was facing an old man who had just appeared behind the curtain, half-hidden behind the lush hairstyle of his female companion, a beautiful young woman with a more than generous neckline.

"What are you doing here, if I may ask?" exclaimed the angry gentleman.

"Excuse me, is this not box 17?" Morillo asked, feigning stupidity in the most convincing way possible.

"Seventeen? This is number 20. You are not too far away. Are you drunk perhaps?" the man said, angrily.

"Maybe I drank a little more than I should, yes," Morillo said, rising quickly and leaving the box. He could not draw more attention to him, especially knowing the Commissioner was on the same floor, a few boxes away.

He went to the bathroom because he needed a quiet place to think. He entered the luxurious room but felt uncomfortable when he met a boy sitting on a wooden stool, offering him wash towels and fragrances.

He pretended to freshen up his face, and when he saw the boy was still there, he had no choice but to go into one of the cubicles and sit on the toilet with the lid down.

If he went back to Agnes now, it would be very difficult for him to justify a new absence later, especially when he would already have a hard time explaining the current one, since a physiological urgency of such duration should have been necessarily fatal.

He didn't know how much time could have elapsed, but they were probably finishing the second act.

Agnes told him that a highlight of the opera was the musical introduction at the beginning of the third act, the famous Ride of the Valkyries, a fragment that had gained enormous popularity, expected with joyful delight by the audience.

He knew during that fragment nobody would move from their seats throughout the whole theater, and he could then make his approach and confront Gisbert.

He got out of the cubicle, and let the water running to give greater realism to his performance, and the boy handed him a towel, which he refused, earning him a look of reproach in which he could read what the boy thought about his lack of hygiene.

"Do you know how when will the third act begin?" Morillo asked, approaching again the employees guarding the access.

"In just a few minutes, sir. I recommend you don't miss it because tonight's performance is special. When the Ride of the Valkyries begins, we will use for the first time ever, a new movie projection system that will project moving images of the Valkyries riding through the Montserrat mountains. It will be the first time in Europe, and for the first in history, all theater lights will go out and there will be total darkness during the projection," the employee said, with understandable pride.

"So I better hurry then," Morillo said, smiling, as he had finally found the right time to surprise Gisbert.

A supervisor appeared and called the two boys to go over their duties once the hall lights went out in just a few minutes.

Morillo left, strolling down the corridor on the right, raising no suspicion from the distracted employees.

Now he only had to wait until the lights went out and force his way into Gisbert's box, the third starting from the end.

Despite his boasting of being thoughtful and a good police strategist, the stupidity of his current plan, or rather the lack of it, surprised him. He had let himself get carried away by his impulses, his emotions, by the horror he had witnessed at the hands of that vicious sleazebag, and that had clouded his reasoning.

What if Gisbert was not the murderer? What if he was a legitimate businessman with excellent contacts in high places, great wealth, and immense power to do with a simple subinspector as he pleased?

He tried to get that possibility out of his head. Deep inside he knew that guy was the one who had confronted him on several occasions, who showed so much evil and caused so much pain.

He just had to get to him and look him in the eyes to be

certain.

CHAPTER 52

The corridor lights flickered. The main hall must have been in silence since he could no longer hear the distant rumble of the powerful orchestra. Morillo wanted to know what was going on inside, but couldn't see it from his position. The doors to all the boxes were closed, and he didn't want to risk opening any fearing a new unwanted meeting.

The corridor lights flickered again, a warning to the public of what would come next. And then he heard it loud and clear. First, it was just a hum lost in the depths of his conscience, but it gradually worked its way up to the surface and he heard it with clarity.

Those notes, those distant trumpets, he had heard them before. He didn't know where, he didn't remember it, but they were very familiar. That melody and its in-crescendo rhythm ignited the soul, lifted the spirit and brought it closer to the gods, to the Olympus of beauty.

The corridor lights flickered a third time and extinguished completely. It was time. Fortunately, he was close to the box, otherwise, he wouldn't have been able to find the door in the darkness.

What he was about to do went against all police logic, not to mention ethics, but for Morillo, there was no going back. He knew what he had to do, what his mission was, what he was doing for all the innocent victims of that maniac.

Praying for the layout of all boxes to be identical, he held the doorknob and opened the door decisively, closing it behind him.

Darkness was complete, but he didn't have to wait more than two seconds to feel something moving beside him. He was in the anteroom, and he knew it was rectangular and elongated to his left.

Whoever was there could only attack him from his left, so he stepped aside and instinctively ducked, feeling like someone hit him on the side as he went past him and crashed into the anteroom wall.

Morillo wasted no time, he lifted his leg, slamming his knee somewhere in his assailant's body, which creaked upon receiving the impact as he let out a muffled scream.

Having lost the element of surprise, the assailant turned on Morillo and held him by the waist, groping in the dark to embrace his body and started trying to suffocate him.

He tried to get up and shifted his weight forward, swinging up to stretch his arm and groping in search of the liquor cabinet.

The sound of broken glass told him he was close, and he was able to hold a bottle with his fingertips, bring it to an upright position and grab it by the neck. It felt more like a wine decanter, but he picked it up and dropped it with full force over the man's head, as he staggered slightly but continued suffocating him.

The music was blaring in the main hall, but it probably was not loud enough to muffle the noise of the fight.

Morillo was running out of steam quickly, both because of his fighting efforts and the crushing of his chest cavity at the hands of that mastodon. His hands kept desperately feeling the liquor cabinet but there no longer was any glass or bottle left alive.

Following a crazy idea, he made a superhuman effort to swing forward, enough to throw them both off-balance with his weight, and moving a few steps to the left.

He reached out until his fingers identified the wooden edge of the auxiliary folding table. With a last desperate

287

effort, he raised the wooden board with his fingertips, and a click told him the stand was engaged properly.

As he lowered both hands, he held on tightly to the head of that human mass, pulling up with what little energy he had left, until he felt he was holding his head in a more or less upright position.

He bent the two legs, leaned his feet against the wall, propelling himself forward with all the strength of his thighs, as if he was about to take off and wanted to cross the wall.

Surprised by the strength Morillo used to push him back, the bodyguard's neck, savagely beat against the sharp edge of the wooden table, whose angle cleanly penetrated several centimeters his skull base.

Morillo felt the warm wetness of blood running through his hands, but he maintained pressure on the strung head, with the little strength his quadriceps could offer him. When he felt the subject's last seizures, as he slumped to the ground, Morillo fell on top of him.

With no time to recover, he stood up. He drew back the curtain that separated him from the box, but in front of him, he only saw the generous neckline of the beautiful woman accompanying Gisbert.

The Ride of the Valkyries was in full swing, and the only light in the main hall came from the flickering reflection of the rough footage shot in black and white that was being projected onto the stage before an audience stunned at such deployment of high technology.

Where was Gisbert? Probably hiding in the darkness of the deepest part of the box, waiting for Morillo to make the first move. The answer came as a terrible punch to his jaw that sent him reeling and knocked several of the empty chairs around him.

Morillo considered using the young girl as a hostage, but he immediately dismissed the idea, not so much for ethical reasons but for the certainty the vicious psychopath would not hesitate to sacrifice her.

He stood before her, trying to be at the center of the box

and from there be able to react jumping to either side, but remembering the physical superiority the man had shown in their previous encounters, Morillo had no choice but to use his gun as the only way to intimidate him.

He grabbed the gun and aimed it at the hidden shadow in the back of the box.

"Don't move and I won't shoot," Morillo shouted, uncertain Gisbert heard him over the din of the music.

As if thrown by a cornered dragon spitting fire, a chair flew from the depths of the box and hit him in the temple, even when he bent down to avoid it.

Morillo saw the chair continue its flight above the railing, plunging into the dark depths of the stalls, surely hitting more than one spectator, but he could not hear it because of the volume of the music.

He pulled the trigger and the brightness of the flash attracted some stares from the stalls and the boxes in front, but there was too much confusion for anyone to notice anything.

Morillo dodged another chair which flew from the back of the box and hit the girl in the face. She clutched her broken nose, which started bleeding profusely, staining in red her dress.

Morillo fired again, adjusting his aim to the right, where he thought the last chair had come from. When he noticed neither movement nor more flying objects, he assumed he had wounded Gisbert and kicking away the remaining chairs he took a few steps forward.

Gisbert jumped like a wounded black panther and both rolled on the box's floor. Morillo was underneath and was getting a monumental beating, as each blow he received on his face resulted in another strong blow of his head against the wooden floor and he was getting very stunned.

Taking the plunge, and in a desperate action, he raised his gun and brought it close to the man's choleric face. He could see his bloodshot eyes, the same that stared at him when he attacked him at the Hospital de Sant Pau, the same eyes that had witnessed life escaping from so many innocent victims.

He brought up the gun barrel until it touched Gisbert's cheek and fired again.

He heard the bullet strike the ceiling, but Morillo hoped it had, at least, gone through his cheek. Gisbert threw a terrible punch to Morillo's jaw and rose.

Gisbert pushed Morillo against the young girl, who was screaming in terror, and she swung over the railing, hanging outside the box.

Several gentlemen down in the stalls missed no detail of the complicated framework of petticoats, clothing folds, and metal rods, among which a pair of beautiful, slender legs in white stockings were shaking spasmodically.

Morillo stood up staggering, and could barely stay upright. Gisbert had just fled, he could see the curtain moving after he went through, and he wanted to run after him, but there was a badly injured young girl about to fall into the void. A stupid young girl? Perhaps. An innocent girl? With all certainty.

Once again, his police conscience dictated what he had to do. He holstered his gun and flipped over the railing to hold her by the arms.

By then, people in the stalls had stood up and the frightened spectators pointed up to the box, women screaming in terror, while some men came closer and stretched their arms and canes, in a futile attempt to help.

Morillo grabbed the girl by the forearms, but she weighed more than her fragile complexion could have suggested. Perhaps it was her dress, or maybe the heavy corset she wore, in which there probably was more iron than in the Eiffel Tower. Forces were abandoning him, for the fight with Gisbert had left him exhausted, and he was not sure he could hold on much longer.

He looked down to see which area would she fall into if he let her go, and he was glad to see the height was not significant, and enough men were waiting for her below to ensure a comfortable landing for her.

He closed his eyes as if by doing so he would get divine

forgiveness.

"Hold on tight, Miss." he shouted, realizing the absurdity of his comment, as he opened his hands and let her fall. The way the young girl squealed made her a worthy competitor to any of the high-C notes hit by the soprano throughout the evening.

The singers stood motionless in the center of the stage, undaunted by what was happening, enjoying for once the show was taking place offstage and not in it.

Morillo looked down to make sure the girl was alive, which was certified by the slapping with which she tried to shake off the hands of all the men around her.

More at ease, Morillo dashed out of the box and into the anteroom and ran down the corridor toward the main stairs.

Many spectators started to abandon the theater, frightened by what they thought could be a reprise of the unfortunate bombing from a few years earlier, and with that tragic precedent in their minds, they ran downstairs between shouts and head-butting.

Morillo addressed the employees guarding the entrance to the boxes.

"Has Mr. Gisbert passed by you?" he asked, almost without stopping.

"No sir, we have seen no one," the more loquacious of the two said, in what Morillo knew was a blatant lie.

"Are you sure? A burly guy with a dark jacket, mustache, and red hair."

The two employees exchanged glances before giving the same answer, which confirmed Morillo's suspicions they were only synchronizing their rehearsed answers, covering Gisbert's back.

After all, it wasn't Morillo who rewarded them generously after each performance and who gave them a bonus for Christmas.

He reached the large main staircase and ran downstairs, throwing elbows and trying to break through the riot.

"SubInspector Morillo, is that you?" he heard a voice calling his name from behind. The voice came from the upper floor, and although he didn't turn to look back, the curvature of the staircase allowed him to see out of the corner of the eye it was Commissioner Pizcueta, who had abandoned his box and headed for the exit.

Just what he needed now. Morillo pretended not to have heard him and ran through the front door toward the Ramblas.

To the number of regular onlookers, many more had joined this time, attracted by the screaming and the flood of people running out the theater, in an overwhelming human tide, a kind of reverse tsunami flowing from inside the building to the exterior.

CHAPTER 53

M orillo squeezed between the large number of carriages and cars awaiting their owners at the entrance, crossed the avenue, and stopped next to several horses quite disturbed by the shouting, while their drivers tried in vain to reassure them.

Then he saw him, about fifty meters away across the Rambla, on the driveway going up the other way. He was getting into a car, a huge Cadillac Model Thirty, the first vehicle to incorporate an electric starter.

Morillo ran after him and crossed the central part of the Rambla, dodging the pedestrians approaching the theater, until he was a few meters from the car. Gisbert turned and their eyes met, as Morillo tried to decide whether to jump on the car or to stop running and draw his gun to shoot.

It was a public place and there were too many people around, so he quickened the pace and tried to reach the car. The driver honked several times for pedestrians to step aside, and Morillo seized the opportunity to jump and hold on to the rear of the vehicle, standing on the leaf-springs of the suspension.

The car revved up and jumped ahead, hitting and knocking down several women crossing the street. Morillo threw several punches on the fabric roof of the car with the only hand he dared to let go, but the car did not stop, it kept going up the Ramblas, gaining speed because there were fewer pedestrians on the driveway as it moved away from the theater.

He had to get inside the car, but first, he needed to set foot on the rear fenders, and from there, climb onto the roof. It was a desperate, risky and stupid solution but he clutched hard to the back of the rear seat and raised one of his legs up onto the fender flap, ready to climb.

The driver began to swerve to throw him off balance, and Morillo had to reposition his feet on the rear leaf-springs to avoid falling to the ground.

He tried again and this time he placed the foot on the flap and propel himself to the roof and grab one of the horizontal bars that kept the canvas taut. With a tremendous effort, he managed to stretch from the waist up over the roof, while his feet dangled kicking into the void.

Several bullets pierced the roof canvas, fired from inside the car. Without letting go of his hands, he rolled to one side, but the canvas didn't hold his weight and tore lengthwise. Instead of falling into the car, he felt a pair of hands pushing him from below and throwing him to the side of the car.

Morillo was hanging from the right side of the car, desperately holding on to a piece of canvas that would soon tear. His feet already dragged on the ground and he could feel the blows of the road cobblestones on his knees, a situation he could not withstand for much longer.

He let go of one of his hands to reach for his weapon while holding on as he could with the other. The car was weaving and he couldn't aim well so he lined up the gun barrel with the tear in the canvas over the back seat and fired,

The redhead's face appeared briefly and looked at him with a look of utter contempt before disappearing. Seconds later he reappeared, hidden behind the barrel of his gun, aimed directly at the subinspector's chest.

Morillo could not fight back, he couldn't aim well, and the only way he could avoid being shot at close range was to let go and fall on the pavement. In a desperate move, he lowered his weapon and fired three times aiming at the vehicle.

Two shots hit the target and the right front tire blew up in pieces, causing the vehicle to give strong jolts, and head directly against the sidewalk, to which the ailing wheel climbed several times while the driver tried to keep the car under control.

The menacing sight of several street lights rapidly approaching towards him was enough for Morillo to let go of the canvas, rolling down the pavement until he lay beside a manhole, as the car of the bloodthirsty bastard rattled over the cobblestones, one wheel short, but maintaining its course and disappearing up the Ramblas.

Morillo rose, helped by several bystanders who had come to his aid. Without identifying himself as a policeman, he thanked them for the gesture and turned to go back to the theater.

His appearance was pitiful. His torn jacket had lost one sleeve and his elegant suit pants had directly transformed into ragged shorts. From the waist down, he was bleeding in several body parts and showed large open wounds and abrasions on knees and ankles.

Limping and dragging one leg, his immediate priority was to find Agnes, although he didn't even know how to start talking to her.

She would be furious at him, for hiding from her the real reason for their presence in the theater, and for having abandoned her in the middle of the play. Either his was the longest physiological urgency in history, or his excuse would be phonier than the Valkyries stage sets.

A human flood was flowing out of the theater, and its waters parted to let that shabby bloodstained man pass as if he were Moses crossing the Red Sea.

Morillo wondered how he would find Agnes. He could not enter the theater looking like that, or rather, the doormen wouldn't let him go past the front door, so he stopped about fifty meters from the entrance and scan the horizon, hoping to recognize Agnes' elegant headdress between the crowd that was hastily leaving the building.

He felt someone approached him from behind and

gently pulled the only sleeve that remained intact in his jacket. Some detective he was. Agnes had found him before he could find her.

Morillo closed his eyes before turning, and said a prayer to all the saints of his devotion, fearing a monumental reprimand from her.

He opened his eyes, ready to face Agnes' fury and dip into the well of his creativity to give all the necessary explanations, when he found himself face to face with another woman, the prostitute with whom he had shared confidences recently.

Not yet recovered from the surprise, instead of talking to her he looked in all directions, to make sure Agnes was not around. If she caught him with that woman, it would be very difficult for him to explain how he had met her and the non-sinful nature of their relationship.

Morillo took her by the arm and dragged her to the sidewalk, seeking to hide behind the useless protection of a thin lamp post, but with his back to the theater, as if that would make it harder to recognize him.

"For the love of God, woman, what are you doing here?"

"I came here on purpose to find you," she said, seemingly frightened.

"How did you know I would be here?"

"It was me who suggested you come, don't you remember?"

Morillo stared at her for a few seconds without saying a word, and finally, his expression relaxed and he approached her ear.

"We shouldn't be seen in public. You know who I am and you know what's at stake, don't you?"

"Yes, I know, and to be honest, I don't want to cause you any trouble, or put you in an awkward position."

"So?"

"I have come to give you information that I think will interest you. But, what happened to you?" she asked, noticing for the first time his shabby appearance. "Have you fallen off your horse or something like that?"

"Something like that," Morillo said, tersely. It was obvious he was uncomfortable in the company of that woman, and he kept looking over his shoulder and turning to the theater, fearing being caught by Agnes.

"When you left, I made some inquiries around the house, I talked to the other girls," she said, grabbing Morillo's attention. "One of the oldest told me something that will interest you."

"Well, I'm waiting for you to tell me," Morillo said, growing impatient.

"I'm also waiting," she added, getting up and ostentatiously readjusting her breasts into what clearly was a suffocating corset that should be squeezing all the juice out of that young body.

Morillo didn't have a clear head, still stunned after his fall from the car, but not enough not to realize she was expecting a reward for her information.

"And how do I know what you're going to tell me will interest me?"

"I know it will. But if I tell you and you're not interested, to prove I trust you, I will give you your money back," she said.

"But I haven't given you any money yet."

"I know, but you're gonna do it now, aren't you? Think about who it is you're looking for. I can help you find him," the girl said, with great aplomb.

"Okay, but I cannot pay you in advance, I'm sorry."

The young girl's look of disbelief, mixed with an insinuating expression and a new pectoral readjustment, were so embarrassing for Morillo, he made his decision quickly.

"All right, wait. This is all I have," he said, reaching for his wallet and taking a single banknote which he had been saving to pay the tram fare for the trip back home with Agnes.

"Enough, for now," she said, taking the note and introducing it quickly into the deep valley of her generous cleavage.

"You'll see," she said, invading without hesitation the privacy of Morillo's personal space. "One of the new girls told me that mister redhead had expressly asked for her and that he wanted to meet her tomorrow night in his chambers. You know what that means."

"That he wants to get to know her better and deeper, right?"

She nodded. "More or less, that's it. Especially the part about knowing her deeper."

"And where and when will the meeting take place?"

"Tomorrow, around eleven o'clock at night. The master chambers are in the main house, on the top floor."

"Could you grant me access to the house?"

"Of course. I can show you where his room is, and can also find a place for you to hide."

Morillo did not respond.

One idea was burning in his mind, and Agnes was not part of it.

CHAPTER 54

Rabassada Road. Barcelona. 1912

I t was the last tram traveling up to the Casino that evening. Morillo got off as the tram began its long descent along the dusty road. As usual, he preferred to walk the last part of his journey, to avoid drawing attention or being easily recognized.

He took advantage of the long journey to self psychoanalyze, trying to find a justification for his actions since that case was becoming an obsession for him. He was working outside the rules of his own police department, almost outside the law, and had been the target of several assassination attempts.

Unable to resort to his superiors, as they were probably involved in that murky plot, he barely had any friends and he knew he was facing a very powerful group with branches in the highest echelons of political and economic power in the city.

But he felt like a knight fighting for the honor of a damsel in distress, he saw himself as a champion of lost causes, a defender of those who had lost all hope and could not resort to the system.

Nothing prevented him from confronting Gisbert directly and arresting him officially at his home or office, but he would only earn the wrath of Lieutenant Botell. Given the lack of conclusive evidence, he would spoil the element of surprise and the limited freedom of movement he enjoyed, at least temporarily, by working on his own.

What he found hardest to cope with was seeing how that crusade to which he had surrendered voluntarily, affected his relationship with Agnes with hard to predict consequences. Meeting Agnes was the best thing that ever happened to him, and for the first time, he saw himself settling down and building a family, with her at the center of his life.

Agnes brought him peace, and a touch of calm sanity with which she addressed all issues. That's why he suffered at the thought if he went ahead with that madness, he risked throwing away any chance he might have with her.

His fanatical obsession with catching that psychopath had led him to ignore Agnes, to lie to her, even to use her shamefully, the episode at the Teatre del Liceu being the most recent and dramatic example of such obsession. Catching that man was his drug, and he had become addicted to it, above anything else, even his relationship with Agnes.

He told himself that night would be the last. He would face him, and after that he would tell Agnes everything. He needed to feel there were no more secrets between them, that she could know him as he really was.

His priorities would change, he had to place her above all things. No criminal case or injustice could be more important than building a life together based on mutual trust and love.

Strengthened by this conviction, he walked for twenty minutes alone, avoiding pedestrians and getting a few meters into the forest whenever he crossed paths with one.

From a distance he could already see the tower rising above the roof of the big house. He reached the great winged lions guarding the main entrance, and walked to the side door.

After saying the code word he had agreed with the young woman, minutes later he was at the reception in the small building, putting up with the fat Madame's oily smile, while she was delighted to have a client back, only a few days after his last visit.

She offered him to meet new girls, but he insisted on requiring the services of the same one he had been with recently. The Madame smiled, with the naughty and knowing grin of those who believe they can read between the lines, discreet witness of a situation already experienced so many times.

The sensual sound of silk sliding over the bare skin of the young girl's slender legs as she walked down the stairs, made him turn his head long before he saw her silhouette against the staircase landing, such was his state of nervous anticipation.

The Madame grinned openly, mistakenly reading his anxiety as the familiar and irrepressible lustful desire so many customers showed at that moment. The descent of the stairs and the first glimpse of the young girl by the customer was her favorite moment, she never tired of admiring the effect the rampaging hormones had in men.

It was the clash between two worlds, the satisfaction of the most basic and universal desires of humanity, seasoned with the salt of the forbidden and the pepper of infidelity, spicing together a dish that was more of a sweet and spectacular dessert for gourmets with a sweet tooth than a coherent and nutritional stew for the day to day.

The girl accompanied Morillo upstairs, and they were soon inside the same room they had occupied days earlier.

"Well?" Morillo asked, unable to hide his anxiety.

"Well what? Relax. You came very early. We even have time to have some fun while we wait, " she said, letting the silk robe open slightly and displaying a generous portion of her half-naked body.

Morillo swallowed and to his surprise, it took him longer than expected to respond, but he concentrated in his mission, in his recent determination regarding Agnes, and pushed away from his mind any temptation.

"At what time are you expecting him?" he asked, walking over to the window to peek outside, hiding behind the curtain.

"It'll take him at least one hour, but you never know. Sometimes he shows up earlier. The girl that awaits him must be ready by now."

"Is there anyone else in the other house?"

"I don't know. I know there are several service people there, a cook, some servants, perhaps a guard, but they rarely stay overnight."

"I need you to take me there. I have to find a good place to hide," Morillo said, heading for the door.

"When?"

"Now," he said, his hand on the doorknob.

She led him to a small service room leading to a narrow staircase, that took them down to an exit door in the building's rear. She went first to check no one was there.

An abundance of plants invaded the space between the two houses, as if the intention had been to create a natural barrier to separate the two buildings.

Even in the dim light of dusk, the back house was an imposing construction. A tower from which you surely enjoyed a breathtaking view of the surroundings topped its roof. Simple floral mosaics, very popular among the predominant Art Nouveau taste of that period, adorned the top of the front facade.

They surrounded the building, remaining sheltered within the plants and turned to a flight of stairs going under a balcony, to a wooden door to what looked like a storage room for gardening tools.

The young girl came to the door and knocked several times, in what evidently was an agreed code. The door opened, and she motioned with her hand to invite him to follow her, as she disappeared inside.

Morillo looked around one last time. He was getting into the lion's den, the lair of the beast, and he only hoped to get out of there alive and be able to hang the bastard's head over his fireplace as a trophy.

What Morillo hadn't noticed was that his house had no chimney.

CHAPTER 55

T he dark and narrow room had a strong musty smell. Out of nowhere, a candle appeared in the hands of the girl and she motioned him to follow her.

They were in an old stone washtub with two large sinks that seemed carved into the rock, one of them filled with dark water to the edge. Moss patches dotted the walls, as if wanting to get through from the outside to invade that oppressive environment.

They walked a few meters deep into what looked like the foundations of the building, and reached a crossroads of identical corridors, with no element to help them find their way.

"Are you sure you know the way?" Morillo whispered.

She did not answer, just kept walking through the maze with such resolve it made Morillo think it was not the first time she visited that place, which he found surprising.

After several turns, they came to the end of a corridor that gradually narrowed until it almost forced them to walk sideways. She disappeared behind the corner and Morillo reached a staircase so narrow he doubted he could climb it, despite not being a claustrophobic person.

Standing sideways, he stepped into the narrow opening and pushed upward, forcing his feet to crawl up the steps, while his shoulders and head rubbed against the walls and ceiling of the constrained space.

He could see the candle glow in front of him, and he pushed forward out of survival instinct, praying deep inside for the passage to widen soon and not get stuck for eternity in such a dreary place.

His prayers were answered when he soon noticed the walls around expanded and he could inhale deeply, which he appreciated and did with fruition.

They were behind a huge vase at the end of a dark corridor, at the bottom of a spiral staircase that ascended to the upper floors.

Without saying a word, she began to slowly climb the wooden steps that creaked under her weight. Morillo went after her, and could not keep his hand from unconsciously going to his gun when he heard the creaking of his own footsteps on the stairs.

They reached a landing in what had to be the second floor, decorated with the same vase that seemed to be in all floors, cloaking the access to the service staircase.

A thick carpet covered the corridor before them, and large paintings hung on both walls, symmetrically placed between delicate Art Nouveau moldings.

She waited a few moments, and as everything seemed quiet, she came out of hiding from behind the vase and tiptoed across the carpet to one of the room doors. A few meters away there was the main staircase of the house, going down to a spacious living room on the first floor.

When Morillo joined the young girl, she brought her finger to her lips to ask for silence and started to open the door. It surprised Morillo she did not check first if there was anyone inside, but he guessed her contacts inside the house had paved the way already. Morillo went in after her and shut the door behind him.

The room was like the ones he already knew from the other building, but much bigger. The prevailing color in the decoration was black, which together with the maroon fabric paneling the walls gave the place a gloomy air. A huge canopy of dark wood covered the bed, reminiscent of the best moments of the reign of Louis XIV. The French monarch would have felt more than comfortable in it.

"Is this where the redhead is supposed to meet with your friend?" Morillo asked, somewhat uneasy.

She pointed to the bed.

"That's where he does it all. You know what I mean."

"Where can I hide?"

"There," she said, pointing to a large black three door cabinet presiding over one of the farthest walls.

Morillo examined it carefully, slowly opening the center door. Inside, only a wooden bar from which several jackets and shirts hung, but the cabinet was deep enough to hide an entire family.

A soft knock at the room door startled Morillo, who jumped into the cabinet and closed the door from the inside with his fingertips.

"Hello, come in" he heard the young girl say, in the sweet sensual tone he was accustomed to hear from her.

He tried to keep the door ajar but was eager to look through the crack. To his relief, it was not the red-haired man, but another girl dressed in a purple nightgown.

She was very beautiful, with a wavy mane spilling over her shoulders in a cascade of jet-black hair. Both girls smiled, hugging and whispering, while Morillo didn't know whether to get out or stay hidden. Did the newcomer know of his presence there? Was she aware of what was going to happen?

He decided it was better not to reveal his presence, although the truth was he wasn't too uncomfortable watching two beautiful scantily clad young girls.

From his hiding place he saw the expression on the faces of the two girls mutate into one of great concern, as they both turned toward the entrance.

The room door opened with a crash. Although Morillo could not see it from where he stood, he heard it hitting a chair placed behind the door.

Morillo froze, trying to guess what was happening. The dark-haired girl disappeared from his field of vision and he could only see her friend, who was still standing in the middle of the room.

The dim light came from a single gas lamp at a minimum, that only let him see a moving shadow dance projected onto the bed and the adjacent wall.

He could hear voices, he even thought he heard muffled laughter, and his eyes were almost out of their sockets from the efforts he made to look through the slit without opening the door.

Gradually the feet of a man slowly came into view, next to the girl's naked thighs, whose immaculate skin glowed in the flickering light of the gas lamp, releasing silk sparks.

The man wore a hat, and had his back to Morillo, thus he couldn't see who it was. He took off his jacket and threw it to the floor, along with his stick, which until then he had been holding in his hands.

He started slowly caressing the girl and signaled Morillo's friend to come closer. She stood in front of him, and the man embraced her, kissing her on the neck while she removed his hat and dropped it on the floor on top of his jacket.

From his position, Morillo watched them in total immobility. He sweated profusely, both from nerves and due to the confined space, and he feared he would let the door slip out, since he was only holding it with the tip of his sweaty fingers.

The prostitute looked up and straight into Morillo's eyes, smiling at him as her robe and nightgown slid on her skin and fell to the floor. The man's hands were quick to disappear behind the girl's bare back, while the other girl cuddled him from his side and clung to him like a leaf to a wet glass window.

Morillo didn't know how to behave, it was a very uncomfortable situation. That scene was raising the temperature inside the cabinet by the minute and he wasn't certain that was the man he was looking for.

If he came out of the closet and was wrong, that would worsen his already precarious professional situation, but if he didn't take action, he would lose a golden opportunity to settle the score with his nemesis.

The man nuzzled the two women to the bed, and stretched them out on the mattress, being partially hidden by the fabric veils hanging from the canopy. He climbed into bed and stretched between them, and a game of petting and making out started, one that Morillo could only glimpse at, because of the distance and the poor lighting.

After several minutes of erotic foreplay, the man stood up and jumped out of bed to go to pour himself a drink from a bottle sitting on a coffee table.

The two girls kept romping and fondling each other as if the man was still there, and they rose in unison, standing at the foot of the huge bed, appearing completely naked before Morillo, whose fingers were sweating and shaking, and not only from the effort needed to hold the door.

He didn't know how long it had been; he had probably spent only a few seconds drooling over those two nymphs, when a brief access of lucidity assaulted him. He had the strange feeling those two beautiful women were exhibiting their naked bodies in a private show directed only at him, and both were smiling at him.

Although initially he felt in seventh heaven, his police instinct reacted immediately. How could they both be looking at him if supposedly only one of them knew about his hiding place? How could they be flashing in front of him without the man finding it strange or stopping them?

The only explanation was both of them had to be working in collusion with the man. And by the way, where was the man?

Upon realizing what was happening, his fingertips immediately released their grip on the cabinet door, which began to open in slow motion as his hand dipped in search of his gun.

He had no time to reach the holster. A formidable roar disoriented him completely. The inside of the cabinet seemed to come alive and writhe. He lost all sense of time and space and spun in a giant blender as he felt he was falling into the void, his body pounding hard against the walls.

Finally, an excruciating pain ran through his whole body from head to toes, like an electric shock of millions of volts running down his spine and reveling in various parts of his anatomy.

He couldn't stand it and closed his eyes.

He thought he had died.

CHAPTER 56

When Morillo opened his eyes, he was in complete darkness. If he had died and he was in Hell, it was not how he had imagined it, but one is never prepared for that.

When he regained consciousness, he started analyzing the situation. He felt pain, had bruises and wounds on his head and arms and his back ached as if he had broken it in several pieces.

He took a deep breath and a mixture of hot and humid air filled his lungs, triggering a painful coughing fit.

Reaching out he felt around. He was lying on a stone floor, probably underground. He could distinguish the bitter smell of wet soil and roots. He sat up and searched in vain for his gun. It wasn't there.

Suddenly a yellowish light flashed next to him, momentarily blinding him. He covered his eyes with his hands and looked around. It was a small space, just two meters wide and a meter and a half high, directly on a huge flat stone that acted as a pavement.

The walls were dug in the soil, with tree roots protruding threateningly and reaching out like tentacles of stalking subhuman beings.

There was a small wooden door with a narrow square opening through which he could see the light bulb shining insolently.

He heard movement, someone was approaching. He

310

tried to gather his strength to launch an attack, but he was exhausted and didn't know where to find the energy reserve he clearly didn't have.

The door opened with a slight creak, but no one appeared. With great difficulty, Morillo got up and crawled out of that claustrophobic prison. His knees ached, and he noticed his hands and legs were bleeding, but he didn't stop.

Before him, there was a long tunnel, crudely dug underground. It was narrow and barely a meter and a half high, and was lit by yellow bulbs evenly spaced every twenty meters.

He crawled through the tunnel, gaining strength as he made progress, not meeting anyone. He was heading toward the unknown, into a possible ambush, to find horror in its purest form, but he had no choice. There was only one passage in front of him, and Morillo did not hesitate to follow it.

His hands looked like two mud stumps, covered with sludge and blood, and to say he was completely disoriented was an understatement.

The tunnel had widened, and it was high enough to allow him to stand. Staggering and leaning against the walls, he kept moving forward, until he reached a fork.

He bent down to examine the ground and noted one of the two paths showed signs of trampling, while in the other, the soil looked more compact and unaltered.

He followed the trampled path, but he heard a noise and stopped. Someone was coming toward him. Morillo retraced his steps and went into the other passage, standing still.

The noise sounded ever closer, the sound of footsteps sinking into the soft muddy ground of the tunnel. They were light footsteps, but he was sure they were of human origin, not an animal.

"Hello, are you there? Answer me."

Morillo froze upon hearing that. It was a woman's voice and despite the lousy acoustics in those catacombs, he recognized the voice of the prostitute. He didn't know whether to get out and meet her or remain hidden.

He took the risk and tried to play the few cards he had left, coming out of hiding.

"I'm here," he said, walking out into the light at the crossroads. She was a few meters away, in the other tunnel, half-naked, her body covered with a blanket hanging from her shoulders. Morillo noticed she walked barefoot.

"What is happening here? Where are we?" Morillo whispered.

"Follow me, there's no time to waste," she said, turning and disappearing the way she had come.

Morillo went after her, not thinking about the possible scenarios he could find beyond. It was a desperate situation and he let his impulses guide him.

After walking for what felt like an eternity, they reached a dark brick wall, on which there was a small door. They were still under the mountain, but humidity was lower and the atmosphere less unbreathable, and he guessed perhaps they were in the basement of one of the mansions in the area.

The girl reached into a concavity in the rock, from which she removed a large iron key, which turned in the lock. The door opened, letting out a thread of light that drew a line on the stone floor, almost to his feet.

She disappeared and Morillo went after her. The door opened into a narrow, dimly lit corridor. The floor was made of dark tiles, with a design pattern he found hard to identify. The passage went down and ended in a flight of stairs crudely carved into the rock.

Morillo approached the girl, who was waiting motionless in the middle of the passage and grabbed her by the wrists.

"Tell me what the hell is going on here. Where are we?" he asked angrily.

"I can't talk now, we're in danger. Go up those stairs and wait for me in the room you will find above. I'll be back with help. Trust me," and pulling away, she disappeared into the darkness of the hallway, leaving Morillo in utter stupefaction.

"Trust me," were the last words the woman had spoken. Morillo wondered if there was anyone in the world he could trust, except Agnes, of course.

Agnes' image materialized before his eyes, and when Morillo reached out to caress her delicate features, it disintegrated like a shattered mirror.

He had come too far to turn back now. Everything he did he did it for her.

It was time to put an end to the obsession that haunted him, and rid the world of the presence of that psychopath, to go back into Agnes' arms and share his life with her, living together, growing old together and, if possible, dying together too.

He sighed, and started up the stone steps with resolve. The stretch was steep and described a sharp curve. When he reached the top, he faced a varnished wooden door, marked with a wavy golden brass figurine.

Slowly, Morillo brought his hand to the doorknob.

"Damn it" he muttered, after instinctively taking his hand to the side to draw his gun and finding once again an empty holster. He grabbed the doorknob and turned it decisively, opening the door slowly.

Inside, a thick carpet covered much of the floor giving the room a surprisingly comfortable look. A quick visual inspection showed him a couch next to a hanger for coats and hats, and a bookcase full of volumes.

In front of him, he saw the silhouette of a person sitting at a small wooden desk, his back on him. The desk was against the wall, whose dark tiles reflected the dim light of two small gas lamps.

Morillo looked around but couldn't find anything he could use as a defensive weapon. He took two steps toward the center of the room, without looking away from the man who appeared to be writing. He was sitting in a swivel chair, wearing a dark jacket and a wide-brimmed hat covering his head.

"Excuse me," Morillo said, raising his voice slightly.

The figure stood still, but he kept walking. He reached out and touched him gently on the shoulder, with no response. He tried again, this time holding his shoulder and shaking it.

Despite the dim light, he realized the strands of hair sticking out under the man's hat had a reddish glow.

The chair began to turn slowly and as the man's body was becoming visible Morillo couldn't help but jump backward upon meeting face to face with Mauricio Gisbert.

In an instinctive movement, Morillo ducked, wanting to fend off an attack that never came. He got up and approached the static body before him, which was leaning dangerously on the chair. Morillo held it to prevent it from falling.

The glazed look in those open eyes seemed to be penetrating his soul and got deep under his skin. The body already had blue skin and his lifeless face held an expression of restrained fury mixed with terror.

Surprise paralyzed Morillo. He had come to the end of the road; he had before him the psychopath he had been pursuing relentlessly, the bloodthirsty murderer who had killed Mrs. Xamot and probably many others, and he was now dead, or so it seemed.

It couldn't be so simple, it couldn't end that way. Someone had beaten him and done the job for him.

At first glance, he saw no signs indicating the probable cause of death, but he would have to examine the body carefully before drawing any theory.

He wondered where the prostitutes had gone and what was their role in all that. Had they been killed too? His brain seethed with so many unanswered questions struggling to grab the attention of his meager and exhausted neurons.

When his hand opened the jacket on Gisbert's corpse, he had to hold back when he saw a giant hole in the place where his abdominal viscera had been.

How could someone have shown so little mercy by

eviscerating a corpse? And what if they had skinned him when he was still alive? Only the thought of that sent a shiver up and down his spine several times.

The murderer had finally found his match, he thought. Until then, he was convinced Gisbert was the sadist behind those murders, but what if he were just another victim? What if the real murderer was someone else?

This new theory began to take shape in his mind, and he was so absorbed evaluating that possibility he did not hear the footsteps approaching from behind.

He barely had time to turn upon hearing them, but it was too late. He glimpsed some vaporous woman's clothes before a dark shadow pounced on him and unbearable pain descended like an unstoppable cascade from his head down to his toes. Next, silence and total darkness.

When he opened his eyes, he was pleased to see he was still in the room, a sign his descent into Hell had not yet taken place, although the excruciating headache he was suffering made him think otherwise.

Visibility was almost nil, since the flames of the gas lamps were almost extinguished.

He was sitting at the desk, and he felt the cold and wet touch of blood running down his face, dripping onto the wooden surface. He was sitting in the same chair in which he found Gisbert's body, which had disappeared.

As he looked to his right, toward the sofa beside the coat hanger, he was startled to see two bodies sitting on it, staring at him motionless.

He was sure one of them was Gisbert, or rather his body, still staring at him with sullen open eyes. Next to him, there was another body, sitting beside him, smaller, probably a woman.

From the color and texture of her open clothes, he concluded it had to be the prostitute who, judging by her immobility, had joined her couch companion in the hereafter.

CHAPTER 57

"I'm sorry we had to reach this far, but you left me no alternative."

A deep voice behind him had spoken the words. Morillo tried to turn but his wrists were cuffed to the arms of the chair.

He struggled to free himself, and when he failed, he propped his feet on the ground and pushed upward to jump with the chair and turn toward the entrance.

"I'm pointing a gun directly at your head. If you don't calm down, I will do it for you, but I'm afraid it will be permanent," the voice said again.

Morillo stopped instantly. "Who are you? What do you want? Let me go immediately or face the consequences," Morillo protested, talking to the wall in front of him.

"You are not in a position to give orders, much less threatening me. From what I know of you, I think you're a man of honor, and as such, you'll give proof of it in the decisive moments."

"What the hell are you talking about? Who are you?" Morillo insisted, struggling gently to loosen the handcuffs.

"There is no time to socialize. The ultimate goal is always the main priority and nothing and nobody will stand in my way," the voice said, speaking slowly.

"Please, I'm a cop, and my fellow police officers will soon be here. Let me go and let's talk," Morillo tried to reason.

"I would laugh if I had time. They say time never stops, even when the handles on the clock do, even when its rusty machinery stops working. Listen to me carefully, because my voice is the last thing you will hear in this world."

Something in the tone with which he spoke those words froze his blood.

"I know who you are, subinspector Morillo. I know your career history, and I know what is left of your family, your mother, your uncles, and cousins. I met your beautiful girlfriend, what's her name? Yes, Agnes. I could have such good times with her, although I suppose she would offer some resistance, that's part of the game, is what excites me, is the essence of the hunt."

When he heard Agnes' name being referred to in those terms, Morillo could not help but squirm in his chair, tugging frantically at the handcuffs, as if he could dislocate his wrists to break free.

"Do not waste your meager forces, since you will need them," the voice said, and Morillo reacted, calming down for a moment.

"Everything becomes irrelevant in reaching the ultimate goal. I am also a man of honor, and I will always respect those who behave the same way. I know you are one of them, and I know you want the best for your loved ones."

Morillo was sweating profusely. He didn't like the direction that lunatic's speech was taking, but he wanted to hear more, know where he was heading.

"Things are always very simple. You have full capacity to decide for yourself. On the table in front of you, there is a letter I beg you to read carefully. It's a proposal, or rather, a gentlemen's agreement. You meet your part of the bargain, I keep mine. Without misgivings, without mistrust, with the full assurance honor is the most sacred thing we have."

Morillo realized for the first time that there was an open envelope on the desk, and a letter sticking out it.

"I will approach slowly and release one of your hands so you can read the letter. Do not try anything, because if you do, it will be the last thing you do in this world. Then I will exit the room and leave you alone so you can meditate about what you just read. If you try to leave the room, you won't get through the door. I will gun you down and you will die like a wharf rat."

Morillo heard footsteps approaching from behind, muffled by the thick carpet and he tensed his muscles, waiting for the best time to jump on him as soon as he loosened his handcuffs.

He felt a hand coming from his right towards the arm of the chair, and he prepared to attack, when he felt a cold razor-sharp steel blade leaning on his jugular and pressing so hard on it he feared it could section it.

Morillo froze. He had never seen a knife of such giant dimensions, which he thought it probably was used to hunt bears.

"Yes, I suppose it must be a surprise. I have changed my mind at the last moment. Guns are too sophisticated. In matters of honor, nothing like resorting to the nobility of the classics, of the ancient weapons brandished by our ancestors since the beginning of time. I hope it will not trouble you and that my choice will be to your liking. After all, it's a weapon that several of your friends and acquaintances have already tried, subinspector Morillo," the voice said, getting closer to his ear and pressing the huge knife blade hard against his neck, whose jugular was so swollen by the tension that seemed it could burst spontaneously at any time.

With a click, the handcuffs on his right hand opened and dropped to the floor with a thud, muffled by the carpet. Morillo did not dare move one millimeter from his position.

"I have the gun in my hand again. Back to modern times," the voice said, releasing the big knife's pressure on his neck, and turning away quickly to disappear.

"Read the letter. It's short, it won't take you long. And from there, the choice is only yours. As I said, life only makes sense if we consider it a matter of honor. You always have the last word."

Morillo heard the door closing behind him and spun. He was alone in the room. With his free hand, he tried to free the other wrist, but it was impossible. He stood up and dragged the chair, hopping and approaching the couch, and he soon found his suspicions were true.

The corpses of Gisbert and his prostitute friend watched him, amiably sitting shoulder to shoulder, with a gloomy, empty gaze, yet with a hint of sympathy, as if they smiled at the irony of that insane situation.

He dragged the chair over to the desk and sat before it. With his only free hand, he took the envelope and pulled out the letter, a yellowed paper bearing the letterhead of the Casino. This was proof that his suspicions were not unfounded, that the connection with the Casino was a fact.

His police mind speculated about the options he had before him, assessing probabilities. He was on the right track, and that excited him greatly.

But something stopped him short, a feeling that arose from the depths of his being, and that he placed above any professional activity.

His life was at stake, but above all, that man had threatened Agnes and his family, and now he could not show any weakness, he had to play that game until the end; he was too deep into it to be distracted with other disquisitions.

Without further thought, he unfolded the paper and read the letter.

"Distinguished gentleman,

Brevity is a commendable virtue, which together with honor define an honest person to perfection. Confronting life with integrity and honor is one of the traits that define the human being and differentiate humans from the rest of the animals.

You have a chance to close with dignity the book of your passage through life. In the drawer in front of you, you will find a gun, whose drum houses a single bullet, a single opportunity to abandon with honor this unjust world.

If you squander the bullet and use it to break free and escape, not only will you have wasted your only chance to die honorably but you will condemn all your family members and loved ones to the most atrocious suffering and most ruthless death.

Choose wisely and do not waste your opportunity. Should you choose to abandon life with honor, your family will not suffer any harm, and they will live the rest of their haphazard lives oblivious to your decision, unbeknownst to them the honorable sacrifice with which you will have saved their lives.

May that be your reward, the satisfaction of knowing that your anonymous sacrifice will allow them to live their lives and die of natural causes when their time comes.

You will never leave this room alive. The question is whether you wish to do it quickly and with honor, safeguarding the lives of your loved ones, or you prefer to endure untold sorrow and extend that suffering to your family to share with them the punishment for your lack of honor.

You have the last word, the decision is always yours."

Morillo's tears started falling on the letter, and the fresh ink ran and blurred the words, making them vanish as if all that was nothing but a nightmare from which he would wake up right away.

He tried to get over it and remain hopeful until the end. He put the paper down on the desk, reached out and opened the desk drawers. From one of them, he took out a small gun and checked it housed a single bullet.

He aimed at the lock on the handcuff that held his other hand and thought about shooting and freeing himself. If he did, that man would be waiting outside to finish him, but at least he would have a fighting chance to break through if only with his fists, that so far had been of little service to him.

The two corpses were watching him as impassive

spectators and he turned toward them as if expecting them to nod and tell him how to proceed.

He aimed the gun back at the handcuffs and put his finger on the trigger, applying more pressure as he closed his eyes.

Something made him stop. It was a premonition, or maybe something he had seen but he was not conscious of. He lowered the gun and put it on the desk and he opened again the two drawers, but this time pulling them out completely. One was empty, but inside the other one, he found a small object he pulled out and stroked between his fingers.

It was a small linen handkerchief with embroidery around. He unfolded it slowly and held it to his face, closing his eyes and breathing deeply, as if to wrest all the essence it carried in its fragrance and make it part of him.

With tears in his eyes, he laid the handkerchief on the desktop, smoothed it with a trembling hand, and with tears blurring his vision he read the delicate letters embroidered in one corner, "Agnes."

He knew what that meant. It was both his death sentence and the realization that he had the chance to carry out the ultimate sacrifice, the anonymous exchange of lives that would end his but would protect hers.

Agnes would never know the truth, would never know how much he had loved her, she would never know that if she was alive, it was precisely thanks to that love, that would live forever in her.

Morillo let the tears run until his eyes welled and he could not take it anymore. He took the handkerchief and delicately held it to his eyes and dipped it in his teardrops, which soon invaded the name "Agnes" and spread across the fabric as if they wanted to conquer its entirety.

He took it to his lips and kissed it gently, trying to retain its fragrance, and letting the scent of her skin draw her image before his eyes one last time. Morillo could see her before him, smiling at him with a serenity that conveyed all the peace in the world, and he knew what he had to do. He closed his eyes to see her better, he smiled back at her and his lips silently uttered three words: "I love you".

His hand picked up the gun again and raised it slowly.

It was true, the choice was his and also the last word, and he had already made his decision.

CHAPTER 58

Barcelona. Today.

To Gerard, the police response to his complaint had been as expected, minimal interest and implication in the case. When he tried to contact Lieutenant Botell they always met his requests with the same runarounds and systematically diverted them to lower rank officers.

He learned they had sent a patrol car to explore the Casino ruins, and after much insistence, he found out the name of the officers sent to the scene.

The professionalism conveyed by agent Vehils pleasantly surprised him, when she shook his hand and invited him to sit in a small visiting room at the police station. The fact she was young and beautiful was an added incentive.

"Are you sure you reached the place I told you?" Gerard asked, in a tone suggesting disbelief.

"I don't think there can be another place like that in the whole city. It took me quite a while to find the entrance, and then I walked along the passage until I reached the fork, and once there, I followed the path on the left."

"Exactly. See how I was not lying?" Gerard said, excitedly, giving a gentle tap on the table.

"I never said you were. In fact, although I shouldn't say it, I'm one of the few in here that give some credit to your story," the agent confessed.

"What do you mean? Do you believe I would make up something like that?"

"There was no body inside the cistern, you admitted it yourself."

"But she was there the first time I went in. I wasn't dreaming, I assure you. It was Eva, and she was dead."

"Can you assure me you were not under the influence of any substance that day?" the agent asked, trying not to offend him with her question.

"Apart from a ham sandwich and a latte I had that morning, no."

"You can joke all you want, but without proof, your story doesn't hold, and at present, I am the only person who can or wants to help you."

Gerard took a deep breath and folded his hands on the table.

"Have you searched Eva's house?"

"No family member has reported her disappearance, only you, and you're not even a close relative nor a friend. We have questioned the neighbors of the presumed missing person and they told us she visited them to say goodbye and told them she would be traveling for several weeks and asked them to collect her mail. As you can see, we have little to hold on to," she argued.

"I know you want to help me, and I appreciate it. You're the only one who has shown interest in this case, unlike Lieutenant Botell, who seems more interested in avoiding me than in doing the work for which he gets a salary we all pay as citizens. We are in a free country and I can express my opinion without getting into trouble, right?"

Agent Vehils replied with a slight nod and a shy smile which Gerard immediately interpreted as a sign she could be attracted to him and decided to investigate the matter as soon as she had a chance.

"I'll keep you up to date, but you must have patience and let us do our work, although, given the circumstances, it may take some time until we can declare her as officially missing".

Gerard thanked her for her dedication and left the police station. He could not understand how in an era of great scientific advances, police could not use DNA analysis, or dogs, or any other technique that could confirm Eva's body had been in that tank.

Days went by with no progress in his research for his article. He felt stagnant, not only professionally but also emotionally.

He was convinced the corpses found in the Collserola forests were victims murdered near the Casino or maybe even inside, dropped in the forest to mislead the police.

The question was to find out whether those murders had been only the result of isolated actions committed by simple robbers, or if they were part of an organized plan. If true, that would be the real news, and he would unveil the plot and bring to light whoever pulled the strings.

The Art Nouveau era had been extraordinarily rich culturally and artistically, but extremely turbulent and traumatic politically and socially.

If he could find a link between those killings, and relate them to the Casino and its administrators, he would uncover a plot that might require rewriting the official history.

To uncover it and tell the world about it was too attractive a challenge for Gerard to let it pass.

He was eating breakfast, sitting at the small kitchen table in his tiny apartment when he heard his cell phone vibrating on the wooden surface.

"Yes, who is it?" he said, in a voice so full of morning mucus that not even his own mother would have recognized him.

He could only hear background noises, as if someone was fiddling with the phone. Suddenly, a woman's voice screamed so hard Gerard had to put the phone away from his ear. Although distorted by terror, it was a familiar voice.

"Help, you have to help me. Hurry, come as soon as

possible," the voice shouted, conveying a level of hysteria as contagious as a cold in a crowded mall elevator on Christmas Day.

For a moment Gerard could not believe his ears. That voice screaming in terror was Eva's.

"Eva, is it you? Eva," Gerard shouted.

"Yes, please come and help me. He's gonna kill me," she shouted between sobs.

"How is that possible? I thought you were dead. Where are you? Who are you with? Where are you calling me from?" he said, realizing immediately those were too many questions.

"Calm down and tell me where you are, I'll pick you up right away," Gerard said, trying to convey a calm he was far from feeling.

"I don't know where I am, but I think I must be close to the place where we parted. I'm in a room, with no windows."

"Calm down. What can you remember? How did you get there?" Gerard asked, overlooking the fact he was sure he had seen her dead body in the tank. Now the priority was to find her, there would be time to speculate with what might have happened.

"They beat me. I don't know how I got here or through where we reached this place, but I heard them talking about an access through the tunnels. There must be some entrance we did not explore, or that we overlooked. Please, come and get me," she said, and her breathing choked with her tears.

"Relax. I'll go get you right now. Are you hurt?"

"I have cuts and bruises, and I have a terrible headache, but I think no vital pieces are lacking."

Eva still kept a sense of humor, that was a good sign.

"Are they watching you? Can you escape that room or give me a more concrete reference, any detail you remember?"

"No, they locked me up here and I cannot break down the door. It's the only entrance. I think I remember that, on

326

the way here, I heard water, like a pool or a pond," she said immediately.

"I'll go to seek help and we'll find the access, I promise."

"Please hurry. They'll be back to get me and take me to another place, I'm sure they'll kill me," and Eva squealed as the conversation ended abruptly and the communication interrupted.

Gerard called her mobile phone several times but got no answer. He wondered which phone could she be calling from, but he would find a solution to that enigma later.

He had to do something quickly, and he knew involving the police would not be the smartest thing, although nothing would have pleased him more than to disembark in the ruins with a team of fifty agents and comb the area until they could find the hideout and put an end to that nightmare once and for all.

Where could that room be? He had no reliable data, nothing to let him know where to start looking.

If he did it alone, he would waste precious time perhaps he did not have. He would have to bring in reinforcements but did not dare to call agent Vehils. He would have to settle for Max.

"I see you haven't learned your lesson with our recent experiences in that damn place, have you? And now you want us to play ghostbusters and go back there to look for a ghostly apparition, a woman who appears and vanishes with the same ease as the positive balance in my bank account," Max said, as they drove to the Casino area.

"Basically, yes. She says they locked her in a windowless room, perhaps a basement in one of the nearby houses. There may be an access through one of the roller coaster tunnels in the old amusement park. The question is finding out which is the one we are looking for."

"Have you considered we're probably facing dangerous professional killers who must be armed, and that we just have our fists as our only defense?" Max said.

"I carry a tool kit in the trunk of the car."

"Oh, what a great relief, I feel much better already," Max said.

"What I don't understand is how could she phone me. Where was she? How is it possible they didn't take her mobile phone? Perhaps she hid it," Gerard wondered.

"We have more worrying matters at this precise moment, like for instance, what are the police going to say when they discover we are once again snooping around in the ruins when they expressly forbade us to go back there."

"We'll deal with that when the time comes. Now let's focus on thinking about the problem at hand. I think there are only three of the old roller coaster tunnels left standing. We already searched two of them on foot and they were empty, I don't remember seeing there any passageway or fork. But there was a third one we did not search because it was bricked up," Gerard said.

"We cannot be sure she referred to the roller coaster tunnels, there could be more hidden tunnels, such as the one we found by the tree. There may be a network of hidden underground passages, it can be a fucking giant anthill," Max said.

"True, but we have to start somewhere. It would take us too long searching for new accesses buried underground; it took us forever to find the one we found, and it was almost by chance. We only have two options, either we continue exploring the tunnel next to the cistern, or we explore the only roller coaster tunnel we haven't explored yet, the one with the bricked-up entrance," Gerard said.

"Do we divide the work or we do it together?" Max asked. "I'd bet my money on exploring the roller coaster tunnel. If we ran into trouble, two are always better than one, but we must work very hard to open a hole in the wall blocking the entrance to the tunnel. I have a question, will we do it with our bare hands, or with our teeth?"

"No problem. I keep a sledgehammer in my toolbox in the trunk of my car," Gerard said.

CHAPTER 59

"Is this what you call a sledgehammer?" Max said, lifting a tiny hammer by its narrow handle, similar to the one used by the shoemaking elves on the Hans Christian Andersen tale.

"The strength has to come from your arm, not from the hammer. The secret is in the technique," Gerard said, closing the trunk of the car and starting to walk along the road ditch toward the entrance to the Casino ruins.

"Do you think your sister will resist the temptation to read the letter?" Max said.

"I wouldn't hold my breath. My sister is more gossipy than you, and we're talking Olympic category gossip here, but I didn't have time to think of anyone better."

Before leaving home, Gerard had written a note to agent Vehils, telling her about Eva's call, where they were heading, and enclosing a copy of an old blueprint of the Casino grounds.

He marked the point where he believed the entrance to the passages could be, based on Eva's words and his own previous exploration of that area. He also apologized to her for not having involved the police earlier and asked her to come to the scene to rescue them, or to pick up whatever could be left of them.

That morning Gerard left the note in a sealed envelope on his kitchen table. From his car, he called his sister Pilar to ask her to pick up the letter and take it to agent Vehils only if they did not return home within twenty-four hours.

His sister asked a million questions, Gerard had to stop, arguing it was a confidential journalistic investigation.

"This will be the first time you come to this place and don't go by the old tower to visit your friend the tramp," Max joked, seeing Gerard took a path in the opposite direction of the Casino ruins.

"I've already had enough, I leave that pleasure to you because you're a little masochistic," he said, as he descended through the forest.

After hesitating and retracing their steps a few times, they finally reached their destination at the bottom of the valley, stopping in front of the bricked-up entrance to what had once been one of the roller coaster tunnels.

Gerard kicked the bottom of the wall with the tip of his boot to check its solidity.

"It shouldn't be too thick. It sounds relatively hollow. Let's hope they didn't build a double wall and there's only one row of bricks," Gerard said, opening the small backpack he carried on his shoulder.

"Do you intend to tear down the wall with that toy hammer, or are you going to blow like the wolf in the three little pigs' tale?" Max joked, seeing him approach the wall holding the small hammer.

"If you want to try it yourself head-butting, maybe we will finish earlier," Gerard said, putting a mark on the brick and starting to hit it.

"The key is to concentrate all the blow strength in a very specific point, to work our way through the brick."

Max turned and disappeared into the forest, while Gerard kept hitting the brick patiently.

A few minutes later, Max stood beside him, holding a huge rock in his arms.

"Step aside, please, or I'm gonna drop it," Max said, taking two steps backward to gain momentum and running to the wall like an Olympic weight thrower, throwing the rock against the brick wall, approximately on the mark which Gerard had been hitting at.

He repeated the same procedure twice, and took several staggering steps and fell on the ground, stretched on his back, very dizzy.

Gerard approached him.

"How are you? Are you hurt?"

"No, but the whole forest is spinning. Stop it, please, before the trees fall over me," Max said, probably watching a private screening of planets and constellations orbiting around his head. Gerard smiled and sat on the ground, waiting for his friend to recover.

"Look, you made a hole," Gerard said, noting the last hit had opened a large hole in the wall, exposing the deep darkness of an opening behind which a more than likely death could await them.

"I had to come and finish the job, otherwise we would have been here until next week if you kept using that ridiculous hammer," Max said, sitting up and smiling contentedly.

"Keep in mind who marked the hole for you and who started the job. You just did the easy part," Gerard said, walking over there and kicking the exposed bricks to make a bigger and more practicable opening.

The smell coming from inside was intense, a mixture of moisture, mild, and the indescribable scent of the unknown, the fragrance of terror.

"Max, did you bring the flashlights?"

Max reached into his pockets and showed him a small flashlight with a manual crank to charge an alternator and generate light for a few minutes.

"Where did you get this?" Gerard asked, taking it in his hands and turning the loud crank.

"I had them in the kitchen. They're very useful and don't need batteries, so we'll always have light, they never ran out," Max said, taking another identical unit out of his backpack.

"I hope we don't have to hide and be silent because with this, they'll hear us coming from at least three kilometers away," Gerard said, turning the crank to turn his flashlight on and starting to walk.

The tunnel was over two meters high, and its vault still showed the remains of the power lines that had once lit the way. It stretched for a few meters in a straight line but soon veered to the left drawing a smooth curve.

"They used this tunnel as a warehouse and cellar after the war, who knows what we may find here," Gerard said.

"Nobody ever leaves anything of value within reach, it's an immutable law of human nature. Do you expect to find the hidden Nazi gold?" Max said.

"What about those boxes?" Gerard said, pointing to some dusty wooden boxes piled up against the wall.

"Maybe this is the cave of Ali Baba and the Forty Thieves after all," Max said, running toward the boxes, covered by a canvas whose color was impossible to guess.

Gerard came closer and lifted the canvas, raising a dust cloud through which he saw two masses fall at his feet, the dried-out bodies of two large rats he kicked away.

"Good kick. Look, not even rats can survive in this place, and they eventually turn into mummies. We won't find anything here," Max said.

The boxes contained construction materials, old sacks of petrified cement that had solidified many years ago, and cobblestones like the ones used in the city streets. Gerard wondered what would they want those materials for, and why did they abandon them inside a closed tunnel.

They kept going, following the weak beam of their famished flashlights, with the musical accompaniment of the sound of the cranks turning every few minutes to recharge the batteries. They soon reached the end of the tunnel, also bricked up similarly to that in the entrance.

"End of the road and false alarm. This is not the tunnel we were looking for. Do you know of any other?" Max asked, seeing the look of frustration on Gerard's face.

"No, this was the last one. There may be more, but their entry must be buried. Finding them will take precious time and we don't have it, and there's no guarantee they exist at all. Eva will die if we don't get to her soon," Gerard said, clearly dejected.

"Maybe we should tear down this brick wall and see where the tunnel leads," Max suggested.

"No, they only built these tunnels for the roller coaster, they're always short and I'm sure it leads into the mountain. It's not worth it," Gerard said, pointing his finger at the roller coaster route on the photocopy of the old amusements' blueprint.

The tunnel was as empty as his head was lacking in ideas, and they were running out of time.

CHAPTER 60

"I don't know what to tell you. You're the one who has investigated these issues. I've run out of ideas," Max said, as soon as they stepped outside.

Gerard was reviewing in his head all the information and data that he had accumulated about the Casino and its surroundings and unceasingly went over his conversation with Eva. If he wanted to see her alive, he had to find some clue as soon as possible.

"Maybe we should call your police friend," Max suggested.

"We have no time, and I'm not looking forward to giving again so many explanations as they will want us to. Eva said she was in a windowless room, probably in the basement in some old mansions that still remain in these mountains," Gerard said, thinking aloud.

"We cannot show up in all the houses in the area and cheerfully ask them to inspect their basements. It pains me to say it, but I think this time this is a job for the police," Max insisted.

"I never thought there would come a day when I would hear you talking like that," Gerard said to his friend. "It must be age."

"Eva told you she heard water, as in a pond or something, right?" Max said.

"Yes, but there is nothing in this area. Near the Casino tower, there's the large water cistern where I appeared after my first encounter with the damn hermit and his dog, but that cistern has been in disuse since the Casino closed, and it was drier than you."

Max ran his hands around his waist, sucking in his belly and holding his breath.

"A hundred years ago there was an artificial lake in the esplanade, where the little Water Chute boats landed, but it shouldn't have been more than half a meter deep, and it was outdoors. There is nothing left, only the concrete base forming the bottom of the lake, covered with soil and grass," Gerard said.

"And in this area, there are no rivers, nor lakes, nor streams, only small fountains and picnic areas for hikers," Max said.

"There must be something we're overlooking," Gerard said.

"Haven't you found anything in all those books you've read about the Casino? Nothing we can use? Not even in the suicide letter?" Max asked.

Gerard took a small notebook out of his backpack and the pages flew quickly through his fingers. He ran through all his notes on the interviews he had done to former Casino workers, trying to find the spark that would ignite the flame.

"*To Hell you must get through water, for it is the fountain of all evil. The black lady guards the entrance,*" Gerard recited several times, slowly, as if savoring every word would allow him to assimilate its secrets.

"What is that, a saying your grandfather told you?"

"Those were Agustín's last words. That old bellboy knew something, and he was trying to tell us. He uttered that phrase as his last riddle before he died."

Between the pages of his notebook, he kept the paper with the drawings Agustín had left him. The house, the mythological animal, the faucet and the water. There was the water, a water sprout; it could not be a coincidence.

Max took the paper to examine the drawings, and as he was holding it, something caught Gerard's attention, and he took it from him and put it before his eyes.

"Max, turn the crank and charge your flashlight to the max."

335

"I don't know what this is about. They barely light up anything when we're in the dark, but here in full sunlight, you tell me," Max said, very surprised, but he obeyed.

"Point it at the paper from behind, right here, come as close as you can," Gerard said, pointing at one of the bottom corners of the paper.

Max shone the flashlight over that point, while Gerard got close to the paper until he almost touched it with his nose.

"It seems there was a drawing, and they erased it, but I can still distinguish traces of it," Gerard said.

"What do you see?"

"It's kind of a letter M, but it's embossed, it has volume. I don't know what it means."

"Maybe it was a draft of what your friend the bellboy would draw next. Many people doodle when they are bored, but it actually has no meaning," Max said, trying to be the voice of reason.

"Yes, but this is too well done to be a doodle, is a very thick letter M, it almost looks like a crown," Gerard said, not looking away from the sheet of paper.

"It may be the initial of a name, Mariano, Miguel, Matías, who knows."

"The answer must be in the water. Agustín mentioned it, it also appears in his drawings, and Eva heard water when they kidnapped her, it cannot be a coincidence."

Several minutes of respectful silence went by, in which the two partners refrained from saying anything that could interrupt the thread of each other's thoughts. Each of them waited for the other to be the first to open his mouth to launch a theory or to suggest what the next step should be.

Gerard broke the ice swatting his backpack while he put all the papers inside and ran down the mountain.

"Follow me. I have a hunch," he shouted to Max, without turning, jumping over fallen tree trunks. He headed toward a wet area where there were no pine trees but trees with a smooth, straight, whitish trunk, typically found on riverbeds and marshes.

Gerard didn't remember having been there before. The vegetation was thick, and the plants broad-leafed and abundant, as if they were better fed. Gloom dominated the atmosphere, because sunlight had to sweat to reach the bottom of the valley through so many green hands standing in its way.

"It seems as if we were in a different forest, almost in another country," Max said, noting the big change in the environment.

"Yes, here it is much more humid. Look at the trees, the plants, the flora we see, they're all different species from those in the upper valley. They have adapted to moisture and water. It's a sign. There must be groundwater, maybe even underground rivers somewhere," Gerard said, with great excitement.

Max was running in circles through the area and suddenly stopped before a big clump of bushes and disappeared inside.

"Gerard, come see this" he shouted, a few seconds later.

It amazed Gerard to see Max standing on a cobblestone floor and next to a railing made of large concrete blocks in the form of stylized hourglasses.

Max cleared the way, tearing branches with hands and feet, and without a word, the two strolled along the narrow causeway that lay at their feet, hidden under thick layers of grass and dirt.

The causeway ran along the true bottom of the valley, describing a gentle curve to the left, limiting on one side with the forest and on the other with a rock wall that they could barely glimpse through the thick tangle of branches, roots, vines and moss growing over it, covering it almost entirely, like a second skin.

Thirty meters later, the causeway widened, in a space reminiscent of a small round square. Among the lush vegetation covering the floor, they discovered a stone structure that stood out in the center of the circle. It was a round stone table, surrounded by a circular bank also carved out of dark stone, partially destroyed.

"This is a damn picnic table," Max said, almost indignantly.

"So it seems. What's wrong with you?"

"It's disappointing. I was hoping to find something a little more mysterious, a magical object or a temple built by an ancient civilization, and not a damn conventional picnic table, for the love of God," Max shouted, raising his arms to the heavens.

Gerard smiled and examined the stone table closely.

"The table is a slab of stone on a cracked concrete base. They build the bank the same way," Gerard noted, and walked away from the table heading for the rock wall. He pushed aside the branches and foliage covering the surface to reach the rock layer. He picked up a stone and hit the wall. Then he took out a small knife and scratched the rock surface.

"It's the same material the table is made of. This wall is manmade," Gerard said, with a triumphant smile, pocketing the knife.

"So what? That means we're not in the middle of the woods but in a bloody Hollywood movie set. Personally, I don't care if the wall is faker and more artificial than a mortadella. How is that going to help us?" Max said, with his usual spontaneity.

"Maybe it won't, but at least we know this area probably fell within the Casino grounds. Help me check out something" Gerard said, beckoning Max to help him clear branches and shrubs and a good part of the rock wall.

"I don't know what you intend with this gardening exercise but, how much longer do we need to be here cutting down half the forest with our own hands?" Max asked after a while.

"We're almost done, let's make sure we clear the top part a little more," Gerard said, climbing over a tree trunk from which he kept pulling branches as if searching for a treasure.

Gerard jumped to the ground and walked a few meters away from the wall area they had cleared.

"Max, what do you see from here?" Gerard asked him, fearing his answer. Max joined him and stared at the wall in its entirety.

"I don't know. If you expect from me an art critique or an expert naturalist opinion, you can sit around waiting... on that picnic table over there. Other than a concrete wall, I see nothing more, nor do I see what relationship it can have with what we're looking for," Max said, snorting.

Gerard approached the wall and ran his hand over its surface.

"They made this wall with cement, molding these forms on top of the mountain rock base underneath. It's very darkened by the passage of time and moisture, but we can still see the effect they intended to achieve, look."

Max was watching but did not follow him.

"Do you see those vertical undulations, like the folds of a hanging curtain?"

Max nodded.

"Don't they remind you of something, or better yet, of a very typical place in the Catalan geography? It's a rather poor imitation, I have to admit, but I'm sure I'm right," Gerard said.

Max reaffirmed his ignorance gesturing with his hands and head.

"Those undulations try to represent the mountain of Montserrat," Gerard said, as excited as if he were revealing the mystery of the origin of life to a group of students.

The mountain of Montserrat was one of the main tourist destinations in the region. A unique mountain in the world, with rock formations eroded by the elements over millions of years, which had carved peculiar shapes that recalled the jagged edge of a saw. In one of its rocky walls, there was an ancient monastery that was one of the main spiritual centers of Catholicism.

"I remember reading that within the Casino grounds there were several walk areas. This must have been one of the Casino playgrounds and they built paved causeways like this for guests to wander through the forest, which was not as dense as it is now."

"Now that you mention it, I do see some resemblance, but even I could have done it with a little more grace," Max said, in a display of sincerity.

Gerard continued with his reasoning. "In those recreational areas, there used to be natural mineral water springs where people could drink straight out of the rock. There has to be one close by."

"I don't follow you one hundred percent," Max said, while Gerard frowned. "Maybe not even fifty percent, or maybe even less."

"Think about what Agustín drew. The embossed M. It was not an M, it was a symbolic representation of the mountain of Montserrat, with its peaks that seem bitten by teeth. He was leading us to this place," Gerard said, trying to convince him.

"I don't know, it's a possible interpretation, but the evidence is a little weak," Max said, shaking his head.

"It's not just the drawing of the mountain, he also drew a fountain and running water, and if we look for it, I bet it must be around here. And not only that, remember what he told me."

"To Hell you must get through water, for it is the fountain of all evil. The black lady guards the entrance," Max recited. "I have a good memory."

"Exactly. He spoke of water, the same water Eva heard. Agustín even mentioned the fountain. The fountain must be the key," Gerard said.

"I'm only interested in the part where he said it was the source of all evil, don't you forget that detail. I have no interest in entering the fountains of the underworld, I assure you. And who is that black lady who he says is guarding the entrance? I don't see any Caribbean mulata standing guard around these parts," Max said.

While Max spoke, Gerard ran along the stone wall, putting his hands through the thick vegetation covering it.

"There's something here. Come."

Gerard bent down and pushed away a thick bush of reeds that covered a hole less than a meter high at the bottom of the rock wall. From inside the hole, a trickle of water flowed into a small stream, almost invisible behind the vegetation.

"Oh, it's amazing, you found a hole and a half-dry fountain. So what does that explain?" Max said, sarcastically.

Gerard placed one foot on either side of the stream and pushed away the thick branches, clearing the upper part of the hole. He turned to Max with a broad smile.

"Max, meet the black lady, the guardian of the entrance," Gerard said, pointing to a small statuette carved in stone, positioned over the opening of the fountain. The image represented the famous Virgin of the mountain of Montserrat, popularly known as the "Moreneta (Black Madonna)," for the statue was totally black.

Max scratched his head, unable to believe what he was seeing.

"It seems as if you staged it all to impress me with your conclusions," Max said, in amazement.

"However, everything fits, the references to water, the drawing of Montserrat, the comment about the black Virgin. This has to be the place," Gerard said excitedly.

Max kept scratching his head.

"I have to admit it makes a lot of sense, but the only thing it proves is that the old bellboy had run around these woods as a child when he worked in the Casino and that he knew this place well. I still don't understand how we will find your girlfriend. This is a picnic area and all I see is a fountain."

Gerard bent down to inspect the opening where the creek flowed, and pushed away all the plants, clearing it completely. The opening was a natural spring that flowed out of a water mine, a crack in the rock through which mountain groundwater made it out to the surface, creating springs that hikers and weekenders enjoyed.

Gerard got into the creek. The flowing water barely covered the sole of his boot, and he bent to enter the opening and try to go up the creek bed.

"Are you going to get in there? There's barely any room," Max said, watching him disappear inside. Gerard turned to him.

"These springs are natural caves. The only artificial part is the exterior. They usually channeled the last few meters of the creek bed and built a small fountain in cement or stone for the public to have easy access to the water. If one walks up the mine river bed you soon get to the natural part, which is usually a crack or a cave, and sometimes there can even be enormous natural wells inside. Let's see how far we can go up this one," Gerard said, disappearing inside.

Max had no choice. He gave several vigorous turns at the crank of his flashlight and prepared to follow in his friend's footsteps.

CHAPTER 61

The passage was very narrow and just over a meter high. They were walking through the water and noticed the ceiling level was going down slowly. The rock projections and sharp edges on the walls sparkled like knives to the light of the flashlights.

"Didn't Agustín say this was the entrance to Hell or something? What was he referring to?" Max exclaimed.

"Those are the exaggerations of an old man with a penchant for the theatrical. Ignore them," Gerard said.

They reached a point where the spring bed deepened.

"Judging by the trickle that flows outside, I didn't think there could be so much water in here," Gerard said, getting in and noting the water reached up to his waist.

"At least our heads will not touch the ceiling and we can walk upright," Max said with relief.

"Let's be careful because we can hardly see anything and there could be hidden underwater wells," Gerard said, pointing his flashlight toward the bottom, but not even the light dared to go through those dark and cold waters.

"The rock wall is dark and I can't see the bottom. It's as if the water were black," Max shouted.

Gerard had stopped and pointed his flashlight toward the end of the passage, a gigantic digestive tract that was swallowing them and seemed to stretch for kilometers.

"I can only see rock walls, water, and darkness. How far do you think we have walked?" Gerard asked.

"Since you had the bright idea to visit these caves, maybe one kilometer, maybe a little less. We've been here stuck in this icy water for the last forty minutes, and my ass is so wet and cold I'll be shitting ice cubes for a week," Max said.

Gerard knew his friend's strength was far superior to what his little patience seemed to suggest, but still, they couldn't go on much longer into the water. There had to be some alternative path in that place, and he set out to find it before giving up and having to return.

"Let's walk for ten more minutes and find a place to get out of the water," he suggested to Max, who replied with an affirmative grunt.

They walked for over twenty minutes until they reached a bend where the rock walls widened and formed natural ledges on which to rest, and they climbed freehand and got out of the water. The river formed a wide haven, and it seemed to be deeper in that area.

"Finally, a break. My legs hurt from so many blows against the underwater rocks and my hand hurts even more from so much turning the damn crank," Max protested.

"It is you who brought these flashlights, probably wanting to save money on batteries," Gerard said.

"And why have you chosen this place to stop What's so special about it? I think you're crazy for dragging me in the darkness into the bowels of the earth, with the water above my navel, and for what? We must be several kilometers underground, with tons of rocks above us and who knows what creatures or monsters may lurk beneath these waters."

Max seemed to be relieved after his last rant, and Gerard waited a few minutes to reply.

"I know we're in the right place, but I thought we would find a diversion or some other passage, but this seems to be an endless crack, with walls of solid rock. Maybe you're right and we should go back," Gerard said, pointing the light to his friend's face, to check his expression.

"I agree with you. This could go on for kilometers and maybe we would end up reaching the source of the Nile. It's better to return. We must be the first humans who have made it this far, but this is nothing more than a giant crack straight to Hell. The old man was right after all."

Gerard stood up and Max was ready to follow him into the water, happy to return, but he stood still when he saw Gerard jumping to the other side of the river bed to approach a rock ledge above his head.

"What the hell is going on? Aren't we leaving?"

Gerard brought his flashlight close to the edge of the overhang from which a rock fragment had broken off, exposing a lighter-colored rock underneath.

"It seems worn, this edge is not as sharp as the rest of the rocks on the wall, don't you think?" Gerard asked.

Max watched him from afar, with little interest.

"I can't even see your hand from here, much less the rim."

Gerard was on his tiptoes, and he reached out until his hand felt the surface of the small ledge and he gave a shout that echoed through the passage as if there were forty more people with them.

"What?" Max said, also standing.

"I don't think we're the first humans to get here, after all. Look what I found," Gerard said, showing him a dazzling red metallic object.

Max turned his flashlight to the other bank where Gerard held between his fingers a modern climbing carabineer anchored to the rock wall using a metal ring hidden above the rock ledge.

"Yes, I really don't think they found many of these in the Altamira caves," Max said. It was his peculiar way of admitting Gerard was right.

"Let me see it," Max said, and jumped to the river bank where Gerard was, but his foot slipped on the wet surface and he fell into the water, hitting his leg against the rock edge. Gerard crouched but couldn't catch him on time.

The river depth at the backwater was nearly a meter and a half. Gerard walked to the edge and shone his flashlight on Max, who had underwater for a few seconds and now splashed on the surface. When he saw he was all right he reached out to help him climb the rock, but Max refused.

"Are you OK?"

"I'm cold, hungry, and I think I must have opened a hole in my knee which can drain all the blood in my body and feed the wild piranhas that must infest these waters," he said.

Gerard was relieved to see his friend had returned to normal.

"Gerard, did you know that these fabulous high tech flashlights I brought, work underwater?"

The question surprised Gerard, who answered with a shrug.

"Let me have yours, please," Max said.

"What happened to yours?"

"It's at the bottom of the river."

"If I give it to you, we'll be in the dark, we won't be able to get out of here without light," Gerard said, with growing concern.

"Do you trust me?"

"I know I'll regret for a very long time what I'm going to say, but yes, I trust you," Gerard replied, reaching out and handing him his flashlight.

From inside the water, Max took it in his hands, turned hard the crank to get a powerful light beam, and disappeared underwater.

The cave plunged into total darkness. That nutcase had ruined their only two flashlights putting them underwater and getting out of there in the dark would be an ordeal.

Gerard waited for what felt like several minutes. Something had happened to Max, and he was about to jump into the water when he thought he saw a faint glow on the river bottom.

He leaned over and saw two light beams dancing and refracting underwater in all directions. Max's smiling face appeared next, and he blinded him shining the two flashlights on his face.

"I can see they do work underwater, but put them away from my face, I can't see a thing," Gerard said.

"So far, they're holding on."

"I thought you were not coming up, I was about to jump in to get you. Since when can you hold your breath underwater for so long?" Gerard asked.

346

"If I told you I can stay underwater longer than Houdini in his Chinese Water Torture Cell, I would be lying. But just as he did, the key is knowing how to control your vitals."

Gerard didn't see where Max was going with what. "I fear the worst," he thought.

"If you want to know how I do it, follow me," and he plunged again, disappearing underwater, but keeping one flashlight pointing toward the surface.

Gerard did not hesitate and jumped into the water, took a deep breath and plunged following the light beam, dancing and scurrying like a fish in front of him.

CHAPTER 62

Gerard dove and reached the bottom of the backwater, covered by a thin layer of dark sand and stones, following Max's flashlight, appearing and disappearing like a lunar eclipse, hidden behind his huge body mass.

Suddenly the light, and Max's silhouette, disappeared. Darkness was complete, and Gerard lost track of space and didn't know what was up or down. He left his body still, to float and figure out which way the surface was, when he saw a faint light beam under a rock ledge.

He would soon have to come out to breathe, but still had energy left to give two strokes and dive to the sandy bottom and look under the ledge.

Under the rock, there was a passage, beyond which he sensed Max's blurred face and the light from his flashlights showing him the way.

In the movies, the protagonists dived into the sea wearing no glasses and had no problem performing all kinds of underwater activities. There he was, diving without glasses in crystalline waters, and he saw everything as blurry as if he was drunk.

With his lungs about to burst, like two tires facing a nail on the road, he opened his mouth as soon as he felt his head was above water. He couldn't see anything, but he appreciated the cold, moist air from the cavern more than finding a soda fountain in the middle of the desert. He breathed deeply several times and when he recovered he looked around.

Max floated beside him, holding their flashlights underwater. He raised his hands and handed him one.

"Look around. What do you think of my discovery? I think I should name the place, as the ancient conquerors did upon reaching uncharted territory," Max said, bursting with pride.

"I'm sorry to disappoint you, but I think someone beat you. Have you forgotten the climbing equipment we have found outside?" Gerard said.

"It's possible they stopped there, and no one has ever discovered this place," Max insisted.

Gerard did not answer. He was fruitlessly trying to get his flashlight to reach beyond two meters, but he only saw darkness at the end of the white light wand.

"We're in a giant cave, I can't even see the ceiling," Max said, pointing his flashlight upward. "This is a true lake. Who knows how far it will go," he said, swimming toward the wall.

"With these flashlights, we won't get very far; besides, swimming and turning the crank at the same time is quite impractical. Since we cannot see where the other shore is, it's better if we follow the contour of the wall," Gerard suggested, moving forward holding on to the rock.

The water was freezing, and both wanted to get out as soon as possible, but no one dared to be the first to suggest it.

Gerard saw a large rock, to which he climbed freehand. Sitting on top of the rock, their bodies recovered some temperature, and they kept walking, jumping from rock to rock, without getting back into the water.

"There might be another way out on this side," Gerard said, trying to be positive.

"Yes, if we finally find a way out, I bet you we will be so far away we'll hear people talking at least in German, or perhaps even in Russian," Max said.

Twenty minutes later they were still lingering over the rocks, occasionally jumping into the water to overcome an obstacle they couldn't go through.

Gerard stopped and lit a spot on the wall in front of them.

"It may be nothing, but I'd say there's a passage there, or at least that's what it seems," Gerard said, climbing up the wall.

It was a natural crevice, like the crack they had followed when entering the mine.

"Look at those marks," Gerard said, pointing to some spots in the rock that seemed to have been rounded with a tool.

"There goes my dream of giving my name to an unexplored lake."

"Yes, it seems someone has widened the passage in those places," Gerard said, reaching the crack and starting down the passage.

"The truth is, I was already tiring of so much water, I'm glad to return to the mainland," Max said, following closely behind.

The passage gained height as they made progress and soon they could stand up and move faster.

After a sharp curve, the passage formed a space where three new narrow passages started.

"Here we go again. Either we split up, or we have to choose one way," Max said.

"We should split up to cover more ground, but under the present circumstances, maybe it's better to stay together," Gerard suggested.

"In other words, you're scared shitless," Max said.

"If this leads to where Eva is being held, it's more than likely we'll be in danger, or we go straight into a trap. There is strength in numbers," Gerard said.

"But there's only two of us. That's some strength and some number. Anyway, I agree. Which of the three paths do we take?"

"Let's try the widest one," Gerard said.

Max walked in front and led the way. The passage was tortuous and very irregular, and after walking for ten minutes they reached a point where it narrowed so much it was impossible to continue. Max reached into the narrow crack and lit the rest of the passage, which continued beyond the narrowing.

"There is no way to pass."

"Let's go back and try another one," Gerard said.

The second passage was wider and soon it ceased to be a crack in a natural cave to become a real tunnel dug into the rock.

"It seems as if we were inside an old mine, but I don't remember having heard of any so close to the city," Max said.

"Barcelona was founded long before the Romans arrived, there were already Iberian and Phoenician settlements, and from many other tribes. But this looks like a mine of recent construction. Look at this," Gerard said, pointing to a pipe in which they had used segments of metal tube, darkened over the years.

Max halted and pointed his finger to the top of the wall.

"A light bulb," he shouted, as excited as if he had discovered a gold vein among the rocks.

"We're close. We must exercise extreme caution," Gerard said, motioning for him to lower his voice.

From there they walked in silence. The light bulbs were spaced every ten meters, but they found no control panel to activate them. The floor was no longer natural rock, but it was covered by a thin cement layer, badly damaged by the passage of time.

They reached a long straight section, which stretched beyond the point where the light of their famished flashlights died. On both sides, they could see several doors, some dark wood, others metallic with rivets.

They walked in complete silence until they reached the first door and stood before it. Gerard put his ear to the wood and listened intently. He could hear nothing inside. He put his hand on the doorknob and turned it softly, but it didn't move. It was closed.

With a gesture, he told Max to keep going, and they tried all the doors, distributing them between the two, to check if they could hear movement inside. To avoid making noise when operating the crank flashlights, they hid them inside their clothes.

They had almost reached the end of the corridor when Gerard motioned for Max to come to his door, a solid dark wood piece covered by a thick layer of varnish.

He didn't hear any noise inside, but the doorknob could turn. It was open.

CHAPTER 63

They turned the flashlights off to preserve their last lighting reserves. Gerard spoke into Max's ear and they agreed it was best to go in blasting and once inside turn the flashlights on at the same time.

In complete darkness, Gerard tapped three times on Max's shoulder in a somewhat rudimentary countdown, but the plan worked.

The door opened more easily than Gerard had expected, which proved it had been used frequently. They entered at once, getting in each other's way and it took them a few precious seconds to activate the switch on their flashlights.

Their entrance was so clumsy Gerard knew there could be no murderers lurking, otherwise they would have had so much time to shoot them at will, they could have turned them into walking strainers.

"Shit, mine will not switch on," he heard Max say.

Gerard lit his friend so he could push the small plastic switch and once he succeeded, they both did a rushed sweep of the room.

It was a small room, dug directly into the rock, like the rest of the passage. The floor was uneven and the first thing they saw was a big rusty metal can, filled with water halfway up.

The second impression they received was olfactory. The room presented its visitors with a unique blend of pestilential effluvia, a musty smell with a strong aroma of urine and feces, mixed with something indescribable but equally repulsive.

The human body can adapt to virtually any environment, but until their pituitaries were used to that stench, a few endless seconds elapsed.

When their nasal cavities seemed to recover from the impact suffered, the third impression they received went straight to the nerve center of their bodies, the heart, which was on the verge of stopping when they pointed their flashlights toward the opposite wall.

A great rock wall towered away into the heights, and from its central part, two thick iron rings arose, deeply anchored into the bowels of the rock. From there, two huge rusty chains hung, whose links must have been part of the anchor of the Titanic.

At the end of those chains a human body dangled, in a state of semi-decay, but given the poor lighting and its pitiful condition, it was hard to guess who could it be.

It was a man's body, hanging from chains attached to the wrists, just skin and bones. They knew for sure because his skeletal arms were skinned and his bones were visible in several places.

A layer of rags, dried blood, and dirt covered his chest, but upon close inspection, they could see the rock wall through the body, and it was not due to the transparency of his flesh but to the fact there was a huge hole in the place previously occupied by his lungs.

They were not in a room; it was a cell in the style of the dungeons in the great classic stories. If at that moment the Count of Monte Cristo himself had shown up preparing his escape, they wouldn't have been the least surprised.

Gerard wondered if he had finally found the suicide room, that horrible legendary place in which so many lives ended. However, the situation in which they had found that poor devil didn't exactly lead them to think in a voluntary death. That was only a mere dungeon.

Max examined the body closely and with the tip of his flashlight, he lifted the head of the deceased to see his face.

"Oh my God, I know who this guy is," Gerard said.

Max turned to him, but the corpse's head swung back and fell off the body, banging on the rock and falling on the floor, where it rolled up to Gerard's feet, making him jump back.

"It seems he has also recognized you and wants to be with you," Max said.

"It's the tramp I met in the tower, the one who attacked me, the owner of the dog," Gerard said.

"Are you sure? I think in the condition he's in, he could even resemble my aunt Margaret."

Gerard moved the corpse's head with the toe of his boot and pointed his flashlight in its direction.

"No doubt about it, I assure you. It's him."

"Well, it doesn't seem it was he who was behind all this, after all."

"No, it does not. Look how vicious they were with him, how they mutilated his body; it seems they ripped his guts," Gerard said, pointing to the remains hanging from the chains.

"I wonder if they did it when he was alive or they only mutilated the corpse," Gerard added.

"It's the difference between pure torture and pathological perversion. I don't know which of the two I would choose if given the option."

"Hopefully we won't see ourselves in the same dilemma. We have to get out of here and keep looking, although this was the last door left for us to check," Gerard said.

"Yes, but the other doors are locked. Your friend could be behind any of them. We cannot knock them all down. In fact, we cannot tear down any, we don't have tools, we have no weapons, we have almost no lighting. That's not the way to go," Max said.

"I suggest we continue exploring this tunnel and see where it leads. We may find more doors or get to the surface".

The rumble of the wooden door closing behind them made them turn in unison. They pointed their harmless flashlights to the door as if they had drawn their Colts in OK Corral. Apparently, the thick wooden door had closed by itself.

They looked at each other without uttering a word. There were no air currents there that could explain that, and they knew what it meant. The door closed from the inside out, so someone had to have approached while they were facing the body and closed the door from the outside. They were not alone, and they had been discovered.

They crept closer to the door and stepped aside, fearing there might be someone hiding behind it. Gerard motioned for Max to wait and gently grabbed the doorknob, turning it slowly.

To his surprise, the door was unlocked and opened smoothly. They waited a few seconds, but silence was all they heard, so they peeked out cautiously.

The passage was empty, there was no one in sight, so they stood outside the door, pointing their flashlights in all directions and recharging them by turning the cranks as if possessed.

And then there was light. As in a divine revelation, the old bulbs along the entire line flickered and came back to life, even if it was a half-life, as their filaments did not quite come to glow and just gave off a poor yellow light.

"Someone is playing with us," Max said.

"Or maybe they want to show us something. If they wanted to kill us, they would have done it when they entered the cell to close the door."

"I won't take a chance. I don't like it."

The high-pitched squeal of a woman ran through the passages and gave them a chill.

"Is that your friend?" Max asked.

"I don't know, I haven't been able to distinguish it well," Gerard said, walking up to the curve at the end of the passage. He peeked out and motioned for Max to follow him.

They walked down several more stretches of passage. The light bulbs allowed them to move much faster than before and they soon reached a point where the passageways multiplied, a hub from which nine passages started in different directions.

The gut-wrenching shriek came again, this time accompanied by a gunshot, which rumbled along those walls, shattering their eardrums.

"Where to?" Max asked.

"I don't know. I'm not even sure which way the sound came from."

"Then we should split up. We each choose a tunnel and entrust ourselves to St. Jude's protection," Max said.

"To whom?"

"St. Jude, the patron saint of the impossible, of lost causes."

"It's not the best way to give encouragement, but if the good saint can help us, I have no objections," Gerard said, while each of them walked toward the entrance to one passage. Before disappearing in his, Gerard turned to Max.

"Good luck. If you find something, or if you run into problems, do whatever you can, shouting, bellowing, kicking, whatever, as long as you let me know. Oh, and one more thing about that St. Jude," Gerard said.

"What?"

"I'm more of a devoted follower of blessed Saint Apapucio," Gerard said.

"And what did he do to deserve it?"

"Someday I'll tell you," Gerard said, smiling, and he disappeared down his tunnel.

Max shrugged and walked down another passage.

CHAPTER 64

Gerard walked through a maze of cracks in the rock and natural passages intertwined with parts excavated or enlarged by man, but apparently leading nowhere.

The roughest sections lacked electric lighting, which he used as a reference to retrace his steps and walk only on the lighted ones, believing that by doing so he would be more likely to reach some inhabited part.

He had the impression of having passed by the same place more than once and began to seriously think he was lost.

He used that time to mentally review all the evidence he had gathered until then. He couldn't take his mind from the suicide farewell letter he had found in Apollinaire's forbidden book, especially his last words.

"*It is time, I must not keep the lady of the house waiting, she should not be infuriated*".

That sentence had always sounded like an epitaph to him, and he was sure its unfortunate author was trying to communicate something through it, maybe clues about the location of the bloody room.

It was clear he feared they could intercept his letter, so not only did he hide it into the back cover of the book, but he also encrypted his message.

It was exactly what he would have done in his place. He had read that letter a hundred times, and he felt that somehow he could relate to what the man felt in his last moments, what went through his head and the logic that had guided his actions.

The "*lady of the house*", who could she be? Neither the Casino nor the hotel had ever had a woman as the owner. The businessman Josep Sabadell had been its main promoter, and a corporation established to commercially exploit them had managed both. What house could he be referring to?

He sensed he was on the right track, but he needed to unlock his mind. He stopped and leaned against the cold rock wall while trying not to lose the thread of his thoughts and keep pulling it.

The suicide victim feared the owner of the house would be angry if he was late and did not complete his fatal mission. What woman would be upset because someone took too long to take his final step toward death?

Who but death itself? Gerard punched the wall, which crushed his knuckles, but was excited by the logic of his reasoning.

Death, that figure always portrayed as a woman dressed in black, scythe in hand, it was she who should not be infuriated nor kept waiting. But in the letter, he referred to her as the lady of the house. Could he be talking about a funeral house, maybe? Or a cemetery?

If death was the lady of the house, he could not be referring to any other place. Maybe the room was within the grounds of a cemetery or in a graveyard. It was a line of research he had to follow as soon as he got out of that maze.

He was convinced the suicide room really existed and had a feeling he was now closer than ever to find it. He opened his backpack and checked for the umpteenth time the old blueprints of the Casino and its surroundings.

At present, none of those buildings was left standing, only the tower and part of the terrace above it, but none of the many sources he had consulted spoke of facilities or underground passages under the Casino or the hotel.

Unless there were secret structures built outside the official blueprints, it had to be outside the Casino enclosure.

He didn't know how far he had traveled along the maze, but considering that the entry through the water mine was at the bottom of the valley, at present he could be anywhere in the mountains west of the Casino, or under the forest, or perhaps under one of the mansions scattered along the road leading to Barcelona.

The lights flickered several times, and fearing they could definitely go out, Gerard put the blueprint in his pocket and sped up his pace, although he didn't know where he was nor where to go.

He followed only those passages that sloped upwards. After all, he was in the Collserola mountain range, not in the Himalayas. The highest point in the mountain should be just a few hundred meters above sea level, so if he kept going up it was more likely he could find a way out or get close to one of the houses in the area.

The strategy seemed to work because he soon reached an area where the passages were wider, the floor and walls covered with a layer of cement and it looked like he was in a network of passages attached to the basement of a house.

The "cavern look" had given way to the "basement look", which made him feel calmer for being close to a possible exit, but also more uneasy for being closer to some potential criminals.

I'm getting close to civilization, Gerard thought, excited to glimpse in the distance a wooden door in one of the side walls.

Gerard thought he heard muffled voices coming from inside the room. He stopped to listen and heard the door beginning to open. He turned around and retreated to crouch and hide behind the next bend in the passage, from where he could peek out to see what was happening.

The door finally opened, and a man dressed in a green raincoat came out, then closed the door and locked it. Gerard waited until he heard the footsteps go away in the opposite direction. He waited one more minute, for safety, and ventured to stick his head out.

His surprise could not be greater as he was looking directly into two dark and menacing eyes, those of a sawed-off shotgun pointed at his face. He rose slowly, drifting and religiously following the movement of the gun, which led him to the center of the passage.

He had never seen that man before. He must have been about forty, showing an unkempt beard, and so many wrinkles his face looked like an orographic map of the region. He kept pointing the shotgun at him but did not utter a word.

"Don't shoot, please, I beg you," Gerard said, with increasing nervousness. The man seemed undeterred and motioned with the shotgun for him to start walking toward the room he had come from.

When they arrived at the door he opened it, and still pointing the shotgun at him, he pushed him hard inside. Gerard fell and hit against the concrete with his knees.

He stood up with difficulty, and barely had the time to turn toward the door, which was already closing. The sound of the key in the lock brought him back to reality. He had let them catch him, and he was locked in a dark room at an unknown location underground. His options were very limited if not nil.

He turned and looked around, and despite the prevailing darkness, he could hear a moan coming from the back of the room. He was not alone. Instinctively he stepped back and fumbled in his pocket until he found the flashlight and turned the crank frantically, pointing the beam in that direction.

A lump moved, sitting on a metal chair. It was a body and appeared to be tied to the seat rest. Gerard ran to the body and lifted its head.

"Oh, my God, Eva," he exclaimed upon seeing the young girl tied to the chair and in a semiconscious state. Her eyes were closed and her head fell as he let go. She seemed very weak.

Gerard stood behind her and hurried to release the bindings on her hands.

"Eva, can you hear me? Talk to me, please," he said, as he released the knots holding her wrists, but she only made soft unintelligible moans.

When he managed to free her hands, he kneeled in front of her and did the same with the bindings on her feet. The knots were in the back, at the height of her heels, and Gerard pulled the rope to bring them to the front and untie them more easily.

In doing so, it surprised him it didn't take him any effort, because the rope was not tense. He pulled the rope further, but the knots did not appear. In fact, it seemed as if there were no knots, as if the rope was not even tied.

He looked up and Eva's bright sharp eyes and her mischievous smile as she stared intently at him, were the penultimate thing he could see, since the last was the butt of a gun moving at high speed to impact against his forehead, making him lose both his balance and his consciousness at the same time.

When he opened his eyes again, the positions had switched, and he was tied hand and foot to the same chair. The yellow light of an old light bulb tried to illuminate the room, but it could not penetrate the thick layer of dirt attached to the glass, acting as a brown filter.

"Eva, what the hell is this? What's going on here?" Gerard exclaimed, very upset.

"Do you think an explanation is necessary?" she said, keeping a bloodcurdling smile.

"What does this mean? I thought you were dead. I saw you in that tank," Gerard said, as he struggled to try to loosen his bindings.

"You only saw what I wanted you to see, and understood what I wanted you to understand. Realize once and for all you have no business here. You've been delving into issues that go beyond you, which you should have let rest in peace, and now you have to pay the price for having done it."

"What are you talking about? Are you crazy? What do you want?"

"Madness viewed in others is only the subjective projection of our own fears and complexes. Madness lived in oneself, that's something else; it's an affirmation of independence, of freedom, of breaking with what the official fate has in store for us, is a liberation that..."

"Enough fancy talk, let me go," Gerard interrupted. "Whatever you're scheming makes no sense, but you can still fix the situation, no one has been hurt."

"Don't be so sure," she said, shining the blade of a large knife that appeared from nowhere. She walked over to the chair, and without preamble, she carved two intersecting straight lines on the skin of Gerard's forearms, which began to bleed immediately.

"What are you doing?"

Eva was moving her hand in the air, in an ethereal dance in which the blade drew ephemeral figures and occasionally descended to Gerard's arms and sank slightly into his skin until blood flowed, and she cleaned the steel blade immersing it in the serum of life.

Gerard struggled and moved the chair, trying to get out of the knife's path, but the blade always ended by reaching its target. It terrified him to see the stabbing, which had started in his arms, had been moving up to his chest and was now dangerously close to his neck.

She muttered something unintelligible as she continued moving the blade with deadly skill and accuracy, and finally stopped, resting it near the jugular, in what reminded Gerard of the classical calm before the storm, which in this case would be deadly for him, who already saw his life slipping away through a red curtain.

"It's a shame you have to go this way, without knowing the truth, with the inexorable feeling of having failed in life, knowing your passage through life will leave no more trace than a bloodstain the earth will soon absorb and will disappear forever," Eva said, applying pressure to the blade, which began to move longitudinally, drawing a thin red line on Gerard's neck, from which blood would soon sprout.

"Gerard, are you there?"

Eva stopped when she heard the voice coming from the hallway. Gerard was relieved but knew it was but a brief pause in his ordeal. Eva lowered the knife and walked behind the door to listen.

Gerard sped up his pace, but it was almost impossible to cut the plastic flanges with just the touch of the rounded edge of the chair, it would take him at least five years to achieve it.

His only chance was to slip one hand under the flange. He would have to pull with all his strength and he knew that doing so the flange would tear much of the skin on his wrist, and he risked ending up with the bony hand of a skeleton.

"Gerard, if you're there, say something," the voice spoke again, in a low, almost whispery tone.

"Max, here," Gerard shouted, instantly recognizing the voice of his friend, but he could not continue because talking with the handkerchief ball Eva quickly tucked into his mouth, was not one of his skills.

With that in his mouth, Gerard could not even growl and he watched in terror as Eva broke the light bulb with the blade of her knife and when the light went off her silhouette faded into the darkness.

"Help, we're here," she said shakily and Gerard understood immediately what she was trying to do.

"Relax guys, I'm here. I'm coming in. Step aside," Max said, slamming the door, without even checking first if it was already open.

Gerard knew it was now or never. When Max came in through that door Eva would stab him mercilessly, so he told himself a skin graft was a low price to pay for his friend's life.

After the second charge against the door, Max decided to try the doorknob, which opened easily. Noting the room was dark and that the dim light coming from the corridor barely illuminated a few steps ahead, he stood under the doorframe, busy turning the crank on his flashlight.

When he turned it on, the light beam fell directly on Gerard's silhouette, writhing in a chair in front of him, and making superhuman efforts to get up.

Without hesitation, Max took a step forward toward him, and just as if by doing so he had activated a hidden mechanism, from the depths of the room, the silhouette of a huge and sharp steel blade emerged, fast as a gale, and traveled the short space between darkness and Max's back, as he ran toward Gerard.

Gerard pushed with his legs and got up dragging the chair while pulling hard to get one of his hands to pass through the flange loop.

The tremendous effort allowed him to spit out the handkerchief stuck in his mouth and the scream he let out was so brutal, he felt his jaw almost unhinging for doing so.

He could not see it, but he was sure his right hand now probably looked like an X-ray image of his bones, because he had felt the flange slicing his skin and subcutaneous tissue as his hand was moving toward freedom.

With one hand free and the other on the way to being freed, Gerard lunged on top of Max, trying to divert him from the knife's path, which had already found his back and was sinking into his lumbar area.

Max screamed as he felt life slipping away through his kidneys, in one of those clairvoyant premonitions that spring from pure animal survival instinct before an extreme situation.

Gerard fell on top of him, dragging behind the chair. Eva was trapped under the tangle of limbs and had to drop the knife to release her arm and get up.

As he tried to sit up, he reached out to hold Eva by the waist of her pants, but she gave him a hard kick in the face and escaped.

He finally stood up, untied his boots and stepped out of them to release his feet more easily. Once free, he bent down over Max, who was lying and bleeding profusely from his back. The knife had fallen to the floor and was not blocking the wound, thus the bleeding was severe.

Gerard took off his shirt, huddled it and placed it against Max's lumbar area, pressing on the wound. He needed something to hold it. He took off his pants and bound them over the clogging, making a rudimentary double knot with the legs of the pants.

He accommodated his friend's body on the floor and approached his face. Max was very pale and breathing with great difficulty.

"Max, hold on, please," he shouted, slapping his cheeks to keep him awake.

Gerard knew if he stayed, there would be nothing he could do for his friend, deep under the mountain, and unable to go out for help. Max's death was more than certain, and probably his too.

His only chance was to leave him there and run for help. It went against all logic or ethical standard of humanity and the principle of humanitarian assistance to those in need, especially with a friend, but he had no choice.

He was positive the passages communicated with a mansion in the area, and he was determined to find an exit and go get help, even if it was the last thing he did, which might well be the case.

CHAPTER 65

Gerard was wandering on a giant spider web, a labyrinth of passageways he navigated desperately taking almost no precautions. Now his priority was to find a way out and seek help to save Max. Everything else took second place.

Even spider webs have defined limits, and the network of tunnels was not infinite. It couldn't be so difficult to get out of there, but he felt bloated, his head increasingly heavier, and he was tired, very tired.

Was it possible Eva could have administered him some drug while he was unconscious? It was the only possible explanation, so he made great efforts to stay alert, although he felt the slumber was catching up with him.

He knew the spider was always lurking, hidden at one end of its web, patiently waiting for its prey to get exhausted or trapped in its sticky filaments, to then appear and devour it.

His only chance of salvation lay in staying awake, alert, and study the signals. Max's life could depend on it, so he fought against the advance of the soporific haze, and building on his last throes of lucidity he walked toward one of the light bulbs illuminating that stretch of passage.

With trembling hands, he unscrewed the light bulb and carefully put it in his backpack, which he then deposited on the floor, a few steps from him. In the darkness, Gerard brought his fingers to his mouth and felt the bittersweet taste of blood dripping from them.

He no longer felt any pain. He could count the bones in his phalanges, exposed and emaciated, but his pain threshold had risen so high that not even crushing them with a steamroller would have made him blink the slightest bit.

Moistening his fingers with his tongue, he felt the rough surface of the rock wall as if caressing the smooth skin of a woman. When he touched the wooden base for the light bulb, he took a deep breath, took two steps back, and jumped in the air, while putting three fingers into the socket.

The electric shock ran the length of his battered body, triggering convulsions that shook all his joints.

His idea was to electrocute himself to short-circuit his nervous system and free it from the rising tide of narcolepsy.

He knew his stiff muscles would not respond to any commands for a few seconds, but after the jump, the weight of his body would drag him to the ground, detaching his hand from the socket before it was too late, trusting the force of gravity would save him, as it did.

Fallen on the ground, he remained motionless stretched next to the wall for several minutes, as a shaky fallen salt statue.

When he slowly regained control of his limbs, he was glad to feel a wave of unspeakable pain running through his body like a tsunami, reminding him both of his own mortality and the fact he was still alive and wide awake.

He got up and made a first quick damage assessment. His whole body ached, and he still suffered from some slight residual seizure but felt more alive than ever.

Reaching for his backpack, still on the floor beside him, he removed the light bulb and screwed it back into the socket, taking care not to electrocute himself again when touching it.

When there was light, he looked down in awe to realize he was barefoot and dressed only in his underpants and a t-shirt that had once been white. A true warrior's armor at its best, Gerard thought.

He examined the Casino enclosure blueprints under the light bulb. He had noticed the passages that had natural rock walls and ceilings were the ones at a greater depth, confirming his logic that by going up he was getting closer to what probably were basements and tunnels connecting various buildings.

The suicide letter described death as the lady of a house that should not be kept waiting or infuriated, Agustín's drawings evoked mythological clawed and winged creatures suspiciously reminiscent of demons. Everything was necessarily related.

His mind was more than awake, the electric shock had restarted his brain systems with brutal hyperstimulation.

He kept walking down the corridor when the epiphany came to him as if a meteorite had fallen in front of him.

Now he remembered where he had seen those mythological beings before, and it wasn't in the terrifying illustrations of a book, or as menacing cathedral gargoyles, or as the tormented characters in a museum painting.

Those were the statues adorning the entrance to one of the Art Nouveau mansions near the Casino.

The first time he visited the Casino ruins he passed by the remains of a beautiful but disturbing mansion, with an imposing entrance gate flanked by two columns.

On top of them, two statues of winged creatures guarded the property, having miraculously survived the passage of time and the general decay of the enclosure.

The mansion was west of the Casino ruins, just over one kilometer down the road, but walking underground as he was, that distance could mean many hours of hard walking. Could that mansion be at the origin of the network of passageways? It was plausible, but there was something he needed to check.

He pulled out of his backpack a notebook bound with a rubber band, where he had been jotting down ideas and details during his hundreds of hours of research. He quickly flipped through the pages until he came to his notes on the mansions around the Casino. The few still standing and preserved in good condition, had been restored and converted into restaurants, foundations' headquarters or private residences.

He read in his notes that the house in question was called Can Torres. In some of the few black and white photographs taken during the few years of the Casino existence, the silhouette of its towers was always visible in the distance.

The origins of the mansion were a great mystery, as was the identity of its owners. Over the years, the building lived several lives, as a guest house, hostel, and even having hosted a discreet brothel. After the Civil War, the house had various military uses and later it even hosted children during vacation periods as a summer lodge for them.

It was fascinating for Gerard to note the striking parallelism between the life of houses and that of the human beings inhabiting them.

Like people, mansions were born at some point, forged their own history, with their hopes and dreams of childhood, the boldness, and insolence of adolescence, the conflicts and contrasts of their mature stage, up to their subsequent decline and final abandonment, death, and ultimate oblivion.

What a fantastic irony that in the very walls that welcomed high society wealthy gentlemen in search of the forbidden pleasures of the flesh, the innocent laughter of hundreds of children playing and enjoying their summer vacations also echoed.

Life and death, always encrusted into a cycle without beginning or end, feeding on one another, but needing each other at the same time. Death was nothing more than a parasite that fed on life, but life without death would be nothing more than constant evolution, since it was death that gave life its value, which gave it a meaning, which made it worth living.

Why was he wasting his time rambling in philosophical reflections when he should do everything possible to seek help? he wondered, and he followed the main passageway, ignoring all side branches he met along the way.

He came to an area where the corridors went through what looked like the foundation of a building. Parts of the walls were made of red brick and in other parts, they had used thick cement.

The main passageway died before a thick iron gate, which seemed not to have been opened in many years, darkened by rust and moisture, and dotted with large rivets outlining its perimeter. For a moment he thought he was at the access hatch to the Nautilus, the mythical submarine with which Captain Nemo sailed along Jules Verne's novels.

The door had no lock nor latch and it looked solid. He hit it hard and heard the same sound as if he was hitting a granite wall.

If someone fled that way, he must have gotten help from the other side. Otherwise, there had to be another way out through one of the countless side passages he left behind, but there was no time to explore them all, and he had to come up with something, and fast.

The concept of death was still chasing him, and he started thinking again on the black woman with the scythe, the lady of the house. Could it be Can Torres' mansion? Was he standing at the basement door of the crumbling mansion? Or maybe it was the gateway to the suicide room, the scene of so much horror?

He went back to his notebook and then he remembered. In a couple of articles he had read, the journalists referred to the house by its popular name, granted by citizens based on its dismal reputation. It was known as "MM", initials for its French name, "Maison de Morte", or "House of Death".

Where did he hear that name before? It felt oddly familiar.

He went through his notes until he found the sentence he wrote after reading the diary of Juana Caballero, Eva's great-grandmother, the Casino employee who abandoned her job because she was terrified.

"*I cannot stay here any longer, they cannot force me. Agus says that the devil dwells in MM and I don't want to end up like the others*".

The quote made it clear, that poor woman believed the devil himself lived at MM. That's what young Agustín, the Casino bellboy, had told her, and it terrified Juana to the point of forcing her to abandon a well-paid job at a time of such hardship.

When she wrote she didn't want to end up like the others, Juana was referring to the deaths that took place in those surroundings.

Gerard was convinced he had found proof that the damn room was close, probably in one of those passages, but in which one?

CHAPTER 66

Trying to open that door banging against it with his shoulder was like trying to get into the Fort Knox Federal Reserve vault head butting. He had no choice but to explore every one of the side passages he saw along the way. There were only six or seven, so he just had to go back the way he had come and try.

He had barely taken a few steps when the lights went out in the tunnel and everything was dark again. Gerard reached for his backpack to look for the flashlight when a metallic sound made him stop.

He couldn't see anything, but he knew it was the big iron gate opening. He turned around and put his back against the wall as if that instinctive movement were to magically protect him from some unknown danger.

It was the sound of heavy hinges scraping each other, but it wasn't the screech produced by a door that hadn't been opened for a century. That door was well greased and seemed to be used frequently.

Hiding behind the first bend, he could not resist the temptation to peek and find out who opened the door. He reached inside his backpack and found the flashlight, which he brandished like a weapon, his finger ready to trigger the power button. He hoped there would be enough charge left in the battery, since he didn't want to use the crank and give away his position.

He poked his head first and gradually the rest of the body. He could see in the distance the silhouette of the door ajar, since a soft red glow emanated from inside casting a triangle of light on the pavement. From there he could only see part of what looked like the hallway of a house.

He took a few small steps toward the light, when he felt a strong blow on his back, knocking him down. He rolled on the ground but sat up quickly.

If it was not humiliating enough to walk through those tunnels barefoot and in his underwear, he now had to add his lack of weapons to defend himself. His only option was to catch his attacker by surprise, faking an injury, so he would come to him and then launching himself on top of him when he approached.

He bent down to pretend he was writhing in pain, with the flashlight clutched between his fingers, like a stone ready to be thrown.

When the shadow of the assailant approached, Gerard jumped and rotated his arm like an Olympic disk thrower, launching his fist against the face of that beast. The flashlight's plastic case crackled inside his hand, just like his finger bones, which crushed against the assailant's jaw.

The brutality of the impact caught the shadow by surprise and it fell backward, disappearing into the darkness. Gerard twisted and turned several times trying to figure out his position.

His attacker moved quickly, and he was soon again behind his back, landing another heavy blow to his kidneys. Gerard collapsed again and fell with his bare knees against the concrete floor. From there, he covered his face with his hands to ward off the next blow to fall on him, but it didn't come.

He looked up and saw nothing, but he knew he was too exposed and the next blow could be the definitive one. He couldn't go on like that for much longer, so he ran toward the light, jumped through the open door, and leaning his back against it, he pushed until it closed behind him.

The door had a lock on the inside and Gerard hastened to engage it. He breathed in relief and saw he was not in a room but in a small corridor, illuminated by a single light bulb. The cement walls had no decoration and the floor tiles showed beautiful geometric patterns, barely visible from the dirt accumulated on them.

At the other end, he saw a dark wooden door, about two meters high, on top of which there was a large golden brass peephole. Two large iron bars blocked the door halfway up, and like the iron door, it didn't have a knob or a latch.

When he reached the door, he stood on tiptoe and admired the peephole. He had seen some like that in old Art Nouveau houses in Barcelona and he knew how they worked. He engaged the mechanism that turned the brass sheet and several slits opened, through which he could see the other side, all dark.

Still holding the battered flashlight in his hand, he turned the crank to bring it to life. He got a flickering beam of yellowish light and introduced the tip of the flashlight in one of the peephole slits.

He could only see what was directly in front of him. It didn't look like a basement, but a hallway in an old house, with fabric paneled walls and old rugs on a wooden floor. The rest were indefinite shadows, suggesting more than confirming forms or bulges, impossible to identify under such poor lighting.

Could it be the Maison de Morte? Was he in the corridor leading to the room he had been searching for so long?

He hesitated whether to unlatch the bolts and find out, but he was afraid to meet any unwanted surprise on the other side. He looked back toward the comforting view of the other metallic door with an engaged lock.

It was more than likely this was the only access and that he would be safe there, but he had not come that far to remain forever trapped between two doors, he had to keep looking for a way out.

Besides, the corridor he saw through the peephole did not look menacing, so he closed it and unlatched the two bolts.

As with the iron door hinges, the locks slid with surprising ease, unbecoming of a door exposed to centennial weathering.

Carefully, he slowly opened the door, which did not put up much resistance, and introduced the flashlight through the opening to light the way. When he could see what was before him, he was immediately transported to the past century.

He was in the corridor of an Art Nouveau home, with wooden floors covered by rugs so worn by moisture and the passage of time, it was impossible to tell what color they were in their previous life.

Several large paintings hung from the walls, also covered by a blackish patina of an unknown nature. In one of them, he glimpsed two cheerful women hugging and smoking huge cigarettes.

The dark arm of a gas lamp came out of the wall as if it craved to breathe the pure air it had been deprived of for more than a century.

Gerard had the very unsettling feeling of seeing everything in black and white, of being in a place visited by death, as if the woman with the scythe had passed her black veil over that corridor that once must have been full of life, banishing all color and turning it into a mausoleum, a monument to putrefaction.

There were several doors in the hallway, and Gerard approached them with the secret hope and fear behind one of them he could find the room he craved to find. He entered each one and found them all empty, except for an army of insects and rodents fleeing from his flashlight's pitiful beam every time he opened a door.

The musty stench was unbearable, and spiders had built a real amusement park in that place, weaving a dense tangle of webs crossing the corridor from side to side. It was obvious no one had been there in decades.

He pushed away the best he could the cobwebs that clung to his arm, and crept around it as if they had a life of their own, and walked to the far end of the corridor, which continued in another stretch at a perpendicular angle.

After turning around the corner, he reached the end of the corridor and came face to face with a brick wall that went up to the ceiling. That access was bricked up, and from the appearance of that construction, it looked like it had been that way for at least half a century. It was no use trying to tear down that wall with his bare hands, and in those rooms, he had seen nothing that could help him do it.

If that corridor really communicated with the ruins of the Maison de Morte, it was impossible to check. He reached a dead end, a mousetrap, and his only escape route was to go back to the iron door and explore the remaining passages.

But if no one had gone through that dusty corridor, how could his attacker have gotten there?

He retraced his steps, stopping at one of the huge paintings hanging on the wall. His ostentatious thick black frame was probably golden, but it was impossible to know for sure. The surface of the painting was also black.

As he ran his hand over the canvas, to his surprise his fingers left a trace of color behind, like the tail of a comet bringing back to life everything in its path, waking up the colors from their centenary lethargy.

The flashlight shone on the top of the canvas. He could make out the proud upright figure of a woman pompously dressed in the purest Victorian style. She was holding an open book in her hand, but Gerard could not read the title. The woman was standing next to a wooden desk, and behind her, there was a bookcase.

He pointed the light beam toward the face of the woman and regretted not having a stronger light source or a stool to take a closer look. The woman's traits were oddly familiar, something in them did not fit with the image of last century women that vintage photographs used to show.

There were more paintings hung along the corridor, but only two were almost life-size, the one with the woman and the book and the painting hanging right on the opposite wall. He turned to the other painting and walked the beam of his flashlight over its surface, caressing the features of the gentleman who watched him from the canvas.

It was a young man, dressed in a black suit and encased in a black cloak. He wore a top hat and held a cane in his hands, smiling in a way that came across as insolent.

He found it interesting the gentleman was posing in front of what looked like the same wooden desk and facing the same bookcase as the painting of the woman. The two shared

377

the same background, but seen from two slightly different angles.

A muffled sound abruptly interrupted his pictorial contemplation. He heard it clearly, and although distant, it sounded like a bang. Gerard grew restless, because in that dark corridor, in that Art Nouveau postcard, in that piece of history snatched to the past, there was nothing or no one that could have caused it, not even a rat.

He had entered all the rooms, and they were all empty, with no furniture or objects that could have caused the sound.

He strolled down the corridor, his flashlight illuminating the walls, while the light beam pranced impossibly through spider webs that gleamed like silver threads.

One after another, the paintings hanging on the walls went by him, like black windows to an outside world in which there was only emptiness and darkness, and which dirt and neglect had covered with that blackish layer that standardized it all, the patina that democratized oblivion.

He heard a thump again, and Gerard stopped to listen. It had sounded even more distant, but he could swear he was not imagining things.

He went back to the wooden door. He had already wasted too much time searching that old basement; he needed to go back and find an exit to the outside as soon as possible, and the only way to do it was through the tunnels.

He pushed the wooden door, but then he stopped. He kept thinking about the image on the woman's painting and had a sudden inspiration. He retraced his steps and stood before the painting.

The delicate but yet energetic face, the sharp nose, high cheekbones, the proud somewhat haughty bearing.

He was watching Eva, it powerfully reminded him of Eva's facial features, and even the proportions of her body could fit hers.

He noticed the coincidence of backgrounds between the two paintings and turned to look again at the painting on the opposite wall, the smiling gentleman.

What was it that captured his attention in that painting? It wasn't the man's face, because he did not recognize him, nor the background shared with the other painting. It was the fact this painting was brighter, it seemed to be more alive.

How was that possible? Then he noticed a detail he missed earlier. All the paintings in the hallway had a layer of dirt so thick it was impossible to see what was painted on the canvas without using the hands to remove that layer.

The gentleman smiled at him from his painting, and Gerard hadn't had to use his hand to clear his face, the painting was cleaner. He examined it closer. Both the canvas and the frame were much cleaner than the other paintings in the corridor, as if someone had recently used a feather duster to remove dust. He pulled the frame and tried to push the painting to the side, but it did not move one iota.

He walked to the painting of the woman and found that, despite being hung by two points, he could move it easily, while the picture of the gentleman was anchored to the wall.

He heard a dull and muffled sound again, but this time he heard it a lot closer and seemed to come from... behind the painting.

Frightened, he took several steps back and turned off his flashlight. It was clear something hid behind the huge canvas. He heard a click, followed by several almost inaudible sounds, but he could make them out in the hallway's silence.

Either he was freaking out or the painting frame had drifted. Gerard jumped and left the corridor, hiding behind the wooden door, which he closed almost completely, since the only light bulb in the corridor was right behind him, and he didn't want the glow to give him away.

He spied through the peephole, and despite the dimness of the ghostly corridor, he saw how the frame moved to one side, and a pair of legs emerged from inside, followed by a dark body, coming out of the wall and standing in the center of the corridor.

So the painting hid an escape route out of that place; it was the route they probably used it to quickly enter and exit the maze. He had to get there, but the black silhouette stood in his way.

The shadow turned and discovered Gerard's eyes spying on him from behind the peephole. In a split second, a huge hunting knife appeared in his hands and sunk in the wooden door, its tip coming out just a scant centimeter from Gerard's face, still glued to the peephole.

The shadow lunged toward him, but Gerard acted instinctively and only had time to push the wooden door and close it, latching the two bolts, thankful that they were so well oiled.

Someone was bumping against the door and beating it fiercely. For the moment, he had escaped.

He looked at the other end of the stretch of corridor. He was trapped between two doors locked from the inside, but without hesitation, he walked to the big iron door, unlatched the bolts, and brandishing his flashlight he returned to the maze of tunnels.

After he closed the door behind him and taking no precautions, he sprinted down the main corridor, heading for the small side tunnels open into the rock.

CHAPTER 67

He didn't know how long it would be until his pursuer reached him, but for the moment two thick doors separated them, and Gerard wanted to exploit his advantage.

Deep down he was convinced that by then Max would not have overcome his injuries and should already be in heaven or purgatory, cheering for him to escape. However, hope was the last thing he would ever lose, so he would give his best to try to find another way out, if there was any.

He explored sequentially each of the side branches he found along the way. Most of them were passages that took advantage of natural cracks in the rock and became dead ends. They had widened some to serve as storage rooms, and in others, he found wooden crates filled with construction materials, similar to those they found in the roller coaster tunnel.

There were barely any more branches left to explore. He stopped and turned around. Either he had not been able to find any other way out, or there was none and his only option was to return to the corridor, open both doors and face whoever was there, to try to escape through the painting.

If he wanted to fight that man, he needed to get hold of a gun, or something hard-hitting that would give him a chance to defend himself, but he had nothing. In that claustrophobic underworld, he had found no object he could use, and his small flashlight could only be used once as a projectile, and of rather pathetically ridiculous effectiveness.

It was not entirely true he was helpless. He remembered the crates containing construction materials he saw in two of the tunnels and headed there to pick up some bricks or look for a shovel or a blunt tool.

In the first tunnel, he found two boxes, and fortunately, it didn't take much effort to lift the thick wooden lids. He cursed his luck, as both were full of cement sacks, which had become so hardened with moisture that they seemed granite blocks from the Cheops pyramid. He could not even move them one centimeter.

Through the second tunnel, he reached a narrow natural crevice in the rock where he found three wooden boxes piled up, covered by a large green canvas.

He lifted the canvas and covered his mouth and eyes to protect them from the huge dust cloud, which would have surprised Lawrence of Arabia himself.

Not waiting for the ridiculous light of his flashlight to fight the cloud of dust and dirt, he climbed over the boxes and opened the one on top, finding only cobblestones inside.

Gerard weighed one, to assess its potential as a deadly weapon, but preferred to keep looking in the other two boxes underneath.

He leaned with his back against the crate and pushed with both feet on the rock wall. Once it started moving, it gained momentum until it got out of balance and fell to the ground.

The box hit the floor by its corner and wooden boards flew up in the air, freeing a cascade of cobblestones that spilled on the floor in a stony wave spreading in all directions.

Gerard leaned back to protect himself from the second sandstorm that stirred in that subterranean desert, hoping his back would find the rock wall, but it didn't, and he fell back.

His battered head poked behind one of the crates. He had fallen into a hidden passageway behind the mountain of crates. He waited for the dust to settle, coughing non-stop and rubbing his eyes, as irritated as if the boxes had been full of onions.

He supposed they had placed there those crates to hide the passage and decided to explore it. He recharged his flashlight and entered the narrow tunnel, which allowed him to stand up and curved to the left.

At the end of the passage, he reached a rectangular space in whose end he saw some rudimentary steps carved directly into the rock. That was a novelty because throughout the maze he had found no other construction of that type.

He walked up the steps, and stopped, very impressed when he faced a wooden door very different from any other he had found until then.

The wood was very dark but shiny because a thick layer of a varnish covered it. In its upper part, a brass figurine caught his attention. The figure had undulating forms, and it looked like the silhouette of a dancer or a stylized woman with her veil to the wind. It was clearly of Art Nouveau style and could have come from any of the many Art Nouveau mansions in the city.

He reached out and his fingers caressed the cold brass surface. That silhouette was familiar, but he could not remember exactly where he had seen it before. Perhaps in some photograph in one of the many Art Nouveau art books he studied. He had seen it before, because the figure was exquisite, and he remembered having experienced the same feeling just a few weeks earlier.

Gerard had a good memory, although it was not good with names or dates. If he crossed paths on the street with some old kindergarten companion whom he had not seen for thirty years, he recognized his face immediately with no possibility of error, but most likely he would not remember his name.

He made an effort to remember where he had seen that figure, and finally remembered an old photo book of the interior of the Xamot House, a magnificent Art Nouveau mansion that belonged to an industrialist's widow. The mansion was famous in its time because the widow suffered an assassination attempt there and eventually died later under tragic circumstances, killed by an unknown maniac.

He remembered having read the mansion survived the tragedy and gone through different owners, to end up being demolished in the fifties as a result of real estate speculation conducted by Porcinoles, a former nefarious mayor of Barcelona, with the connivance of powerful construction lobbies. One of so many wonders of the city that had succumbed to the ignorance and greed of certain political and business classes of the time.

Several old photographs showed the same figure carved on one of the outer walls of the mansion, near the main door, and also reproduced in one of the very elegant multicolored stained glass windows adorning the wall of one of the great halls of that impressive mansion.

He wondered how such a delicate figure could have gone from the Xamot House to a door in a damp, dark catacomb such as that.

Putting his hand on the doorknob, he turned it slowly. The door was heavy, but pushing with both hands he opened it.

His first impression was as if he had opened a portal into interstellar space, into the dark void.

That strange sensation gave way to a feeling of being before an invisible force, as if a magnetic field stood between him and the interior of the room and prevented him from moving forward.

Was it a force field that blocked him or was his own fear of what he might find inside?

CHAPTER 68

Darkness was impenetrable, so he pointed his flashlight forward and made a sweep from side to side before taking a step. The musty smell was strong, and it surprised him to find fewer cobwebs than in the corridor at the basement of the Maison de Morte.

He crossed the threshold and leaned against the inner door frame. Without great expectations, he rotated the ancient porcelain lightswitch.

Seconds later the only one light bulb in the room blinked, awoken from its slumber by the electric current still traveling on a thick fabric-lined electric wire, supported by insulating porcelain caps placed along its route.

He pocketed his trusty flashlight and examined the room carefully. It was a simple room soberly decorated, and just by entering it Gerard felt a strange mixture of opposing feelings.

On the one hand, he felt as if he had crossed a portal that allowed him to travel back in time to the early last century, but at the same time, that room greatly disturbed him.

Despite the Art Nouveau scent given off by the surroundings, the walls were not lined with the ubiquitous fabric but tiled with black varnished tiles, spitting back the reflection of the flickering light bulb as if it was a black starry sky.

The four walls covered with black tiles gave it a cold, industrial look, like a gym locker, the communal showers in a bathhouse, or... a municipal slaughterhouse.

He felt something soft under his feet and noticed a thick carpet, which could not be a hundred years old since it was in relatively good condition, showing it had been placed there recently.

A bookcase leaning against the wall struck him. Its shelves were empty and from where he was he could distinguish the layer of dust and cobwebs covering it.

Next to the library, a small French-style sofa seemed to wait for someone to sit down on it, but this one should have been waiting more than a century, for its fabric was threadbare and had lost all its pattern design.

A wooden chair in front of an antique writing desk with a bureau on it was the only other furniture in the room. On the desk, he saw an old black Bakelite telephone with a rotary dial. Gerard ran to the phone and picked up the receiver, but there was no signal. He dropped it in anger.

He examined the desk surface. The wood was varnished, but it had lost its natural gloss, an effect of time and humidity. He could not help snooping into the small drawers in the bureau. They were all empty except for one, from which he took several sheets of yellowed paper with whimsical green geometric motifs scattered over its surface, drawn by mold and fungi that had grown roughshod for decades.

He took a sheet, rubbed one corner with the tip of his index finger to remove the layer of mold and turned on his flashlight, placing it behind the paper sheet to look at it against the light.

He could not believe what he was seeing. Those sheets had an embossed letterhead, and he believed it could be the Casino de la Rabassada logo.

If that sheet of paper belonged to the official Casino stationery, it could be the evidence proving that was actually the room he was looking for, it could not be a coincidence.

What if that was the cursed room, the suicide room?. He refused to believe he had finally found it, but that's what the evidence suggested.

Otherwise, what could be the sense in building such a room underground? What could its purpose be? It was such a big nonsense he saw no possible explanation other than they had built it for evil, with a purpose as dark as its walls.

The room was devoid of any ornament or decoration; it lacked personality, conveying a depressing feeling of abandonment and death. Metal arms emerged from the walls, in what must have been gaslights, fallen into disuse many years earlier. He approached the empty bookcase, reinforcing the sense of abandonment and decay of the place.

A bookcase without books was like a body without a soul, like a hollow, superficial, and uninteresting person. He ran his hand over the shelves, letting his fingers impregnate with the thick layer of dust covering them. He reached out and when he ran his hand over the top shelf, his fingers came upon a paper, which he had not seen before.

It was a piece with jagged edges, ripped heedlessly from a newspaper page. On one side, it had a printed text that was part of an article, and on the other side, it showed part of a black-and-white photograph.

He couldn't recognize what it was or the date of the issue where it came from, but he put the clipping into his backpack to examine it later more calmly if he could get out of that place alive.

At that moment he thought he heard a cry in the distance and turned to listen carefully. It sounded like the howl of the wind blowing through castle battlements, but he was now in a maze of underground tunnels and there were no visible air vents.

It felt like a cry, and although he didn't know whether its source was human or animal, it gave him goosebumps throughout his body, even in places where he had no hair.

Images of the wild black dog attacking him crossed his mind again, and it mortified him to relive those bloody moments until his common sense told him that was enough.

He sensed this could be the place he had been looking for, but his initial enthusiasm was soon watered down when he didn't find much more to examine there, apart from the austere furnishings.

Overcome by his growing disappointment, he went back to the main passage to take a closer look at the area where he found the crates.

He put the sheets of paper bearing the Casino seal into his backpack and turned to head for the door, but a sixth, seventh or eighth sense, allowed him to capture a slight movement at the periphery of his vision and he instinctively ducked.

A big black mass was coming down on him and he could feel the air stream it moved just before receiving a brutal impact that knocked him down. It stunned Gerard, he could not prepare for the hit and his coccyx had struck directly against the tile floor.

He leaned on the floor to stand up, but a pair of black boots landed on his shoulders and held him against the floor. He grabbed one of them and pulled with all of his strength and could move it aside. After releasing himself, he then rolled on the floor to one side and jumped up.

In front of him, there was an imposing figure, wrapped in a large black cloak reaching down to the floor. A black mask covered his face, molding to his facial physiognomy as if made of elastic mesh, disfiguring him completely. A wide black hat crowned his head and swung like the wings of a giant condor.

"Who are you?" Gerard shouted, trying to reason with the beast rather than keep fighting, while he breathed deeply and took the opportunity to recover from the shock.

The only response from the bulky individual was to push the cloak aside and let out a huge machete whose blade shone even under the dim light from the light bulb.

"What do you want? What are you going to do?" Gerard shouted again, getting no response, while the black figure took a step forward, bringing the machete close to his frightened face.

Watching him move forward, Gerard looked in all directions, not finding any object with which to defend himself. He reached out and lifted the wooden chair by the backrest in the true classic style of the lion tamers, trying to surprise him.

The man didn't wait and with no notice, he leaped forward and lunged with the knife pointing toward Gerard's chest, as he immediately discharged a chair blow on the attacker's arm, and although he did not make him drop the machete, at least it put him off balance.

Gerard seized those seconds to take the only sensible decision he could take then, to run out of there. He took two strides and arrived at the door, but he stopped when an obstacle blocked his exit, pointing to his stomach with a gun.

Eva was standing in front of him, her face bloodied and showing unequivocal signs of struggle.

"Eva, that gun..." were the last words he uttered, before receiving a new and final blow to the head that made him lose consciousness and his body collapsed to the floor a second time.

When he raised his eyelids again, for a moment he thought he was in a nightmare from which he could not wake up. When he opened his eyes and saw he was sitting in a chair at the desk, still in that gloomy room, he realized that the current reality was as tragic as the one he had left behind before losing his consciousness.

It took a few seconds for him to realize his hands were not bound, and as soon as he was aware of it, he flexed his legs, ready to take a leap and try to get to the door.

The cold and unpleasant pressure of the huge machete blade against his jugular made his muscles relax almost faster than what took them to contract.

"I wouldn't want to use it. Do not force me, please."

The voice sounded behind him, grave and deep, and the words fell slowly, almost with liturgical precision.

Gerard shook his head to clear the mental cobwebs that still hindered his reasoning.

"I'm not moving, I assure you, nor do I intend to," Gerard said, noting how the pressure on his jugular decreased.

"If you try to turn or move if only a muscle, I'll let the knife do its work and skin you alive, and I'm talking literally," the voice said, in a tone that left no room for misunderstanding.

"What do you want from me?"

"I want nothing. I'm here to help you."

"Help me? Some help. What do you mean by help?"

"Helping you to put an end to your suffering, help you give meaning to your life. In short, to help you abandon this world in a fast and definitive manner."

"What makes you think I want to leave this world?"

"No matter what I think, all that matters is that the balance be restored, that order may rule again."

"On that, we agree. I don't know what you're talking about, but I assure you I agree with you," Gerard said.

"Surely you think I'm crazy, that this is nothing but an absurd nightmare. Nothing further from reality. I'm a facilitator, my mission is to help those who, like you, have lost their way and failed to establish their priorities. I help them rectify and find their place in the universe."

"I have lost nothing, I know exactly where I want to go in life."

"Nonsense. You've been sniffing around for too long, squandering your efforts pursuing ghosts and waking up beasts that were already sleeping the sleep of the just. You are an anomaly that must be eliminated, as have been all those that preceded you."

"What are you saying? Whom do you mean?" Gerard said, turning toward him, but the tip of the knife stuck in his neck forcing him to look ahead while a trail of blood gushed and slid down his bare chest.

"It is of little consequence if now you know because you will take your knowledge with you to the grave. For many years I have been preparing to carry out my mission, just like my father did before, following on the footsteps of his father. It's a tradition that cannot get out of the family circle."

It was confusing to Gerard, but he had to keep the man talking.

"What is your mission?" Gerard asked.

"It's been over a century and it has evolved over the years, adapting to modern times. Initially, it was about protecting society, keeping it safe from dirtbags, corrupt politicians, greedy businessmen who exploited the working classes while squandering their fortunes in sex, pageantry, and gambling. They committed so many injustices during those turbulent times, there was no shortage of candidates. But someone crossed the red line, and that mission became a personal matter, a family matter better addressed from within."

"What the hell are you talking about?"

"I've talked too much, it's time to get down to it," the voice said, getting away from Gerard's back.

CHAPTER 69

"There is a letter in front of you. Read it."

Gerard saw a sheet of yellowed paper on the desk and unfolded it slowly.

"*Distinguished gentleman,*

Brevity is a precious commodity, and a commendable virtue, which together with honor, define an honest person to perfection. Confronting the reality of life with integrity and honor is another of the traits that define and distinguish humans from the rest of animals.

You have before you the possibility to close with dignity the book of your passage through life. In the drawer before you, you will find a gun. Its drum houses a single bullet. A single opportunity to leave this unfair world with honor...".

Gerard kept reading, the same letter dozens of unfortunate souls had read before him, and who like him, faced the terrible dilemma of having to choose between their life or that of their loved ones.

"*...but you will condemn all your family members and loved ones to the most atrocious suffering and most ruthless death...*".

Gerard could not believe what he was reading, it was so surreal he felt as if attending a contemporary theater performance, in which he would soon hear the applause and the room lights would turn on.

"*Choose wisely and do not waste your opportunity... your anonymous sacrifice will allow them to live their lives and die when their time comes, of natural causes...*"

Was that how suicides happened? Forced by the pressure of a psychopath or a whole family of lunatics?

"...You will never leave this room alive. The question is whether you wish to do it quickly and with honor, safeguarding the lives of your loved ones, or you prefer to endure untold sorrow and extend that suffering to your family to share with them the punishment for your lack of honor...".

Gerard refused to believe that play could have a tragic end. He told himself he would rewrite the end of the story, even if it was the last thing he did, which was an incongruity in itself, but he was determined to do so no matter what.

"... You have the last word, the decision is always yours" the letter ended, and Gerard slowly placed it down on the desk.

"Do you understand what we expect of you?" the voice asked.

Gerard knew well what the letter meant, a kind invitation to commit suicide, wrapped in a pretentious speech about honor. He refused to give up so easily.

"Very interesting, but what makes you think I will be stupid enough to do what the letter says?" Gerard said, without turning around.

"Indeed, you may be stupid, but not enough to jeopardize the life of your sister and your niece."

Gerard could not contain himself and turned, pouncing on that individual, who dodged the onslaught with some difficulty and hit him in the side with the machete.

Gerard fell on the floor, pushed the overturned chair aside, and tried to sit up, taking his hand to the side.

"Don't you dare to get anywhere near my sister or my niece," he shouted, pointing his finger at him.

"Enough is enough," the assailant said, and pushing his cloak aside with a quick wave of his hand, he grabbed the huge machete and lunged at Gerard, who tried to raise an arm, which the assailant twisted as he stood on top of him, putting his heavy boots against his back and smashing his face against the floor.

"The conversation is over, now things get serious. You will not see your family alive again, that is a fact, but the question is whether the lost life will be yours or theirs. You have the power to decide. If you sacrifice yourself for them, they will no longer hear from you, they will think you abandoned them, but at least they will live their miserable lives until death catches up with them when their time comes. If you choose to play the hero and not be a man of honor, be prepared to accept the consequences of your choice. I will visit your sister and I will make her remember the day your niece was born. I'll make her relive the pain of childbirth, only this time without anesthesia, and I will perform a cesarean section in vivo using this machete as the only surgical instrument," he shouted in his ear, while he crushed his face against the floor with his foot.

"I will spend a little more time with your niece. As she is young and has had no children yet, I'll give her a master class about how children come into the world. I will rape her as many times as necessary until she begs me on her knees and prays for me to end her life. Then I'll come for you and kill you with my own hands, but not before describing in great detail what I have done with your two loved ones. Are we understanding each other?" and after finishing the sentence, he lifted his boot from Gerard's head and turned away toward the door.

"It is totally impossible to escape from this room, no one knows you are here, no one can hear you, and nobody cares. You have twenty minutes to meditate and take your decision; as you can see, I'm not an inconsiderate man. When the time is over, I will make a call to that phone. If no one answers, I will understand you have made the right decision, and as the gentlemen and men of honor we are, I will honor my word, and the women in your family will never know of my existence. If, on the contrary, you answer the phone and are still alive, I will launch the plan I have outlined for you, and I assure you when you see me again you will regret a thousand times not having pulled the trigger, but it will be too late and you will endure unspeakable suffering. The clock is already ticking, don't you hear it?" he said, and left the room, closing the door behind him with a loud bang, followed by the sound of locks latching.

Gerard wondered how could he have gotten in that situation. The least he could have expected when he started the investigation was that anyone in his family could be harmed. Not even in his worst nightmares could he have imagined the blood oozing from that case could splatter his sister and niece, let alone that the blood could be theirs.

What that psychopath was asking of him was of unimaginable cruelty. Giving up his own life to safeguard that of his family, sparing his loved ones from untold physical suffering, in exchange for subjecting them to unspeakable psychological suffering, not seeing him again. It was a sick and macabre proposal, and Gerard would not accept it without a fight.

He would not let that lunatic get away with it. He would try to get out of there before reaching the twenty-minute deadline, and when the time was about to run out... then he would decide what to do next.

Gerard stood up, ran to the door and tried to open it. He hit it several times with hands and feet but the door sounded solid. He looked around and all he could use as a blunt object was the chair, but its thin wood would have shattered at the second blow.

He approached the desk and opened all the bureau drawers, which had been empty during his first inspection. In one of them, he now found the gun mentioned in the letter, and checked that indeed there was a single bullet in the cylinder.

He considered shooting at the door, but with a single bullet there was little damage he could inflict, plus the door had no lock accessible from the inside.

His eyes lingered on the old gas lamps. They were two wavy metal arms, simulating a tree branch with leaves. Gerard hung from them with both hands and yanked them off from the wall. They were not very thick, but at least they were two iron bars that could be useful.

He jammed the bars on the door frame and levered, but he could barely make a dent in the wood. He hit the door with the bars but soon realized it would take him forever to break through that way. According to his watch, over five minutes had already elapsed, and he was sure the psychopath would keep his word.

Gerard tried to stay calm and consider his options, but he couldn't avoid seeing the faces of Max, his sister and his niece dancing around him, breaking his concentration. He tried to block them out and concentrate on solving the problem at hand before the hourglass dried out.

Bending down, he lifted the carpet in one fell swoop, and stomped the floor as a flamenco dancer, looking for trapdoors or underground passages, but the floor was solid.

He ran to the couch, pushed it aside and examined the tiled wall, it seemed normal. He did the same with the desk, but the wall behind it also seemed solid. He was in an underground room, and the walls seemed carved into the rock and later covered with tiles.

The only piece left to examine was the bookcase. He checked his watch. It had been over ten minutes. He didn't have much time, but he still had options. He went to the bookcase and pushed from one side, but could not move it, which surprised him because the bookcase was empty.

Pushing again didn't move it one millimeter. He supposed it was attached to the wall, but he couldn't separate it to examine it from behind.

He bent down and examined the lower shelves, knocking on the wooden panels that formed the back wall. Instead of sounding like hollow wood, they had an unusual thickness for that type of furniture. He picked up one of the gas lamp metal arms and swatted the back panel, without making a dent in the wood.

It was all very strange. Why would they fix to the wall precisely that bookcase and not the other pieces of furniture? It made no sense unless the bookcase was there for a reason, such as hiding or protecting something.

He glanced at his watch again. He only had six minutes left, but he tried to be positive and think it was an eternity. He knew the bookcase was hiding something, and he tried to isolate from everything to concentrate on the analysis of the problem by reducing it to its most elementary parts.

If he assumed as certain the bookcase was there to protect something as if it were a door, it should have a lock or at least an opening mechanism. He quickly felt around all sides of the bookcase, pressing the wooden planks for some loose plank, but found none.

He climbed on the chair and examined the top of the bookcase, but everything seemed solid. The shelves would not move either, they were solid planks glued to the side walls.

The mechanism could also be away from the bookcase. He ran his hands along the wall against which the cabinet was leaning, but found no trapdoors or hidden switches or cables. He was getting very nervous and started to manifest it externally.

Since he wore no shirt, he rubbed his forehead with the back of his hand to remove the sweat drops sliding down on it.

According to his watch, he only had three minutes left, which could well be his last three minutes of life, even though Gerard refused to surrender.

If the mechanism was not in sight, it would be impossible to find it in just a few minutes, unless he found a clue, and perhaps it was closer than he thought.

Once again, he closed his eyes for a moment and let his intuition carry him away. He threw his backpack on the floor and rummaged inside until he found the paper in which Agustín made his drawings.

He stood under the light bulb and noted once again the drawing of the house, the winged animal, the water and the boat, and then he noticed some faint lines drawn in one of the page footers. He had seen it previously but did not give it any relevance.

A square with a flame drawn inside. The flame rose above a horizontal line, like a lighted candle lying flat.

A lighted candle might represent a church, a chapel, a cemetery, but he couldn't see any candle there. He looked around again and had a second of brilliant inspiration.

Perhaps the square represented the room, and perhaps it was not a candle in a horizontal position but a metal arm on whose end a gas flame was burning.

He got up without even daring to look at the watch again. He would fight to the end, no matter what.

He went straight to pick up one of the metal arms he had ripped from the wall and dragged a chair next to the wall. He climbed on it and introduced the metal arm back into the original hole in the wall.

The bar was loose, and he spun it until he found a point where it held tight. He let go, and the bar remained horizontal. He had found a fit.

Keeping the bar embedded, he moved it in all directions, from top to bottom first and horizontally later, sensing some resistance. When he kept pushing, he felt the resistance beginning to give way, and he kept moving the bar horizontally until it was flat against the wall.

Nothing happened, and everything would end in just a few seconds. Discouraged, he couldn't help looking at his watch.

The clock hands let the last thirty seconds go, disappearing from the dial and Gerard's life as it moved, erasing also all hope for his family.

He let go of the bar and collapsed on the chair. He took a deep breath and prepared to await developments with resignation, determined to battle until his last breath.

He picked up the gun from the table and clasped it, waiting for the hand of the clock to complete the circle.

A snap startled him and made him turn toward the wall, and he aimed the gun at the point the sound had come from, the bookcase.

Everything seemed in order, but he was sure he heard it right. He got up and walked to the bookcase and immediately noticed something had changed. The rear edge of the bookcase was slightly separated from the wall, whereas before it had been impossible for him to move it even a millimeter.

He rested his hands on the side of the bookcase and pushed, and his heart sank when he noticed the bookcase slid easily to one side, exposing an opening in the wall, a dark

398

space barely one meter high, through which a person could pass if crouching.

Gerard did not even hesitate for an instant. He put the gun into his backpack, climbed to the chair and pulled the bar to take it with him, and jumped down to the floor and disappeared crawling through the hole.

One second later, his hands reappeared through the hole and pulled the bookcase to bring it back in place, where it fitted with a new snap.

In the silence of that gloomy room, the phone started ringing with its intermittent moan. Gerard could hear it through the wall, like a distant echo, and he stopped to listen for a second.

It was a call nobody would answer, although that was not exactly what the sinister psychopath expected to happen.

Gerard didn't know what to expect from that point on, but life had given him a second chance, and he would not waste it.

CHAPTER 70

The passage was only a natural vent, an almost vertical crack in the rock, manually widened to barely allow the passage of a person. Gerard took out his flashlight, and after charging it by turning the crank, he held it in his mouth as he used hands and feet to climb the crack.

Slits and small rock ledges, flattened to provide support for hands and feet along the way, facilitated the ascent. He soon reached the top of the crack, which opened to the floor of a new stretch of artificial passage, covered with a thin layer of cement and having a higher ceiling.

Not knowing which way to go, he chose at random. He had only walked for a few minutes when he thought he heard a door closing. He stopped immediately, turned off the flashlight and reached into his backpack to fumble for the gun.

He had never fired a real one, the closest he had been to do it was with shotguns at the fair, although at present shooting would not be the most difficult part, but wisely administering the only bullet he had at his disposal and deciding when to use it. He would not have a second chance, and he wanted to save it for the psychopath who had threatened his family.

Once his eyes adjusted to the darkness, he walked along the passage until he saw a closed door and light filtering out through the slits. Confident, he abandoned the protection of the corner behind which he was spying and walked up to the door.

He could clearly hear the noise someone was making on the other side of the door. Apparently, someone was moving a heavy object.

The door had a doorknob, but he didn't know whether it would be locked. If he tried and found it locked, he would then betray his presence there, a risk he was willing to take. Feeling the gun in his hand, although he only had a single ridiculous bullet, gave him a strange peace of mind.

The noise had stopped, but Gerard put his hand on the doorknob, raised the gun, mentally counted to three, and turned it decisively.

To his relief, the door opened with no resistance, and Gerard jumped inwards and ducked to dodge the likely hail of gunfire that always accompanies that gesture in every action movie. He waited there crouching but nothing happened, and when he opened his eyes, he saw he was in a small warehouse filled with wooden crates.

There was nobody there. Could it be possible they had escaped through a door at the other end of the room? Gerard walked up to there to check. He found another small door and got ready to open it following the same technique he had successfully used to enter. He raised his gun, put his hand on the doorknob and did a mental countdown.

"*One, two and three.*"

"Do not move if you want to stay alive," he heard a voice say behind him, while he felt the cold touch of a gun barrel against his neck.

Gerard released the doorknob, lowered his hands, and turned slowly.

"Eva, what do you want?" he said, when confronted by the girl, who was pointing at him with a gun larger than his.

"Drop your weapon and kick it."

Gerard dropped the gun at his feet and kicked it just a few meters away.

"Eva, put the gun down and let's talk, please."

"We have nothing worth talking about."

"It's not true. What about your great-grandmother and how much she suffered? What about figuring out what tormented her at the Casino?"

"I already know what tormented her, and I assure you my great-grandmother's soul already rests in peace. We already took take care of that a long time ago."

"We took care? Why do you speak in the plural? Whom do you mean?"

"I mean the shadow, the Casino ghost, the dark soul who wanders through its ruins waiting to avenge so many forced suicides."

"An avenger? Is this is how you now call one who's just a simple psychopath murderer?"

Eva grinned openly and seemed to relax a little.

"There is so much you don't know."

"Why don't you tell me then? For instance, what do you have to do in all this?" Gerard asked, stepping forward, which made her raise her weapon again and put it against his chest.

"Go back immediately. I will not hesitate to empty the clip on you if you come near me again. Although now that I think about it, I must do it anyway, even if you don't come near me so, what difference does it make? Sit over there," she said, pointing the gun at some crates.

Gerard stepped back and sat on them.

"What's in here?" he asked, slapping his hand on the crate beneath him.

"None of your business. You know you ask too many questions? That's your main problem. That, and your exaggerated and morbid curiosity. Although it cannot be said I am not curious too. When you came to see me, I met with you out of pure curiosity. I knew what you were after, but I needed to confirm my suspicions and find out how much you knew, how far you had gotten in your investigation."

"What are you talking about? What are you hiding from me? What's going on here? Can you please explain?" Gerard demanded aloud.

"You're in no position to demand anything, especially not using that tone. But since these are your last minutes alive, never let it be said I did not grant the prisoner his last wish. Whatever you may think of me, I'm not a heartless woman," she said, lifting her foot and resting it on one crate.

"As a child, I grew up hearing stories about my great-grandmother. Not the official history but the forbidden version, the one my mother and grandmother told in confidence, which they shared with me when I became an adult. A story that was passed exclusively from mothers to daughters and that could only be told on the deathbed."

Gerard listened intently, ignoring where Eva's story was headed.

"My great-grandmother Juana worked at the Casino, she had a position of responsibility as a housekeeper and in charge of room service, and she met many of the most powerful and influential people in the society of her time. She was a very beautiful woman and soon caught the attention of many of those idle men who tried to convince her to offer services far beyond those stipulated in her contract. Let's say she got to know so many bedroom secrets that she became a potentially dangerous person to many of them.

During the time she worked at the Casino, she discovered one of its best-kept secrets, the existence of a forbidden room, a temple of horror where they took all those who wished to leave this world after having gambled and lost everything, unable to overcome the embarrassment of confronting their families and the public scandal that would entail. It was the easy way out for them, and without judging if it was morally reprehensible, the Casino offered them an honorable escape route."

"Do you think helping people to commit suicide is honorable?" Gerard said.

"I told you I don't do moral judgments, I simply listen to the facts and collect all the evidence at my disposal. My great-grandmother did the same, she did not judge anyone and kept at her work and routine. Eventually, she discovered that what seemed a discrete and macabre service offered by the Casino, went far beyond. It covered up a sinister network dedicated to identifying potential wealthy victims, whom they attracted to the Casino through all possible means of persuasion, to then separate them from their money at the gambling tables.

Subsequently, they offered them a way out of their economic problems by inviting them to leave this world in a quick, honorable and discreet manner, but during that process they suffered extorsion, blackmail and were forced to divest any assets and properties, under terrible threats of death, rape and all kinds of atrocities, targeting their family members, usually the wives and children of the victims.

They forced them to transfer funds and properties and write them to the name of individuals associated with the circle. They asked them to change their wills and introduce new beneficiaries, to sell businesses and properties, acquired at bargain prices by frontmen of the group."

Gerard was speechless. That confirmed his suspicions; the incredible story matched the evidence he had been collecting in his research. For instance, the deal they offered him earlier in that room, should not differ greatly from the one they put in front of the poor souls who ended up in that same situation one century ago.

"My great-grandmother didn't want to know more; it was a criminal organization that had blackmailed businessmen, politicians, and aristocrats of all kinds, but when she refused to collaborate with them, she began to fear for her life. She had become a threat to that secret society, but they couldn't touch her because she still kept contacts and powerful friends.

There came a time when she was so terrified by what she had seen and everything that was happening there that she quit her job at the Casino, hoping she could get away from it all, and for a while, she succeeded. He married a good man, a glass craftsman who took care of her and fathered her two daughters.

Years passed, and I suppose many of the important politicians and businessmen who protected her died of old age, so my great-grandparents left Barcelona city to get away from the many powerful people who could still feel threatened by her presence and who could still want her dead.

Her world apparently went back to normal, and after the Civil War, she reoriented her life and devoted herself to helping her husband in the family business, a glassware store they had set in a small town in the province of Girona.

However, in 1945, a sad November day, my great-grandfather called the police because that morning she had not come to open the shop and had not shown up in all day. They searched for her for weeks, and some even said maybe she had fled with some of her former lovers, but all was in vain.

A year later, two hunters found human remains rotting in a nearby forest, close to where she had lived. It would appear those could be my great-grandmother's remains.

The body was in very poor condition, several limbs were missing, which they attributed to the action of forest vermin, but I always believed them to be vermin of the two-legged kind. The autopsy revealed they had used extreme brutality on her and that her suffering must have been unimaginable.

Something everyone missed during the brief and ridiculous investigation police carried out, was what they found in one her skirt pockets. A two pesetas token from the Casino de la Rabassada.

The police settled the issue by saying it must have been a souvenir from the time she worked there, that she was wearing as a good luck charm. I knew that token brought her nothing but the worst of luck and that it was a sign planted by those who had finally found her and had silenced her, a warning to anyone who tried to follow in her footsteps."

"It does not differ much from the current modus operandi of the mafia," Gerard said, although Eva ignored his comment and continued her story.

"My great-grandmother left a diary which she hid in a safe place for her daughter to find, my grandmother, at the time of her death. In the diary she explained in great detail everything she knew about the macabre activities of that group of powerful people operating in the Casino, providing names, both for the public figures who made up the group, and for many of the victims, many of whom never were declared officially dead, only as missing.

That diary had been the reason my great-grandmother was murdered. For years it had been her safeguard, her life insurance, but as her protectors started dying, at some point it became her death sentence.

The information contained in that diary, if made public, would have ended the career and life of many supposedly honorable people and model citizens. There were politicians, businessmen, judges, police chiefs, aristocrats and big names of the public life of the period, all directly or indirectly involved in the killings and the extortion network, and all of them benefitting financially from all that horror."

"Is that the same diary you showed me the day we met for the first time? There she only wrote about personal issues and mentioned her intention to quit her job at the Casino."

"Do you think I would have let you read the true diary? That was a transcript I made myself, reproducing the most harmless pages. Some pages in the original diary are so hot that the paper catches fire just from reading them."

"And your great-grandfather suspected nothing?"

"As I said, it was something only handed down from mother to daughter. Fortunately, women prevail in our family. You men are weak by nature and not to be trusted. We have always been strong, and great-grandmother Juana was a model for us, she showed us the way. She did it in life, with her strength and courage to write her diary, and continued to do it after her death, by showing us which was the only way to put an end to all that and avenge all the damage done to so many families like ours."

"Which way do you mean? What the hell are you talking about?"

"My grandmother found Juana's diary and was so impressed by what it recounted, that she dedicated the rest of her life to fight all those who had brought hell to my great-grandmother's life and that of so many other families. My grandmother had university studies, she was a historian, and devoted her life to secretly investigate everything that happened in the Casino and the society during those turbulent years. Using the precious information in Juana's diary, she tracked down the names that appeared there, investigating the origin of their fortunes and following the thread of all transactions and operations they carried out in those years.

She discovered many of them had enriched dramatically in a short period of time, by alleged inheritance, or speculating in reclassifications of land acquired at very low prices. They received Art Nouveau states and buildings of great historical value as donations, only to demolish them without hesitation with the connivance of corrupt politicians and builders, to build impersonal grisly story buildings on the empty lots, buildings they subsequently sold, earning them huge profits."

"And why didn't she go to the police with the diary?"

"Are you not listening? I said the list included politicians, police authorities, judges, it was like reading the society pages in a newspaper of the time; it listed members of the crème de la crème of Spanish society. Going to the police with that would have amounted to suicide."

"Which wouldn't have looked out of place, considering the issue at hand," Gerard joked.

"You even dare to make jokes about this. The only thing that saves you is that this will probably be your last joke in this world, and it will be precisely me who gets the last laugh," Eva said, staring intently into his eyes.

"Besides the famous names involved in that scandal, my grandmother discovered something that would change her life and that of all women in the family who have come after her."

CHAPTER 71

Eva smiled at him, managing her silences with the mastery of someone who controls the art of public speaking, keeping the audience interested and in suspense.

"She investigated the murderers, but also the lives of many victims and determined that not all of them were wealthy, some were middle-class persons who had become a threat to the organization, and were invited to commit suicide.

She interviewed the descendants of many victims but developed a very special relationship with one of them. She discovered that, on top of being the son of one victim who disappeared in the Casino, he was dedicating his life to discovering the truth, just like her.

They got to be so close my grandmother showed him Juana's diary.

After reading it and finding the name of his father among the list of victims, something inside of him awoke, feeding a thirst for vengeance that turned him into a beast, up for anything just to kill those who had provoked such horror, a beast that had the unconditional support of his new partner, my grandmother."

Gerard had not moved since Eva started talking. He didn't know if what she was explaining was true, but although it was incredible, it made sense and he wanted to know the rest of the story.

"From that moment on they worked together, both as a professional and romantic couple. They explored the Casino ruins, and following the indications in the diary, they found the cursed room and the network of underground tunnels that start at the Maison de Morte, a remarkable feat you also achieved on your own, a sad waste of talent."

Gerard winced, not knowing whether to be flattered by the compliment or fearful by the veiled threat.

"They located the perpetrators mentioned in the diary who were still alive, and also the descendants of those who had died because of age, and they carefully planned how to kill them all, making them pay for their actions or those of their ancestors, in exactly the same way they had done it in the past.

Their technique consisted in abducting and locking them in the suicide room. There they terrorized them and finally forced them to commit suicide in exchange for respecting the life and physical integrity of their loved ones, just as they did to so many innocent people."

"What if they did not cooperate and refused to commit suicide?"

"I must admit their arguments proved most convincing, as most ended up accepting the deal. For those that did not, their bodies appeared in the mountains a few days later, seemingly quartered by wild animals."

"Don't you find their hypocrisy to be sickening, eliminating the children of those murderers, becoming murderers and extortionists themselves, rising exactly to the same level of those they both hated so much?" Gerard said passionately.

"Don't be stupid, you know nothing of what happened. The real hypocrites were those who appeared to be respectable members of society, while cheating on their wives with their mistresses, ripping off their business partners, killing innocents and taking advantage of the lowest instincts of the human condition for their personal gain. My grandparents never profited financially from anyone, never took a penny from any of their victims, they only sought justice, and avenge the memory of those who died," Eva said, furious.

"How many children did they have?"

"As I said, their relationship went beyond the professional, and they had an only daughter, my mother," Eva said.

"They devoted their lives to cross off names from the list in my great-grandmother's diary. Sometimes it took them years to identify their prey, but they had the infinite patience of the professional hunter. They were a perfect tandem, seamless, and their modus operandi was impossible to detect by the police, the perfect crime."

"Perfect? If I could get to them, others will too, and certainly the police as well," Gerard said.

"You think you've gotten to them? Don't be naïve. First, I don't think you're in a position to be giving lessons or get to anyone, when I will die in a few minutes. And second, they are no longer active, they died years ago, but their secret is still alive, my grandmother passed it on to my mother on her deathbed, and my mother passed it on to me, and I have followed the family tradition."

"Then, is your mother the one committing the crimes, the one who goes around dressed in black?" Gerard said defiantly.

"No. She never wanted to intervene, although she understood our mission and supported us. It was she who encouraged me to continue the work of my ancestors. She was a good mother and never betrayed us. When she died, I promised her I would complete the mission entrusted to us by my grandmother, and it is an honor for me to be taking her place.

"Then, do you work alone?"

"No, someone has taken my grandfather's place. If you knew who the person hiding behind that cloak is, you would regret not having gladly accepted his offer and pulled the trigger when you had the chance. Now you must suffer the consequences, not only for yourself but for your sister and her daughter."

At the mention of his family, Gerard could not restrain himself and lunged at Eva, who pulled the trigger.

The sound of the shot bounced off the walls of the small room and was deafening. Gerard fell sideways, having taken the shot in his left shoulder.

Eva got up and approached him, still pointing the gun at him.

"You're pathetic, and above all, so predictable. If only you had used your wits and perspicacity to work with us instead of wasting your time chasing ghosts, we could have completed our task already and it would all be over. Chasing us was a very serious mistake, one you will pay with your life, and that of your family," Eva said.

Gerard gripped his shoulder, trying to plug the wound, which started bleeding.

"I just wanted to get to the truth, find out the reason for those deaths, know the true story of what happened in the Casino. My interest was only journalistic," Gerard said, in a voice filled with pain.

"Nothing you can say matters to me. Say your goodbyes and be thankful it's me that's ending your life and not him, for he would not be so considerate with you. I think he prefers to save his energies for your sister and her daughter," Eva said, howling with laughter.

Gerard felt the sweet taste of blood in his mouth, from biting his lip hard trying to hold back and not jump on Eva. He knew if he tried she would shoot him again and he would run out of options. He needed to keep her busy, perhaps with a little white lie.

"Eva, just one more question, please," Gerard begged, raising his hand from the ground, in surrender.

"The last wish of a sentenced to death. I cannot refuse."

"What happened with your great-grandmother's diary? Where is it now?"

"Is that your last question? You really are strange, but I'll tell you. I have it, I'm the one who checks it and who crosses off names on the list as they are being executed. The truth is few of them remain alive because it's often difficult to locate their descendants after so many years, but we'll go on till the end. I keep it in my house, in a safe place. Satisfied?"

"It's not the only diary in existence," Gerard said.

411

"Nonsense, you're ranting. My great-grandmother only wrote one. That, I am sure of, and I have it."

"I'm not talking about her, I'm talking about your grandmother."

"My grandmother wrote nothing, don't be a liar."

"Why would I lie when I'm about to die? Your grandmother wrote a letter I found into an old book that came from the Casino, most likely from the same bookcase still standing in the cursed room," Gerard said.

Eva approached him and squatted near his shoulder.

"You're lying to me, I know. You just want to buy time to delay the inevitable, to add a few more minutes to your miserable life, but it won't do you any good."

Gerard sat up and kept talking.

"I'm telling the truth. It's a letter she wrote years ago, in which she mentions one victim they forced to commit suicide. The initials of the victim were V.P. and he died on January 6, 1912, leaving a wife and daughter," Gerard said, making up a half-truth.

Eva's cold stare did not betray her thoughts, but she seemed startled by that revelation.

"Perhaps you didn't know about the existence of that letter, but if you really have been dedicated to this for years, you will know the data on the victim is correct. Am I wrong? Do you know who is hiding behind the acronym VP? For once in your life, tell me the truth."

Eva held Gerard's gaze, before she closed her eyes, took a deep breath and started to speak.

"They forced Catalan businessman Victor Papiol to commit suicide on that date, leaving a wife and a daughter. They probably believed he had abandoned them to run away with another woman, to another country, taking with him his fortune and family assets and condemning them to a future of deprivation, aggravated by the Civil War, during which the mother died. His daughter lived a miserable life until her death twenty years later, single and childless," Eva said, not showing any emotion, as if reciting a memorized text.

How did you find out about those initials? Only my great-grandmother knew those details. Where do you keep that letter? Where is it? I need to read it," Eva said.

"It's kept in a safe place, in case something happened to me. Let me go and I'll let you read it," Gerard said.

"I cannot do it, I no longer can, it's too late," Eva said, shaking her head in despair. Gerard sensed that if he kept pushing her that way maybe he could crack her shell.

"Your grandmother seemed to suffer a great deal from the tone in which she wrote it. I think she was struggling in a sea of doubt about her mission."

"Gerard, please, I need to read it. It means a lot to me," Eva said, in what sounded more like a plea than a statement.

"Let go of me and I'll take you to her."

For a moment, Eva seemed to consider Gerard's proposal, but her face shifted from tension to pride in a few seconds, smiling uneasily.

Nothing prepared Gerard for what came next.

"I must admit you have showed a great ability finding out about VP and unraveling what happened until his well-deserved end," Eva said, "but I'm sorry to tell you you have fallen short of your deductions, so much you have not even scratched the surface of what hides under this gigantic iceberg."

"Where are you going with this?"

"I want to rub the truth on your face so you feel once and for all in your flesh what this means to us. It's a true crusade, in which we are the warriors of Christianity. It's not about revenge, it's about doing justice.

"Revenge is nothing more than the search for a substitute for justice, for desperate people like you," Gerard said.

Eva laughed openly, which further unnerved Gerard, who tried to control himself.

—All right, I'll be honest with you, because it will really be the last thing I do and I don't care if you know. Are you sure it was Victor Papiol who appeared in the letter you found?

"I told you, I found information about his family, and everything matches. The letter is authentic," Gerard said.

"I know, and his story too, but that's not what I mean. Are you sure those were the initials, VP?"

"The ink is discolored and the strokes are weak, but I assure you it's readable."

"Are you completely sure?" Instead of VP, couldn't it have been VB? The difference is minimal, just a tiny leg in a single letter," Eva said, going back to her most serious countenance.

"And even if it were, it wouldn't change anything of what happened, nor would it make it less reprehensible."

"What if I told you those initials might correspond to Valentín Bach? Does the name ring a bell, Mr. Gerard Bach?"

Gerard didn't know what to say. That name was familiar, he vaguely remembered hearing it mentioned at home, when his parents were still alive. He was one of his father's ancestors, perhaps his own great-grandfather.

If he believed those ravings, a completely different and frightening scenario opened before him, his family directly involved in that monstrous plot. He could not give credit, however, something inside prevented him from dismissing it as the raving of a deranged woman.

"If you and I had worked together, we would have rewritten history. But it's too late now, you will never know how close you have been to discover the big secret, to which you would partly deserve to have access in your own right."

"Can you tell me what are you talking about? Eva, please speak clearly. What does my family have to do with all this?"

Eva didn't answer anymore. With a lost gaze, and teary eyes, she whispered the words.

"A pity…, it's too late…, you'll never know…"

The door opened with a heavy blow, a black figure framed under the doorway.

CHAPTER 72

Eva and Gerard turned to the black figure in unison and their shock seemed rehearsed, perfectly synchronized.

This time Gerard could take a better look at him than before. A black mesh covered his face, and what he first thought was a cloak, was a black cloth wrapped around his body.

"I see you did not answer my phone call after all," he said, with a deep voice.

"Didn't you leave a message on my voicemail? Sorry. If you did, I haven't had time to listen to it. I've been a little busy during the last hour," Gerard said.

"I'm glad to see you still keep your sense of humor. It's the only thing you'll keep, besides your teeth, but not for long. I'm sorry to have interrupted you, for I know the lady was about to show you the way out of this room, wasn't she? To find it, you only have to come and look through the hole in the barrel of the gun she is pointing at you. Look through it and you will soon see the light at the end of the tunnel," the masked figure said.

Eva was crouching next to Gerard and her body prevented the murderer from having a direct view of Gerard's face, while he was trying to get Eva to read his lips.

"I'll give you the letter, but you have to help me escape," he said, again and again, gesturing slowly without uttering a word, hoping she would understand. Eva stood motionless, staring at him with glazed eyes, in which tears began to well.

"Eva?" the murderer said, becoming impatient at her passivity.

Gerard knew those were his last seconds. No matter what happened, he wouldn't have more than a small window of opportunity, so he seized Eva's hesitation to reach out slowly, taking delicately the hand Eva was using to hold her gun, and she offered no resistance.

Leaning on his other arm, he stood up, and taking Eva's hands in his, he turned the gun toward the dark figure, joined Eva's finger on the trigger, and pulled hard.

The shot deafened him again for a few seconds, while Eva's body fell on him and they both rolled on the ground. He sought her arm to grab her gun and shoot again, and got it easily, too easily.

Eva's body lay limp. He took the gun in his hands and fired twice toward the darkness of the door, which was already empty. His shoulder hurt more and more, he didn't know how much blood he had lost, but he felt weakness was taking over his movements.

He held Eva's body by the shoulders while he turned it and saw a large bloodstain spread through the fabric of her blouse as if someone had thrown a pebble into a pond.

Gerard opened her blouse by pulling all the buttons and was speechless at seeing the tip of the huge machete poking its head between Eva's breasts, only the handle sticking out of her back.

Eva parted her eyes and barely a few words could escape from her lips, interwoven with her last breath of life.

"Everything I did was for the family. Never give up. Don't let… "and her eyes closed as her body disconnected from his vital functions for good, and her head tilted.

Gerard dropped her gently on the floor and struggled to his feet, holding the gun in his hands. The murderer could return at any time, and his strength was abandoning him as quickly as the toilet water after being flushed.

Why in such a dramatic moment, an eschatological metaphor had come to mind was anybody's guess, but he suspected it was but a prelude to madness from hypovolemic shock. He had to find the exit once and for all if he didn't want to end up like Eva.

He staggered toward the second door on the opposite end of the room, but he could not resist checking what was in those boxes. He used the metal arm of the gas lamp as a lever to lift the wooden lid in one of them.

Expecting to find again bricks or sacks of hardened cement, to his surprise he found a few small plastic packages. He reached over, took two of them, and put them in his backpack. There was no time for more.

He came to the door and opened it taking no precautions. He found a tortuous passage, built from a natural cave but reinforced with cement. The musty smell was strong, and lighting was poor, as had been the norm.

He walked with the waning agility with which his legs could move, which was not much, until he reached a point where the passage widened to form a small hall. The wall in front of him was built with cement-coated brick, was about three meters high and had a single metal door.

Gerard walked to the door and listened carefully, but could not catch any noise from the other side. He put a hand on the doorknob, grabbed the gun with the other, and pushed the door open a few centimeters. He waited a few seconds and ventured into the darkness of that new room.

He couldn't see anything, but from the echo and the way his footsteps resonated when walking on the concrete floor, he had the feeling he must be in quite a large room.

Reaching into his backpack he pulled out the small flashlight, but it could hardly illuminate beyond one meter. The curved walls and its dimensions, suggested it was a giant cistern, much bigger than the one he had known days ago when he was trapped in it.

His feet splashed on several small puddles of water, suggesting the tank could have been recently active.

He pointed the flashlight towards the ceiling hoping to see some opening through which the water could come in, but saw none. It seemed it was a sealed tank with no entry point other than the door, which meant he would not have any other escape route either.

Suddenly, the ground seemed to open beneath his feet and swallow him into a dark abyss. He was so concentrated looking up, he had not seen a giant hole in the tank's floor, right at its center. Gerard fell on it but clung with arms and elbows to the edge of the gaping hole, avoiding a more than certain death.

His feet dangled in the void, and he tried to support them on the slippery smooth walls. His injured shoulder did not allow him to use his arm strength to climb freehand, so he had to lift one foot to the edge and get out, before collapsing exhausted on the ground.

He caught his breath for a few seconds, and tried to gather his power, but the only one he had left was willpower.

He sat up and looked for the flashlight, which luckily had not gone through the hole, and pointed it at the opening.

It was a giant sinkhole, a circular well almost two meters in diameter, probably used to empty the tank. He poked his head over the edge and pointed the light down but saw nothing but utter darkness. He searched his backpack for some small object and chose a coin, which he threw at the center of the hole.

He listened for the moment the coin hit the bottom, mentally counting the seconds, but the time never came. It was not possible, it couldn't be a bottomless pit. He threw another coin and listened intently, but he got the same result.

With the third coin, it was the same, and in view of the high cost of the experiment, he canceled it at the fourth coin before bankrupting his finances. There had to be another explanation, but at that moment he couldn't think of any.

If that well was a drainage, there had to be a water inlet somewhere, he thought. He walked to the far end of the tank and run around its perimeter, his hand on the wall, until he reached the starting point, the metal entry door.

He decided to get out and explore another passage, but when he tried to open the door, he found it locked.

He was sure he had left the door open when he entered, as a precaution. It was a metal door that had no doorknob from the inside, so although he pounded hard on the door, all his attempts to open it were in vain.

Trapped him in a cistern for the second time in a few days, unbelievable. If there was a water drainage, maybe he could use it as an escape route. He went back to the center of the room to inspect the well more closely.

"You have turned out to be a bigger nuisance than I had anticipated. Maybe I underestimated you a little."

CHAPTER 73

The voice echoed inside the tank and seemed to come from all directions. Gerard turned off the flashlight and when he saw a small hatch opening on a corner in the ceiling, he ran in that direction and stood right underneath.

It was a square hole through which a person would hardly fit, but he could see someone watching from above. He knew whom that voice belonged to.

"What do you want? Why did you lock me here?" Gerard shouted.

"Eva will not enjoy seeing the culmination of our work, you have deprived her of our big moment, and now you will pay for it."

"What are you talking about? I did nothing. I'm just a journalist in search of the truth."

"You say you only seek information, and I'll give it to you. In fact, I'll give you a scoop, a headline for tomorrow's news. "*Nosy journalist drowns under mysterious circumstances*". Or better this one "*Reckless journalist disappears after savagely killing his sister and niece.*" Although as usual, perhaps the best solution is a combination of both "*Mediocre journalist disappears after his sister and niece are found drowned.*" What do you think? Which one do you like best? It's not that I'm letting you choose, but I want your opinion," the voice shouted from above.

"What do you think of this one? "*Psycho murderer found dead after a century-old organization dedicated to the extortion of personalities and businessmen is exposed,*" Gerard said.

"I think it's weak, lacking hook, and above all, untrue but, what else can you expect from a shitty journalist like you? I'll give you all the information, the pure facts for you to write your story. Too bad no one will read it unless you write for the fish, the only ones which will read you from now on."

At those words, Gerard feared the worst, that the psychopath would begin letting water fall through the ceiling hatch to fill the tank.

"It won't have slipped by you the fact you are in one of the old Casino tanks. Impressive, isn't it? It has a capacity for several million liters of water. Despite your stupidity, you must think I will fill the tank for you to drown in it. If so, you are correct."

Seeing the size of the small trapdoor, Gerard did a quick mental calculation and estimated that if a water jet the size of the hatch fell through it, it would take many hours to fill that huge cistern, perhaps more than a day. More than enough time to find an exit.

"When the water level reaches where I am, you'll be history. You will regret not having dared to use the gun to end your life quickly and honorably when you had the chance. Now you will have to do it the traditional way, with suffering and pain, a slow and harrowing agony."

The mention of the gun reminded Gerard he also had one, although he had lost it when he was about to fall into the pit.

Since the tank was in complete darkness, probably that individual could not see him from up there, he could only hear his voice.

He did not dare to turn on the flashlight, to avoid giving his position away, but he kept talking, as he bent down and patted the surrounding ground, looking for the gun.

"Why are you doing this to me? Let me out and I promise to tell your version of the story, you will have a chance to let the world know what happened in the Casino," Gerard shouted.

"It's an interesting offer which honors you, but it comes too late, perhaps some fifty years late. It would only attract crowds of onlookers like you and would make my life unnecessarily difficult, especially now that we are so close to making it. You see? I'm still talking in the plural, as if she were still alive and working by my side."

Gerard could not contain his excitement when his fingers felt the barrel of the gun and he picked it up quickly. He did not remember how many shots he had fired, so he couldn't be sure how many bullets were still left, if any, but he didn't dare to check to avoid making noise.

He positioned himself under the hatch and kept on talking, to let the voice of the murderer guide him since the eco was very disorienting and made it difficult to pinpoint where the original voice came from.

"Eva didn't want to go on with you, she was tired of it all and wanted to quit. She confessed it to me before dying," Gerard shouted, which made the man furious.

"You're talking nonsense," he shouted with an angry voice. "She would have never betrayed her family, her great-grandmother's legacy and that of her ancestors, the same way I'm loyal to mine, to the task my great-grandfather began, whom this city owes so much and who did so much good."

"Blackmailing and killing innocents is doing good? What good did your crazy great-grandfather do for them?" Gerard said, trying to provoke him to keep him talking.

"And what about all the people he saved? So many patients who owe him their lives, so many families to whom he returned their loved ones. And how did they pay him? They fired him from the hospital, dragging his name through the mud. The great Professor Papiol, turned into an outcast, a pariah of society. They ruined his life and sullied his honor, but his revenge has lived through the years, and it's not over yet. I'll put an end to all this. More and more people are becoming interested in the Casino's history, and it's only a matter of time before someone finally gets to us, as you did. That's why the time has come to disappear. I will blow this whole place up, destroy every passage, every room, every trace of our presence and no one will ever find anything that could shed light on our sacred work.

"What are you saying? What is it you want to blow up?"

422

"I have placed explosives at key points in this network of passageways and the large groundwater reserves. When the charges explode, the few passages that have not collapsed will end up completely submerged, erasing all traces of what could have taken place here in these past hundred years. When the water in the tank reaches this room up here, it will activate a trigger system that will detonate the main charges, setting the deflagration in motion.

It is even possible part of the mountain may crumble, changing the topography of the area. Heck, from tomorrow they will even have to amend the maps of the province. Too bad you will not be there to watch it from the outside, like me, although you cannot complain, because you will be front-line witness to one of the biggest explosions, one that will send you up so high your nose will touch the stars."

"You are nothing but a madman, you don't know what you're saying."

"Then I'll disappear, but I'll keep operating under a new identity. Nobody knows me, nobody knows I exist, only Eva knew my identity. I swear I will return to complete my task, to put an end to all unfinished business."

Gerard couldn't wait any longer. Being completely in the dark, it made no sense to keep his eyes open, so he closed them. He tried to concentrate solely on the voice speaking to him from above, to isolate it from the bouncing echo and to locate its source.

When he thought he had succeeded, he kept his eyes closed, held his breath and raised his arms. He held the gun with both hands and aimed in the direction his senses suggested, hoping Eva's gun would at least have one bullet left in its chamber.

The echo of the shot multiplied as if he had fired a machine gun, which was a sign that indeed there was ammunition. He kept his arms straight, firing a second time, but he stopped before firing a third. He could not waste more ammunition shooting blindly.

All he could do was wait. The voice no longer spoke to him, but he couldn't be sure whether he had hit the target. A noise echoed through the cistern, the sound of the trapdoor shutting. That meant he had missed his shots and the guy was still alive. He had to try to open that damn door at all costs.

As he passed by the pit, he heard a distant sound rapidly increasing in intensity. Its frequency was becoming sharper until it reached a point when it became inaudible.

Gerard stepped back and turned on the flashlight. At that moment, a huge water jet emerged from the center of the pit and went up in the air like a geyser, an underground volcano spewing water instead of lava.

The water jet almost reached the ceiling and fell back down like heavy rain that began to fill the bottom of the tank. Gerard ran to the metallic door and banged on it, but it seemed solid. The water level had risen and already covered the instep of his feet.

What he had believed to be a drainage hole was actually a pressure water inlet. He didn't know where it could come from, probably from one of the underground lakes he had discovered with Max. At that rate, it wouldn't take more than a few hours for the water level to get to the ceiling.

He wondered what could have become of poor Max. It had been several hours since he left to seek help, and all he had achieved was being trapped several times and spend his last minutes of life drowned like a rat in the hold of a sinking ship. Some help he had provided his friend.

He had to keep fighting to get out of there. That's what Max would have wanted, what he would have expected of him, so he would not disappoint him, even if it was the last thing he did.

He would try to force the door with the help of the metallic gas lamp arm. When the water reached the top of the door, he would have no choice but to stay afloat until the rising water level would bring him close to the cistern ceiling.

Then he could open the trapdoor, hoping it would offer less resistance than the metallic door, and try to defuse the explosive charges.

On paper, it was a good plan. With very little chances of success by not having any tools at hand, but it was a good plan.

CHAPTER 74

He spent endless minutes trying to pry the door open with the metal bar, but it appeared the door was watertight because as the water level rose, it did not escape through its slits.

The water level already reached halfway up the door. Gerard had run out of ideas. He decided to save his energies and wait for the water to lift him to the tank ceiling and try his luck with the trapdoor.

He relaxed and concentrated on staying afloat holding on to the walls, shaking his legs as if he were in the open sea. The momentary inactivity made him aware of the pain in his shoulder, and he wondered whether he could withstand the several hours it would take him to reach the ceiling of the tank.

The water was freezing, and he began to feel thousands of pins sticking into his legs. He hugged his backpack and leaned his head on it to get some rest while he waited. The contents of the backpack made it stiff and wouldn't let him lean his cheek on it, so he reached inside to reposition them.

He took one of the packages he had previously put there and held the flashlight in his mouth as he examined it.

The adhesive plastic wrapping made it waterproof, and he was sure it had to be a cocaine package. That must be how those fanatics financed their terror operations, trafficking with drugs they hid in those unexplored underground passages, he thought.

It was a perfect setup; nobody knew that place, nor the Casino's history, nobody bothered them, and they could go on with their plans knowing they were untouchable, having access to the substantial resources obtained from the drug trafficking.

With much difficulty because of his wet hands, he peeled off part of the protective adhesive wrapping and revealed one end of the package. To his surprise, it contained no powder inside, but a mass of clay-like consistency. There were black numbers printed on one side, indicating a possible serial number or manufacturing batch.

If water had not been so cold, he would have felt the chill running down his back when he realized what it really was. He was carrying two packs of plastic explosive in his backpack.

His fear and respect for explosives soon became excitement. He was holding something that could get him out of there if he only knew how to use it properly and didn't blow himself up.

He tried to remember what he had read about how to manipulate those materials, but the truth is he had barely read anything about it. What he knew he had learned from movies and novels, and those might not be very reliable sources.

If he could blast the metal door and empty the tank, even if he succeeded and survived the explosion, he would be back to the starting point, the passageway leading to the storage room, where the murderer would sure be waiting for him. There was no way out from that side.

His other option was riskier, to keep waiting for the water to lift him and to place the explosive on the tank ceiling hatch. Once it exploded, he could flee through the trapdoor and try to override the detonation system before the rising water activated it.

He chose the second option, although he was entering unknown territory for him.

The first thing he needed was a detonator to blow it up while staying at a far enough distance not to blow himself in pieces; floating in the dark inside a cistern was not the ideal situation to think about it.

The water level had already risen above the height of the door. Gerard estimated he had, at most, two hours before reaching the trapdoor to climb through it. Enough time, but first he had to blow it up without dying in the attempt.

He neither had a fuse, nor rope, nor a measly cigarette lighter to build a detonator, and in the aquatic environment where he was, he couldn't use them, anyway. There was only one thing he could do.

Holding the flashlight in his mouth, he pulled the gun from his backpack and checked if there were any bullets left in the chamber, begging God there were.

He thanked his guardian angel for having listened and stroked the only bullet left in the gun, his only chance to get out of there. His life and that of many people might depend on that small piece of metal.

If he placed the package of explosives in the trapdoor and shot it from afar, diving quickly afterward, he could detonate it and let the shock wave travel through the air, minimizing its impact underwater.

He didn't know if his reasoning was correct, but he had to trust his film culture, which dictated this was the most sensible solution.

For the first time, he let go of the tank wall and swam until he was right under the trapdoor, shining it with his flashlight. It was a metal trapdoor coated with a layer of thin bricks to camouflage it with the rest of the ceiling.

He could see the gap between the hatch and the frame, and that was where he would place the explosive, pushing it into that space, following the entire lid perimeter.

The waterproof canvas of his backpack had kept the interior relatively dry. He had two packages of explosives but didn't know which was the right amount he would need.

If he used too big a load, he risked causing a nuclear mushroom that would send him and what remained of the Casino into the stratosphere, but if the load was insufficient, he would waste his only chance to survive and would drown and die.

Better too much than too little. He opened the second package and carefully cut it in half and mixed it with the first, gently crushing the material, as if kneading biscuits for tea.

He could almost touch the ceiling, so in a few minutes he would be ready to place the charge. He carefully inserted the explosive all around the trapdoor, a much bigger effort than expected, as he had to stay afloat kicking with his legs underwater, like a dolphin in a zoo show.

When he finished placing all the load, he made sure it was thick enough to make it visible from afar to allow him to aim the gun.

Without losing sight of the trapdoor he swam backward toward the far wall, keeping the flashlight pointing to that spot. He held on to the wall, gathering his strength for a few minutes. He was running out of time; he had to act now.

He closed the left-over explosive package and dropped it into the water to let it sink like the Titanic to the bottom of the tank.

He drew his gun and stroked it as if showing affection toward a weapon would increase his chances of success or help his shot reach the target. He turned the crank as hard as he could, to charge the flashlight to the maximum, and held it to the top of the gun, in the best style of American detective series.

It was the moment of truth. So many things could go wrong, a wet projectile, an expired explosive, his trembling hand, his poor aim, an insufficient amount of explosive, and so many more, that he preferred not to be so optimistic and forget about everything.

Once again, he trusted his instinct, which normally didn't fail him. He relaxed, closed his eyes, took a deep breath, leaned back against the wall, and opened his eyes slowly, concentrating only on following the light beam and aligning the tip of the barrel with the whitish mass of explosive.

He let his body follow the swing of the water, but he secured his feet on the wall behind him, and as soon as he felt it was the right time, he strained his legs, held still, aimed at the explosive and squeezed the trigger gently.

It all happened in a split second. The gunshot echoed inside, but Gerard was expecting to hear an even bigger noise, the explosion.

If he wanted to have any chances of survival, he couldn't wait to check his aim. As soon as he felt the gun had fired, he dropped it in the water, dipped his head and pushed down with both legs, diving on a diagonal that took him to the bottom of the tank.

He didn't know if he had succeeded, but he looked up after feeling a very strong tremor that traveled underwater, accompanied by the distant drums of a huge explosion.

The flash reached him through the water, confirming the charge had exploded, but the blast hit him despite being several meters below water, pushing him toward the powerful water jet coming up from the well at the bottom of the tank.

His body cavorted up and down, spinning like a leaf in a submarine swirl for a very long minute.

Stunned by the explosion and the underwater dance and weakened by the cold temperature and the blood loss, Gerard made a Herculean effort to wake up, and do a self-assessment of damage.

His head was about to burst from pain as if he had placed the charge inside his skull, a sharp buzz lived inside his eardrums, and he was dizzy, disoriented and convinced he had swallowed more liters of water than those the tank contained.

After taking a few deep breaths, the pain he felt when he noticed the hot air and smoke penetrating his lungs made him come alive. At least he was now floating on the surface.

He coughed several times, spitting blood and perhaps some teeth, but looked up. He had lost his flashlight, the ridiculous but indispensable gadget that had helped him so much, but in the distance, he could see a faint glow coming in through the huge hole opened in the tank's ceiling, and he swam toward it.

The explosion had blown up the hatch and part of the ceiling had collapsed, but there was an electric light up there. He couldn't wait for the water level to rise further, he had to reach the edge of the hole as soon as possible. He reached out as far as he could, but without finding support for his feet, he could not reach the edge.

He was only one foot away from it, so he swam in circles around the water jet rising from the depths, calculating where was its center, and without hesitation, he swam into it.

The force of the water threw him against the wall. Gerard plunged again and tried one more time. He dove closer and as soon as he felt the force of the water, he entered the jet, which again expelled him out.

With the acquired practice, Gerard tried it for the third and fourth time, until he finally managed to remain steady and upright in the center of the jet, contracting every muscle in his body, adopting the shape of a human missile.

The force of the water pushed him up and this time he could maintain the trajectory, and he hit against the ceiling of the tank while his fingertips clung to the bricks at the edge of the hole.

It was the defining moment, so he drew strength from where there was hardly anything, and climbed up freehand until he could lift one leg, bring it through the hole, and pull his whole body through it.

Not knowing where he was, he collapsed and lay there for several minutes, his eyes closed, concentrated only in his breathing and in giving thanks for having escaped from that deathtrap.

He opened his eyes and saw the blurred silhouette of a yellowish light bulb hanging from a cable. He was in a small chamber directly on the ceiling of the tank.

CHAPTER 75

The roar of water bubbling under his feet brought him back to life. He looked at the black eye of the gaping hole and could feel the turbulence of the dark waters underneath boiling furiously, trying to get to him.

He remembered where he was and what he was looking for. He stood and searched for the water-activated detonation system, but the only thing that could fit the description was a plastic box attached to the wall.

The box had holes on the side and bundles of wires coming out of it, disappearing through a small hole that ran through the wall, next to a door.

Inside there was a set of thin metal sheets just one millimeter thick, connected to wires. He guessed that when the water got to the box, the metal sheets would come into contact and close a circuit triggering the detonation of all charges placed along the corridors.

It was a very rudimentary system, and Gerard assumed the murderer was not expecting company, so he did not use a timer. If he was right, all he had to do was to open the box and pull out those wires to deactivate the detonation.

He needed a sharp object to open the box without the sheets coming into contact due to vibration. She rummaged into his battered backpack and found a small plastic card with which he loosened two screws that held the housing, lifting it enough to expose several sheets.

Not wanting to touch them, he needed to find something to insert between them to prevent them from coming into contact. He thought about using the same plastic card, but there were many sheets and he only had one card, so he could not isolate them all. He checked around the room and found nothing he could use.

He approached the edge of the hole, and noticing water was spreading across the room floor, he picked up several pieces of rubble from the explosion, with traces of cement and plaster attached. He held them above the metal sheets and rubbed them against each other tightly.

Remnants of grit fell on the sheets as a fine dust rain, interposing between the sheet surfaces and isolating them from each other.

"This should be enough to avoid their coming into contact accidentally," Gerard thought, already feeling the cold water covering the soles of his feet.

With the sheets isolated, Gerard dared to manipulate the wires coming out of them. With his fingertips, he pushed them back and forth several times, until he pulled them out, leaving the rest inside the tube that ran through the wall.

When the water would come up to that level, he could not avoid their making contact, but since they were on the top part of the door, perhaps he had bought himself an hour.

He had to find a way out once and for all and had the feeling it couldn't be too far away.

A thunderous crackling mixed with the regurgitant sound of thousands of liters of water in motion shook the room. Gerard gripped the doorframe, noting with dismay the floor was giving way and collapsing. The ceiling of the tank had collapsed and was traveling down towards the bottom.

Gerard pushed his back against the doorframe, his fingertips resting on the base, just a few centimeters from the huge mass of water that roared at his feet.

With a trembling hand, he let go of his right hand and brought it to his back, fumbling until he found the door handle. He hoped it was open, otherwise, he would take a dip again, and this time it would be his final one.

The doorknob turned easily and Gerard fell back when the door opened. A small water tide splashed over him until he sat up. He pushed the door hard and could close it, although a rivulet kept flowing from under it.

Something about the door caught his eye. There were bloodstains around the doorknob, and he could also see more on the concrete floor, getting away toward a passageway.

A wave of satisfaction came over him. At least one shot had hit the target, he had wounded the murderer.

The passage retreated in two directions. He only had two choices, keep going following the blood trail or do it in the opposite direction.

He guessed that the murderer, confident as he was in his superiority, must have walked into the tunnel network to perform final checks on the explosives.

If so, it was better to take the opposite direction which, logic dictated, would have to lead him to an exit. He had no weapons, nothing to defend himself or fight back, so he let caution show him the way, and started running in that direction.

An unsung dead hero would serve no purpose to society if he could not make public the horror he was experiencing there.

The passage sloped upward, and soon it branched out again. Gerard let his instinct guide him and took the detour that had the steepest slope, hoping it would take him faster to the surface.

However, his logic seemed to crash against the rock wall Gerard found at the end of the passage. Determined to go back and take the other detour, he realized he had gotten there with no artificial light, without there being any light bulb in sight.

He walked the passage up and down trying to find the light leakage. Finally, next to the rock wall he found an opening in the ceiling hidden behind a sharp rock. It was a natural opening, a chimney in the rock that rose several meters to a gap through which he could see the brightness of what had to be the sunlight.

Without hesitation, he climbed the rock, and securing his hands to the ledges, he began his ascent along the natural chimney. His bare feet and toes bled upon contact with the sharp rock edges, but his desire for freedom made him impervious to pain.

When he had traveled more than halfway, one of his feet lost its support. He shook his leg but couldn't find any ridge.

A sharp sting in his foot felt as if he had struck hard against a rock. He looked down and saw horrified a huge black figure into the chimney, climbing after him.

The sole of his foot was bleeding and the excruciating pain was a sign the psychopath's machete had severed part of his musculature. Caught in that mousetrap he would now end skewered like a kebab.

"You won't get away," his attacker yelled.

"I defused the explosives, you won't make it, damn you," Gerard said, kicking blindly and pulling hard with his arms to climb faster.

He felt another stab, and this time the pain came from his ankle. That guy would rip out his legs with his machete, and soon he wouldn't have but stumps. He broke free momentarily and climbed freehand the final stretch.

He looked up and noted the passage widened less than a meter away, opening directly to the outside, but found the exit was closed with an iron grate with bars, covered by vegetation.

Gerard climbed to the wide section and held on to the grate bars pushing up with all his might. The grate would not budge, it was very rusty and probably had not been used in decades.

It looked like a rainwater drain, the kind of grate usually not anchored or welded, kept in place by its own weight.

The machete reappeared next to his foot, but this time Gerard saw it coming and kicked it away. He picked up a loose rock at hand, hit the machete blade, and threw the rock against his pursuer's head, and he backed down the chimney.

Gerard took advantage of the break to stretch under the grate. He put his battered feet against the iron bars, pushed the grate up and was happy to see it moved.

He redoubled his efforts, but it was very heavy and swayed dangerously. Like a circus acrobat holding with his feet a wooden board with his partner on it, Gerard did the same with the huge grate, which swung menacingly.

Gerard feared his strength would abandon him and his legs would give way, dropping the grate on his face and crushing him. Once he had it in the air, he started moving his back to the side to get the grate out of its housing and place it on the ground so he could get out through the hole.

He was about to succeed when he felt the steel blade of the machete approaching his neck and sectioning part of his earlobe. He screamed and made a huge effort not to release the grate, as he swiped aside with his hand to push the machete away from his neck.

Lying on his back, holding with his feet an over fifty-kilo iron grate, and having a psychopath stabbing him from behind, he couldn't have imagined a better way to start the day or to finish it, it was all a matter of perspective.

The machete approached his neck again, and this time Gerard had no strength to keep putting up a fight with his hands, so he kept moving his back until the grate was in a perpendicular position.

He gave one last push up with his legs, but Gerard raised his outside leg and contracted the inner one, bringing the heavy grate to lean toward the hole in the chimney, and then he gave it the final touch.

A small kick and the grate slid from his feet heading down the hole, falling by its narrowest side, roaring at high speed.

The murderer only had time to look up and see the heavy iron mass heading straight to his face. Gerard didn't look down but could hear the wet and dull noise of iron pounding against soft tissue, before hitting the rock bottom.

Gerard stood and got out, staggering as he walked through the thick bushes that had hidden that drain for years. He thought he saw the remains of a wall or an old building, but his brain no longer registered what he was seeing.

He walked aimlessly under a blinding light, bumping against tree trunks and stumbling on branches and stones, but he kept walking up the mountain, always going up. He knew salvation consisted in always going up.

At that moment, an earthquake shook the ground, trembling under his feet. The trees bent before the force of nature that was shaping the terrain at will, creating new headlands and depressions, swallowing into its guts what until then had been a reality, creating a new and different reality, a new scenario, and wiping out in one move what time had patiently built.

He no longer felt the ground under his feet, he was flying, he was sliding down a new and wonderful land, where there was no pain, no obstacles, no stalkers, where he could finally rest, safely, in peace.

CHAPTER 76

The music sounded insistently. Gerard hated those melodies so repetitive that when they get into your head, stay there for ages. He wanted to switch the channel, tune another station, but he couldn't find the source, couldn't find the radio set.

Could it be the alarm clock what was bothering him so much? He reached out and touched the surface of the nightstand but found nothing. He would have no other choice but to open his eyes and look for it.

It startled him to feel a hand holding his wrist and forcing him to stay in bed. He opened his eyes and tried to sit up, but someone held him by the shoulders.

"What's happening here?" Gerard shouted, able to release one arm and swiping his hand left and right. All was in vain, and they soon pinned him down to the bed again.

That was not his bed, nor his bedroom, and he was not at home. A young woman dressed in a light blue blouse held his wrists squashing him against the bed, bent over him, leaving her ample cleavage perfectly aligned with his field of vision.

As his friend Max would have said, the contemplation of the wonders of nature is one of the great pleasures life has to offer. Being enraptured by the beauty of the nurse's neckline probably did more to reassure him than any painkiller administered intravenously.

Gerard slowly became aware he was in a hospital room, and when he turned his head, he saw they had connected him to a monitor, which produced the annoying intermittent beep he had tried to silence.

From that moment on, questions accumulated in his mind until it overflowed as a dam above its capacity.

"Where am I? How did I get here? How long have I been unconscious?" he asked, turning to the nurse, who still didn't dare to let go of his wrists.

"If you calm down, I'll call the doctor and he'll come and talk to you," she said, in a tone that made him understand it was better to obey and not look for more trouble.

"Okay, forgive me. You can let go, I'm not a threat."

The nurse seemed convinced and loosened her grip.

"Have you news about my friend Max? He was with me in the cave, he's very badly injured, you have to get him.

"As I said, the doctor will talk to you right away," she said, motioning to her partner at the nurse's station.

A few minutes later a doctor entered the room, fitting perfectly with the stereotype of a young doctor in need to assert himself in public. White coat, stethoscope around his neck and hung over his shoulders, artificial smile and a facial expression wanting to give the impression of being very busy and having little time to waste.

The doctor greeted him with the usual condescending tone with which many of them treat patients, addressing him as if speaking to a child, which always bothered Gerard.

"Do I have any serious medical condition?" Gerard interrupted, "because if not, I need to get out of here and seek help for my friend. It's an emergency. How long have I been here?"

"Calm down, please, all in due time. You've been here almost one full day. They brought you here yesterday afternoon and now it's almost noon."

"Damn, a whole day. Max didn't have that long. Listen to me, please. It doesn't matter what happens to me, but my friend Max is badly injured and needs immediate medical attention. Can you send an ambulance for him and incidentally call the police?"

The doctor seemed upset at Gerard's insistence.

"We'll call the police if there is evidence you have had a stroke or been assaulted, but for now it looks like yesterday's earthquake in Collserola dragged you down. It's amazing an earthquake of such magnitude may occur in this country, which is not in an area of seismic activity; and to top it off, some of the victims are hikers who were in the mountain," the doctor said.

"I'm not a hiker, and I assure you there was no earthquake. It was an intentional explosion. My friend is very badly injured, he has a stab wound in the lower back, that is, a gash in the kidneys, and needs urgent help."

"If you don't calm down, we will have to sedate you," the doctor said, motioning to the nurse to be ready.

"Can you call the police, agent Iolanda Vehils, please? It's a real emergency."

The doctor nodded, and the nurse ran out for the phone.

"Doctor, what are the chances of surviving a stab wound to the kidneys?"

"It's difficult to determine not knowing the extent of the injury, nor the impact on other vital organs, or if there was massive bleeding."

"I tried to plug the wound, which was bleeding, although I cannot judge whether it was a little or a lot. I went out for help. Staying there would have been like committing suicide," Gerard said.

"Given your pitiful condition, one would say you have already been actively trying," the doctor added.

"We must send help, and only I know how to get to him," Gerard insisted.

"Let's wait for the police and let them decide. You are in no condition to accompany anyone anywhere. You have several broken ribs, a stab wound in the foot sole and so many wounds and bruises you look like a Nazarene in an Easter procession."

Gerard tried to laugh, but the pain in his side prevented it.

"Now you'd better rest, you have lost a lot of blood, and your body needs to rest more than anything else. If you need painkillers, I have prescribed you some and the nurse will administer them as needed," the doctor said, preparing to leave the room.

"Where did they find me?" Gerard asked.

"Some hikers found you in the Collserola woods, near the road to Sant Cugat, half-naked and ranting. If it weren't for the number of wounds you had, I would have sworn you were drunk and hangover, coming back home after a crazy party," the doctor said.

"A crazy party in the middle of the mountains? Don't make me laugh, doctor," Gerard said.

"We will notify you when the police arrive," the doctor said and left the room.

Gerard closed his eyes. Now that he had regained consciousness, he was attending in his head the screening of several movies at once.

Everything that happened in the tunnels, the discovery of the lake, Max's stabbing, the encounters with Eva, her version of the story, the attacks of the psychopath dressed in black, his escape from the tank, and above all, the macabre discovery of the suicide room.

He regretted not having explored it further, but at least he had verified its existence, watch it closely, and escape from it alive.

It was not an urban legend nor a myth created by the press; it was a reality he had verified personally.

If the room existed, it was more than likely much of what Eva had told him were also true, and that the sinister organization created by her family and colleagues to continue killing for decades, was also real.

That certainty opened up an exciting new line of research for him, the possibility to investigate directly not only the disappearances occurred early last century but also all those that took place during the following decades until the present.

The crimes kept being perpetrated, although in an anonymous way to society, under the cover of the almost complete prevailing ignorance about all events related to the Casino.

That would be the investigation of his life, the project to which he would devote the next years, until he could clarify all the facts, or reached the end of his days, whichever came first.

He owed it to Max, and also to the victims, families, and descendants of so many unfortunate people forced to commit suicide and remain anonymous.

He knew in some cultures suicide was as an act of honor, whereas in Western culture it was a socially reprehensible act, generally associated with cowardice.

Now he could personally claim that, within the four walls of that room of horror, suicide had ceased to be a reprehensible act, to become the ultimate expression of love and devotion for so many men defending their loved ones.

When all of that would come into the public light, the moral and ideological debate was guaranteed.

His breathing became increasingly slow and his snores soon engaged in a meaningless competition with the beeping of the monitors.

"Are you awake?" a familiar voice asked, interrupting his sleep.

CHAPTER 77

Gerard opened his eyes. He didn't know how long he had been sleeping.

A nurse placed two pillows under his back to help him sit up, and left the room, closing the door. Agent Vehils came to the foot of the bed.

"You see what happened to you for not listening to me and playing the detective," she said, although Gerard ignored her comment.

"Thank God you came. We have to look for Max. He is trapped in the tunnels and very badly hurt. I'm the only one who can guide you there, we must waste no time," Gerard said, showing his feet under the blanket and trying to get up.

The agent walked around the bed and stopped him.

"Not so fast, we have to talk first."

"There's no time, Max's life depends on us."

"From what the doctor told me, your friend's life should no longer be a concern, and I'm sorry to talk to you like that."

"How can you say that? I asked them to call you because I can't trust anyone else. You can't tell me this now."

The agent pulled up a chair and sat beside him.

"I appreciate your trust, but there's a protocol we must follow. As much as I want to help you, and believe me, I do, I need you to tell me everything that happened. Give me evidence, and I'll do all I can to help you."

Gerard had no choice but to calm down and to recount all the events from the beginning, skipping no details, except for the existence of the diary, which he preferred not to share with her yet.

The agent listened intently, interrupting with some questions and taking notes in a small notebook. When Gerard's story got to the part where they found him in the forest, the agent could not suppress a smile.

"What?" Gerard asked.

"I'm trying to imagine what the hikers thought when they found you naked and ranting through the woods. The doctor told me they are still under treatment in the emergency room because of the shock they suffered seeing you that way," she said.

"You're hilarious, did you know that? Are we going to search for Max or not?"

"Think about what you just told me. If we tried to access the tunnels from the water mine, the rescue team would have to overcome several underwater passages, to reach your friend. Not to mention having to walk all the way back, diving and carrying his body on a stretcher. From what you explained, you could hardly go through yourselves. How could a stretcher fit through the narrow passages?"

Gerard said nothing, he was trying to find another way to convince her.

"We could try to access it from the outside, from the forest. We would only need to retrace the steps I took when I escaped. Enter through the grate on the ground, go down the chimney, reach the tank, dive into it and burst the door to empty it, and then follow the corridors to get to the place. I think I would remember the path I took," Gerard said, excitedly.

"Use your head. What you're suggesting implies several days of work, with no guarantee of success. Also, don't forget there has been a huge explosion that must have collapsed most of the tunnels, and a fire has devastated part of the forest. Firefighters are still working in the area and we cannot get close until they officially declare it extinct. And even if we could have access, do you believe you could find the entry? Do you remember the exact spot where you came out to the outside?"

Gerard remained silent. He didn't remember it. In his mind, he only saw the iron bar grate and the sunlight outside, but from that point, he remembered nothing more, just having seen a low wall, as if it were part of some ruins. He couldn't be sure of anything.

"Keep trusting me. We have cordoned off the entire area, but from what you have told me about the explosives you saw in the storage, it could be an act of terrorism, and we must inform the President, who will activate the defense protocol against terrorism."

"But it has nothing to do with it, they're not a terrorist group, but a group of psychopaths," Gerard interrupted her.

"What's the difference? I promise you that as soon as we can access the area, I will personally visit the place and immediately send a rescue team to look for your friend, but now you have to be strong and face reality. Both your friend and your mysterious attacker are probably dead and buried under the rubble. Meanwhile, I will do some digging about Eva and the other names you gave me," the agent said, rising to leave.

"Thanks for your help. You believe me, don't you?" Gerard asked, holding her hand.

"Yes, although I know I should lock you up for disobeying authority, destruction of private property, and God knows how many more infringements. But there is something about all this that I don't like, and I won't rest until I find out what it is. Get some rest, I'll need you soon," the agent said, and left the room.

Gerard closed his eyes and tried to rest, but he couldn't erase from his mind the image of that man chasing him, and he also saw Max, stretched over a pool of blood, looking into his eyes with his eternal smile, without reproach, resigned to die.

He couldn't just stay there doing nothing. He put his feet on the floor and leaned on them to get up, but his injured foot hurt and his legs could barely hold him. Sleeping one full day had done him good, but he was still very weak.

The door opened, and a nurse entered carrying some pills in her hand. Seeing him standing, she ran toward him and put him back in bed.

"You must not get up yet. The doctor has not authorized it. I brought you some painkillers for your shoulder pain. Take them and you will sleep well," the nurse said, showing him several pills in a plastic cup.

"With your permission, my bladder is about to burst, and if I don't empty it soon, I will make a mess here. Give them to me, I'm going to the bathroom and I'll take them there with some tap water," Gerard said, extending his hand.

The nurse gave him the pills and helped him up, waiting in the room as he headed toward the small bathroom and locked himself inside.

He couldn't trust anyone. He let the faucet water run, as he threw the pills down the toilet and flushed it. He freshened his face and two minutes later he left the bathroom, displaying the most convincing relaxation expression he could fake.

"Thanks, I have already taken them and now..." but he stopped when he saw the room was empty. The nurse was gone.

He sat on the bed and put his legs on the mattress to rest a few minutes. He wondered if Max would have survived, but he could only find out visiting the place, something they wouldn't let him do for a long time.

The door opened and the nurse who had assisted him when he first woke up entered the room.

"I see you're feeling better, but don't get up until the doctor says it's okay. If you're hungry, we'll soon bring you some food, a light diet."

"Thank you, having a bite to eat to regain strength will do me good."

"Good, I'll go get the tray. If you need the painkillers the doctor offered, ask me and I'll bring you the pills," she said, turning around.

"No, thanks, I already took them."

"You already took them? But I still haven't brought them to you," she said, stopping at the door.

Gerard was confused, but soon realized what had happened.

"It's all right, I'm still stunned by the blow. If I need them I'll ask you, don't worry," he said with a smile. The nurse smiled back and left the room,

Gerard got up immediately. He knew what that meant. Fortunately, the pills the fake nurse had brought were now happily traveling towards the sewers' mouth in the Mediterranean Sea.

His closet was empty. He forgot he had spent most of the last twenty-four hours wearing only his underpants, which he didn't even keep. With a hospital gown and his bare ass, he wouldn't get very far.

He had to get out of there; he feared for his safety, and what was worse, he didn't know who was behind this.

Upon hearing the rattle from the tray cart he ran into bed and pulled the sheet right at the moment the door opened. The nurse came in with a succulent menu of boiled cabbage and fish soup with a single slice of hake.

"Had I known the food here was so delicious, I would have tried to be admitted a lot sooner. Next time I'll bring some friends, this deserves to be enjoyed in good company," Gerard said, slurping a spoonful of the gray soup.

"Your good humor is a very good sign," the nurse said, "the doctor will be pleased. If you like soup so much, you can have another bowl. If you want, I can bring you one more."

"No, that won't be necessary, I don't want to deprive other patients of this succulent delicacy. There has to be enough for everyone's enjoyment. Thank you very much," Gerard said, slurping the soup loudly, to displease the nurse and get her to go out.

When he was alone, he removed the tray and lifted the sheets to take a piece of paper he had found on top of his bed when the nurse entered.

The short anonymous message read: "*The offer still stands, the clock is still ticking. You will soon receive the call. The choice is yours.*"

It had no signature, but it didn't have to. The psychopath or any of his colleagues had placed the letter there. It was not over yet, in fact, it had just begun.

He picked up the phone and tried to access an outside line but he could not. Soon a voice from the nurse's station replied. Gerard asked them to urgently call agent Vehils on her direct line and the nurse assured him they would do so.

After hanging up the phone he sat on the bed and waited. Not even five minutes had gone by when the door burst open and a blond woman dressed in a white coat and reading a medical record entered the room.

Gerard was uneasy to see a new face. It could either be a new doctor or someone purporting to help him get down to the morgue on the fast track. He slipped one of his legs under the sheets and set it on the ground, ready to jump and run, if necessary.

"Who are you?" Gerard asked.

She lowered the medical record folder, brought the hand to her head and yanked out her scalp. Gerard winced but said nothing.

Under the wig, a short stiff mane of brown hair shone under the fluorescent light and a pair of small mischievous laughing eyes watched him.

"I cannot believe it, agent Vehils. This is what I call police effectiveness. You know how to make a grand entrance. I am honored you have come to my call so fast."

"What call? No one has called me. I tried to come up here without attracting too much attention. Put this on," she said, throwing him a bundle of clothes in a plastic bag.

"What's the matter? Why the rush?"

"Have you taken a liking to run around naked like Tarzan?" she said.

"That's not what I meant, I was asking about the disguise. I like blondes, but your natural hair color suits you better," Gerard said.

"Get dressed fast, I'll explain on the way."

Gerard dropped the hospital gown to the floor, but immediately picked it up and covered his parts, motioning with his hand for her to turn around.

"For God's sake, I have three brothers. There's nothing you have that I have not seen a thousand times before," she said.

"I could reply with a thousand witty remarks, you made it easy for me, but I'd better bite my tongue," Gerard said, trying to get into a pair of pants several sizes too small.

"Where did you get these pants? Did you borrow them from your little brother?" Gerard said, struggling to zip up his fly.

"Actually, I thought I had guessed your size correctly, but I was wrong," Iolanda confessed.

"Again, I will refrain from making easy jokes, but please don't go down that road or I won't be able to restrain myself."

Agent Vehils put on the wig again and waited behind the door.

"I'll get out there to stir things up a bit. Count to sixty and leave the room and stop at nothing and nobody. Walk to the end of the hall, and out the door leading to the inner staircase. Go down to the first basement and wait for me on the landing.

The agent adjusted the wig and went out, leaving the door ajar behind her. Gerard started counting but lost count when he heard alarms going off in the monitors in several of the rooms at the other end of the hall. The hubbub of nurses' steps on the run faded away in the opposite direction.

Gerard didn't know whether he had already made it to sixty or gone beyond, but he didn't hesitate and went out resolutely, stuffed in those high school student clothes and headed for the emergency exit.

CHAPTER 78

Gerard heard someone coming down the stairs in a hurry.

He had reached the basement landing ages ago and didn't know what to do or where to go. He looked up at the stairwell and could only see a hand coming down and leaning on the railing. He hoped it would be agent Vehils, but he held the door ajar in case it wasn't her and had to leave in a hurry.

"Go, go, get out and follow the hallway," Iolanda shouted, jumping the steps three at a time. They ran along a corridor painted in gray and reached a lobby with two metal doors, one of which connected with the parking.

"This way," she said, and they reached the first level of the parking. "Walk slowly now. I have a vehicle on that side, next to the columns," she said, pointing to the farthest side.

Gerard could barely move in a pair of pants that cut off blood supply to vital parts of his body and was glad to be getting to the car.

"Which one is it?" he said, pointing to two modern Mercedes Benz parked next to the columns.

"That one," she replied, pointing to a small Seat 850, the most popular car model in Spain in the sixties and seventies, and now a collector's item.

"That one? My father owned one of those when I was born over thirty years ago, and even then it was already an antique. Where did you get it?" Gerard asked, not knowing whether to get excited or alarmed.

"It's my father's. He keeps it that way since he bought it. It's immaculate. Get on," she said, opening the door and throwing the wig on the back seat.

"Why didn't you bring a patrol car? Why the disguise?"

"I'll tell you when we're on our way," she said, starting up the car and heading for the exit. "Wait here, while I go to the pay booth."

Gerard waited for her sitting in the passenger seat, remembering his childhood family trips, during the summer vacation, the car loaded like a ten-ton truck, the roof rack cluttered with bundles piled in a stack larger than the Cheops pyramid, all tied under a tarp held in place with a few rubber bands ended in hooks, popularly called *octopus*.

Inside that car, there was always room for the whole family, regardless of how many members traveled, its capacity had no limits. There were no seat belts either, probably because in case of an accident no one would be ejected since all passengers were crammed in there like sausages under pressure.

Iolanda returned with the parking stub and sat behind the wheel. Once away from the hospital, she drove uptown. They arrived at the famous Güell Park, designed by the architect Antonio Gaudi and Iolanda drove around for a while until she found a place to park.

They approached the park entrance, and she showed her police badge to allow them access without going through the ticket office.

Once inside, they mingled with the numerous groups of tourists and finally sat in one of the immortal benches tiled with fragments of broken pottery, the famous Gaudinian "*trencadís*", from which they enjoyed a spectacular view of Barcelona.

"You were right, Mr. Bach," she said, looking into his eyes.

"Please, call me Gerard."

"You were right, Gerard. I know everything you told me is true," she said.

"Did you doubt me? My whole body aches, I've been shot, stabbed at, chased, drowned, blown up in the air, and

450

probably my best friend has been murdered, and all in just a few hours. Do you think you I could make up something like that?" he said.

"Sorry, I'm a cop. I have to suspect everything and everyone, I can't help it. But I know that what you say is true. When I left you at the hospital, I went to the police station to start a rescue operation, but all I found was resistance. Some of my superiors want me to forget about the case and the investigation."

"But they assigned you to the case, didn't they?"

"No. Remember it was you who requested me. As soon as they heard what happened, Lieutenant Botell put that Cro-Magnon of Guzman in charge of the case and they want to take me away."

"That proves nothing, it may be part of the internal policy in your department, don't you think?"

"No. Guzman is the biggest useless asshole I've ever met, besides being a repressed fascist. His mission is to hinder my work, not to cooperate with me."

"When will we be able to access the fire zone?" Gerard asked.

"We won't."

"What? And what about Max's rescue?"

"There will be no rescue. It's what I'm trying to tell you. The fire is almost extinguished, but they have sent units of the Special Forces to investigate in the area, and it's already outside police jurisdiction. And Guzman is the liaison with them. I'm officially out of the case."

"Is there any way we can get there at night? You were in the tunnels, you reached the lake, you know that all that exists," Gerard said.

"I know it's very hard, perhaps even cruel, but get used to the idea that Max is dead. Yesterday I was in the area. Half the mountain disappeared after the explosion and the fire. There must be no trace left of all that was down there. If the forensic teams find any evidence of the presence of human remains they'll let us know."

"And what's that got to do with me?"

"You're an inconvenience for them. For the police department, you're nothing but a nosy reporter who stuck his nose in police affairs and ended up getting it burned, but nobody will take it any further, except those with vested interests. I have the feeling this involves very important people in this, even within the police department. They think taking me out of the case will stop me, but they underestimate me. The good thing is now they don't suspect I may have any leads, and it's in our best interest they keep thinking that."

"Did you say *our*?"

"Don't you want to find out why Max is dead? Don't you want to know who's behind this plot? How far the rot reaches?" she asked.

"Of course, but to be honest, I'm more interested in pulling the thread and finding out what happened in the last hundred years, than unmasking those who may pull the strings today, except for the lunatic that killed Eva and Max. I want to interrogate him myself," Gerard said.

"So we split the job. I'll deal with the present and you investigate in the past, but in any case, we'll finally bring it all into the light. I can find out many things from the inside, especially if they forget about me and I don't draw too much attention," she said.

"But how will I go unnoticed? They have tried to kill me in the hospital, and look what I found in my bed," Gerard said, showing her the note.

Iolanda read it and put it in a plastic bag.

"Let me analyze it, maybe I can find traces. Do you think the same guy who locked you in the room wrote it?"

"I'm sure of it. Apparently, he still expects me to commit suicide. The thing is, he threatened to rape and kill my sister and her daughter. Can you offer them police protection? They are in danger."

"I don't know how to justify it internally without having to reveal all the details about the suicide room and everything that happened there. I'm not sure whom I can trust within the department. However, if they had wanted to kill them, they would have done it already. We still have leverage; they

452

don't know how much we know, and they will not hurt your family at the risk you go public with the information you have," Iolanda said.

"The easiest would be to kill me as well, getting rid of all of us."

"Trust me. They will not dare to touch any of you."

"Do you mean they will not attack my family, but I'm not good for them dead either?"

"I want to think so, that they need you alive, to find out what you know. That's your trump card."

"What a trump card it is, how lucky I am. That's why they send killer nurses to visit me."

"Maybe that woman was working alone and is not related to the psychopath who attacked you. Let me look into it. Meanwhile, if you know someone who lives far away from the city, in the mountains, now it would be a good time to disappear for a while. You can spend your time doing remote research, all you need is a good Internet connection. I'll be your link with the city and help you with everything."

"But, what about the police? I mean, what are you going to do with me? Will you prosecute me, will you call me to testify?" Gerard insisted.

"Nobody has filed any charges, no one has reported anything, and not even you have officially gone to the police. You called me directly, nobody is looking for you, no one has incriminated you, and also it was me who started this investigation, so it is my report the one Guzman will take into account when he takes over the case, and in that report, I think I will forget a few things," she said with a smile.

"What you say makes sense and I guess it's the best solution, but I can't stop thinking about Max, that I have failed him, that I have abandoned him."

"On the contrary, you're doing it for him. He would have wanted you to finish what you two had started together, that you carried the investigation to the end, that you discovered the truth and brought all those bastards to justice. You are doing the right thing," Iolanda said, resting her hand on his.

"All right. But keep me informed if there is news or about anything you may find in the Casino."

"Don't worry, I'll be your eyes on the ground and you'll be my brain from the mountains," she said.

"It's an image I find difficult to visualize, but I get what you're saying. Well, it's time for me to go. I'll change my mobile phone, I'll get the new number to you. We'll contact online through a secure server that I'll set up soon. We can meet when we have to, but I'll let you know how and where. And thanks for everything, really," Gerard said, rising from the bench.

"You know where you're going?"

"I have an approximate idea. You'll hear from me soon. Thanks again," he said as he was leaving, but he stopped and smiled.

You know what? If you weren't a cop, I would kiss you. That's why you must settle for a hug," he said, with a smile, and taking a few steps forward he hugged her tightly.

Iolanda allowed the embrace, and when his arms began to let go, she held him for a moment, brought her lips closer and kissed him on the cheek, a warm and moist kiss, and held her lips there several seconds longer than it would have been mandatory, which didn't go unnoticed to Gerard.

No one could ever erase the guilt that plagued him for having abandoned his best friend to his fate. But at the same time, he felt he was doing the right thing, to take that investigation to the end and to recover the memory of so many families torn apart by such a dark and infamous organization.

He had risked his own life, had his best friend killed, and threatened the integrity of his sister and niece, but the fight had just begun.

At the bottom of his heart, he felt comforted in feeling he was doing what his conscience dictated. He knew he would spend what remained of his life pursuing it, he had finally given meaning and purpose to his life.

And he was not alone, beside him he had a woman of resources, an exceptional woman.

Together they would achieve what nobody had in a hundred years, to unmask those who hid behind the mask of terror, those who used their power and social position to gamble with the life and the fate of innocent families, getting richer along the way with no scruples.

He had found the mythical suicide room, and although it had probably disappeared in the blast, he now realized the symbolism of that room could no longer be confined within its four walls.

The horror that room symbolized, the lowest level to which the human race could drop, would not disappear because its walls had been demolished.

Unfortunately, the evil that room represented, could be found every day anywhere in the world, in any country in which innocent people were forced to act against their will, to prostitute themselves, to give up their principles and dignity, forced to take it to the limit to defend their loved ones.

For Gerard there was no more universal feeling than the power of love, giving yourself without reservations, and he thought there was no greater sacrifice than giving our most precious asset, our life, for those we love.

It had been so since the beginning of time and so it would remain for as long as the human race still existed, for in the end, is what defined us, what identified us, what made us what we are, what made us human.

EPILOGUE.

Sant Julià de Cerdanyola. Six months later.

The peacefulness of the village was only altered some weekends and during summer, when vacationers coming mainly from Barcelona disembarked, but the rest of the year the village barely had a few hundred permanent residents.

Hidden at the top of a remote mountain, the houses scattered over a beautiful valley as if sprinkled from heaven with a giant salt shaker.

Six months earlier the village had added one more inhabitant to its census of permanent residents. Gerard found there the peace, and above all the discretion he needed to carry out his work.

Close enough to Barcelona to travel there when necessary, but far enough to be safe from prying eyes.

He had become one more in the village, the writer, as this neighbors called him, having welcomed him with no suspicion.

The anxiety Gerard had experienced during the weeks following the explosion in the Casino ruins slowly disappeared as the days passed and nobody bothered him.

As Iolanda had expected, the police investigation was not very thorough. In the routine report she handed out to inspector Guzman, she made Gerard look like a mere accidental witness, so the investigation went no further and they never required his presence.

The Special Forces maintained the Casino area as a restricted area for months, and supposedly, it either would become a restricted military area or it would be open to the public again, in which case Gerard and Iolanda would be the first to go there to investigate on the ground.

Max was officially declared as missing since his body never appeared, although Gerard was sure they didn't look very hard.

In the quietness of the pre-Pyrenees village, Gerard made a lot of progress in his research.

With Iolanda's help and the police resources she discreetly handled, he could put a name to some people declared missing at the turn of the century, and to some of the many corpses found in the Collserola mountain range.

One of his main objectives was to identify the signatory who hid behind the initials V.P. in the suicide letter he found in the book.

Just like Eva confessed before dying, it could well be Catalan businessman Víctor Papiol, disappeared in 1912, leaving a wife and a daughter, who could not maintain their comfortable lifestyle and had a tragic end.

What surprised him the most was to find that Víctor had an older brother who was a physician, Dr. Oleguer Papiol, who at the time was the Head of the Digestive Surgery Department at the Hospital de San Pablo in Barcelona.

Dr. Papiol, who until then had enjoyed some fame as a specialist, fell from grace and was expelled from the College of Physicians and lost his job at the hospital for complaints about the alleged practice of therapeutic killings on some patients, a primitive form of euthanasia that could never be proven with certainty.

The doctor's tribulations ended when he introduced the barrel of a gun into his mouth and the found his body next to a suicide note in which he confessed his actions and claimed to repent from them.

Gerard discovered Dr. Papiol had been involved as a physician in several high-profile cases at the time, such as the attack suffered by Mrs. Xamot, a wealthy widow from the upper part of Barcelona who was admitted to the same Hospital de San Pablo, where she was the victim of a second attack, which ended her life.

Gerard was convinced this was the same Dr. Papiol the psychopath had mentioned when he told him about his great-grandfather. It was very plausible they had transmitted the thirst for revenge in macabre inheritance from father to son up to the great-grandson, who took matters into his own hands and put it into practice.

Was it possible for generations the family had been killing the descendants of those who had accused the patriarch, the illustrious doctor fallen from grace? Were they part of an organized group that could include figures of social relevance of the era, hiding dark economic interests?

Gerard felt there were too many suspicious coincidences in that story. Besides Dr. Papiol's involvement, the person responsible for the investigation had been a certain Captain Casimiro Botell, who as Iolanda discovered, proved to be the grandfather of Lieutenant Botell, her current direct superior.

That only reinforced the need to maintain maximum discretion during their investigations, since it was impossible to know how far the network of influences reached and the actual scope of that organization.

Eva's posthumous words had made a dent in Gerard. The possibility that the initials in the letter were VB.

Finding out all he could about his potential ancestor, Valentín Bach, became a new obsession for him. Unfortunately, Gerard could no longer turn to his parents to gather information about his past, so climbing the branches of his family tree would be much harder without them.

Was it possible someone in his family could be part of that awful plot? The mere possibility took away his sleep and turned all his work into a personal matter.

And what could Eva's role be in all of that? They invested a lot of effort to investigate her and her environment. A police raid of her house ordered by Iolanda cast no light on the case, nor provided any evidence. It was as if nobody had lived in the house for a century. They never found neither a diary nor any documents.

It was as if she had never existed. A birth certificate and a death certificate to her name from when she was three, were the only documents Iolanda could find.

But Gerard knew Eva not only existed, but she had played a crucial role in the story. He knew Eva's participation in those murders was not the result of psychopathy but to something more profound.

His intuition told him Eva's motivations responded to an irrational desire for revenge, which could only obey to reasons of the heart or the blood, meaning, family revenge.

Now his task was to find out what event in her past could generate such irrepressible hatred in her, that she wanted to erase that past in a bloodbath.

The key to unraveling what happened lay in that mysterious diary in which her grandmother had written both the names of those who disappeared and of those who could run the plot, and which had become the roadmap followed by the psychopathic murderers during the past century, up to present time.

Until Gerard could not find the diary, he could not be sure of anything.

He had to find an old diary from the turn of the century which no one knew existed, and which had been in the possession of a woman who supposedly died in her childhood.

All to unmask those who at present were running a monumental conspiracy, involving politicians and relevant people for over a century.

A period during which businessmen, public figures and their descendants, had been systematically and secretly harassed and murdered by a group of avengers who seemed to recreate the macabre modus operandi of the alleged organization operating at the turn of the century in the Casino, having as their operations center a mysterious and legendary room whose existence everyone doubted.

The challenge was tremendous, but Gerard faced it with the passion and determination that came from knowing that would be his life's work.

Max's disappearance, so many unwarranted deaths, so much horror, the potential implication of some unknown member of his own family, it was imperative someone clarified it all and brought truth to the light.

And that someone would be him, with the invaluable help of Iolanda, working incognito from within the police force.

Revenge had fed all the horror on both sides for more than a century, and Gerard knew that in his case, retaliation would also continue to feed his research and his commitment to the truth.

It was not his only motivation, but he could not deny he felt comfortable giving in to it.

Human nature had not evolved over millennia, and it would not change now, no matter how much he wanted it to. If he had managed to discover and prove the existence of the real suicide room, he could also unravel what happened in the Casino and its surroundings during the last one hundred years.

And as for that phone call he was expecting, maybe they were the ones who would have to wait.

With all that was at stake and his new mission in life, it would have been suicidal to have suicidal thoughts.